JON COURTENAY GRIMWOOD

THE FALLEN BLADE

Act One of THE ASSASSINI

orbit

www.orbitbooks.net

Orbit
Hachette Book Group
237 Park Avenue, New York, NY 10017
www.HachetteBookGroup.com

First U.S. Edition: January 2011

Orbit is an imprint of Hachette Book Group, Inc.
The Orbit name and logo are trademarks of Little, Brown Book Group Limited.

Library of Congress Control Number: 2010933805
ISBN: 978-0-316-07439-1

10 9 8 7 6 5 4 3 2 1

Printed in the United States of America

For Sam,
who found Venice stranger than she imagined . . .

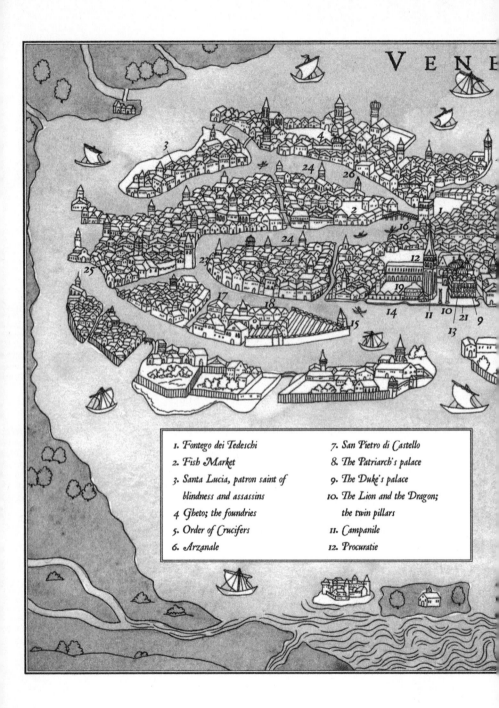

VEN...

1. Fontego dei Tedeschi
2. Fish Market
3. Santa Lucia, patron saint of
   blindness and assassins
4. Gheto; the foundries
5. Order of Crucifers
6. Arzanale

7. San Pietro di Castello
8. The Patriarch's palace
9. The Duke's palace
10. The Lion and the Dragon;
   the twin pillars
11. Campanile
12. Procuratie

I A

22

6

7

8

20

The Millioni family tree

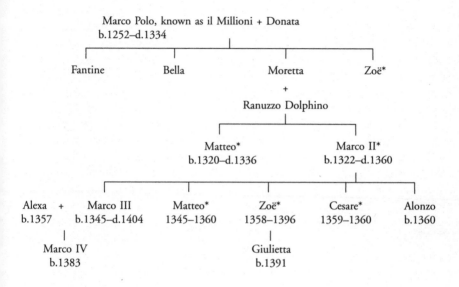

Marco Polo, known as il Millioni + Donata
b.1252–d.1334

Fantine   Bella   Moretta   Zoë*

+

Ranuzzo Dolphino

Matteo*   Marco II*
b.1320–d.1336   b.1322–d.1360

Alexa   +   Marco III   Matteo*   Zoë*   Cesare*   Alonzo
b.1357   b.1345–d.1404   1345–1360   1358–1396   1359–1360   b.1360

Marco IV   Giulietta
b.1383   b.1391

* Murdered

First Republic
1336 –1348

Second Republic
1360 –1362

Dramatis Personae

Tycho, a seventeen-year-old boy with strange hungers

The Millioni
Marco IV, known as Marco the Simpleton, Duke of Venice and Prince of Serenissima
Lady Giulietta di Millioni, the fifteen-year-old cousin of Marco IV
Duchess Alexa, the late duke's widow, mother to Marco IV, sister-in-law of Prince Alonzo
Prince Alonzo, Regent of Venice
Lady Eleanor, Giulietta's cousin and lady-in-waiting
Marco III, known as Marco the Just. The late lamented Duke of Venice, elder brother of Alonzo and godfather of Lady Giulietta

Members of the Venetian court
Atilo il Mauros, ex-Lord Admiral of the Middle Sea, adviser to the late Marco III, and head of Venice's secret assassins
Lord Bribanzo, member of the Council of Ten, the inner council that rules Venice under the duke. One of the richest men in the city

Lady Desdaio Bribanzo, his daughter and sole heir

Sir Richard Glanville, Cypriot envoy to Venice and knight of the Order of White Crucifers

Prince Leopold zum Bas Friedland, the German emperor's bastard. Secret leader of the Wolf Brothers

Patriarch Theodore, Archbishop of Venice and friend of Atilo il Mauros

Dr. Hightown Crow, alchemist, astrologer and anatomist to the duke

A'rial, the Duchess Alexa's *stregoi* (her pet witch)

Atilo's household

Iacopo, Atilo's servant and member of the Assassini

Amelia, a Nubian slave and member of the Assassini

The Customs Office

Roderigo, Captain of the Dogana, penniless since he refuses to take bribes

Temujin, his half-Mongol sergeant

Street Thieves

Josh, fifteen-year-old gang leader

Rosalyn, his thirteen-year-old companion

Pietro, Rosalyn's young brother

PART 1

"... what a hell of witchcraft lies
In the small orb of one particular tear ..."

A Lover's Complaint, William Shakespeare

1

Venice, Tuesday 4 January 1407

The boy hung naked from wooden walls, shackles circling one wrist and both ankles. He'd fought for days to release his left hand, burning his skin on red-hot fetters as he worked to drag his fingers free. The struggle had left him exhausted and — if he was honest — no better off than before.

"Help me," he begged, "I will do whatever you ask."

His gods stayed silent.

"I swear it. My life is yours."

But his life was theirs anyway; even here in an enclosed space where his lungs ached at every breath and the air was sour and becoming sourer. The gods had abandoned him to his death.

It would have helped if he could remember their names.

Some days he doubted they existed. If they did, he doubted they cared. The boy's fury at his fate had become bitterness and despair, and then turned to false hope and fresh fury. Maybe he'd missed an emotion, but he'd worked his way through those he knew.

Yanking at his wrist made flesh sear.

Whatever magic his captors used was stronger than his will to be free. The chains with which they bound him were new, bolted firmly to the wall. Every time he grabbed a chain to yank at it, his fingers sizzled as if a torturer pressed white-hot irons into his skin.

"Sweet gods," he whispered.

As if flattering the immortals could undo his earlier insults.

He'd shrieked at his gods, cursed them, called for the aid of demons. Begged for help from any human within earshot of his despair. A part of him wanted to return to shrieking. Simply for the release it would bring. Only he'd screamed his throat raw days ago. Besides, who would come to his grotesque little cell with no doors? And if they did, how would they enter?

Murder. Rape. Treason . . .

What else merited being walled up alive?

His crime was a mystery. What was the point of punishment if the prisoner couldn't remember what he'd done? The boy had no memory of his name. No memory of why he was locked in a space little bigger than a coffin. Not even a memory of who put him here.

Earth strewed the floor, splattered with his own soiling.

It was days since he'd needed to piss, and his lips were cracked like dry mud and raw from where he tried to lick them. He needed sleep almost as desperately as he wanted to be free, but every time he slumped his shackles burnt and the pain snapped him awake again. He'd done something wrong. Something very wrong. So wrong that even death wouldn't embrace him.

If only he could remember what.

You have a name. What is it?

Like hope and freedom, this too remained out of reach. In the hours that followed, the boy hovered on the edges of a fever. Sometimes his wits were sharp, but mostly he inhabited a blasted wasteland inside his own skull where his memories should be.

All he saw in there were shadows that turned away from him; and voices he was unable to hear clearly.

Pay attention, he told himself. *Listen.*

So he did. What he heard were voices beyond the wooden walls. A crowd from the sound of it, arguing. And though what he heard was little louder than a whisper it told him they spoke a language he didn't recognise. One voice snapped out an order, another protested. Then something slammed into the wall directly in front of him.

It sounded like an axe or a hammer.

The second blow was even harder. Then came a third, his wooden world splintering as sweet air rushed in and fetid air blew out. The light through the narrow gap was blinding. As if the gods had come for him after all.

2

Late Summer 1406

Almost four months before the boy woke to find himself trapped in an airless wooden prison, a young Venetian girl hurried along a ramshackle *fondamenta* on her city's northern edge. In some places in that strange city the waterside walkways were built from brick or even stone. The one here was earth, above sharpened logs driven into the silt of the lagoon.

After sunset everywhere in Venice was unsafe, particularly if you were fifteen years old, unmarried and out of your area. But the red-haired girl on the *fondamenta* hoped to reach the brine pans before then. She planned to beg passage on a barge carrying salt to the mainland.

Her burgundy gown was already dusty and sweat stained.

Despite having walked for only an hour, she'd reached another world entirely. One where silk dresses attracted envious glances. Her oldest gown was still richer than the *campo gheto*'s best. Her hopes of passing freely ended when a small group of children stepped out of the shadows.

Opening her cloak, Lady Giulietta yanked free a gold locket from around her neck. "Take this," she said. "Sell it. You can buy food."

The boy with the knife sneered at her. "We steal food," he said. "We don't need your locket for that. Not from round here, are you?"

Giulietta shook her head.

"You Jewish?"

"No," she said. "I'm—"

She was about to say . . . something stupid, knowing her. It was a stupid kind of day. Being here was stupid. Stopping was stupid. Even treating his question seriously was stupid. "I'm like you," she finished lamely.

"Course you are," he said. On either side, others laughed. "Where did you get this anyway?"

"My m . . ." She hesitated. "Mistress."

"You stole it," a smaller boy said. "That's why you're running. Nasty lot, the Watch. You'd be better coming with us."

"No," Giulietta said, "I'd better keep going."

"You know what happens if the Watch take you?" a girl asked. She stepped forward to whisper in Giulietta's ear. If even half were true, someone of Giulietta's age would be better killing herself than being captured. But self-murder was a sin.

"And if the Watch don't get you, then . . ."

The youngest shut his mouth at a glare from their leader. "Look around," he snapped. "It's getting dark. What have I said?"

"Sorry, Josh."

The older boy slapped him. "We don't use names with strangers. We don't talk about . . . Not when it's almost nightfall." He switched his glare to the girl who stood beside him. "I'm going to cut him loose. I swear it. Don't care if he is your brother."

"I'll go with him."

"You'll go nowhere," Josh said. "Your place is with me. You too," he told Giulietta. "There's a ruined *campo* south of here. We'll make it in time."

"If we're lucky," the girl said.

"We've been lucky so far, haven't we?"

"*So far, and no further,*" said a shadow behind them.

Old and weary, the voice sounded like dry wind through a dusty attic.

Unwrapping itself, the shadow became a Moor, dressed in a dozen shades of grey. A neatly barbered beard emphasised the thinness of his face and his gaze was that of a soldier grown tired of life. Across his shoulders hung a sword. Stilettos jutted at both hips. Lady Giulietta noticed his crossbow last. Tiny, almost a toy, with barbed arrows the size of her finger.

With a sour smile, the Moor pointed his crossbow at Josh's throat, before turning his attention to the young woman he'd been following.

"My lady, this is not kind . . ."

"Not kind?"

Bunching her fists, Lady Giulietta fought her anger.

She'd become used to holding it in in public, screaming about her forthcoming marriage behind closed doors. She was two years older than her mother was when she wed. Noble girls married at twelve, went to their husband's beds at thirteen, sometimes a little later. At least two of Giulietta's friends had children already.

She'd been whipped for her refusal to wed willingly.

Starved, locked in her chambers. Until she announced she'd kill herself. On being told that was a sin, she'd sworn to murder her husband instead.

At that, Aunt Alexa, the late Duke Marco III's widow, had shaken her head sadly and sent for hot water to which she added fermented leaves to make her niece a soothing drink. While Uncle Alonzo, the late duke's younger brother, had taken Giulietta aside to say it was interesting she should mention that . . .

Her world became a darker, more horrid place. Not only would she marry a foreigner she'd never met. She'd be taught how to kill him when the bedding was done. "You know what they expect me to do?"

"My lady, it's not my place . . ."

"Of course not. You're just the cur sent to round up strays."

His eyes flared and she smiled. He wasn't a cur and she wasn't a stray. She was Lady Giulietta dei San Felice di Millioni. The Regent's niece. The new duke's cousin. Duchess Alexa's goddaughter. Her whole life defined by how she was related to someone else.

"Say you couldn't find me."

"I've been following you since I saw you leave."

"*Why?*" she demanded. Only in the last half-hour had she felt herself watched. She couldn't believe he'd let her travel right across Venice by herself, knowing he would stop her before she could escape to the mainland.

"I hoped you might turn back."

Rubbing her temples, Giulietta wished they'd sent a young officer she could shout at, or beguile with her charms, meagre though they were.

"How can I marry a man I haven't even met?"

"You know . . ."

Giulietta stamped her foot. She understood. All daughters were assets. Princely daughters more than most. It was just . . . Maybe she'd read too many poets. What if there was someone she was *meant* to marry? She regretted her words the moment they were spoken. The Moor's quiet contempt for her question ensured that.

"And what if he lives on the world's far edge or is not yet born? What if he died centuries ago? *What if he loves someone else?* Policy can't wait on a girl's fantasies. Not even for you . . ."

"Let me go," Giulietta begged.

"My lady, I can't." He shook his head sadly, never letting his crossbow's aim stray from Josh's throat. "Ask me anything else."

"I want nothing else."

Atilo il Mauros had bought her her first pony. Dandled her on his knees. With his own hands he carved her a bear fighting a woodcutter. But he would return her to Ca' Ducale because that was his duty. Atilo did his duty without fear or favour. It had made him the late duke's favourite. And earned him Alonzo, the new Regent's, hatred. Giulietta had no idea what Aunt Alexa thought of him.

"If you loved me . . ." Her voice was flat.

Lord Atilo glanced at the bow he held, looked at the ragged thieves and shifted Giulietta out of their hearing, without letting his aim waver.

"My lady."

"*Listen to me.*" She felt sick in her gut. Tired and fed up and close to tears. "King Janus was a Crucifer. A Black Crucifer."

"I know."

"And I had to learn it from servants' gossip. They're going to marry me to an ex-torturer, who broke his vows of poverty and chastity. Who abandoned *the purity of pain.*" Her lips curled in disgust at the words.

"To become king," Atilo said simply.

"He's a monster."

"Giulietta . . . The Germans want Venice. The Byzantines want it too. The Mamluks want your colonies. Even my people, the Moors, would happily see your navy sunk. King Janus was Black only briefly. Cyprus is an island we can use."

"*Use?*" she said in scorn.

"Venice's strength rests on its trade routes. It *needs* Cyprus. Besides, you have to marry someone."

"It might as well be him?"

The Moor nodded, and she wondered if he could read the fury in her eyes. Anger kept her fear at bay. Her fear of what being bedded by a Black Crucifer might involve.

"My lord," Josh interrupted.

Atilo raised his bow. "Did I tell you to speak?" His finger began tightening on the trigger.

"*Let him speak.*"

"My lady, you're in no . . ."

". . . position to demand anything?" said Lady Giulietta bitterly. She'd never been in a position to demand anything as far as she could see. At least not since her mother was murdered. Giulietta was a Millioni. A princess. She had one of the most gilded childhoods in Venice. Everyone envied her.

She'd swap all of it for . . .

Lady Giulietta bit her lip so hard it bled. There were days when her self-pity nauseated even herself. This was turning out to be one of them.

"Let's hear what he has to say," she suggested.

Atilo lowered his tiny crossbow. A nod said the boy was reprieved, for now. "This had better be good."

"We should get off the streets, my lord."

"That's it?" Atilo sounded astonished. "That's your contribution? You're a split second away from death. And you think we should get off the streets?"

"It's almost dark."

"They're afraid of the Watch," Giulietta said.

She wasn't surprised. *Beat you and violate you, smash your face and twist your arms if you don't do everything they want.* That sounded as if the girl spoke from experience.

"Not the Watch," the younger boy said dismissively. "We ain't afraid of them now. They don't go out after dark."

"They're the Watch," Giulietta said.

"Got more sense," he told her. "Not with what's out there."

"And what is out there?" she asked. Perhaps the small boy didn't see Atilo's warning scowl. Perhaps he wasn't bothered.

"Demons."

"No," his sister said. "They're monsters."

"Atilo . . ." She shouldn't be using his name like that. Not without "my lord" or whatever title he held since the Regent had stripped him of Admiral of the Middle Sea, which had been his position under Marco III . . . The late, and very lamented Duke Marco III. Since his son, Marco IV, her poor cousin, was a twitching simpleton.

"What?" His tone was sharp.

"We can't just leave them."

"Yes," he said. "We can." Atilo stopped at an owl's hoot, his shoulders relaxing slightly. When he hooted back, the owl hooted in return. "It's you we can't leave." There was bitterness in his voice.

"But you would if you could . . . ?"

"I have fifteen blades out there. The best I've trained. My deputy, his deputy, thirteen others. Good soldiers. If half come through this alive I'll be grateful."

Giulietta didn't recognise him as the old man who had carved her a wooden toy as a child. This was the Atilo people saw in battle.

"Are we heading for safety?"

He turned, looked at her. A hard glare that softened slightly. "There is no safety tonight, my lady. Not here and not now. The best I can do is hope to keep you alive."

"And the children?"

"They're dead already. Leave them."

"I can't . . . We can't . . ." She plucked at his sleeve. "Please."

"You want them saved?"

"Yes," she said, grateful. Thinking he'd changed his mind.

"Then let them be. They stand a better chance of living if they hide now. Not much, admittedly. But staying with you will certainly get them killed."

Lady Giulietta looked sick.

"It's you our enemies want. Well, it is now."

Taking a stiletto from his hip, he reversed it fluidly, offering her its handle over the edge of his forearm. *Sweet Lord*, she thought. *He's serious.* From the knot in her guts, her body was ahead of her brain. She was afraid the knot would let go and she'd disgrace herself in front of the old man.

"Find a tanner's pit," Atilo snapped at Josh's group. "Shouldn't be hard round here. Squat in it up to your necks. Don't move. Keep silent until morning."

"The demons hate water?"

"They hunt by smell. You stink of piss already. Find a tanner's pit and you might get lucky." Atilo turned without further thought. They were gone already as far as he was concerned.

"Stay close," he told Giulietta.

Atilo used a *sottoportego*, an underpass beneath a tenement building, to reach a tiny square. At its far edge, the square was prevented from crumbling into a narrow canal by oak stakes along its bank. Slicing a rope to a shabby gondola, Atilo kicked it away from the side to make a makeshift bridge. Once Lady Giulietta was over, he cut the remaining rope and jumped for safety as the boat drifted away.

"Where are we going?"

"I have a house," he said.

"Ca' il Mauros?" Her heart sank. To reach there from here, they'd need to cross the Grand Canal by gondola twice, or walk round it, which would double the distance and take them down one of the most dangerous streets in Venice.

"A different house," he told her.

When he reached for her hand, it was not to comfort her, but to grip her wrist and start dragging. He wanted her to walk faster.

"Atilo, you're . . ." Giulietta shut her mouth. The old man was trying to save her. He was furious, in a way she'd never seen, his face a battle mask, his eyes hard in the darkness.

"I'm sorry," she said.

He stopped, and Giulietta thought . . . For a second, she thought he'd forget himself and slap her. Then there was no time to think more of that, because a grotesque figure watched them from a square ahead.

"This way."

A yank on her wrist hurled her towards an alley. Only that

way out of the new square was blocked as well. As were the other two exits.

"Kill yourself," Atilo said.

Giulietta gaped at him.

"Not now, you little fool. If I'm dead, and they're dead . . ." He pointed to silhouettes appearing in the shadows. Some stood near the grotesques who blocked the exits, others stood on rooftops or balconies. "Don't let yourself be taken."

"They'll rape me?"

"You can survive that. What the Wolf Brothers do you don't survive. Although you might be more use to them alive and unharmed. Which means you must definitely kill yourself."

"Self-murder is a sin."

"Letting yourself be captured is a worse one."

"To God?"

"To Venice. Which is what matters."

Serenissima, the name poets gave to the Serene Republic of Venice, was an inaccurate term. Since the city was neither serene nor, these days, a republic.

In Atilo's opinion, it was most like a bubbling pot into which some celestial threw endless grains of rice. And though each morning began with the bodies of beggars against walls, new born infants in back canals, paupers dumped to avoid the inconvenience of burying them—those unwanted, even by the unwanted—the city remained as crowded, and as packed, and as expensive, as he remembered it ever having been.

In summer the poor slept on roofs, on balconies or in the open air. When winter came, they crowded squalid tenements. They shat, copulated, fought and quarrelled in public, seen by other adults as well as by their own children. The stairwells of the tenements had a permanent odour of poverty. Unwashed, unloved, stinking of sewage, and a greasy misery that oiled the skin until it looked and smelt like wet leather.

A dozen scholars had drawn maps of Venice. Including a Chinese cartographer sent by the Great Khan, who'd heard of this capital with canals where roads should be and wanted to know how much of it was true. None of the maps were accurate, however, and half the streets had more than one name anyway.

Running through what he thought of Venice, Atilo il Mauros wondered, in retrospect, why he felt reluctant to leave it and the life he'd made here. Was it simply that this was not the way he'd intended to die? In a squalid *campo*, near a ramshackle church, because every *campo* had one of those. Although not usually this run-down. A church, a broken wellhead, ruined brick houses . . .

He'd hoped to die in his bed years from now.

His wife, beautifully stricken, backlit by a gentle autumn sun; a boy at the bed's foot, staring sorrowfully. To have this, of course, he'd need a wife. A wife, a son and heir, maybe a couple of daughters, if they weren't too much trouble.

After the siege of Tunis, Duke Marco III had offered him a deal. The duke would spare the city and Atilo would serve Venice as Admiral. If Atilo refused, every man, woman and child in the North African city would be slaughtered; including Atilo's own family. The great pirate of the Barbary Coast could turn traitor to those he loved and save them, or stay loyal and condemn them to death.

Bastard, Atilo thought with admiration.

Even now, decades later, he could remember his awe at the brutality of Marco's offer. In a single afternoon Atilo uttered the words that divorced his wife, renounced his children, converted his religion and bound him to Venice for life.

In taking the title of Lord Admiral of the Middle Sea, he had saved those who would hate him for the rest of their lives. In public, he'd been Marco III's adviser. In private he'd been the man's chief assassin. The enemy, who became his master, ended as his friend. Atilo would die for that man's niece.

This was the biggest gathering of Wolf Brothers in Atilo's lifetime—and he was shocked to discover so many in his city. Well, the city Atilo he'd come to love. Atilo knew what this battle meant. To fight *krieghund* in the open like this would destroy the Assassini, quite possibly leave him without an heir. Destroying the Assassini would leave Venice without protection.

Was her life worth that much?

He knew the girl behind him had caught the moment he wanted to slap her. Fifteen-year-old princesses were not meant to run away, unhappily betrothed or not. They were not meant to be *able* to run away. A savage whipping would await her if she lived; assuming Atilo told the truth about her flight. Alonzo would see to the whipping even if her aunt objected. For a woman so fond of poisoning her enemies Alexa could be very forgiving where her niece was concerned.

"My lord . . ."

A black-clad man appeared out of the darkness, sketched a quick bow and instinctively checked what weapons his chief was carrying. He relaxed slightly when he saw the little crossbow.

"Silver-tipped, my lord?"

"Obviously."

The man glanced at Giulietta, his eyes widening when he realised she carried Atilo's dagger.

"She has her orders," Atilo said. "Yours are to die protecting her."

There were twenty-one in the Scuola di Assassini, including Atilo. In the early days he'd given his followers Greek letters as names, but he drew his apprentices from the poorest levels of the city and many had trouble with their own alphabet. These days he used numbers instead.

The middle-aged man in front of him was No. 3.

No. 2 was in prison in Cyprus on charges that couldn't be proved; he would be released or simply disappear. Knowing Janus it would be the latter. No. 4 was in Vienna to kill Emperor

Sigismund. A task he would probably fail. No. 7 guarded their headquarters. No. 13 was in Constantinople. And No. 17 was in Paris trying to poison a Valois princeling. In theory, only one of them needed to survive to ensure the *scuola*, the Scuola di Assassini, continued unbroken.

Sixteen Assassini against six enemies.

With those odds victory should be certain. But Atilo knew what was out there: the emperor's *krieghund*. His blades would die in reverse order. The most junior trying to exhaust the beasts so their seniors had a chance of success. Atilo was arbiter of what success entailed. Tonight it meant keeping Lady Giulietta out of enemy hands. "Go die," he ordered his deputy.

The man's grin disappeared into the night.

"Numerical," Atilo heard him shout, and hell opened as a snarling, silver-furred beast stalked into the square, leaving a screaming, vaguely man-shaped lump of meat in an alley mouth behind.

"What is it?" Giulietta asked, far too loudly.

"*Krieghund*," Atilo snapped. "Speak again and I'll gag you." Sighting his crossbow, he fired. But the beast swatted aside the silver bolt and turned on an Assassino approaching from its blind side. The kill was quick and brutal. A claw caught the side of the boy's skull, dragging him closer. A bite to the neck half removed his head.

"I thought they were a myth," Giulietta whispered, then clapped her hand over her mouth and backed away from Atilo.

The Moor grinned sourly. She was learning. Give him the girl for a few months and he'd give her aunt and uncle something worth keeping, and not just keeping alive. But they didn't want something to keep. They wanted something unbroken they could trade.

In a miracle of luck and poor judgement the third most junior Assassino hurled himself at the creature in front of him, ducked under a claw and managed to stab his sword into the beast's side before the *krieghund* struck. The young man died with his neck broken and his throat spraying blood.

"Kill the beast," Giulietta begged.

"I don't have arrows to waste." Sweeping his gaze over the small, dark square, Atilo concluded fifty people must be watching from behind shutters. Houses this poor lacked glass. So they could hear as well.

None would help. Why would they?

"Look," he told her, pointing at the *krieghund* on its knees. As she looked, the beast began to change, its face flattening and its shoulders becoming narrower. Giulietta took a second to understand what she was seeing. A wolfthing becoming a man, who stopped howling and started trying to shovel loops of gut back into his gaping stomach.

"Now we kill him."

Out of the darkness came an Assassino, his sword already drawn back to take the dying man's head. Blood pumped in a fountain and fell like rain. The battle was ferocious after that. Beasts and men hacking at each other. And then men lay dead in the dirt. Most in riveted mail, a few naked.

"My lord . . ."

Giulietta was finding her nerve, addressing him politely now. She still looked pale in the moonlight. They all looked pale to him. At least she'd stopped shivering and now held his dagger more confidently. There was an old-fashioned Millioni princess in there somewhere.

"They're advancing . . ."

"I know," he said, raising his bow.

The officer who took orders originally glanced over, bowing slightly in reply to Atilo's nod, to acknowledge whatever passed between them. He signalled to those of the Assassini who remained and they attacked as one.

The last stages of the fight were brief and brutal.

Swords slashing, daggers sliding under ribs, blood spraying. The stink was the stink of the abattoir; of shit and blood and open guts. The men died well, but they died, and, in the end, most corpses were clothed, a handful were naked and one furred half-corpse lurched towards Atilo, a dagger jutting from its ribs.

"Kill it," Giulietta begged.

Sighting his crossbow, Atilo fired for the creature's throat.

The beast staggered, but kept coming. Straight into a second arrow. Hooking back his string, Atilo slotted a third, and would have fired had the *krieghund* not slashed the bow from his hand.

Never thought I'd die like this.

The thought came and went. There were worse ways to go than facing a creature from hell. But he had Marco III's niece behind him and he couldn't just . . . "Don't," he shouted. He was too late, however.

Stepping out from behind him, Giulietta rammed her stiletto into the *krieghund*'s side, twisting hard. She went down when the creature cracked its elbow into her head. It was stooping for the kill, when a piece of night sky detached itself, dropping in a crackle of old leather and dry clicks. Atilo took the opening. Stabbing a throwing knife into the beast's heart.

"Alexa . . . ?"

The square of leather bumped into ground-floor shutters, crawled between rusting bars and hung itself upside down. Wings folding to a fraction of their previous size as golden eyes glared from a face disgusted with the world.

"Giulietta's still alive?"

Kneeling, Atilo touched his fingers to the girl's throat. "Yes, my lady."

"Good. We'll need her now more than ever." The bat through which Giulietta's aunt had watched the battle turned its attention to the *krieghund*'s death agony. "You've upset him." The words were thin. A whisper of wind forced from a throat not made for speech.

"He's dying."

"Not him, fool. His master. Leopold will try stealing her again."

Atilo considered pointing out that the German prince hadn't stolen her this time. Lady Giulietta had stolen herself.

"Then we hunt Leopold down and kill him."

"He has protection," whispered the bat. "He will be more cautious now. He will move more carefully. And he will rebuild his Wolf Brothers. And then all this will start again. Slaughtered children and the Night Watch too scared to do their job. Until we grow tired and beg for the truce he keeps offering us."

"This is our city."

"Yes," said the bat. "But he's the German emperor's bastard."

The second time someone didn't come when he knocked, Atilo kicked the door off its hinges and entered with a throwing dagger in his hand.

"Boil water," he ordered. "And fetch me thread."

A combination of the blade he carried, his air of command and his absolute certainty he would be obeyed was enough to make the householder put down an iron bar, bow low and order his wife into the kitchen at the back.

"Who sleeps above?" Atilo pointed over his head.

"My daughter . . ."

"Bring her down."

"My lord."

Atilo caught fear in his voice. "I don't want your damn daughter," he said brusquely. "I want her bed, and privacy. Leave hot water, a needle and thread outside her door."

"Thread, sir?"

The Moor sighed. "Find a horsehair, boil it in the water, and the needle while you're at it. Knock when they're ready." Disappearing into the night, he returned carrying Giulietta, her legs hanging over his arms, her head thrown back to reveal blood in her hair.

"You know who I am?"

The man, the woman and their newly arrived daughter shook their heads. The daughter was about twelve, wrapped in a blanket, and flinched when he turned his attention to her. "Did you see the battle?"

"No one here saw anything, my lord."

"Right answer," said Atilo, pushing past towards the stairs.

3

New Year 1407

In the days then weeks and finally months that followed that autumn's pitched battle between the Assassini and the Wolf Brothers—a battle known only to a few—plans went forward for the marriage of Lady Giulietta to Janus, King of Cyprus.

As the year dragged towards its end and another was born, on 25 December, the same day as the Christian Lord, Atilo il Mauros—who wasn't quite sure which god he acknowledged—licked his wounds and wondered how to keep the destruction of his Assassini secret.

The girl they'd died protecting simply waited to meet her new husband. Although she should have realised he wouldn't come himself. Instead, he sent an Englishman, Sir Richard Glanville, as his envoy.

Arriving in mid-December, the envoy spent Christmas at the ducal palace, while terms were negotiated and arrangements made for Lady Giulietta's departure. When these were agreed, Sir Richard celebrated by offering a hundred gold coins as the prize for a gondola race. A foreign noble's traditional way of ingratiating himself with the Venetian public.

However, his generosity failed to impress Lady Giulietta, who resented having to leave her warm quarters for the chill wind of a winter afternoon, and made little attempt to hide it. She had no idea that Monday 3 January would change her life. As far as she was concerned, it was the day sleet frizzed her hair as she turned out to watch the end of another stupid race.

"They say Crucifers prefer men."

Sir Richard's simple breastplate was half hidden by the cloak of his order. His only jewellery was a ring marrying him to his priory. By contrast, the captain of Giulietta's escort wore red hose, scarlet shoes and a brocade doublet short enough to show his codpiece. Both men were watching a merchant's wife.

"My lady. Are you sure about that?"

"Eleanor . . ." Giulietta started to reprimand her lady-in-waiting and then shrugged. "Perhaps Sir Richard's the exception."

"Perhaps the rumour is wrong."

"You like him!"

"*My lady.*"

"You do!"

Eleanor was thirteen and Giulietta's cousin. She had the dark eyes, black hair and olive skin of those who mix northern blood with blood from the south. She was loyal but quite capable of answering back. "He's a White Crucifer."

"So?" Giulietta demanded.

"Crucifers are celibate."

"Supposedly."

"What do you think they're discussing?" Eleanor asked, trying to change the subject. Although all that happened was that Giulietta's scowl deepened.

"My engagement. All anybody talks about."

"She's interesting."

Captain Roderigo regarded the merchant's wife with surprise. She was certainly blonde, and pink-skinned, big-breasted and big-boned. With thighs made to cushion a man's head. But interesting?

"I meant your Lady Giulietta."

Both men glanced towards the Millioni princess.

Her family had worn the *biretum*, that oddly shaped cap adopted by the doges of old, for five generations. Earlier dukes were elected, however corrupt that election. Marco Polo's descendants claimed it by birth. Their palace was grander than the Medici's. Their mainland estates wider than the Pope's own. They were aggressive, avaricious and scheming. Essential qualities for a princely family. To these they added a fourth, *murderous*. Their arm was long. The blade it held sharp.

"The Millioni have kept us free."

"From whom?" Sir Richard asked, sounding surprised.

"Everyone. Venice balances on a rope, with predators waiting in the pit below. They see us dance elegantly, pirouette daintily; dressed in our gaudy clothes. And never ask the reason we stay high on our rope."

"And who are the predators?"

Roderigo regarded him sharply. "We have the German emperor to the north. The emperor of Byzantium to the south. The Pope has declared the Millioni *false princes*. Making them fair game for any penitent with a sharp dagger and a guilty conscience. The Mamluks covet our trade routes. The King of Hungary wants his Schiavoni colonies in Dalmatia back. Everyone offers to protect us from everyone else. Who do you think the predators are?"

"So you marry Giulietta to Janus because it will help protect those trade routes? Poor child . . ."

Finding them watching her, Giulietta turned away.

"She makes no pretence to be pleased," said Sir Richard, then shrugged. "Why would she? Janus is years older. I imagine she dreams of the Florentine."

"Cosimo?"

"He's . . . what? A few years older than her? Educated, loves music, dresses well. He's even said to be handsome."

"She fancies no one," Roderigo said. "Not even," he said, trying to sweeten the truth, "a ruggedly handsome, war-hardened veteran like me."

Sir Richard snorted.

"Anyway, she can't marry the Medici. Florence is our enemy."

"So were we until your ambassador proposed this match at the funeral of our late queen. Janus was surprised by your timing."

Roderigo wasn't.

Venice's ambassador to Cyprus had the patience of a baited bear and the subtlety of a rampaging bull. He'd been given the post because Duchess Alexa couldn't stand his presence in her city any longer.

"Look," said Roderigo. "You should tell Giulietta that Cyprus is beautiful. That Janus is struck dumb by the beauty of her portrait."

"I'm a Crucifer." Sir Richard said ruefully. "We don't lie."

"You have to entice her."

"You've visited Janus's island? Then you know the truth. The summers burn, the winters are bleak. The only thing he has in abundance are rocks and goats. I won't embellish the truth to impress her."

Roderigo sighed.

"On to other matters," Sir Richard said. "Who takes the tenth chair?"

Glancing round, as if to indicate that simply asking was unwise, Roderigo muttered, "Impossible to say. No doubt the decision will be a wise one."

"No doubt."

The city's inner council had one seat vacant. Obviously enough, that seat was in the gift of Marco IV, reigning Duke of Venice and Prince of Serenissima. Unfortunately, Marco had little interest in politics.

"Surely you have some idea?"

"It depends . . ."

"On what?"

After another quick glance, Roderigo said, "Whether the Regent or the duchess get to choose." They walked on in uneasy silence after that. Until Sir Richard stopped at a proclamation nailed to a church door.

Wanted.
Axel, a master glass blower.
Fifty gold ducats to anyone who captures him. Death to anyone who aids his escape. This is the judgement of the Ten.

The glass-blower was described as thickset, heavy of gut and white at the temples, with a lurid scar along his left thumb. If he had any sense, he'd crop his hair. Moreover, skulking in fear for his life should shrink his gut. The scar would be harder to hide, however.

"Will you find him?"

"We usually do."

"What happens to his family?"

Roderigo checked that his charges were walking arm-in-arm ahead; one sullen, the other watchful. Being Giulietta's lady-in-waiting was an honour, but not an easy one. "They'll be questioned obviously."

"They haven't been already?"

"Of course they've . . ." Roderigo's voice was loud enough to make Lady Eleanor look back. "Yes," he hissed. "They've been questioned. One son-in-law and a grandchild are dead. The Council examines the others tomorrow."

"And then . . . ?"

"Death between the lion and the dragon."

Two columns marked the lagoon edge of the *piazzetta*, a small square attached to San Marco's much larger one. One topped by a winged lion, the other by Saint Todaro slaying a dragon. It was here that traitors died.

"Why kill them if they know nothing?"

"What do you know about Murano?"

"Little enough. You don't encourage strangers."

"The glassmakers' island has its own courts and cathedral, its own coinage, its own bishop. It even has its own Golden Book. A good portion of Venice's wealth comes from its secrets."

Captain Roderigo paused to let that sink in.

"It's the only place in the world where artisans are patrician and skill with your hands earns you the right to wear a sword in public."

"This comes at a price?"

Honesty kept Roderigo from lying. Glass-blowers couldn't leave Murano without permission and the penalty for a Muranesq caught trying to abandon Venice was death. "Didn't you need your Prior's permission to leave Cyprus?" he added, refusing to concede the point entirely.

"I'm a Crucifer." Sir Richard's voice was amused. "I wake, sleep, piss and fight on the orders of my Prior. And we should stop talking. Ignoring Lady Giulietta makes it hard for her to ignore us."

Roderigo laughed. "She's young," he said. "And Janus has . . ." He hesitated. "A strange reputation."

"For liking boys?"

"Also pain."

"The last is a lie."

"Yet he married his late wife for love?"

"Bedded her once. And was stricken when she died. Your Lady Giulietta will not have an easy time of it."

First out of the Grand Canal and already speeding towards the *piazzetta*, a curly-haired boy and his Nubian companion were far enough ahead to have a length between them and the first of those behind.

Maybe the lightness of their boat made up for the slightness of its crew.

Two boys rowing, where others had three, five or even seven working an oar. All stood, using a single oar each. There were ten thousand *gondolini* in Venice and each was taxed yearly. That was how their number was known.

A hundred and fifty craft had set out, hoping to race round the city's edge, before returning along the reversed S of the Canalasso, as the Venetians called their largest canal. Although most were *gondolini*, the boat in front was not.

"What is it?" Sir Richard asked Roderigo. Then, remembering his manners, added. "Perhaps her ladyship knows?"

"Eleanor?"

Her lady-in-waiting didn't know either.

"A *vipera*," Roderigo said. "Mostly used for smuggling."

"It's a *vipera*," Giulietta said flatly. "Mostly used for smuggling."

"Equally pointed at both ends?"

Roderigo nodded. "Instead of turning his boat, the oarsman turns himself, while my men are still turning their *gondolini*. It's rare to see one used openly."

"And the name is from *viper*?"

"Because they strike fast."

"Smugglers who strike fast. Or maybe such boats have other uses?"

Roderigo smiled at the dryness in Sir Richard's voice. Venice was known as the city of gilt, glass and assassinations. The whole of Italy knew why the boats racing towards the finish were black.

Eleven years earlier, in the year of Our Lord 1396, a gondola had drawn alongside the ornately painted craft carrying Giulietta's mother, Zoë dei San Felice. The crossbow bolt that killed her passed through her oarsman first. When the oarsman crawled to her side, the late duke's only sister was dead.

A sumptuary law passed that evening instructed that all *gondolini* be painted black. This was not death's colour in Venice, that was red. But in honour of Zoë's elegance, all vessels would be her favourite colour. The truth was that Marco III had wanted the safety *gondolini* looking alike would bring his family.

The boys in the *vipera* were extending their lead when the boat closest behind rocked suddenly and tipped, losing its crew with a splash. Glancing back, the curly-haired boy shouted something and his Nubian companion started to laugh.

"That was Dolphino taking a ducking," Roderigo said, as if this explained everything. "He can't bear losing."

"You mean . . . ?"

Lady Giulietta curled her lip. "That was no accident."

"By tonight," added Roderigo, "Dolphino will have been closing the gap and about to win. And the boys who just stopped will have sacrificed their second place to help a friend."

"Let's get this over with," Giulietta said.

Gathering her gown, she stepped from a wooden walkway on to slippery brick and headed for the finish line. Sir Richard followed, wondering how King Janus would deal with his strong-willed bride.

"Your names?" Roderigo asked.

"Iacopo, my lord." Cheaply dressed but freshly razored, the curly-haired boy bowed with lazy grace, as if born to court rather than the poverty his jacket suggested. "And this is . . . a slave." The slave bowed low in the Eastern style, silver thimbles dancing at the ends of a dozen tight braids.

"Well done," Sir Richard said.

The curly-haired boy smiled.

A wide face and brown eyes. Strong arms and . . . His virility made obvious by the tightness of his hose and the salt spray that soaked them.

"Eleanor," Lady Giulietta said. "You're staring."

The girl flushed with embarrassment.

"The distance?" Sir Richard asked quickly.

"Nine *mille passum*, my lord. Seven thousand paces around

the edge, and two thousand back through the canal. The waves were tough to the north, but she's good . . ." He nodded to the *vipera* in pride.

"Yours?"

"My master's."

Realising the silence following was a question in itself, the boy added. "Lord Atilo il Mauros. He's . . ."

Sir Richard knew. "Your winnings," he said, offering a purse.

The young man bowed again, and couldn't resist weighing the purse in his hand. His grin showed white, and crinkled the edges of his eyes.

"Eleanor . . ."

"I'm not the one gawping."

Giulietta glanced sharply at her lady-in-waiting.

"And have this," Roderigo added hastily, shucking himself out of his brocade doublet. It was outdated and darned, but the victor's eyes widened and then he scowled.

"Silver thread, my lord."

Tattered brocade he might get away with. However, silver thread, like gold thread, fur, enamel, silk and embroidery, was denied to servants by law.

"I doubt the Watch will arrest this afternoon's winner before nightfall and you can have your woman pick it clean by tomorrow."

"I don't have one, my lord."

"You will tonight," Sir Richard promised.

4

Grateful to be free of the wind in their faces, Lady Giulietta's party were walking away from the salt spray and the bobbing boat of the victors when Roderigo became aware of footsteps behind him.

"My lord . . ."

Turning, he found the curly-haired boy. "Iacopo, isn't it?"

The young man was pleased the captain remembered his name. "Yes, my lord. Forgive me. You know Lady Desdaio, I believe?"

Roderigo nodded.

"Intimately, my lord?"

The captain's scowl was so fierce Iacopo stepped back.

"I have no doubt of Lady Desdaio's honour," Roderigo said fiercely. "*No one* has any doubt about her honour. Understand me?"

Nodding, Iacopo bowed low for causing offence. After which, he chewed his lip and shuffled his feet like the street urchin he'd probably been. His was a face found everywhere in Venice. A curving mouth and knowing eyes framed by curls. His straight, unbroken nose was less usual. It said that either he disliked fights or fought well.

"What about her?"

"She is betrothed to my master."

Roderigo was not a man of tempers.

He did his job well and both the Regent and duchess used him when they needed a good officer. He'd reached his post as head of the Venetian customs by hard work, having entered as a junior lieutenant. All the same, there was a blackness to his gaze as it swept the herringbone brick of the *piazzetta* that made people look away.

"When did this happen?"

"Yesterday, my lord . . . I learnt this morning when preparing for the race. Lord Atilo came to wish me luck."

"I see," Roderigo said tightly.

Full-breasted, plump and buxom, Desdaio Bribanzo was his ideal of beauty. Hell, she was the city's ideal. Only her hair let her down. This was chestnut rather than the reddish blonde Venice favoured.

Unlike other girls, she refused to dye it.

At twenty-three, Desdaio combined huge eyes, a sweet face and sweeter smile with being heiress to a vast fortune. Her father imported more pepper, cinnamon and ginger than any other noble in the city. Obviously enough, she had more suitors than any of her rivals. One of whom was Roderigo. They'd known each other since childhood. He'd thought they liked each other well enough.

"Why tell me this?"

"I'd heard . . . Your kindness. The coat . . ." Iacopo stuttered to a halt and went back to shuffling his feet.

"Lord Bribanzo approves?"

"He's still in Rome, my lord."

"In which case we'll see what he says. She wouldn't be the first to give her heart to one man while her father gives her body to another."

"This case is complicated." Iacopo chose his words carefully, keeping his face neutral as he waited for the captain to ask why.

"So tell me," Roderigo growled.

"She has moved herself into Ca' il Mauros."

"My God. Her father will . . ."

"Be furious, my lord. None the less, if she stays even a single night there unchaperoned. No parental fury can undo the damage that does her."

"She has gold." Roderigo said flatly. "It will be enough."

Iacopo sucked his teeth, as if to say the ways of women, particularly noble and rich ones, were beyond him. And if the brave captain said this was the case, who was he to disagree?

The Ca' Ducale was built using pillars, window frames and door arches looted from other cities. Its style, however, was unique. Round arches from the Orthodox East combined with mauresque fretwork and pointed windows from Western Gothic; mixed in a fashion only found in one city in the world: this one.

This theft of materials was not the insult.

Nor was the fact that the palace and its basilica both used materials stolen from mosques, synagogues and even churches. How could one expect better of a place where *Venetian first, Christian second* was said daily?

The insult was more subtle.

The palace said to foreign princes, You hide behind fortified walls in ugly castles. I live on islands in the sea. My power is so great I can afford to live behind walls so thin they could be made from glass. That fact had not occurred to Captain Roderigo until Sir Richard pointed it out to him.

"Sir Richard, perhaps you could . . ."

Indicating Giulietta discreetly, and then the nearest palace door, Roderigo said, "I have official matters waiting."

"You're not dining with us?"

"As I said, duty calls."

Sir Richard scowled. "I don't suppose . . ."

"Me," said Roderigo, "the duke can manage without. You, he

is expecting for supper. Well," he added, more honestly, "I'm sure the Regent and Duchess Alexa expect you. His highness . . ."

There was no need to say more.

"This business had to do with the customs office?"

Roderigo jerked his head at a dozen ships moored on a stretch of lagoon reserved for those in quarantine. Since God's wrath killed half of Venice sixty years before ships now waited offshore to make certain they carried no disease.

"We think one of those might already have taken the glass-blower aboard. We'll be boarding the ship tonight."

"Which one?"

"See the last?"

Sir Richard peered into the sleet. After a second, Roderigo realised that Giulietta and her lady-in-waiting had joined them.

"Moorish," Eleanor said.

Giulietta shook her head. "Mamluk," she corrected. Seeing Sir Richard's surprise, she added tartly, "When there's nothing to do but watch ships you learn their flags quickly enough. Any fool can work it out."

Sir Richard's face went blank.

He had to confirm a treaty, collect his king's new wife and escort her to Famagusta, where she could watch ships headed north for the Venetian ports strung like pearls between Rhodes and the city itself. After this, Giulietta's temper was the king's business. Sir Richard didn't look upset at the thought.

"What did the ship do wrong?"

"Absolutely nothing," Roderigo told Lady Eleanor. "It arrived, waited as told, and followed our pilot without arguing the price . . ."

"That's it?" Giulietta's lady-in-waiting sounded surprised.

"Paid harbour dues, bought fresh water. They didn't even try to bribe their way out of quarantine . . ."

Lady Giulietta snorted. That was suspicious indeed.

5

Inside the customs house, Venice's famous Dogana fortress, men had been gathering since sunset. Roderigo was the last to arrive.

"Hey, chief . . ."

The man who spoke was shorter than his commander and half as broad again. He had the wide face, Mongol eyes and tallow skin of his father. After fifty years on God's earth, he still spoke like his mother, a Rialto fishwife.

"What?"

"Guess that answers that."

"Answers what?"

"I was going to ask if you were all right."

Roderigo had found Temujin drunk in the street begging for alms. In two years he'd gone from mopping floors to sergeant. He fought dirty, drank hard and paid his debts; and the troop respected him for it, or had the sense to keep any doubts to themselves.

"Everyone here?"

"One's ill. I've borrowed him instead."

Temujin pointed to a rat-faced man in a Castellani smock, overlaid with a leather jerkin so filthy he could pass unseen on a moonless night. The composite bow over his shoulder fired arrows of a kind the captain hadn't seen in years. Taking another look, he noted the shape of the man's eyes.

"I can find someone else."

"No need." The Mongols kept a *fontego* in the city. A trading post where Mongol law applied. Like every other race, they left their bastards.

Taking another salted fish, Roderigo chewed it until it was just about soft enough to swallow. He wanted wine to remove the aftertaste, but once ordered the temptation to drink would be impossible to bear.

Atilo il Mauros had to be sixty-five at the least. His name wasn't in the Golden Book, the list of noble families with a right to sit in Council. Worse, he wasn't even from Serenissima. He spoke Italian with an Andalusian accent.

"Find me wine," Roderigo demanded.

Temujin looked at him, but sent a trooper for a fresh jug and a squat tumbler on which fading saints stared ghost-like. Having filled his glass, Roderigo returned the jug. "Tip the rest away."

"Chief . . ."

"All right. All right. Share it around. But if one man gets drunk I'll have him whipped. If someone dies through his folly I'll have him hanged. Make sure they know that."

The men filled their mugs anyway.

"The boats are ready?"

Of course the boats were ready. The boats were always ready. But Temujin made do with a brief nod before asking if there was anything else his captain wanted.

Other than the head of Atilo on a spit?

The upstairs office to which the Captain of the Dogana took himself had a fire laid, and a stout woman knelt before it. Who, Roderigo suspected, could be laid with little enough trouble herself. Maria was Temujin's woman and the customs house's unofficial maid.

She had an almost full set of teeth, wide hips and low breasts that shifted as she moved to light his fire. Still crouching, she turned and he saw darkness between her thighs. "Is there anything, my lord . . . ?"

"*No*," Roderigo said.

He wanted Desdaio. Who didn't?

In the corner stood a pair of grinding wheels.

One was coarse, the other so fine he'd never seen another like it. Their combined weight was hard to start rolling but they kept revolving longer than a single stone. Sharpening his sword with casual competence, Roderigo honed edge and point until both could slice leather, this being what most sailors wore as armour.

Temujin knocked as midnight struck.

"Ready when you are, chief."

The sergeant had checked his men's weapons but Captain Roderigo rechecked them anyway. Temujin would be disappointed otherwise. After the fug inside the fortress, the night felt colder than it was. Drizzle coming in sheets on the wind. With luck, it would turn to sleet and fling itself in Mamluk faces, providing cover and allowing Roderigo's men to approach less carefully.

Staring into that wind, Roderigo felt tears fill his angry eyes and cursed himself for stupidity, glad of the darkness. He'd watched Desdaio grow from pampered child to a young woman desperate for the freedom her young cousins still had.

Of course, her fortune would have helped his. His own house was a ruin, his salary from the Dogana less than he spent. All the same, Roderigo hadn't lied when he told Desdaio he loved her. For her to sneak into another man's house . . .

Into another man's bed.

"Chief . . ."

"*What?*"

His two boats had drawn together in the swell, and Sergeant

Temujin was gripping the sides of both to keep them steady. At his anger everyone froze. Now was the time Roderigo was meant to say some words. Choose who boarded first. Tell them what he expected to find.

"Any special orders, chief?"

He and Temujin had searched a hundred ships before. Everything from visiting Moorish galleys and trade ships from Byzantium to Rus boats and even a felucca that sailed all the way from the mouth of the Nile. Why should this one be any different? Roderigo felt he owed his sergeant some explanation.

"A girl I know is getting married."

"That's it?" Temujin looked disgusted.

"There's red gold," Roderigo replied. As if his last words were unspoken. "Also Mamluk silver. They're on the manifest. Three leopard skins, sky stone for hardening steel and a box of rubies. All declared. It's what they're hiding that worries me. I mean, for a Mamluk not to try to barter . . ."

"Chief, can I say something?"

"I don't have to like it."

"You won't. Whoever she is. Forget it. She's just a slit, pretty or not. You can't go into a possible battle moping. It's the quickest way to die."

He hated it when Temujin was right.

As the boats separated and one headed into the wind bound for the far side of the *Quaja*, which was the Mamluk vessel's name, Sergeant Temujin kept up a count as steady as the Watch's steps on Piazza San Marco at midnight.

"Fifty," he said.

Pulling a wide sash from his pocket, Roderigo draped it over his shoulder and adjusted the weight that kept it at his hip. A Venetian officer boarding a foreign vessel had to wear a city sash. It made an insult to the officer an insult to the city. An insult to the city was an insult to the duke.

This simplified matters.

"One hundred," Temujin said.

"Take us in."

A swirl of oars carried them close, the *Quaja*'s side looming so large it threatened to crush their lugger in the swell. An anchor rope hummed with tension above them. That was where they would board.

"I'll go first."

"Chief . . ."

"You heard me."

Even Temujin, sworn to protect Roderigo, knew better than to query an order given in the field. When the captain reached deck, he found a man from his other lugger already standing over a dead Mamluk.

"Sweetly done," Roderigo said.

At his gesture, others climbed aboard.

"Right," Temujin said, keeping his voice low. "You and you by that cargo hatch, and you by that door . . . *And you, why isn't your crossbow loaded?*" This last hiss because a string wasn't ratcheted back.

"Give me a . . ."

One second the sergeant was glaring, the next shock replaced anger in the hiss of an arrow from high overhead. Temujin stared at the shaft in his chest.

"Rigging," Roderigo said.

As Temujin fell to his knees, blood running between his fingers, the troop's newcomer planted his feet, raised his own half bow and hesitated.

"Dead or alive?"

"Kill him."

The man put an arrow between crows nest's boards, through the Mamluk archer's foot and into his groin. The lookout fell with a thud. He should have fired the moment they appeared or held his element of surprise.

"Alive was better." Temujin's words came from between

blood-frothed lips. "So any bastards we leave living could kill him for being useless. Good job he was, though. We'd be fucked otherwise."

"Help Temujin up."

Two soldiers did as ordered. The arrow was a yard long, with its point exiting from Temujin's lower back. Sighing with relief, Roderigo confirmed the point was unpoisoned and snapped the feathered end without saying what he intended to do.

"Bind the arrow in place," he told a guard.

"Sir . . ."

"Seen it." A door was opening. As half a dozen crossbows shifted in that direction, Roderigo said, "Wait on my order."

Opening a little more, the door suddenly started closing and then stopped. The man behind must know it offered minimal protection. Steel-tipped quarrels would rip straight through.

"In the name of Marco IV," Roderigo said. "Show yourself. We search for a missing glass-blower. And have reason to suspect he may have come aboard. Any attempt to hinder us will be regarded as an act of war."

The door shut with a bang.

"My God," one of the men muttered. "We've found him."

It looked that way. Roderigo hoped it was true. Although the glass-blower would die horribly, his children and grandchildren—those left living—would be spared a similar fate.

Strange words came from behind the door.

Guttural and impassioned, the man speaking sounded young to captain a ship, never mind a vessel as large as the *Quaja*. When Roderigo didn't reply, the sentence was repeated, as far as Roderigo could tell word for word. Problem was, Roderigo had no idea if it was a question, a statement or a boast that the *Quaja*'s crew would fight to the death. "Anyone understand that?"

The newcomer nodded.

"What are you called?"

Bato sounded like a nickname.

"Tell him I'm looking for a glass blower. We think he might have been smuggled aboard this ship."

"They haven't got him," Bato said eventually.

"What's the language?"

"It's Turkic. Good Turkic. Formal. Very proper."

"Tell him I'm Dogana chief and I *will* search his ship. If what he says is true, he can wait out his quarantine, or sail on tomorrow's tide. We will count his dead and my sergeant's injury as the cost of a misunderstanding."

The answer when it came was calmer.

No glass-blower was aboard the ship. The manifest of goods given to the Dogana was accurate. All the same, they would let the Venetians search where they liked. Since they had nothing to hide.

"Tell him, if it was up to me I'd take his word and leave now."

Untrue, of course, but any honeyed words that helped get this over with, and Temujin to Dr. Crow, were fine with Roderigo. As he watched, the door opened and a fine-featured Mamluk stood blinking in the moon's rays. His robe was rich with silver thread and a scarlet turban wrapped his skull.

He looked little more than a boy.

Identifying Roderigo by his sash, the Mamluk touched his hand to his heart, mouth and forehead in formal greeting and gestured the Dogana captain inside.

The vessel's layout was like dozens of others he'd searched before. A captain's cabin at the stern and quarters for crew below deck. Half of that area being put aside for cargo. Below this was a crawl space where the hull curved towards the keel. Under that, a stinking slop hole filled with stones for ballast.

Roderigo checked the lot. All the time carrying the weight of Desdaio's betrayal like stones in his own heart. Two of his troop were helping Sergeant Temujin towards the upper deck when

Roderigo stopped. At a growled order, his men did likewise and a flicker of blind panic filled the Mamluk's face.

The crawl space was twenty-one steps long. The cargo deck nineteen. Had it been reversed Roderigo could have dismissed the difference as loss for the curve of the prow. But that way round?

"Tell the man we're going to break this down."

Roderigo pointed at the bulkhead of the stern. A torrent of impassioned Turkic greeted this news. And the Mamluk went to stand in front of it.

"He says his ship will sink and we'll die. It will be your fault and his country will go to war with Serenissima. A thousand ships will sail up the Adriatic sacking every Venetian colony on the way."

"Tell him it's a risk I'll take."

It took five minutes to find a large enough axe. In which time the Mamluk's crew gathered, silent ghosts watching uneasily. Only the loaded crossbows of Roderigo's men kept them from attacking.

"Now," he ordered.

Bato swung the axe.

"And again."

A second blow widened the crack.

"No water yet," Temujin growled.

The planks were too thin to be the *Quaja's* outer skin and their timber too green. Venice's own shipwrights used wood from trees stored for at least two years before cutting planks that had to dry in their turn.

"Hack the lot down."

Planting his feet, Bato swung a blow to behead a horse. His next opened darkness. And a tanner's stink of shit and stale piss hissed through the gap. Not waiting for more orders, Bato gripped one edge of the planking and tugged. Wood split and a plank creaked free from battens behind.

Another plank followed just as noisily.

"Light," Roderigo demanded.

Stepping between the wreckage of Bato's handiwork, he entered a fetid compartment behind the wall. A moment later, the Mamluk followed.

Roderigo was thirty years old. He'd fought his first battle at fourteen and taken his first girl a year earlier. He'd lived through cities sacked, and seen a Florentine spy torn apart by wild horses. He expected the missing glass blower. He got . . .

The captain crossed himself.

A naked boy hung in chains, his wrists raw from fighting shackles. In life, the boy must have been about seventeen. Nineteen at the most. Long silver-grey hair half hid a face so beautiful it belonged to an angel. The corpse had the sheen of wet marble. Almost alabaster in its translucence.

Black earth strewed the deck beneath him.

Lurching past his commander, Sergeant Temujin lifted the boy's head to the light.

Amber-flecked eyes snapped open.

As the foreign captain shouted a warning, the sergeant drew his dagger, and turned to slash the Mamluk's throat, drenching himself in blood.

"*Temujin* . . ."

"Kill them all," Temujin shouted.

Outside, his troop obeyed without question. Crossbows snapped, arrows flew, daggers found hearts. Fifteen seconds of hellish slaughter ended in the stink of blood, Mamluk corpses, and Bato leaving, bow in hand, to hunt down stragglers.

"Burn this boat."

Roderigo stared at his sergeant.

"Chief . . . Steal what you need to keep the Regent and duchess sweet and burn everything else. Him included. Because I know what *that* is and it cannot be tamed. The Khan owned one in my grandfather's time. It killed him."

"*Sergeant.*"

Temujin stopped talking.

His eyes were bright with the onset of fever, and the crude bandage around his ribs dark with blood. Only willpower and his need to convince Roderigo kept him conscious.

"You want to tell me why you killed that man?"

It hurt Temujin, probably more than it hurt to drop to a crouch, but he did it anyway. Opening buttons at the dead Mamluk's neck he revealed the swell of breasts, and said, "She's got to be someone, chief. To command this ship and carry that."

Temujin meant her prisoner.

"We can't let anyone find her. And, believe me, you don't *want* anyone to find that. Kill it, fire this damn ship and get us out of here."

"I wish it was that simple."

"It is."

Roderigo shook his head.

Halfway across the lagoon, while the Dogana troop concentrated on getting their badly wounded sergeant to Dr. Crow for treatment, the boy made his move. He simply stood, and tipped backwards into the water with a splash.

"Kill him," Roderigo shouted.

Not a single man had his crossbow cocked.

By the time Bato slotted an arrow, his target was being swept away by the cross-currents that made Venice's lagoon so unpredictable. Had the burning Mamluk ship been close enough to light the scene Bato might have had a better chance. He fired anyway.

6

The shock of an arrow striking blew breath from the boy's body. And the pain in his shoulder opened the boy's mind to a vision that swept in like smoke.

In the smoke a veiled woman smiled, then scowled and began to protest as her image blew away, leaving him spitting water. When she reappeared, she was sitting on a squat throne with a thin young man in black clutching her knees.

"Join us."

"Where am I?" he asked.

She looked puzzled, as if this was not what he was meant to say.

But already he was thinking other things. Clutching at passing fragments of memory, he tried to recall why he'd been locked behind the false bulkhead of a ship. *Fire and ice, earth and air.* Fire started this. A blaze swept through some building. A man killed another. A sour-faced woman hated him worse than ever. He fought to remember who she was.

Who he was.

But the foul-tasting lagoon swallowed the boy before he could remember more than a single word: *Bjornvin*. The word made no more sense to him than his vision of the veiled woman. Since the men who hacked him free were heading in one direction, the boy let cross-currents sweep him in the other.

He wondered what would happen. He'd die, he supposed. Perhaps he should stop swimming to see how sinking felt?

Stopping kicking, the boy let his shackles pull him under.

And, tasting salt, let himself sink further. Opaque above, darkness below. His toes squelched on soft mud in a channel. Minor canals in Venice were cleared every ten years, waterways and large canals whenever necessary. He knew nothing of this. He simply felt softness beneath his toes.

Sinking deeper, he felt gravel.

His lungs pulled life from the water rushing into them.

Flickers of lightning twitched his limbs as fire lit behind his eyes and he felt his body fight itself, without understanding how it won the battle for life. Slamming into an ancient wreck, which crumbled as he snatched for it, he let a brutal undercurrent sweep him sideways before kicking for the surface.

The burning ship was far behind and buildings lined the horizon ahead of him. Above, in gaps between the clouds, was a bowl of stars. More stars than any man could count. Should he be able to count beyond his fingers.

The boy had reached the Grand Canal without knowing where it was, what it was or anything about it. As his eyes struggled to focus and his body shivered, and his guts retched filthy water, he accepted the embrace of an incoming tide. Then a spasm locked his stomach, and the sky became purple, the moon hurt his eyes, and bitterness filled his throat.

"*There you are . . .*"

The words were not his.

They came uninvited into his mind. With them an image of the woman he'd seen in his head earlier, when he was drowning. An old woman with a young woman's smile. A young woman with an old woman's eyes. Thin wisps of smoke across her face like a veil, which blew away as he stared harder.

"Alexa?" he said.

"Who told you my name?"

Having no answer, he felt her try to pull clues from his ruined memories. All she found were the names others had once called him.

"*White hair* is descriptive. *You* is a pronoun. *Tadsi* is an Old Norse pun on shit, and *Tychet* means idiot. Here we've Latinised it to *Tycho*." She sounded darkly amused. "Keep the last. It suits you."

Tycho forced her voice away.

7

Moonlight glimmered on the Canalasso, the elegant waterway bisecting the city to which the burning ship had delivered Tycho. It glimmered in blanket-sized scraps of silver leaf. And the reflection this glimmering created lit the walls of a fish market opposite. But the three children staring down the slimy steps at the edge of the Grand Canal saw none of this beauty.

They were concentrating on a tidal area, beside the steps, where flotsam gathered. Tonight's catch was a drowned girl, long silver hair rippling in the gentle waves.

"Get her then."

Rosalyn guessed Josh meant her. Since she was the one he glared at. Hooking her smock to her hips, she stepped into the filthy water. "It's cold."

"Just do it."

Corpses could be sold, Josh said.

Necromancers, probably. Rosalyn couldn't see who else might want one. She gasped as the water climbed her thighs, realised she still couldn't reach the floating girl and stepped down again, grabbing hair. "Give me a hand then," she protested.

When Josh didn't move, her brother Pietro did, wading into the canal to help her drag the body nearer the steps.

"My God," Rosalyn said.

Scowling, Josh came to take a look.

A boy, his genitals flopping sideways, his chest entirely flat, his belly button an intricate coil. If not for the belly button, he could have been an angel with his wings cut off. She'd never seen anyone so beautiful.

"He's been shot."

"As if that matters."

She yanked the arrow free anyway.

"We can't sell that," Josh snapped. "What's round his wrist?"

Rosalyn dropped to a crouch, seeing her moonlit reflection in the metal's surface. "A shackle, some of it's silver."

"Don't be stupid. No one would . . ."

Shuffling closer, Rosalyn snapped her knees shut. She didn't like the way Josh was leering at her. After a second, she knelt.

His temper had never been good. After that night in Cannaregio, when they hid in a tanner's pit while demons fought, it was worse. He was less forgiving each day of what had happened to her with the Watch. Maybe, her gut relaxed slightly at the hope, this would keep him happy. The dead boy was pale and very dead, with a ring of ruined flesh where his shackle scraped bone.

"What's so interesting?"

Her guts locked again. "Look," she said. The blood trickling from his arrow wound was blackish, its exact colour hard to determine in the darkness.

"So he's foreign." Turning to Pietro, Josh said, "Give her your knife . . . And you, stop pissing around and chop off his hand."

This was a test, Rosalyn knew it was. Josh spent most of his time telling her she was too stupid to live on her wits like him. Her brother was coming to believe it too. "I'll cut off the shackle."

There, she'd failed. As he expected her to.

"Rosalyn . . ."

Now was when he'd order her to remove it at the wrist, like they'd split a pig's knuckle they stole. Surprisingly, he just sucked his teeth in disgust. "Hurry it up."

Bending the corpse's elbow, she gripped the shackle. It was hard wood, inlaid with bands of silver wire, and it was hinged, clasped and soldered, instead of locked, which was even stranger. In the end, she hacked at the solder wondering why he hadn't done that himself. Maybe he lacked a knife.

Shouldn't be here, she told herself.

Shouldn't be with Josh.

Rosalyn was cold, sodden from the canal, dressed in rags that clung to her legs, hips and buttocks, and scared. Her bladder hurt, her guts said she'd bleed soon, which was a blessing. "Almost there."

"About time."

Dragging her blade, Rosalyn freed the weld and sliced her finger to the bone, feeling instantly sick. She rocked back on her knees, but not before blood splashed on to the dead boy's face.

"What now?" said Josh, as she gasped.

She'd jumped back when dark eyes, tinged with amber flecks, flicked open to glare at her. She felt her stomach turn over as the dead boy examined her face. Then he shut his eyes again. "Cut myself," she said weakly.

"Kick him back in then."

"Someone's coming," Rosalyn said. "We've been lucky so far. Let's just leave." Fortunately, Josh agreed with her.

8

Street children. She should feel sorry for them, Maria knew that. Instead, they simply made her nervous. Listening carefully, she heard them arguing as they moved further away from her towards a warren of alleys.

Ahead was another shrine. This was not good. Five shrines in the last few minutes meant this parish was dangerous and the patriarch wanted to remind everyone that God watched everywhere. In Serenissima, he'd probably gone beyond shocked by what he saw. That naked body by the water steps for a start.

Just another murder the Watch would ignore.

Stranglings and suffocations were rare in Venice. Because Venetians believed a curse passed to the murderer if flesh touched flesh. Knifings were common, however. Why risk throttling someone when a dagger could keep their ghost at bay? So many in Venice believed this, that to beat someone to the edge of death and then knife them was regarded as simple common sense.

Pausing at a statue of the Madonna, Maria the cordwainer's wife muttered a prayer for the dead boy she'd just seen. And finishing, turned to find him standing behind her, water still dripping into the dirt at his feet.

She couldn't help yelping.

Although her yelp ended as he spun her round, fixed one hand over her mouth and dragged her to a doorway. One second, she stood at the Virgin's shrine, the next she and the youth she'd thought dead watched a drunk wander from a tavern, stare around him and disappear the way he'd come.

The strange-looking youth didn't have Mongol eyes. He was far too pale for a Moor, and he wasn't Jewish, although she'd be embarrassed to admit how she knew. If Maria had to describe him, she'd say his cheekbones were Schiavoni, those incomers from Dalmatia colonising her city. Reaching out, he took her face and turned it to the shrine's light. Amber-flecked eyes gazed into hers.

"Doesn't that hurt? she asked, touching her finger to the wound in his shoulder. And suddenly she was held from behind, his face nuzzled her neck. He removed his hand from her breast the moment she burst into tears.

"Don't hurt me."

". . . hurt me." His voice echoed her plea.

Maria—who had no last name, because people like her didn't—was fifteen and a half, being born in high summer. She was in a parish she barely knew, long after she should be home, in an alley with more shrines than a single street should need. As she registered this, Maria finally realised where she was.

Rio Terra dei Assassini.

I should concentrate, she decided.

Not least because the strange youth now stood in front of her again. She was a married woman out after dark and he was obviously foreign. When she tried to step around him, his face tightened, and she remembered his nakedness, the speed at which he moved, and how her father scowled before he lost his temper.

"You should let me go now."

Releasing her, he watched her hurry away.

She kept her panic in check until she believed herself safe. Then her sobbing began, so loud and so open, the boy almost missed the point at which other steps began to follow her. Since most of those crowding the alley around him seemed to be ghosts — hollow-eyed and helpless, waiting to see what he would do — and this woman was undoubtedly alive, he decided to follow her too.

9

"Captain . . . over here." A young whore shushed the voice, shocked at its impudence.

Roderigo recognised its owner despite his gaudy mask. The whore on his arm and the flagon he waved suggested Atilo's servant had spent his prize money with glee. Like most Venetian men, Roderigo used whores. This one was shapely, only half drunk and grinned prettily.

"Iacopo."

"My lord . . ." Turning, Iacopo said, "This is Captain Roderigo. He's head of the Dogana."

The whore shot a glance to say, *Don't be stupid*. Then realised her client meant it and curtsied deep enough to reveal her breasts, which improved Roderigo's temper slightly.

The Riva degli Schiavoni lined Venice's southern shore.

It was the quay where captains sought supplies for their ships. There were food stalls, rope chandlers, and barrel-laden carts with water from the cisterns that collected the city's rainfall. Slaves were sold, crews recruited. It was to the Riva that sailors went to find whores. Here was where Atilo's handsome servant had come to celebrate his victory in the previous day's regatta.

In the course of the night just gone, he'd lost Roderigo's doublet and the hat Sir Richard gave him. In their place, he sported a black eye and an ornate dagger that undoubtedly broke the sumptuary laws. Also two whores.

Although the second, arriving as Roderigo noticed the dagger, proved Iacopo hadn't lost the doublet at all. It was draped over the shoulders of his friend, who needed it against the cold, since her breasts were bare.

"Did you see that ship's fire, my lord?"

"Yes," Roderigo said. "I saw it."

"They say Mamluk spies burnt a Cypriot ship."

Did they now? Roderigo smiled grimly. He'd told his men to say nothing of what had happened, but this was better than expected.

"Why so?"

"Well . . ." said Iacopo. "Lady Giulietta's marrying Cyprus." His elbow missed a ledge, almost tipping him to the ground. "And Cyprus," he added heavily, "is Byzantium's ally. And ours, now, of course."

Byzantium and the Mamluks were enemies, as expected of neighbouring empires. And Venice was Byzantium's ally, theoretically. At a push, if drunk, you could build a plot from that.

"Almost right. But it was a Mamluk ship and I'd put my money on the Moors." Why not? They were the Mamluk sultan's other enemy.

"I heard . . ."

"Believe me. Moorish spies."

Opening his mouth to disagree, Iacopo shut it when one of the whores dug her elbow in his ribs. He was very drunk indeed. "I'll buy you a drink."

"Another time . . ."

"You off to bed?"

Captain Roderigo nodded.

"Then you need help to heaven, don't you?"

It was too late to stop Iacopo's recitation and after the first line the whores joined in. "*He who drinks well sleeps well, he who sleeps well has no evil thoughts, he who has no evil thoughts does no evil, he who does no evil goes to heaven. So drink well . . .*"

"And heaven will be yours," Roderigo finished for them.

After five minutes of one-sided conversation, Roderigo knew that Iaco had been in Atilo's service for eight years. He wanted a promotion. He deserved promotion. There were days—and this was secret—he felt little better than a slave. Atilo's people had slaves. He was sure the captain knew that.

So do we, Roderigo thought. Half the men working cranes outside were indentured to Schiavoni gang masters. The peasants on the mainland were bound to their lords. Did Iacopo think the whore on his arm worked freely? Taking a gulp from his glass, Roderigo winced at its bitterness.

Halfway down the jug, Roderigo realised why the wine was so bad.

If his mind had not been on last night's disaster he would have realised men came here with other things on their mind. To share taverns was a Serenissiman tradition. The rules governing brothels were more complicated. In being here he was breaking half a dozen laws.

"I should leave . . ."

"You sent my whore to check on your sergeant."

So he had, Roderigo remembered.

Taking his hand from between her thighs, Iacopo patted the remaining whore's knees. Her shrug making it clear that losing his attention meant little.

What am I doing here? Roderigo knew the answer the moment the question entered his head. He was behaving as any Venetian noble would when invited by the victor of the previous day's race to have a drink.

"My lord. You look as if the wine doesn't agree with you."

"It doesn't," he said flatly.

When Iacopo returned it was with a different flask. "Frankish," he promised. "The best they have. I'm sorry, I should have realised."

"Realised what?"

"That a nobleman would not have the stomach for the wine we drink. It was thoughtless of me."

Feeling shamed, Roderigo said, "It's not your wine. Yesterday's news about Lady Desdaio has unsettled me . . ." Toasting Iacopo, he discovering the man was right: this wine was better.

Raising his head from the table, Roderigo watched a serving girl approach. Did she work the stalls? He decided he didn't care. She'd come to his bed right enough. He was a patrician with a palace on the Grand Canal.

A small one, admittedly. A thin, three-storey building between two fat ones. But still a palace and still overlooking the Canalasso, that watery road Venice chose for its heart. There were times he didn't like himself and this was one of them.

Last night had begun well enough, only turning sour when Temujin took an arrow. Turning sourer still with his discovery of that boy.

Who knew where he was now?

Drowned, with luck . . .

Early morning sun crinkled on the lagoon and the tide flowed as sluggishly as molten lead. Somehow, without Roderigo noticing, the room had emptied and his companion was gone.

"*Iacopo?*"

"A girl is murdered. Iaco went to look."

In a city where passers-by stepped over bodies most mornings this sounded passing strange. "What makes this killing different?"

"The murderer. A boy was seen nearby. Naked, with silver-grey hair. The Watch believe he was her attacker."

10

Tycho woke with his bladder full, his penis hard and his balls so tight they ached. And when he pissed against a wall his urine was so rank it shocked him into wondering if the stink was something else.

Until he realised everything smelt extreme.

The smoke from fires banked low for the night, the smell of pies and casseroles baking in the public ovens that dotted every other street. This new world was a mix of opulence and filth. And people, thousands of strangely dressed people, living their lives to rules denied him.

Here the horizon was flat, when it could be seen beyond the mist. Because there was always mist. So these might be the last islands in the world. Or the only islands in the world. Or perhaps all the world there was.

The roof above him leaked, and half of the warehouse where he slept was full of rubbish. The other half was piled with drying wood. A side canal, which once served its landing stage, was silted and stale. A bridge across its mouth, blocking entry, was old, the decaying warehouse older.

On the fourth night after Tycho found this hiding place—

the sixth night of the city's rioting, and the first of the snows—
he headed south, driven across the roofs by hunger, and a realisation he needed more than one bolt hole in this city.

He learnt to use the shadows, his breath never disturbing falling
snow. Men, youths and older boys let him pass unseen. He was
the dagger over their heads and the silence above. Girls, cats and
old women were less easy, but everyone knew they saw things
anyway.

The Nicoletti were at war with the Castellani.

If the ship-workers had guild pride, the Nicoletti prided themselves on being from San Nicolò dei Mendicoli, the toughest
parish in the city. No one really knew what had started their
hatred, but the street battles it spawned had simmered for four
hundred years. And the dukes, while not actively approving, did
not disapprove. Should parishes one side of the Canalasso rise,
parishes the other side could be relied on to crush them.

The cause of tonight's fight was real, for once.

The red-clad Castellani accused the Nicoletti of the slaughter
of Maria, a cordwainer's wife. The black-clad Nicoletti accused
their enemy of trying to extract blood money they couldn't afford
and didn't owe.

And so, at midnight, with snow falling so fast rioters lost sight
of the canal edges, the battle resumed. At midnight, because that
was tradition. And it began, as tradition also demanded, with
the previous night's champions meeting on a bridge, scraping
away snow to reveal footprints carved into the bridge's floor, and
tossing a coin to chose who threw the first punch.

In the hour before midnight, while those preparing to fight
were finding their courage in alcohol, and refuelling their anger
with tales of how virtuous Maria had been, or how wicked it
was to demand blood money falsely, Tycho reached a chimney
on the roof of the Fontego dei Tedeschi north of the Rialto
bridge. For company he had a dead pigeon and a live cat, the
pigeon having died to keep the cat alive for another few days.

Around him were a dozen chimneys, twice his height, and topped by fluted stone funnels from which warmth drifted. He'd been drawn here by a noise he'd heard on his first night in the city. A mechanical heartbeat.

Unthreatening but steady, it drew him to the far edge of the *fontego* roof, on to icy tiles two floors below and into an alley where frozen mud cut his feet through a covering of snow. The heartbeat was loud as it echoed off the alley walls. Opening a door without thinking, he stepped through. The machine shop was in darkness, except for a candle in the far corner. A question came from behind the candle.

The voice of the man asking was proud and old. He sounded not at all worried by the arrival of a stranger, where no stranger should be. Tycho knew later what he asked, regretting how he came to know.

"My machine prints."

The book master had the belly of a man who ate well and walked little. His cheeks flapped, as if he'd once been larger, and his eyes were pale and watery. His hair was thick, though, for all it was grey.

"The only printing press in Serenissima."

Tycho looked at him.

"You don't understand?"

He didn't. Although he would reconstruct the conversation in flashes and slivers, as he fled the building. But that came later.

"The Chinese invented this. I changed it to harness water power." The man indicated a moving belt that vanished through a slit in the floor and reappeared a pace later. It turned a wheel, which worked gears that shuttled sheets of paper under a falling square. This was what Tycho had heard outside.

"The future. That's what this is. We can print fifty pages of Asia Minor as the tide rises, change the plate and print fifty copies of China as it falls."

There was pride in his voice. A pride Tycho was to understand later, when the old man had no further use for it. Having explained what it was in Venetian, and seen how hard Tycho struggled to understand, the old man tried mainland Italian, German, Greek and Latin. Finally he shrugged and reverted to his original choice.

"Engraved by a Frank, printed on a Chinese press, adapted by a Venetian. Based on the best facts of Portuguese, Venetian and Moorish navigators. I'm hoping Prince Alonzo will buy my first atlas."

Next to the press was a trestle holding a title page. A fish, that was what its picture looked like. A fish, with a canal's northern opening as its mouth, the sweep of the canal, and the southern exit as its gills.

"San Polo," the man said, pointing to its head.

Cannaregio was the spine.

Dorsoduro, San Marco and Arzanale its belly. The island of San Pietro made its tail. It took Tycho a while to realise he was looking at this new world in which he found himself. And the hope flooded his heart and his face softened.

"*Bjornvin . . . ?*"

Watery eyes examined Tycho. The book master made him repeat the name. Then, turning to the end of an atlas, where a dozen printed lists crossed the page like prison bars, the old man ran one finger down its list of tiny names . . .

He shook his head.

"*Bjornvin.*"

"All right, all right . . ." Pulling down a book so old its cover flaked under his fingers, he ran down a different list, this one handwritten. The third book was no better. The fourth gave an answer.

"A town in Vineland. It burnt a hundred years ago."

The man read the entry, read it again and shook his head. "There's a record of finding ruins." Shuffling across to a collection of manuscripts, he unrolled one. "Sir John Mandeville writes of meeting a merchant who saw them. That would be fifty years ago. It had been burnt to the ground."

His words meant nothing to Tycho.

"*Bjornvin.*"

The old man sucked his teeth. "Why would you be interested?" He stopped to examine Tycho, suddenly noticing how strange he looked. "Impossible. You'd have to be . . . ? What, eighteen now? Plus a hundred."

For the first time he looked worried.

"Buy yourself food," he insisted. "Find somewhere to sleep out of the cold." Digging in his pocket, he found small coins and folded them into Tycho's hand, jumping back as Tycho hurled his offering to the floor.

One had been silver.

As Tycho broke Maitre Thomas's neck, the old man's memories flowed into Tycho's mind. And with them language, a sense of where Venice was, and knowledge of what had just happened, seen from the other side.

11

The snow along the *fondamenta* had the feel of marble polished by the feet of others and was so cold and hard it burnt Tycho's bare toes.

He hardly noticed.

Maître Thomas's memories filled his head. And the knife he'd grabbed escaping the print shop was forgotten in his hand. He found himself on the edge of a street fight by accident.

That night in January was the night Tycho met three women who'd change his life forever. If you could count an eleven-year-old, red-haired *stregoi* as a *woman* . . . At eighteen, the Nubian slave counted. So did the fifteen-year-old Giulietta di Millioni, but Tycho met her last and only briefly.

"No blades . . ." The voice was outraged.

A girl black as a moonless night, her braided hair ending in tiny silver thimbles, stood glaring. She had the eyes of a predator and the stare of one too. One hand rested on her hip, the other gripped a frosted tree on a *fondamenta* edging the canal. Nodding at the knife in Tycho's hand made her silver-tipped braids dance some more. Blood oozed from above her eye.

"What?" she said. "Never seen a Nubian before?"

"No, never."

Even though touching a silver-tipped braid would burn him, Tycho lifted his thumb to her eyebrow and touched the blood. A steel grip stopped his thumb from reaching his mouth. "Don't," she said.

Her braids swayed like poisoned weed in the canal, holding him back as her scent drew him in. He could smell wine, garlic and a stink rising from her. Despite her filthy feet, and a dress hacked to the knees, she looked dangerous and elegant. Mostly dangerous.

How old was she?

Old enough to be in a street brawl, obviously. Lifting the knife from his fingers she tossed it casually into the canal beside them.

"You know the law."

He did, because Maître Thomas had known it. And the book master's memories were now his, transferred in the moment he broke the man's neck. Although many of them had already begun to fade. When Tycho glanced up he found the Nubian watching him, her eyes glittering in the starlight. She thought him Castellani because of his stolen tunic.

"Which is your parish?"

All and none. He lived everywhere and nowhere. Out of the way of strangers and the Watch and those who'd hurt him or needed hurting. Probably not the answer she was looking for. "What's your name?" he asked instead.

"Amelia," she said, grinning at his change of subject.

"And where do *you* live?"

"Near here. I'm a lady's maid. Well, since Lady Desdaio moved in." The girl didn't look like a lady's maid to either of them. Although Tycho only knew what one was because of fragmenting memories.

"Lady . . . ?"

"Desdaio, my mistress."

"What's she like?"

Amelia gave a huge sigh. "Sweet," she said, "with added honey, and an extra spoonful of sugar. I'd hate her, but that's impossible."

"Sounds hideous."

"Should be," Amelia said. "But she isn't. Big eyes and big tits. I get scared for her. She's also a walking mint. Although, obviously enough, men don't simply want her money and body . . ."

"She's rich?" Tycho interrupted.

Amelia rolled her eyes. "Of course she is. She's old man Bribanzo's heir. Boxes of jewellery, chests full of coins, endless velvet dresses, bolts of shot silk, paintings . . ."

"What else do the men want?"

"You know what happens to innocence?"

"It dies?"

"Someone kills it."

"That what happened to you?"

"Shit," she said. "What kind of question's that?" Lifting her face, she grinned at him. Her eyes glittering in the light of a flaming brand fixed to an arch behind him. The pulse of blood in her neck clearly visible. "Kiss me then."

He fled her. Outrage following him in shouted insults as he lost himself in a nest of serpentine backstreets, ducking through an underpass to find a wide alley beyond. As he fled, the night sky changed from the red it had suddenly become to a more normal blue-black, the houses lost their glittering edges and the tightness in his gut released slightly.

He had enough sense to know the anger and his hunger were interchangeable; different ways to describe what soured his mouth when the Nubian girl raised her head to expose her throat.

Statues, and frescoes and marble inlay.

The palaces lining the Canalasso were the grandest in the city. The buildings were rich, decorated with carvings and tiny squares of coloured glass. Many palaces painted. The carvings and the varied stones and the paintings like nothing he'd ever seen. In his fractured mind buildings were wood or earth.

The walls of a great hall, doubled skinned with logs filled with pounded dirt. A turf roof over crude beams. In winter, snow kept warmth in the hall. The snow in Venice was so thin Tycho barely recognised it.

How could his home be burnt for a hundred years? Bjornvin was there in his memory now. Not perfect, certainly not that, but real and recent.

After that . . . ?

He could remember an axe cutting into a ship's hull. His brief blindness as someone thrust a lamp into his prison. Until the light reached him he hadn't known how his eyes had changed. And until he threw himself backwards off the little boat he hadn't realised he moved faster than other people. Everyone here seemed to move clumsily, stumbling through dark alleys, barely seeing what was there.

At first, he'd wondered what was wrong with them. Who these clumsy people were. Now he had fragments of memory back, and Maître Thomas's memories too, he was coming to wonder if he was *people* at all.

"Who goes there?"

Tycho fell into the darkness. He could feel it shimmer, and colonnades lighten as the darkness closed around him. Conical steel caps, straw-stuffed jerkins with scales of cheap steel. There were five guards, two of them carried daggers and two had pikes, their sergeant had a war hammer hanging from his belt. All wore boots studded with rivets against the ice underfoot.

"I saw someone."

"Where?" The question was dismissive.

"Over there," insisted a youth, pointing to where Tycho stood in the shadows. Their sergeant peered into the darkness.

"Boss?" one said.

"Nothing," he replied. Cuffing the boy across the back of his head, the sergeant said, "Scared of his own shadow."

Tycho trailed them around the expanse of a snow-skimmed square, moving silently and unseen behind them, and keeping his steps within the slush their boots churned from the virgin snow. He would have completed the circuit had he not looked up and seen horses.

Four of them.

Striking the air with their hooves as they leapt from the balcony of the Basilica San Marco. He knew the horses instantly. Because Maître Thomas had known them. How could he not? Looted from Byzantium, who stole them from Athens, where they'd decorated the original Hippodrome. He'd never seen a horse close to.

Thanking the masons who carved the basilica's façade, Tycho used one foothold after another to scale a column and roll himself on to the balcony's balustrade. Behind him he left stone angels with muddy toe prints on their heads. The four bronze horses he expected. The red-haired child sat beneath he didn't.

Looking up, she grinned.

"Well," she said. "What a surprise."

The child huddled over a fire, which flickered in the night wind. Its flames were trapped in her cupped hands and burnt nothing, unless it was the empty air between them.

Her hair was greasy, her green eyes unreadable as he hesitated, half over the balustrade, one foot still on the halo of a stone angel. "Impressive, aren't they?" She patted a stallion's leg. "Stolen from Greece by the Romans, stolen from Rome by Romanised Greeks, stolen from them by us . . ."

"Us?" Tycho asked.

"Well, them really." The girl looked at him, hanging half on and half off the balcony, and raised her eyebrows. "Afraid of witches?"

When Tycho scowled, her grin widened. So he rolled himself over the balustrade wishing he'd kept the printer's knife.

"Strange city," she said. "Strange hungers you didn't know you had . . . You're right to be scared. I don't blame you."

"I'm not scared."

"Of course you're not."

Closing her hands to quench the flame, she pulled a scrap of bread from her smock, revealing ribs like twigs as her smock fell open. Eleven, he thought, maybe twelve if starved. "Take, eat," she said, mockingly. "Or is it a different kind of salvation you're after?"

He grabbed the bread, stuffing it into his mouth. Its crust was old leather, the middle sawdust. It tasted of ashes and coal.

She laughed. "Apparently so."

Climbing to her feet, the girl scooped slush from the balcony floor and offered him that instead. He drank from her hands, wondering why. The slush was fresh, if gritty, but it didn't change the taste in his mouth.

"You shouldn't be here," she said.

"Nor should you."

She laughed. "You should go home."

Tycho's eyes filled with snow. Snow and fire and ashes.

"Ahh," she said. "You remember that much." She paused, and for the first time looked uncertain. "Alexa thinks you drowned. Should I tell her you didn't?"

He didn't know the answer. But then he didn't really understand her question. Or how she'd moved from offering him water to standing there. All he knew was she moved as swiftly as he did. Maybe sunlight hurt her too.

"I've tamed death walkers." Her words were bitter. "Seljuk mages, *krieghund* even. A skill much needed last autumn, I gather. But you . . ." Without hesitating, she bit her wrist deep enough to draw blood. Then she took a deep breath and held it out to him.

"Bind yourself."

The world turned red.

Bronze horses leapt through scarlet mist. Hunger hollowed out his guts, his throat tightened at the taste of blood flowing from broken gums where his dog teeth lengthened. As his senses heightened, Tycho rocked back on his heels. Stunned by the onslaught of what he suddenly saw, heard and smelt.

"You stop when I tell you. Or else."

Tycho's intuition said she doubted she could deliver on that threat. A hundred thousand rivers of blood flowed beneath her filthy skin and he could sense them all, for a second they were all he could see of her.

Grabbing her arm, he suckled at her wrist. A second later, he was spitting at the floor, scrubbing his lips with his hand. Curdled milk barely described the taste of her blood. Nothing he'd eaten came close. The red mist was gone, swept away by shock, and the night was dark around him. He felt like crying.

The girl sighed.

Blood ceased to well as she licked her wrist, scabs closing over bite marks. She dipped her chunk of stale bread into a puddle and tore half free, offering it to him. "Sometimes one magic doesn't like another."

Tycho nodded, not trusting himself to speak.

He was still chewing the last of the bread when she walked to the edge of the balcony, and stared over the darkened expanse of Piazza San Marco. "Dawn soon," she said. "We should both go."

"Tell me your name."

She grinned. "I offer you my blood. You want my name as well? It's A'rial, I'm Alexa's *stregoi*. Her pet witch."

Before he could answer A'rial was gone.

12

Patting his stallion's neck, Tycho slid from its bronze back to stand at the balcony's edge, with the wind in his face. Below him, a chair waited, its link men shuffling against the cold. In the distance, the Watch still scuffed their way round the piazza, while cutpurses slunk behind its colonnades, hidden by black cloaks and masks.

Out on the lagoon half-furled sails snapped in the wind. Five men approached the *piazzetta* in a low, lean *gondolino*, saw the Watch and changed their minds. The slight splash of their retreat muted by falling snow.

Tycho listened harder.

Concentrating, he caught a sound from within the basilica itself. A young woman crying, and, tied to her sobs, a scent so compelling it hooked him through the guts. He'd turned towards her before he realised. Desperate to make his way inside the building.

Ducking under a lintel, he found a locked door beyond. The door was solid and the lock firm. So, without thinking, he slid his fingers under the door and lifted it off its hinges. Leaving it against a wall, he entered an attic beyond.

Stones stairs were blocked by a wrought-iron gate, with a better lock and hinges. So he took a corridor that led to an internal balcony high above the basilica floor. A rat paused in its scavenging, only to resume when he moved on.

The balcony stank of dust, damp wood and sweet smoke from a censer hanging over the darkened nave. Below it, mosaics swirled away in patterns that mimicked a Persian carpet, unless it was the other way round.

Christ, his mother and apostles whose names Tycho struggled to place watched from the domed ceiling. Their faces stern, their noses aquiline and their resemblance to long dead Roman emperors unmistakable. Every one of them stared at a girl kneeling below.

Tycho understood why.

She was beautiful, her hair as red as her dress. The Virgin she knelt before stood silent, as stone virgins do, but the supplicant's shoulders heaved with anguish, her sobs rising to heaven. From the desolation on her face she doubted the Virgin would help. It was a low, urgent and very one-sided conversation.

"Please, my lady," she begged. "If you don't . . ."

A heart-shaped face looked up, blue eyes fixing on heaven. Tycho had no idea what she looked for, but he saw a desperate girl pull a knife from her cloak. Gripping its handle, she folded her fingers over the pommel as if this was something she'd been taught and put the point to her chest.

When she lowered the knife, Tycho felt his heart restart.

Only to stop again when she undid a gilded clasp on her cloak and let the garment slide from her shoulders. Next she undid her dress, exposing a white shift beneath. A bow at the neck undid this. Regaining her knife, she slid the dress and shift from one shoulder to reveal a breast.

He didn't know whether to watch the blade or the girl as she put the knife to her heart. He saw her hesitate, watched her wince as she jabbed slightly, blood tricking down her ribs.

"Sweet God," she whispered.

And Tycho's senses exploded, hunger overflowing desire as his world narrowed to the half-naked girl, and her alone. The night-time nave was daylight bright, the smell of incense viciously cloying. Meltwater dripping overhead was loud enough to startle. The gap between him and the censer vanished in a single leap, its chain swinging wildly, until he dropped and its swing ended.

Only when he reached the censer did the girl look up.

Some fifth sense where Tycho now had a dozen. One hand rose to hide her breast and she opened her mouth to scream. Before she could, Tycho dropped, closing the gap between them. Grabbing her knife, he tossed it away.

"*Don't*," he snarled.

He wanted . . . her, but how?

His dog teeth ached, sweetness flooded his mouth. Her neck was freckled and perfect, her exposed nipple pale and pink, the breast it tipped small but ripe. She wore rose petal scent. *That* was what hooked him.

Not just her nakedness. Not just her beauty.

The combination of roses and blue eyes reminded him of . . . Who? Because they reminded him of someone. Shuddering, he traced one finger up the trickle of blood on her ribs, only stopping when he reached the underside of her breast.

"Do you know who I am?" she demanded.

How would he? All he knew was that sucking her blood from his finger sent shivers up his spine. Blood must be what he wanted. Blood must be what he hadn't allowed himself since arriving in this strange city.

"Well . . . ? Do you?"

Furious eyes glared from a heart-shaped face as she freed her wrist, and Tycho let it happen. As he watched, dumbstruck, she raised her shift to hide her breast, blood blossoming in a run of roses across its surface.

"Do you know what my uncle will do to you?"

No, and he didn't care either. He caught her wrist before she could slap him for lowering her shift again. He wanted to hurt and protect her. Strip her naked, take her screaming on the cold floor. And die keeping her from harm. Just looking at the trickle of her blood made him drunk.

"Did you hear what I said?"

"What's your name?"

She glared, convinced he was mocking her. But he wasn't. He wanted to know her name. Needed to know it more than anything he'd ever needed to know.

"I'm Lady Giulietta di Millioni."

"Giulietta?"

"My uncle will flay you."

"I don't care . . ." That was the truth. He didn't.

Outside, guards stamped their feet against the cold, and an oxcart rumbled and creaked over melting snow. Daybreak was near, and Tycho needed to hide. But he stayed instead. "I saw a man flayed once," he said, remembering.

Lady Giulietta scowled ferociously.

"I mean it. He'll have you nailed to a door. Or boiled in oil." She glared at Tycho. "Maybe you've seen a man boiled in oil?"

"No," he said. "Does it last long?"

She hissed in fury. "How would I know? I haven't seen a man flayed either. I'm barely allowed out of the palace." She caught herself. "This is ridiculous. I don't know why I'm even talking to you."

"Because you can't help it."

"That's . . ."

"True," Tycho said. He let her raise her shift again.

Blood still seeped from her slight wound, darkening cloth where it trickled down to her red velvet dress. Giulietta did nothing when he touched the largest stain, though she froze as he lifted her breast, finding the source beneath her shift with his thumb. Carrying her blood to his mouth, he sucked until the ball of his thumb was clean. Then he brushed his thumb across the stain again, and watched in surprise as the trickle lessened and stopped.

Behind him, a door began to open.

"Go," Giulietta begged.

He went, taking the scent of roses, the memory of her heart-shaped face and the taste of her blood with him.

13

When she looked the boy was gone. Despite herself, Lady Giulietta glanced at a huge marble pillar, seeing movement where it met a balcony. But the light in Basilica San Marco came from candles or oil lamps, and she couldn't be sure it wasn't just shadows shifting.

"My lady . . ."

Captain Roderigo looked tired, and worried at how he found her. Since his scars said his courage wasn't in question, she assumed he hung back to give her time to pull up her dress. He said nothing as she fixed her cloak and bent for the dagger, sliding it into a secret hiding place.

"What?" she demanded.

"I have a message for you."

Lady Giulietta sighed. "So?" she said flatly, and watched the captain's eyes tighten at her rudeness. As if she'd care.

"The Regent is asking where you are."

"What did my aunt tell him?"

"My lady, I wouldn't . . ."

"Of course you would," Giulietta said crossly. "Everyone in the palace knows everything. They just pretend they don't. It's a prison."

It wasn't. She'd been inside a prison.

As a child she'd been taken to see a toothless and naked patrician, who huddled in a freezing cell, filthy with his own faeces and sitting in a puddle of his own piss. Nicolo Paso led a rebellion in his youth. The so-called Second Republic, which lasted three years and saw a hundred senators beheaded in a single day when it fell. Paso was spared.

His condition an object lesson in what awaited those who challenged the Millioni dynasty. She'd heard the Byzantine empire funded Paso's treason. But then she'd heard the German emperor was to blame. And the Hungarian king, and the Mamluk sultan . . . Clearly, no one considered Paso might have thought of the rebellion himself. She kept that opinion to herself.

"I've seen Paso's cell," she said, by way of apology. She couldn't help being rude. Well, she probably could, but she wouldn't know where to start or why she would . . .

"Bother," Giulietta said, fumbling a button.

Roderigo's apparent fascination with her face obviously turned on the fact that her fingers struggled with buttons at the neck of her dress, and her hands wouldn't stop shaking. "My lady," he said. "Lord Paso's conditions are good." Before she could disagree, he added. "There are far worse . . ."

"Worse than that?"

"Much worse," Roderigo said. "The Ca' Ducale is *not* a prison. In comparison with the worst this city has, Lord Paso's cell is almost a palace."

"As I would know if I'd need a *real* prison?"

"Yes, my lady."

Giulietta hated being patronised. "Tell me the worst then."

Roderigo considered her demand, then shrugged and obviously decided he had nothing to lose in answering. "The pit of the Black Crucifers. It fills with water each tide and requires hours of labour to empty. Prisoners work in shifts to remove the water before the next tide comes."

"And if they don't succeed?"

"They drown."

"Well," she said, fastening her last button. "I'd still rather pump water there than be here talking to you." Captain Roderigo looked as if he wanted to slap her. That was fine; most days she wanted to slap herself.

Smothering a shiver, Giulietta ordered him to escort her back to the palace. Where she discovered Aunt Alexa and her uncle now separately abed, and retired to her own chambers on the palace's family floor. Dismissing Lady Eleanor, who'd stayed awake to help her undress, she struggled out of her blood-stained dress, pulled off her undergown and changed it for a fresh one, hiding her bloodied shift under her mattress. Falling into bed, Giulietta dragged a heavy fur over her and dreamed of snows and wooden buildings burning.

Next morning she woke, pissed in a cold pot and dressed as quickly as her buttons and ribbons and Lady Eleanor's slowness allowed.

"Eleanor."

"My fingers are frozen."

Her lady-in-waiting was fumbling the ribbons on the sleeve of an overgown when she stopped, with the ribbon half tied. Pulling back the sleeve she revealed a bruise on Giulietta's wrist.

"My lady."

"What?"

"It looks . . ." Eleanor hesitated.

"Well?" Giulietta said crossly. "What does it look like?"

"Finger marks."

Lady Giulietta slapped her.

And having slapped her, she sent Eleanor to her room and tied the ribbons herself, pulling them too tight and making a mess of the bows. She considered recalling her lady-in-waiting to tell her she was dismissed for good. But Giulietta couldn't face that, and Eleanor probably didn't want to go to Cyprus anyway and would only be glad of the news.

So she said nothing and kicked her heels in the map room, endlessly examining a fresco of Cyprus, which showed pitiful little ships sailing in all directions. The artist depicted her future home as rocky and barren, with few towns and fewer cities. This made her no happier than arguing with Eleanor.

It was absurd and ridiculous. It made her sound like a maiden in a troubadour's song, but Giulietta couldn't shake the feeling that the touch of the boy in the basilica had set hooks into her soul. As if he'd stolen a part of her and left a part of himself in its place. A part that tasted bitter, unforgettable.

Aunt Alexa was too busy to be disturbed.

So Giulietta spent the rest of the day practising her harpsichord with fearsome intensity, until the guards in the corridor winced at every repetition. It was next morning before the girls spoke, and three days before they made up their quarrel. Without discussing it, both avoided mentioning the bruises again.

14

"Where is my aunt?"

Roderigo looked into Lady Giulietta's anxious face and opened his mouth to say he didn't know.

"You don't know, do you?"

"No, my lady."

"Idiot," she said crossly. "Everyone's an idiot this evening. I know she's not with the duke, because he's in his room." Permission was needed to visit Marco after dark, even for Giulietta, so Roderigo avoided asking how she knew.

"Have you asked the Regent?" he said instead.

Giulietta turned on her heel.

Wrong suggestion, obviously. "My lady," he called after her. "Shall I mention your wish to see her should I meet the duchess?"

"Yes," came the answer. Although Lady Giulietta didn't bother to stop or turn and thank him for the thought. *Why would she?* he thought. She was a Millioni. A member of the richest family in Europe. And he . . . ? A minor patrician, who squatted one room of a ten-room palace because the other nine were colder, damper and even more disgusting than the one he used.

His meeting that afternoon with her uncle had been worrying.

There was something not being said. Something that had Prince Alonzo trapped between fury and worry, with the Mamluk ambassador's reactions almost identical. The men were sparring nervously. Roderigo would have been happier, and more secure, if he had known about what.

The Mamluk ambassador demanded the Ten investigate the burning of his master's ship, and refused to accept the ship hadn't been ransacked and its cargo stolen before being set on fire. He refused, flatly, to accept it was an accident.

"Mamluks don't drink wine," he said crossly, when Duchess Alexa suggested a drunken crew member tripped over an oil lamp and brought disaster. There were just enough drunk Mamluks, Arabs and Moors in the taverns along Riva degli Schiavoni to give that the lie. But in general it was true.

The ambassador's position was firm.

His master did not take kindly to his trade ships being burnt. Nor would the sultan take kindly to the Ten's refusal to investigate. The duchess hoped that wasn't a threat. The ambassador, with the cold pride for which he was famous, declared it a warning, nothing more. Although he suggested Venice take his warning seriously.

"You already know," Alonzo said, "my respect for your master."

"The sultan has been your friend in the past."

Maybe Roderigo was the only one who read *but that is now over* into this sentence. "I would hate to be disappointed," Prince Alonzo said. "To feel my overtures, my offers of friendship were being rejected."

"Disappointment is a fact of life."

Prince Alonzo looked at the ambassador in shock. "Both our countries will lose if this is not resolved smoothly."

"As God wills," the ambassador said.

At this, Prince Alonzo seemed to regain his temper. He repeated that the fire aboard the Mamluk ship had been an accident. Captain Roderigo was certain of this, wasn't he?

"Of course," Roderigo had said.

"My lady . . ." The voice behind her was oily. *Unctuous*, Lady Giulietta decided, shivering at the word's suggestion of greasy ointment. She increased her pace towards the stairs.

"His highness is looking for you."

"The duke?" she said, spinning round.

The Regent's secretary swallowed, and shot a nervous glance at a nearby guard. "Forgive me," he said. "I meant, his excellence, Prince Alonzo . . ."

She knew her uncle was looking for her. That was the reason she was looking for her aunt. Lady Giulietta had begun to fret about the way Uncle Alonzo eyed her. And his constant suggestions that they have a quiet talk soon, alone. Her worry wasn't helped by her aunt's reply when told this earlier.

"We must talk too," Alexa said. "In the meantime, light a candle for your mother, every night. You can rely on her to guard you."

Everyone wanted to talk. No one specified when and time was running out. Sir Richard left on tomorrow's tide and took Giulietta. The treaties were signed, the banquets were over. The courtiers wanted her gone. She could see it in their eyes. They wanted her moping, and her anger and her misery, out of their lives.

Aunt Alexa was so elusive that Giulietta now wondered if she also wanted her gone. The duchess knew how she felt about this marriage, because everyone at court knew how she felt, even those who usually found safety in knowing nothing. So why was Alexa refusing to see her? *If you had any guts you'd kill yourself.*

The voice was small, still and her own.

"My lady."

"*What?*" Her uncle's horrid little secretary was still there. Looking like a weasel, with his watery eyes and balding head.

"I really think, my lady . . ."

"Well, don't." He'd never dare express an opinion if she wasn't leaving tomorrow. But she'd be gone by the following noon, so what did he have to fear from her now? Her aunt was nowhere to be found and she could hardly complain to . . . "Where is my uncle?"

"Della Tortura."

"He's torturing someone?" She wouldn't put it past him. He often claimed to miss the mud, blood and brutality of the battlefield. *So much cleaner than politics.* You were meant to believe he was a reluctant ruler. But he plotted and schemed and lied with the rest of them.

The Sala della Tortura was on the fourth level, below the roof and above the armoury and chambers of government. Since she was on the second level she had two sets of stairs to climb and a dozen or so guards to pass. No doubt each would sneak a look at her face, wondering what was wrong this time.

The stairs were cold and wind rippled the tapestries ordered by the last duke. These were French and showed the highlights of his reign. The first outlined Marco III's overthrow of the Second Republic as a young god, with his enemies crabbed and bitter. The second his marriage to the Khan's granddaughter, who became Alexa di San Felice il Millioni. She arrived with three boxes of gold, a case of black tea and a dozen imperial pigeons. Her grandfather relied on the breed to carry messages about his conquests, issue orders to his armies and send to the rear for supplies or reinforcements. Tīmūr, the new khan of khans, did the same.

The third and final tapestry was divided into Heaven, Hell and Earth. On Earth, Marco III sat with Alexa and his son. In Heaven, Princes Matteo and Cesare, murdered by the Second Republic, smiled on their brother's new family. And below, in the bowels of Hell, republicans were tortured by demons, while their sons and daughters were violated with spits or hung like joints of meat.

That one gave Lady Giulietta the creeps.

The stairs to the next floor were narrower and far less grand. Flaking murals no one cared about lined the walls. The tapestries had holes. She liked these stairs better. Neither of the guards by the Tortura door readied to open it.

Giulietta was about to be furious when she remembered she'd told them she could open doors for herself the last time she came here. She decided to be furious anyway.

"Open it, then."

They did as ordered.

A fire burnt in a brazier and sweet smoke filled the air. The room was double height. A balcony ran down both sides, with wooden chairs for councillors who wanted to watch a questioning. A single rope dangled from high above. It was the rope from which suspects were suspended. The Sala's walls were bare wood, darkened with smoke and age. The floor was old stone. An incongruous leather bed was pushed into one corner, covered with a Persian carpet. Next to it stood a portable desk, overflowing with papers and cut quills, while an ink pot had its lid open. The man sat at the desk was sketching a horoscope with confident strokes.

"You're here at last," Dr. Crow said.

"Where's my uncle?"

"Busy." Alonzo's voice came from an alcove behind curtains.

"I'll come back later."

"No," he crossly. "You'll wait. I sent for you an hour ago. Your lateness could have made matters . . ."

"What?"

"Unnecessarily complicated."

Hearing the door open behind her, Giulietta glanced back, expecting her uncle's secretary or one of the guards. A sour-faced *abadessa* in the white wimple of her order stood there instead. And next to her, a drunk so blowsy she could have been scooped from the stalls of the nearest brothel. Sweat and alcohol rose from her filthy skin.

"*You*," she hissed, seeing the alchemist.

Dr. Crow smiled. "Mistress Scarlett." The air crackled with the early stirrings of a storm. Only to settle when the nun glared between them.

"We're all here, then."

Dropping the curtain behind him, Prince Alonzo stepped out of the alcove holding a goose quill. It looked like a pen, except it was missing a cut nib and lacked the feathers usually left to balance a pen's upper end. "You're certain the time is propitious?"

"A day off the new moon," Dr. Crow said. "No time better."

"What about her?"

"If what her linen maid says is true. Scarlett can check."

Stepping towards Giulietta, the blowsy drunk scowled when the young woman backed away from her. "This will be easier with your help."

"What will?"

"Everything," Prince Alonzo said heavily. "Believe me. It will be easier for everyone if you cooperate. *Abadessa* . . ."

Grabbing Giulietta, the abbess spun her round and dug a thumb into the soft flesh of Giulietta's arm, shocking her into stillness. "Struggle, and I'll press harder."

Piss spread in a puddle around Giulietta's feet.

"With the Regent's permission," said the abbess. "We'll begin. Mistress Scarlett, if you'll confirm we're not wasting our time?"

Lifting Lady Giulietta's gown and undergown, the wise woman pushed her hand between the girl's thighs and sniffed her fingers. "Close enough. The quill's fresh?"

"What do you think?" Alonzo said, lacing his codpiece.

"It would be surer to . . ."

The Regent's face darkened. "Do you *want* me damned?" he snarled. "It's against the rules of consanguinity. I might as well burn churches and eat meat on a Friday."

"*You can't* . . ."

And then Giulietta said no more, because the sharp-faced nun dug her thumb so savagely into Giulietta's arm she wet herself again, shame spreading in a growing puddle across the floor.

"Stop snivelling," the abbess told her.

"I'm not sure," Dr. Crow said, "that was necessary. And I'm not sure," he added, looking reproachful, "you mentioned your niece was unwilling."

"If she'd bothered to answer my summons we'd have had time to discuss this. As she didn't . . ." Alonzo let his comment hang. He obviously considered Giulietta's ignorance of his plan her fault. "And I don't explain myself to my mage."

"Duke Marco's mage," Dr. Crow said quietly.

Lady Giulietta thought her uncle would strike him. When the Regent held his tongue she knew it meant one of two things. The alchemist was more powerful than she suspected. Or her uncle wanted this over, whatever *this* was. Neither choice made her happy.

"Put her on the divan," Mistress Scarlett said.

It didn't matter that Giulietta struggled. On her back, with her dress and undergown round her waist was where she ended. Although it was only when she began to scream that the Regent lost his temper. "Fetch the bitch a gag."

"We don't have time."

"Deal with it," Prince Alonzo ordered Dr. Crow.

"As you wish." Touching both sides of Giulietta's jaw, he whispered, "Silence." And that was that. Lady Giulietta's jaw locked and her tongue froze in her head. When Mistress Scarlett began to force her knees open, the alchemist looked away, then headed for the alcove where the Regent had been earlier.

"Where do you think you're going?"

"To get wine. You do have wine, don't you . . . ?" Dr. Crow muttered something about bloody well hoping so. And then he was gone, the curtain was in place and Mistress Scarlet was raising the girl's ankles while the abbess held her wrists.

"This will happen," the wise woman said, apologetically.

"Struggling only makes things worse. So be kind to yourself and behave."

Although she hated her own cowardice Giulietta did as she was told. Mistress Scarlett spoke the truth. All Dr. Crow had to do was pass his hands across her hips and those would be out of her control as well.

"Do it," the Regent ordered.

Taking the quill, Mistress Scarlet pulled a fish bladder from her sleeve, blew into it and pushed it on to one end of the quill. The other, she slid between Lady Giulietta's thighs, cursing when the young woman began bucking hard enough to free one wrist.

"*Hold her.*"

The grip on her captive wrist grew savage. "Such a fuss," the nun said. "You'd think you were the only girl to do her city a service."

Repositioning the quill, Mistress Scarlet squeezed the bladder to free its contents. "See," she said. "Not so bad. And you're as intact as the day you were born." She smiled, as if this should make the difference.

"*Alchemist.*"

"It's Dr. Crow to you, woman."

"My part's done," Mistress Scarlett said. "I'll be taking my money and going."

The Regent opened his mouth.

"I'll take my money and go," she repeated.

Prince Alonzo threw a purse at her. "Witch," he muttered, as the door shut behind her.

"If you will," said Dr. Crow, moving the *abadessa* back from the divan and indicating that Giulietta should remain where she was. Since the nun blocked her escape Giulietta did as ordered.

"A son," the Regent said tightly. "You understand? She's to bear Cyprus a son. If she fails I'm going to be angry. In fact, you'll find I suddenly agree with the Pope in Rome's opinion that you're a heretic."

Dr. Crow ignored him.

"My lady," he said. "First babies are often late. Cyprus will never suspect your child is not his. And you will never tell him. In fact . . ." The alchemist glanced at the Regent, who nodded. "You will never talk of what happened here."

The mage held Giulietta steady until she stopped shivering and then touched her face, letting his fingertips brush her jaw.

"How could you?" she demanded.

"I need corpses to dissect, my lady. The Regent provides those and keeps me safe from those who regard my work as abomination."

The *abadessa* left next. And Giulietta was made to lie for half an hour with her knees up and a cushion under her hips. Although the nun's contemptuous parting gift, which was to rearrange Giulietta's gown, at least meant she had her decency. But when Giulietta was at last allowed up, and turned for the door, her knees weak, her guts vomitous and her bowels on the edge of emptying, her uncle called her back. Her job was more than simply giving Cyprus the son his first wife had not. There were other considerations, matters of policy. He wished to explain exactly what was required of her when she arrived at her new kingdom.

15

Stumbling from the room, Giulietta heard footsteps and walked faster, but her stomach was water, the hem of her dress stank of piss, and vomit filled her throat. She refused to believe Aunt Alexa knew of what had just happened. But if she didn't, why had her aunt been unwilling to see her?

It was, Giulietta knew, only a matter of time before her guts released at one end or the other. And when they did, she wanted to be anywhere but on cold stairs watched by needlepoint demons.

"Wait," Dr. Crow called.

Lady Giulietta increased her speed.

He caught up with her at the end of stairs leading to the loggia. This was easy, since by then, she was on her knees outside the Sala dei Censoi, vomiting up her supper. All Dr. Crow had to do was walk up to her and wait.

"It's the shock," he said.

She stood slowly. Slapped him hard.

"You didn't see that," Dr. Crow told a guard coming towards them. The man carried a halberd and wore a thick cloak, as befitted someone whose duties involved walking down an open-sided corridor in mid-winter.

"Saw what, sir?"

"Good man. Now, get me drinking water."

The guard wanted to say fetching water wasn't his job. He was right, his job was patrolling the loggia. But Dr. Crow had turned an enemy to a black cat, and drowned him. Added to which, he treated the new duke in his moments of madness. About which nobody was meant to know . . .

"My lady."

Taking the cup from the guard, Giulietta sipped slowly. A second later she remembered to dismiss the man with a nod. Turning, he marched into the wind, his cloak billowing like a shroud. So much in this palace had to be kept secret. No doubt he'd seen worse.

"Chew this, my lady."

She looked at the sticky pill Dr. Crow offered.

"It will settle your stomach and balance your humours." Dropping the pill into her palm, the alchemist folded her fingers around it. "You should sleep, get your strength for tomorrow."

"I can't. Not yet."

The mage had an old man's eyes, clouded and watery. But Giulietta felt, as she always did, that he could read her thoughts. And she couldn't shake the feeling he knew what she'd say before she did. If so, he must realise how furious she was. How revolted. He must also know what else she had to do.

"I need to light a candle for my mother."

"In the morning, my lady."

"There won't be time," she said bitterly. "Sir Richard, Lady Eleanor and I board at noon, and sail on the tide. There will be farewells first. A formal breakfast in the state room. I will need to say my . . ."

She fought back tears.

"Your own goodbyes?"

Lady Giulietta's nod was abrupt.

"My lady, this is not . . ."

"Don't you dare," she shouted. "Don't dare say I'll see the city again. That this is for everyone's good. That what you did to me in there . . ." Her voice folded into sobs and hiccups.

"It would be the truth."

"That this is for everyone's good?" Lady Giulietta said through tears.

"No. You will leave this city and you will return. Both will be hard but the second will be harder than the first . . . Now, think about going to bed. Your uncle will be unwilling to provide guards for a journey at night. You know they'll not stir without a signed order."

"It's not a *journey*," she said. "It's a hundred paces. And they're not his guards. They're Marco's."

"You'll still need them."

"No, I won't." Opening his mouth to say she would, he shut it when she said, "I'll use the way into the Lady chapel."

Dr. Crow looked shocked.

Because she knew about the passage, Giulietta realised. He knew obviously enough. She was meant to be ignorant of it.

"The door will be locked."

"You can open it."

"My lady . . ."

"Or shall I tell everyone in Cyprus you cut up bodies?"

Apart from locking her jaw, for which she'd never forgive him, this was the first time she'd seen him perform magic. The first time she'd ever seen anyone perform magic. If one ignored producing fire from your fingers, because every mountebank in Piazza San Marco could do that.

The door was behind a tapestry at ground level in a wall that adjoined the basilica. Kneeling, the old alchemist rubbed his hands together. Then he placed his fingers on the key plate, while Giulietta kept watch for guards.

"Hurry up," she whispered crossly.

There was a sharp click as a spring let go and a bolt ratcheted back. Opening the door, Dr. Crow put his hand on the far side of the lock and muttered under his breath. "Shut it when you leave," he said. "It will lock itself."

With that he was gone, in a shambling shadow of grey velvet and the mustiness of an old man with no one to wash his clothes.

Basilica San Marco, the most beautiful basilica outside Byzantium itself, was the duke's personal chapel. Open on saints' days and high holidays, it was reserved for the Millioni at all other times. It was begun when Venice was still an imperial city and the mainland beyond owed its loyalty to the Eastern emperor.

At that time, there was no emperor of the West. At least none Byzantium was prepared to recognise. So, for a while, the Eastern emperor was simply, *the emperor*. This changed with the rise of the Franks who founded the Tedeschi empire, otherwise known as the Holy Roman empire. The Franks were French and the Tedeschi were German, so Lady Giulietta wasn't sure how this worked. But Fra Diomedes used his cane willingly and she'd learnt not to interrupt his lessons with questions.

And so Venice, trapped between two powerful rulers, became sly. She became sly because only this kept her safe. Having changed her saint to one not claimed by the Tedeschi, the Papacy or the emperors in Byzantium, she announced she owed loyalty to no one and would trade with all.

And so matters remained.

The same slew of glass stars circled the Virgin's head, and the same soft smile greeted Giulietta as she bobbed a curtsy, before heading towards a jewelled screen that hid the high altar from public view. She wanted Fra Zeno, one of the few Mamluk converts allowed into the priesthood. Fra Zeno was young, and smiled when he saw her. He would listen without getting cross. But she found the patriarch instead. Or, rather, Patriarch Theodore found her.

"My child . . ." His quavering admonition from the darkness made her jump. "What," he asked, "are you doing here at this hour?"

"I . . ." She was about to say looking for Fra Zeno, when she realised that was tactless, open to misunderstanding, and it didn't matter which priest she talked to. And Theodore was patriarch, after all.

If he didn't know what she should do . . .

"Seeking help."

The old man looked around him and smiled. "There are worse places to seek it," he agreed. "And a troublesome mind is no respecter of the hour." Taking an oil lamp from a shrine, he turned and Giulietta realised she was meant to follow him into the area beyond the altar.

"That's . . ."

"The warmest place here."

In a tiny sacristy she'd never seen stood a gold chalice, decorated with emeralds and rubies. Slabs of lapis were set into the bowl and its rim was ringed with sapphires. The cup rested on a chest containing priestly vestments. An old Persian carpet covered half the floor, and a tattered battle flag hung from one wall. In the bowl of the chalice was a wedding ring.

She knew it instantly. It was the ring with which the Duke of Venice married the sea each year to calm the waters and give fair wind to her ships. Not a year had passed since the city was founded without the marriage taking place. That was what she'd been told by her tutor anyway.

"How old is the ring?"

"How old is an axe if you keep replacing handle and blade? The ring's been repaired this year. And the chalice has had a new base, a new stem and new stones in my lifetime alone. The originals would be six centuries old. Perhaps less. Records undoubtedly lie about which duke first married the sea."

The old man laughed at her shock. "You didn't come here for

history lessons. So tell me why you're here and by a secret entrance. I didn't realise you knew about that door."

"I discovered it."

She wondered why he smiled.

"The devil makes work for idle hands. And between them, Aunt Alexa and Uncle Alonzo have kept you idle for longer than is wise. Still, there are worse things for girls your age to discover than secret doors."

For a moment, Giulietta thought he'd lean forward and ruffle her hair, but he simply sighed and balanced his stolen lamp beside the chalice, looking round for a chair.

"So," he said, finding one. "Tell me what upsets you."

Maybe he expected doubts about her wedding; God knows she had enough of them. Or maybe doubts about leaving Serenissima, because she had those too. But his smile died and the twinkle left his eyes within seconds. By the end he watched with the stillness of a snake. Although his fury was not for her. Giulietta realised that when he did his best to paste a smile into place.

"Let me think for a moment."

She'd avoided all mention of Mistress Scarlett, the hatchet-faced *abadessa* and the goose quill, fearing Dr. Crow told the truth. To speak of them would steal her voice forever. But what she said was bad enough.

"Perhaps you misunderstood?"

"No," she said firmly. "Uncle Alonzo's orders are clear. Once an heir is born I must poison my husband and rule as Regent until he is old enough to rule for himself. My uncle will tell me what decisions to make."

"And how are you . . . ?"

"With these." Giulietta produced two tiny pots from beneath her dress. One was small, the other smaller; no bigger than a thimble. "This," she said, holding up the larger, "has three hundred fly specks of poison."

"To kill your husband?"

"No. To *habituate* myself from the poison in this one."

She stumbled over Dr. Crow's strange word and Archbishop Theodore looked thoughtful. Maybe he heard the alchemist's echo in her voice. The patriarch always greeted Dr. Crow with a steely politeness Giulietta now recognised as hatred.

She watched the patriarch unscrew the smaller pot. The paste inside was sealed against the air with wax set in a swirl. "Rose balm to colour your lips. When you're certain the baby is healthy, you simply . . ." He mimed applying balm to his lips. "And then you greet Janus warmly for a week?"

Lady Giulietta nodded.

"It's slow-acting?"

"Mimics plague . . . I'm to be his food taster, with Eleanor to taste mine, and a taster to test hers before that." Giulietta's gaze was bleak. "I will remain healthy, so no one will suspect poison. Particularly if I insist on nursing Janus." Dashing tears from eyes, she asked. "What should I do?"

"Stay here."

"In Serenissima? But my ship leaves tomorrow. Sir Richard will never stand for it."

"No. Stay here now. Don't move until I've talked to Alexa. I can't believe she knows about this. And I'll be taking these." The patriarch took the tiny jars of poison, then paused. "You don't think Alexa knows, do you?"

Considering how hard it had been to find her aunt, never mind talk to her, Giulietta thought she might. Although she hoped she didn't. Every time she'd gone looking Aunt Alexa was busy or not where her servants said she would be. There had been wariness in her aunt's eyes the last few times they'd met.

"I'm not sure."

"You're not . . ."

Taking a deep breath, Giulietta said, "Aunt hates Uncle Alonzo as much as you hate Dr. Crow, maybe more. He wants the throne.

She wants the throne for Marco. All Marco wants, of course, is to be allowed his toys. So if Alonzo wants this, I'd expect her to object."

"But . . . ?"

Giulietta hesitated. "It was Aunt Alexa who suggested I marry Cyprus in the first place." The thought of it made her want to burst into tears again.

"How old are you?"

An odd question, Giulietta decided, from the man who presented her to the crowds gathered in Piazza San Marco on her naming day. "Fifteen."

Archbishop Theodore smiled sadly. "And already you know how Venice works. You should have been . . ."

"What?" she demanded.

Sent to a nunnery, whipped more often, drowned at birth like a kitten? Those were her uncle's usual suggestions. She'd survived her share of whippings. It was the Regent's contempt she found harder to take. Aunt Alexa wished she'd been Marco's brother. That way, two Millioni would stand between Prince Alonzo and the throne, two heirs being harder to murder than one.

Giulietta simply wished she'd been a boy.

She'd wanted to be one for so long she'd forgotten when it started. Certainly before Aunt Alexa suggested marrying her off. And long before Uncle Alonzo decided she should murder her husband.

"I wish," the patriarch said. "Your mother had lived. *Do* you think Duchess Alexa knows about this?"

"It's possible."

As the clock in the south tower struck one, and their stolen lamp continued to gutter, its flame always on the edge of dying, but struggling back to life, Patriarch Theodore sighed. "Then I'd better start with your uncle. Maybe Aunt Alexa knows, maybe she doesn't. But talking to Alonzo is where I'll start."

16

The first time the beggar girl nodded to him Tycho thought it was an accident, the second he knew it was intentional. She glanced from beneath lank hair, nodded and kept walking.

The night streets were full of those who caught each other's glances and looked away. A quick glance and a slight nod. He'd acquired membership of a clan for whom this was enough. No one tried to talk, no one *wanted* to talk. The nod simply meant, *I'm not your enemy*. He knew, looking at the girl, that she wasn't his enemy. Her spirit was too thin to make her anyone's enemy but her own.

He wondered, however, how she knew he wasn't hers.

The third time they crossed she smiled. A fragile flicker, demanding he comfort her in some way, maybe simply by returning her smile. The days were far too bright for him, the light too dangerous for his eyes. He wondered what her excuse for living in the night world was. This city was full and it was empty. That thought led to separate iterations of *empty*.

Back from the busy thoroughfares were other, emptier streets in this city of the living; because although the obvious places were crowded, there simply weren't enough of the living to crowd the edges. There was, however, *another* city. Really empty, behind this one. It shared identical streets and brick-floored squares, identical churches and squat fortified towers. When Tycho entered it the living disappeared and the sky became silvery. The world in the empty city looked solid close to, but thinned and became translucent immediately beyond. Those in the city of the living showed in the streets of the other city like shadows.

Tycho had reached a point of wondering if all this had some deeper significance; or if was simply how this world was. For days dead children had followed him, shouting pleas he couldn't hear. And then one night they were gone. He had another memory, of a Nubian with silver snakes for hair. Unless she'd been one of the ghost children. And now most of that memory was gone too.

She was young, the beggar girl on the night street. With a filthy smock and bare legs and rags wrapped round her feet and tied at her ankles with twine. Sometimes she was alone, at others with a glowering older boy. Occasionally, a younger boy was there too.

The time she smiled she was alone.

In the time it took the moon to swell from new to quarter full Tycho had discovered how to move between cities, hide himself in the shadows and steal all the food he needed. This would have been something if he'd been able to enjoy it.

Everything he ate tasted like ash.

He drank water from habit, fed when he remembered. But his piss was almost black and it was days since his bowels had worked. He should be starving to death. Instead, he simply felt hungry. If only his stomach knew for what . . .

"You," he said.

She stopped, turned herself and smiled.

"You know me?" he demanded, and watched the smile drop from her filthy face. Without knowing it, she looked around her. Checking for exits. The alley behind the fish market was long and narrow, and more of the crowd were moving against them than going their way. She tried to shrug his hand from her shoulder, then let herself be gripped by the arm and dragged to a doorway.

"So," he said. "Do you?"

"Yes . . ." His expression must have scared her, because she began shaking her head almost immediately. "I mean no. I mistook you for someone else."

"How do you know me?"

She looked at him, debating her answer. In the end she told the truth, perhaps because she was scared by now. Of what he was. Of what he might do to her. Or of the fact he might know the truth already.

"I pulled you from the canal."

He stared at her.

"Don't you remember? I thought you were dead. And then you opened your eyes and looked right at me . . ." She blushed, the change to her skin unseeable in the darkness for anyone but him. Not that there was anyone wanting to see.

"*You* pulled me from the canal? The night I . . ."

Turning her face to the fragile moonlight, he stared into her eyes and watched her blush deepen. A salt mix of fear and arousal rose from her body. When he sniffed, her blush deepened again. Only his grip kept her in place.

Her breasts were tiny beneath her thin smock. Its hem showing more leg than was decent in a girl of her age. Tycho tried to imagine her naked, or half exposed with one breast visible and a trickle of blood beneath.

"You're hurting me."

No, if he was hurting her she'd know.

"Your name?" he demanded.

The girl hesitated, wincing as his fingers gripped tighter. "Rosalyn," she said. "And I'm sorry about your shackle . . . Josh sold it," she added. "I stole it, but Josh sold it. I'm sorry."

"What shackle?"

She really looked at him then.

Tycho knew there had been chains. They trapped him in darkness and held him fast. He had fleeting memories of those chains. Fire, then chains.

"The shackle that was hurting . . ."

Reaching his wrist, Rosalyn lifted it into the moonlight, gaping at the perfect skin where scars should be. The shock in her face was enough to make Tycho remember scars should be there too. He would have said so, but she had already dragged herself from his grip, and was pushing through the crowd, with her head down and her shoulders hunched, careful not to look back.

Tycho let her go.

17

The lamp was about to burn out when Giulietta heard footsteps beyond the sacristy door. Warmest room in the basilica or not, she was frozen and fed up with waiting. Her fingers were so cold her knuckles ached, and she'd been reduced to folding her arms over her chest and tucking her fingers into her armpits.

"Well. What did Uncle Alonzo say?"

She didn't expect the patriarch to have much success. He was allowed into San Marco at will and his unofficial palazzo, behind the basilica, shared a small garden with the ducal palace; but those were concessions Marco Polo offered for acceptance of his family's legitimacy. San Pietro di Castello, Venice's official cathedral, and Theodore's formal palace, were on the city's edge for a reason.

Mostly Uncle Alonzo got what he wanted. Unless, of course, Aunt Alexa objected strongly. If she did, she'd have stopped this already. That was the conclusion Giulietta had reached as she nursed her frozen fingers, shuffled her feet and wished she'd thought to visit the privy before this.

Here came Theodore to give her the bad news. Only the hooded figure in the doorway was not the patriarch. For a second, Giulietta believed that the silver-haired boy was back. But he wasn't this tall.

Other hooded figures appeared behind the first.

Wolf Brothers, she thought, feeling her guts lurch. Then she heard a clang as the man in the doorway turned and his dagger hilt hit the arch, and knew she was wrong. *Krieghund* went armoured. At least the ones that inhabited her nightmares did. When the man drew his dagger, Giulietta grabbed an altar cross, muttering an apology to God as she reversed it to use as a weapon.

The man laughed.

So she swung the cross hard, its base denting his vambrace as he threw up an arm to protect herself. The blow rang like a bell. His dagger landed on the sacristy floor.

"Laugh at that," she said.

When he retreated, Giulietta saw his face in the lamplight. A hooked nose, a sharp beard and a smile so cruel she shivered. "You burnt our ship," he said over loudly. "So now we kill you. Or you come with us . . ."

A man behind raised a crossbow.

"First," she said. "I must replace this."

Replacing the silver cross, Giulietta lifted the chalice from where it rested on the vestment chest, kissed it as if obeying some obscure rite and put the chalice carefully on the altar beside the cross. As she did, she palmed the wedding ring it contained.

"You're sure she's the right one?"

Grabbing her, their leader wrapped his fingers in her hair, and yanked back her head to take a better look. She would have tripped if his grip hadn't kept her upright. She found herself staring at a man with a golden earring.

"Oh yes," he said. "This is her."

Oars slapped against water and Lady Giulietta felt the boat rock as it drew away from a jetty. A man spoke once, his words guttural and only half heard through the darkness of the rug wrapped around her. All she could hear after this was the creaking of the boat which stole her away.

Later she realised her hand was still clenched. Pins and needles stabbed it, but clutching her fingers confirmed something she hadn't dared hope. She still had the ring she'd grabbed from the altar.

Uncle Alonzo might have spent his life demanding demons take her. But he'd come after the sacred ring, Giulietta had no doubt of that. Without it, how could Marco marry the sea?

18

"*Well?*" The Regent's fury could be heard through the door of the Sala Scarlatti. In fact it could be heard down the corridor outside. And since the corridor was open to the courtyard, it could be heard by the stair guards, servants in the kitchen and a cat crossing snow-smattered flagstones in the courtyard.

Only the cat reacted, twitching in irritation. The guards and kitchen servants knew better. They heard nothing and saw nothing. "*Well?*" Prince Alonzo's voice was quieter this time. Hardly more than a bellow.

"My lord . . . We are searching."

"Search harder."

Captain Roderigo withdrew, risking a sigh as the door shut behind him. It could have gone worse. He'd walked out with his life. Something that had been by no means certain when he walked in. He would issue orders that his men should search ships faster. It would make little difference. They were searching as hard and as fast as they could.

In San Nicolo and Castello, the Watch swept through parishes that had hardly been policed in fifty years. Rookeries scattered, child brothels shut their doors, hazard dens threw loaded dice into canals. The frenzy lasted until the beggar kings, panders and den owners realised they weren't the target.

The Watch were both frenzied and tight-lipped. The whole city, from lowest to highest, knew they searched for something. Only a handful knew what. Some imagined the Ten had news of the missing glass-blower. Others insisted a philosopher's stone had been hidden in the city. A monk caused a riot by announcing Dr. Crow had disappeared, having spent the city's treasure trying to create an elixir of life. Cooler heads suggested the Watch hunted a spy.

Many wondered why the Watch hunted where it did. In the foreign sections of the city. Among the Mamluks, the Seljuks, the Moors and the Jews. Among those who kept their women's faces covered, and their mothers, sisters and daughters locked behind doors. Captain Roderigo could have told them. But he kept his secrets, and hoped this would be enough to let him keep his life.

"We should have moved them . . ."

Antonio Cove was a black beetle. A small, old and hunch-backed one. If dung beetles became human this was how they would look. In his defence, the count was rich, and knew where most of the bodies were buried, having helped Duke Marco III, and lately Prince Alonzo, bury many of them himself. He was the oldest member of the Council of Ten, who controlled Venice under the duke. As such, his opinions had to be respected. No matter how hard that sometimes proved.

"Moved whom?" Alonzo asked.

"The Jews. The Schiavoni. The Mamluks. The leather-boiling workshops. Those stinking urine pits their tanners use. Why don't we just banish them all to the mainland? We could . . ."

"*Count.*"

The man stopped talking.

"We have more important things to discuss."

"Yes," said Duchess Alexa. "We have. Explain again why my niece Giulietta was hiding in the basilica. While you met the patriarch here? And how you came to escort Archbishop Theodore back to his palace in San Pietro with a troop of your own guard? I'm sure my son would love to know."

Duke Marco IV, theoretical head of the inner council, looked more interested in his fingernails.

"It's a spiritual matter," the Regent said.

"Which is why Theodore has taken to his bed?"

"He's old. The shock of hearing about Giulietta." Prince Alonzo looked thoughtful. "I wouldn't be surprised if it doesn't kill him. We should be concentrating on getting her back."

"First we need to know who stole her."

"Indeed," said Alonzo. "I was going to ask you if you had an opinion on that." He held Duchess Alexa's gaze.

"The Abrahams," Count Cove's voice was bitter. "Who else? I dread to think what those fiends . . ."

Foam flecked the corners of his mouth.

"I doubt it," Duchess Alexa said. "This is one of the few cities where they're allowed to live in peace. Why foul their own nest? There has to be a better answer. Remember what Marco always said?"

Prince Alonzo's scowl showed what he thought of dragging his brother into this. Since this was who she meant. No one was about to start quoting the thumb-sucking fool kicking his heels in her late husband's place.

"No doubt you'll tell us."

"*Who gains?*" Duchess Alexa said calmly. "That was always Marco's question after an attack or murder. "Who gains from this?"

"No one," the beetle said triumphantly. "That's why it has to be . . ." A hard knock at the door stopped Count Cove before Alexa had to.

Kneeling to the duke, Roderigo bowed to Prince Alonzo and Alexa, and nodded to the rest, his apology for interrupting their meeting. His face was pale beneath his curling hair. He had trouble meeting anyone's eyes.

Marco IV, Duke of Venice, stopped kicking his feet. A beautiful smile spread across his face. "Y-y-you've found my butterfly?"

"No, your highness."

Everyone was so shocked Marco had spoken, they almost forgot to listen to Roderigo's answer. "But we found this." Producing a dagger from under his cloak, he placed it carefully at the duke's feet.

As guards hurried forward, Alexa waved them back.

"You know the law," Prince Alonzo said. "No weapons in this chamber."

"Yes, sir. I thought . . ."

Duchess Alexa was out of her chair, the others standing as she rose. Dropping to a crouch she flicked back her veil to examine the weapon. "Mamluk," she said. "Maybe Seljuk or Moorish. Where was this found?"

"Below the Riva degli Schiavoni."

She waited for him to explain the significance.

"If Lady Giulietta's abductors headed north, through the patriarch's garden, then chose Zalizzada San Provolo, they would have been able to cut south and reach the Riva without raising suspicion. At that time of night . . ." Everyone knew. At that time of night the Riva would have been filled with drunken crews from ships anchored in the lagoon.

"Anything else?" Alexa asked.

"An unflagged ship slipped through the sandbanks before dawn. Its oarsmen rowing against the tide."

"Galley slaves, you mean," Alonzo said crossly.

Serenissima's galleys used freemen. The Mamluks and Moors, Byzantines, Cypriots and Genoese used slaves. Some Venetians captured at sea served the Barbary pirates. But they were few.

Marco III had extracted such revenge for attacks on his fleets that fewer Venetians now languished under the whip than ever before.

"How could you let this happen?"

A question on which Roderigo's life hung.

Although Roderigo knew it was already lost if anyone discovered what had really happened out on the lagoon the night the Mamluk ship burnt. A Mamluk princess killed. Now a Millioni princess abducted in revenge. A new ship slipping away at night. Roderigo needed to avoid laying these strands at Duke Marco's kicking feet. Only to have Prince Alonzo tie them neatly into a knot.

"You saw this ship leave yourself?" Duchess Alexa sounded acid.

"No, my lady. I was told."

"What nationality?"

"We don't know." Roderigo swallowed.

"Why not?" the Regent demanded. "What's the point of a Dogana chief who doesn't register vessels as they arrive in our lagoon?"

"My lord, there are five hundred ships out there. It often takes us more than a day to give them a place in the quarantine line."

"I'm not interested in excuses."

"We can deal with details later." Duchess Alexa was firm. "If Captain Roderigo has been lax he will be fined. If his men have failed they will be flogged. If treason is involved people will die. That is not the issue. Assume the Mamluks took Giulietta. Now ask, *why*?"

"W-w-why why?" Duke Marco asked. "Even, w-why why why?"

"Because," his mother said patiently. "If we don't know *why* they've taken her. How will we know what they want to give her back?"

"She's nice. Perhaps they'll keep her."

"Does he have to be here?" Prince Alonzo hissed.

"Without him there is no Council."

"Enter," the duke shouted. "Sweet bird."

Prince Alonzo and the duchess were still glaring when a guard suddenly knocked and the door was thrown open. In bustled a soft-faced man in scarlet, dragging a dark-haired girl behind him. She dressed as one might for walking. Since she was plump, pink and healthy—and he was old—she obviously allowed herself to be dragged. Her embarrassed yet defiant expression suggested to Duchess Alexa that this was her father. She had some experience in such matters.

"Lord Bribanzo . . . ?"

The old man let go long enough to bow, turning back as if expecting his captive to be sprinting for the door. "I'm sorry to be late." He hesitated. "I have family problems of my own. Of course, if now is an inopportune time . . ."

The smile Prince Alonzo fixed into place belonged to a man who had borrowed fifty thousand gold ducats from Lord Bribanzo and had yet to repay them. "For you, we always have time."

"And this is your daughter?" Alexa said.

"It is, my lady."

Yes. She rather thought it was.

"She's joined our Council without my being told?"

There was an edge to the duchess's question. Even a man as distracted as Bribanzo understood that. "No, my lady. Of course not . . ."

"But you consider her a matter for the Ten?"

Being a matter for the Council was two-edged. They were the law in Venice, and in the city's fiefs on the mainland and in her colonies beyond. They found in your favour. Or they found against you. There was no appeal.

"I have been wronged," Bribanzo said.

"An unwelcome suitor, perhaps?"

"*That's one way to put it . . .*" Catching his temper, Bribanzo spread his hands apologetically. "This has political implications for the city, my lady. I've been in Milan, with Prince Alonzo's permission."

Have you now?

Alexa scowled "The Duke of Milan is our enemy."

"Alliances change," said Alonzo. "Milan needs access to the Adriatic. We could use an ally in the north. The ill will between our cities makes little sense. To me it never has." This was as close as he'd come to outright criticism of his late brother's policies.

"So you approved Lord Bribanzo's journey?"

"We gain an ally and lose an enemy. In Desdaio, Milan gains a duchess. A Venetian-born duchess," Alonzo stressed. "Whose father is a member of the Ten."

And Duke Gian Maria Visconti gains Desdaio's dowry?

Nothing else would persuade Milan's new duke to agree. Gian Maria had just fought a ruinously expensive war. So Bribanzo's gold would be welcome. His daughter's links to Venice less so.

"Months of negotiation," Bribanzo protested. "Weeks on the finer points." He meant how much Gian Maria wanted for making Desdaio a duchess. "All wasted unless we can hush this up."

"Hush what up?" asked Alexa.

"A heathen has ruined her. Stolen the flower of my pride and . . ." Bribanzo stopped, unable to finish.

"Wronged her? Or wronged you?"

The young woman was staring at the floor, blushing to the roots of her curling chestnut hair. She was pretty in a lush way. Breasts young men would like, full and firm. Wide hips and a soft stomach. Alexa had no doubt her bottom wiggled as she walked.

"They are betrothed," her father said furiously.

The duchess could see how that might upset him. Lord Bribanzo's strongroom was apparently so stuffed with gold ducats that his palace had needed new foundations. As well gold didn't tarnish in salt water. Since Ca' Bribanzo was as prone to flooding as the next house.

"Gian Maria Visconti was your idea?"

"Or Cosimo de' Medici. He'd do."

Someone snorted and Bribanzo's chin went up. He was unapologetic about his ambition. How had Cosimo's father secured Florence if not by being rich and ruthless?

"You don't think Venice has young men to offer?"

Lord Bribanzo knew he'd strayed on to treacherous ground. This time he took longer to answer, and his voice was calmer when he did. "My lady, many worthy Venetians have wished for a union. Any one of them would have been preferable to this . . . Mamluk."

"*He's not a Mamluk.*" These were the first words Lady Desdaio uttered. "And I'm not ruined . . ."

"What is he then?" Alonzo asked.

She dropped the Regent a curtsy. "A Moor, my lord."

Alonzo snorted. "Not much difference. They're all more trouble than is wise. It's time we reminded the heathens of our power. Venice is a great city. A kind city. A good city . . ." He glanced round, checking he had the court's attention. Bribanzo and Count Cove were nodding. Even the guards at the door looked attentive. Despite tradition demanding they hear nothing. "But we don't want our kindness mistaken for weakness." Opening her mouth to refute him, Alexa decided not to bother. She'd heard it all before.

"You'll punish him?"

Lord Bribanzo wanted more than his daughter back. He wanted his pound of flesh for the insult to his ambitions. He wanted a warning issued to anyone else who thought they could trick their way to his fortune. "A public flogging at the least?"

"Guards," Alonzo said. "Fetch this man!"

"My lord . . ." Bribanzo was meant to look grateful not embarrassed by this gesture of support from the Regent. "I've already sent for him."

The Regent considered this. Lord Bribanzo was within his rights. Any member of the Ten could demand the attention of anyone in the city.

"Then we wait," Alonzo said.

The grounding of spears on marble outside the chamber announced that guards had crossed their halberds, barring entrance to the prisoner and his escort.

Alexa heard one demand their business.

The answer had metal creaking, as a guard turned the huge handle of the council chamber door. That was when Alexa realised her son was grinning. Sprawled like a skinny black spider across his throne, Marco had one leg dangling over its gilded arm, his shoulder twisted at an ugly angle, and was grinning fit to burst.

When his mother looked worried, he winked.

"Marco . . . ?"

The duke nodded towards the door.

The old man entering wore a Moorish gown, a turban round his head, and turned-up leather slippers. A silver sheath jutted from his belt, but its blade was gone, removed on his arrest. His beard was dyed, although grey flecked his temples.

"*Atilo* . . ."

The duchess was on her feet before common sense kicked in. Sitting, she gripped her chair.

Prince Alonzo smiled.

"You knew about this?" she asked angrily.

"About what?" Turning to Bribanzo, he said, "Are you saying this is the villain responsible . . . ?"

Atilo stepped forward.

"Later," Prince Alonzo snapped. "You will be told when to speak. I am addressing Lord Bribanzo. Well?"

"It is, excellence."

"Then the betrothal is void. You cannot have a betrothal where marriage is banned. Suitable candidates for Lady Desdaio's hand include foreign princes and families in the Golden Book. Lord Atilo is neither a recognised prince nor in the Book. We do not grant permission."

By *we* he meant the Ten. At least, Alexa hoped he did.

"However," Alonzo added. "My brother, the late duke, had faith in this man's abilities. Because of that he will be spared public punishment."

Lord Bribanzo scowled. A quick scowl, speedily swallowed. "No punishment at all, my lord?"

"He has done my city some small favours."

Your city? Small favours?

The duchess was glad to have a veil to hide her anger.

Atilo had won a dozen battles. Never mind the services he rendered as head of the Assassini. And hadn't he sacrificed almost every one of his men to keep Giulietta out of the hands of the Wolf Brothers? What more did Alonzo want?

Alexa wished she'd followed her instincts the morning the late duke died, and had Alonzo killed immediately. If only her husband hadn't made her promise to let him live. Marco III had been known as the Just and the Wise. In this, she doubted both his justice and wisdom.

"I *am* right," Alonzo was saying. "Your name isn't in the Book?"

"No, my lord." Atilo shook his head, his face tightening behind his beard.

"Then this matter is done. Lord Bribanzo may take his daughter. And you can be grateful for our mercy. Now let the Ten consider more important business."

"You can't make me."

Desdaio's protest echoed off wood-panelled walls. Both her father, and Atilo, moved to comfort her and stopped, glaring at each other. While Desdaio stood uncomforted between them, her shoulders shaking with sobs.

Little idiot, Alexa thought.

But a buxom little idiot. Of the kind Venetians find irresistible, burning themselves like moths against her need. Looking into the eyes of her late husband's favourite, the duchess saw real pain. Atilo il Mauros, the man who turned back German cavalry on the marshes of the Veneto, had fallen for the ephemeral charms of a woman a third his age.

Duchess Alexa sighed.

Throwing herself at the feet of Duke Marco's throne, Desdaio gripped its carved legs as if guards were already trying to drag her free. "*Please*," she begged. "*Help me.*"

The duke kicked his heel hard. He glared at his mother. He glared at Atilo. He glared at a spare chair. An empty, gilded chair. Sitting back, he rammed his thumb into his mouth, scratched his crotch openly and scrunched his eyes.

"I think . . ." Alonzo began to say.

But the duchess was standing. Moving swiftly, she stopped opposite Atilo as the court pushed back their chairs, hurrying to stand in their turn. Pausing just long enough to heighten their expectations, she clapped Atilo on the shoulder.

"There is my choice," she said loudly. "My husband's old adviser, this city's faithful servant for the Tenth Chair."

Utter silence filled the room.

"Alexa . . ." Prince Alonzo hesitated. Obviously choosing his words with care. "This is not wise. You know there are reasons why . . ."

"It's my turn."

"No," said Bribanzo. His fleshy face red with the effort of controlling his temper. "You can't."

"My lord . . ." Alexa's voice was icy. And Bribanzo went stock still. He might only be five years older than Atilo, but there the likeness ended. Lord Bribanzo was a coward, albeit an ambitious one.

"You presume to tell me what I may do?"

After Bribanzo had grovelled, Alexa glared round the room, daring anyone else to disagree and, for a second, her gaze halted at the sight of her son smiling sweetly. She could swear he blew Desdaio a kiss.

"Do you accept the chair?" Alexa asked Atilo.

"My lady . . ."

"*Do you?*"

Sinking to his knees, Atilo il Mauros kissed the ring her husband had placed on her finger on their wedding day years earlier. "As always, I am yours to command." Amending this, he said. "As the duke, the Regent and you command."

"Delighted to hear it," Alonzo said.

Turning to a scribe, Alexa said. "Have Lord Atilo's name entered in the Golden Book immediately. He will lead the hunt for my niece."

"Roderigo will accompany him." Prince Alonzo's voice was firm.

To Bribanzo, the duchess said, "Make your peace. My niece must be found and this seat needs filling. Atilo is a trusted servant. As are you." The compliment sounded hollow even to her.

It would help if she could put warmth in it. Give Bribanzo a smile he could interpret as the promise of her future favour. Unfortunately, she loathed the man. Alexa liked her favourites lean and hungry.

"My daughter?"

"Milan will not take her now," Alexa said flatly. "As for other suitors . . ." If they have any sense, she thought, they'll accept defeat to avoid upsetting the Ten's newest member; a man dangerous in ways most didn't know.

An ignorance that came close to bliss.

"You may g-g-go," the duke said. He'd taken his thumb out of his mouth and was pointing at Bribanzo. "N-n-now."

At the door, Lord Bribanzo turned, and his words were heard by those in the chamber, and by those in the corridor outside. By nightfall, they were known everywhere in the city. A declaration of hatred for Atilo, although he directed his venom at his daughter.

"You, I disown."

His voice was the hiss of a snake. His eyes flat, beyond fury, in a state where he would kill her without regret. "You were never mine. It is not that you died for me this day. You were never born."

19

News of Bribanzo's feud with Atilo was overshadowed by rumours that the Mamluks had abducted Lady Giulietta il Millioni to prevent her marrying King Janus, because an alliance with Cyprus would have given Venice the mouth of the Nile. Rumours that grew from abducting, to abducting and probably raping, and then to abducting undoubtedly, raping and probably murdering, as days turned into weeks.

The Cypriot ambassador said goodbye.

Regretful but implacable, Sir Richard Glanville boarded his ship and hoisted his king's colours, and the colours of his Priory, and slipped through the sandbanks at the mouth of the lagoon into the Adriatic beyond.

His was the only vessel allowed to leave.

The ship that had sneaked from the lagoon was chased, stopped and boarded. It turned out to be Mamluk, but Lady Giulietta was not aboard. And its crew swore they had not put ashore since leaving Venice. Their captain died under questioning, still protesting he knew nothing about an abduction. He was a simple smuggler.

Trade ceased on the lagoon for the first time since Marco the

Cruel overthrew the Rebel Republic fifty years earlier. Gulls still swept the waves, cormorants dived from posts holding fishing nets. They were the only movement. Food piled up on the mainland. Night soil was not collected. *Cittadini* made deputations citing loss of profits. Leaving shocked by Prince Alonzo's contempt for their worries.

The city's fishing nets, as famous as San Marco itself, hung from crossed poles, dry and unused. The small boats that should have collected the dawn catch remained beached on Venice's mudflats. Ships at anchor remained there. Those waiting to enter stayed beyond the lagoon or found another port. Salt barges were refused leave to set out for the mainland. New barges, loaded with dried fish, salted beef and wizened fruit stored the previous summer remained on their mainland moorings, their produce slowly rotting.

"You must show yourself," Duchess Alexa told the Regent. "Let the people see you. Reassure them."

"You show yourself."

"I'm in mourning."

"It's three years," he said crossly. "Enough of the hiding in darkened rooms and refusing to appear in public. Take Marco and let the city see you."

"Impossible," the duchess said. "You know . . ."

"He can't be let out in public?"

"*Alonzo* . . ."

"It's the truth. And, speaking of truth, are you behind this?"

"Behind what?"

"Giulietta's abduction?"

"Why would I do that?"

"*Answer me.*"

"If you remember," Alexa said tightly, "I suggested her marriage to Janus. We need Cyprus to secure our trade routes. In fact, our future wealth depends on it. You seem over-friendly with the sultan's ambassador. Should I be asking you the same?"

"Believe me, that's changing."

Stamping to the balcony, Alonzo glared through fretted shutters at a crowd on the Molo, the palace's water terrace. Beyond them, to his left, the Riva degli Schiavoni was equally thronged. Most of those gathering were Arsenalotti. "Venice needs a duke who can control it," he said.

"You, you mean?"

"It can't be you."

"Because I'm a woman?"

"And a Mongol. You know how they feel about that."

The deal Marco Polo had struck with Kublai Khan to import goods from China made the city richer than ever before. Gratitude from the richer merchants had secured Marco the throne. The doge became a duke in power as well as name. The Council became the duke's servant and not his master.

The price Kublai extracted was twofold. A *fontego di khan* near the Rialto from which to trade. And a guarantee that Khanic law would apply to all Mongols in Venice, whatever their crime and wherever that crime was committed. Marco III's marriage had sweetened the deal on both sides. But Marco's grip had been iron for all he claimed it velvet.

"They need a real duke," Alonzo said.

"They have one."

"Whom they see once a year. Heavily sedated. Painted white like some whore, drugged with opium, with his hands twitching like broken wings."

"My son will never abdicate."

"You mean," Alonzo said, "you will never let him . . ."

It was what his niece's absence represented, not the abduction itself, which drove the Regent to fury. All his plans, all his brilliance, simply wasted. He wouldn't put it past the little bitch to get abducted on purpose . . .

20

Rolling over, Giulietta scooped up a blanket and stood. Only to sit back down when the little room began to spin. Hunger hollowed her guts. It stopped her sleeping. Today she would make herself eat.

A fire already burnt in her grate, a large bowl of warm water stood on a stand, ready for her to wash her face. A smaller bowl would be waiting on the table at breakfast so she could wash her hands. As one had been waiting on the table at supper. This was not what she expected captivity to be like.

The first day she'd refused help dressing.

But the old woman in the doorway looked so forlorn that yesterday Giulietta relented and let her help a little. Of course, Giulietta still only had the one dress. And that now looked tired, although still cleaner than it had that night in the basilica when she *got blood on it*.

That barely came close to describing what happened when the strange grey-haired boy dropped from the basilica ceiling and found her half naked. Perhaps, she thought, he would have let her kill herself if he'd known what Uncle Alonzo intended to do to her.

Feeling her eyes fill, Giulietta rubbed them angrily.

The chamber in the Ca' Ducale had been well named. What they did to her in her in the Sala della Tortura *was* torture. The memory of having her knees forced apart filled her with helplessness. She couldn't bear to think about it and she didn't know how to stop herself thinking about it. Every time she recalled the violation she felt sick. And Dr. Crow's magic had worked; she couldn't even talk to herself about it.

At least not aloud.

But since the old woman who looked after her now was deaf as well as dumb it made no real difference. Her husband was the same. It was hard to put an age on them. To Giulietta everyone older than her looked old.

The old woman dried Giulietta's tears carefully, washed her face with a damp cloth and helped her dress, tying the ribbons with shaking hands. Giulietta did the buttons herself. Otherwise the food would be cold.

Her breakfast today was fresh bread, cheese, a wizened apple, a slice of warm sweetmeat tart, and hot wine with nutmeg to keep out the chill. Her wine tasted heavily watered. To the old couple she was obviously a child. The apple was already cut and the pie sliced. Knives had not been laid today.

"I'd like a walk," Giulietta said.

The man looked at the woman, who was the one who made all the decisions. The woman tipped her head to one side, considering. So Giulietta went to stand directly in front of her, and said, "please."

Both of them could read her lips, which told her they understood Italian. She'd already decided they'd once been able to speak or hear, or both. That made her wonder who they were. She was a prisoner. There was little doubt about that.

A prisoner in a warm, sweetly decorated prison in the middle of . . .

And that was where Lady Giulietta's knowledge fell apart.

Obviously, she was somewhere. Since she had yet to go outside, and the shutters were locked, and the skylight showed only cloud, how could she escape if she didn't know what she was escaping from?

"Please," she said. "Let me take a walk."

Maybe it was the *please* that did it.

They must have known it was not a word to drop easily from the lips of a Millioni princess. Because the old man looked at the old woman and something passed in the silence between them. The woman nodded, and the old man fetched a coat of purest white fur. And this puzzled Lady Giulietta more than ever. Because a coat that rare must be priceless.

All she'd seen of her prison was her bedroom and the little room where they ate. But then the woman reached into her pocket for a key, glanced at the old man for reassurance and unlocked the world beyond.

The small hall was so full of furniture Giulietta had to turn sideways to slide between a wooden chair and a chest on her way to the door. Unhooking a heavy key from a nail, the man unlocked the front door and stepped back.

She was imprisoned in a tiny temple.

A tiny wooden temple surrounded by a walled garden run to seed, snow-flecked and stripped bare by winter. Half the trees seemed desolate, the other half looked dead. Giulietta wasn't sure she recognised any of them. The wall enclosing this desolation was higher than she was. Much higher.

"Where am I?"

The old man looked at her.

"Tell me." Since he was dumb, Lady Giulietta wasn't sure how she expected him to answer. Then she noticed him glance towards a post and she wondered if this was her answer. Two horsetails hung from a pole jammed into the snow. Since the silver decorating the pole was black she guessed it had been there for a while. The sky looked familiar and the air smelt as salt as it should.

"Am I still in Venice?"

When the old man turned away, she walked round to the other side of him and he sighed. Giulietta decided a straight question might be better.

"I *am* in Venice, aren't I?"

The old man shook his head, then nodded.

"What's that meant to mean?" she demanded. His smile was kind, but no more use than his conflicting shake and nod. So she headed towards the wall, hearing him hurry to keep up. There was a single door. Needless to say it was locked.

"Open this for me."

The old man shook his head.

"Please," Giulietta said. "Let me see what's on the other side."

To escape she needed to know exactly where she was. And for that she needed him to open the gate. But he simply shook his head when she asked. Lady Giulietta quickly realised he could shake his head as often as she could asked. It made no difference if she begged, wheedled or commanded as a Millioni princess. He wasn't prepared to unlock the gate.

"Has someone ordered you not to open it?"

The old man nodded.

"Who ordered you?" she demanded.

It seemed he could shake his head equally well for every name she offered. Although whether that was because she suggested the wrong names or he had no intention of telling her, she had no way of knowing. So her day dragged to an end, with her feeling scarily like she was trapped in a fairy tale. One of those her mother had told her when her mother was alive. After an early supper, Giulietta decided she needed another walk.

"Please," she said.

The old man looked at the old woman, who shook her head.

"It will help me sleep later," Giulietta persisted. "You want me to be able to sleep don't you?"

At the old woman's sigh, the old man smiled. He collected the key from the wall by the door, while the woman fetched the fur coat. Once they had her safely wrapped, the old man opened the door to let in the darkness.

And a demon entered with it.

21

The Regent's temper when he showed himself to the people by walking the streets at dusk was worse than ever. Fierce enough for Roderigo to fear still for his own future. Prince Alonzo held Roderigo responsible for the delay in finding Giulietta. If he'd done his job properly, the unflagged Mamluk vessel would never have been allowed to leave port. Days would not have been wasted chasing it. The real search for Giulietta could have begun earlier. How he squared this with the fact that the Watch had turned the poor parishes of the city upside down was a mystery.

The mood in the taverns was ugly. The Nicoletti claimed the Castellani helped Mamluks carry out Lady Giulietta's abduction. The Castellani declared they would die to the last man before letting Nicoletti scum accuse them of treason.

Unofficial chains had gone up across canal mouths to lock parishes off from each other. Barricades were being erected. Bricks being prised from *campi* floors as street gangs began to stockpile ammunition.

"So," the Regent said. "How would you suggest we handle this situation?"

"Call out the Watch, my lord."

"There are going to be riots, Roderigo. Do you consider the watch is sufficient?" Prince Alonzo looked from under lowered brows. "That was a question, Captain. Do you think the Watch will be sufficient?"

"No, sir."

"The Watch, plus your men?"

The Dogana guard were few in number. But well-armed, well-disciplined and regarded with a certain fear by the city's poor. They'd provide a backbone, but Roderigo couldn't pretend their spine wouldn't be broken eventually. Even adding the palace guard to the mix would be insufficient. And Roderigo doubted the Regent was prepared to leave Ca' Ducale undefended anyway.

"You could hire mercenaries, my lord."

"They cost, Roderigo. And finding good ones takes time."

"What do we do, my lord?" It turned out to be the right question. Prince Alonzo's shoulders straightened and he glowered, as if he was already on a battlefield viewing enemy deployments.

"We give them an act of utter brutality."

"*My lord . . . ?*"

The parishes had long memories, and memories festered into open wounds in this city in a very Venetian way. Money might keep the *cittadini* sweet. And the Castellani hatred of the Nicoletti, and the Nicoletti's hatred of everyone else, keep the parishes of the poor at each other's throats. But an act of brutality by the Millioni would be remembered. More than one patrician had died for the sins of his ancestors.

"Not the parishes, you idiot."

Alonzo's father, grandfather, one brother and his sister had fallen to the dagger. Both Republics began and ended with murder. In Rome, they joked that assassins were more common in Venice than canals. The Regent obviously had no desire to inspire a third republic. What little remained of his good temper was gone.

"Have you searched the Fontego dei Mamluk?"

"Yesterday, my lord."

"We'll do it again. Properly this time."

Roderigo bowed, without bothering to say it was searched properly last time. If Prince Alonzo wanted the Mamluk warehouses re-searched that was his business.

Near la Volta, on the left bank of the Grand Canal, dangerously far into Nicoletti territory, they found an armed band of Castellani mixed with Arsenalotti. "You," Prince Alonzo said. "With me."

The mob fell in, nudging one another when they realised who the barrel-chested man in the breastplate was. Some carried swords, others daggers, one had a shipwright's adze. When they met a gang of Nicoletti, battle was averted. The black caps being stunned to a sullen truce by the Regent's presence.

There was a growing sense of excitement. No one knew what was going to happen. But everybody knew that something was. And Roderigo began to realise it was more than a simple search Alonzo had in mind for the Mamluk *fontego*. His suspicion proved right when they stopped in front of the building.

"Break down its door," the Regent ordered.

Half the black-clad Nicoletti rushed round to the *fontego*'s *porta d'acqua* to make sure nobody escaped via one of the side canals. The red-capped Arsenalotti fanned out around Alonzo. If the Regent wanted to be seen, it was working. As a mason with a sledgehammer stepped up to the land door, the street behind began filling with spectators.

"Shouldn't we announce ourselves, my lord?"

"If the sultan's subjects do not want to be a friend to me, then they will find I am not a friend to them, or their master. If they wanted to welcome me, Roderigo," the Regent said, "those doors would already be open."

Only, thought Roderigo, *if they want to die.*

The Mamluk merchants had probably hoped they could remain unobtrusive until the city's temper cooled. It had taken courage to open their *fontego* to Roderigo's guard yesterday. But they knew

Roderigo and had dealings with the Dogana. The arrival of Prince Alonzo with a crowd meant only one thing.

Lady Giulietta had not been found.

Now the mob wanted revenge. Personally, Roderigo doubted the Mamluks had done it. The sultan might be ruthless—he'd strangled his elder and younger brothers, after all—but everyone said he was a brilliant tactician. Surely a strategist of his ability would be ashamed of such a clumsy move? What could he gain from making an open enemy of the Venetians?

The Sultan's *fondak* was huge. Built around three sides of a central courtyard, it had one side open to the Grand Canal, where a small *riva* let Mamluk barges unload with trade goods for selling. Some of the mob—Nicoletti, probably—were already launching luggers. They claimed they wanted to prevent the barges escaping. It was more likely they intended to loot them later.

Faced with Istrian stone, the *fontego*'s endless rounded arches lightened its façade. Most large buildings in Venice used colonnades to lighten their weight. Otherwise the wooden pilings of their foundations simply sunk into the mud.

The secrets of such work were jealously guarded and patricians and *cittadini* who ignored advice from the Masons' Guild found themselves owners of expensive piles of rubble. It was a huge man in a mason's leather apron who stepped up to the iron-bound door of the *fontego* and raised a sledgehammer.

Prince Alonzo nodded at Roderigo, who nodded at his sergeant. Leather and horn scales hid Temujin's half-healed shoulder. His pain was obvious, however, in the sweat beading his forehead. "Do it," he ordered.

Spitting, to make clear what he thought of being bossed around by someone half Mongol, the mason pounded his hammer into the stone arch, about three-quarters of the way up.

"Attack the door," Temujin growled.

"No," Roderigo muttered. "He knows what he's doing."

The third blow cracked stone.

So the mason pounded again and the block shattered, leaving an iron bolt jutting from broken stone. It looked almost as new as the day it was fitted. A crack of his hammer drove the bolt inwards, creating a gap at the edge of a huge door.

"Arrows ready."

At Temujin's order, eight Dogana guard ratcheted back their crossbows and slid quarrels into place. Without being told they fanned out, providing cover. Their weapons pointed slightly downwards.

"Now," said Roderigo. "He'll break the lock."

As if to prove him right, the mason swung his hammer into the key plate. Metal rang and the door rattled. A second blow buckled the iron plate and inside someone shouted a warning.

"Should have opened it earlier," Alonzo spat.

Around him the mob nodded, as if the prince might require their agreement. His voice sounded fired up with passion, fury and outrage at his niece's disappearance. His eyes, however, were ice. When he glanced at the captain, Roderigo looked away.

"Stay watchful," Roderigo hissed.

A moment later, Roderigo's sergeant relayed the order, his version centring on what he'd do to their daughters if they failed. When the mason swung his sledgehammer one final time, the lock broke free. For a second the door remained upright, supported on its remaining hinge, and then it toppled. Metal screaming as the hinge tore itself free.

The first arrow from inside hit the mason.

I'd do the same, Roderigo thought.

Dropping his hammer, the mason touched the arrow in disbelief, not daring to pull it from his throat. The Mamluks would die. Shooting the mason ensured it would be fast. At least, Roderigo hoped so. After the siege of Luca he'd seen what happened when angry men decided to kill slowly. That he'd been in the mob and the Lucans its victims made no difference in his dreams.

"Sack this place," Alonzo ordered.

His supporters didn't need telling twice. Swarming past the Regent, they charged the archway. At a nod from his captain, Temujin let them go. The first three through the arch stumbled back with arrows in their chests.

A single archer from the look of it.

Mamluk bows were half as long as English, made from layers of hardwood and horn. Their arrows had three flights and barbed points to make freeing them more dangerous than pushing them through.

"You want me to deal with their archer, boss?"

Roderigo shook his head. Let the crowd do it. That the Venetian mob pushed forward had little to do with courage. The weight of those at the back made it inevitable, whether the front wanted to advance or not.

"We keep the Regent safe."

Temujin nodded.

Not that Prince Alonzo faced much danger. A breastplate covered his chest, while a gorget protected his throat and a crested helm was crammed on to his skull. Vambraces protected his forearms. Across his shoulders hung his broadsword. A dagger sat at his hip. With his beard and armour he looked like a *condottiero*.

Intentional, no doubt.

Grabbing a fisherman's gaff, a squat man hefted it, found its balance and threw with the casual skill of an old soldier. His makeshift spear arcing above those ahead of him to hit its target. Temujin grunted his approval. "Now we go in!"

Since the Regent was freeing his sword and loosening his dagger it looked like the sergeant was right.

"Let me through," Alonzo growled.

One Castellani pushed back, until he glanced round and realised who his rival was. Grabbing the man's red scarf, the Regent tied it to his arm, grinning at the man's shock and the crowd's roar. *I'm like you*, Alonzo's expression said.

Apart from the palace, obviously. The Millioni millions. The fact the law was blind when those who angered the Regent disappeared.

"Boss . . . ?"

"Nothing," Roderigo said.

A merchant in a striped robe barred their way.

Behind him stood half a dozen Mamluk soldiers. The maximum a foreign *fontego* could keep to protect itself from thieves. Six for a foreign *fontego*. Eleven for a Venetian one. Thirteen for a patrician. The rule was clear and ruthlessly enforced.

"Planning to shoot me too?" Alonzo demanded.

"My lord . . ." The merchant bowed, decided his greeting wasn't reverential enough and adjusted it. "Your highness."

The hunger those words fired in the Regent's eyes was frightening. For a moment, Roderigo thought the Mamluk had bought himself life, maybe even freedom. His next words ruined it.

"Could your niece have run away?"

A growl of anger rolled through the mob as those in front carried his comment to those behind them. She was a Millioni princess, about to become a queen, how ignorant could the Mamluk be. Not ignorant, *insulting*.

The Regent dealt with the insult himself. Drawing his great sword, he stepped forward as the merchant began to plead for his life. The sword slashed down anyway.

"Now," Temujin ordered, and his troop cut down the Mamluk soldiers before they could begin to fight back. High above, Roderigo saw two boys manoeuvre a money chest on to a balcony's balustrade, their bodies foreshortened as they struggled to push it over the edge.

"*My lord . . .*"

Flinging himself forward, Roderigo shoulder-slammed the Regent so hard that Alonzo staggered, dropping his bloody sword. And then the flagstones exploded behind them. The chest landing where Alonzo had stood. As one, the mob began chasing the rolling coins across the hall floor, stuffing their pockets with silver dirham. The chest had been the heaviest object the boys could find.

"You saved my life," Alonzo said.

Perhaps Roderigo only imagined he sounded surprised. Although Roderigo was shocked himself, when the bear of a *condottiero* grabbed him, hugging him close.

"Name your reward," Alonzo said.

"My lord, about Lady Giulietta. That Mamluk vessel . . ."

"God's sake, man," the Regent said. "Ignore it." They were talking about different ships. "Your mansion is falling apart?"

"There's not a room that doesn't leak."

"Then it's settled. Two thousand ducats. Tell the treasury I order them to release that amount. What's your rank?"

"Armiger, my lord."

"I make you a baron. Subject to Marco's approval, obviously."

While the crowd scrabbled for dirham, and the Mamluk boys stood frozen on the balcony above, too scared to move, Roderigo bowed low. He bowed low to stop Prince Alonzo from seeing his face.

As Roderigo followed the Regent up the stairs, he considered the implications of accidentally choosing sides in the feud between Alonzo and Alexa. He now had money enough to mend his roof, and a title. One alone would improve his chances of marrying well. Two made it a certainty. Although Desdaio would always be beyond him. Roderigo hadn't intended to choose one faction over another, however. Something he doubted the duchess would believe.

The Fontego dei Mamluk had three levels. At ground level, cargo was unloaded, goods were stored and deals made. An area of hall behind them held booths selling spices and scarlet leather. The booths were kindling now.

The floor they approached had family rooms. A library, most

likely. But it was the floor above the mob wanted to reach. The kitchens were on the top floor, so oven smoke could escape through *fumaioli* to the sky. Here, too, valuables were kept, both living and non-living. The doe-eyed beauties of rumour.

So beautiful they had to be kept veiled like novice nuns, unable to stand temptation. It was this thought that carried Alonzo's followers up two flights of stairs. Behind them they left the Mamluk boys dead on their balcony.

"You cannot enter."

A fat man waddled towards them. He was bald, hairless and wearing scarlet silk pantaloons and a sleeveless jacket, embroidered with peacocks picked out in blue and silver thread. A gold ring hung from his ear.

"A eunuch," Temujin whispered.

Roderigo had worked that out for himself.

"My lords." Planting his feet apart, the eunuch tried to block Prince Alonzo's entrance to the harem. "This is not fitting. Please . . ."

He died. An arrow in his throat.

"Not ours, boss."

A Castellani had helped himself to a Mamluk hunting bow. Roderigo imagined the Regent knew he'd have to disarm the mob once this was over. But for the moment Prince Alonzo flattered them. "Help yourselves," he said.

Did he mean, help yourselves to the women? To the food in the kitchens? Or to the gold hidden in the strongrooms beyond? The crowd decided he meant all three.

Roderigo wondered if they realised Venice had just declared war.

22

"You got Mamluk blood?"

Tycho shook his head.

"Told you," Pietro said triumphantly. He swept straggles of black hair from his childish face, spreading the dirt more evenly. "They're killing Mamluks," he explained. "Rosalyn thought . . ."

He glanced across.

"Well, the City Watch want you. And a black girl with braided hair. So Rosalyn thought you must be Mamluk . . ."

"If he's not," said Rosalyn, "he must be a slave."

"That's it." Josh nodded. "Your master's important enough to use the Watch." He looked suddenly worried. "He's not Ten, is he?"

Rosalyn scrambled to her feet.

She bared her teeth when Tycho stopped her. Behind him, Pietro grabbed half a brick. "*You hurt my sister . . .*"

"I won't." Tycho put his fingers to Rosalyn's head and saw Josh's eyes narrow and his face harden at the sight.

"*I mean it,*" Pietro said.

Tycho nodded, but kept his fingers in place.

I can do this, he told himself. *If it can happen by accident, it can happen intentionally.* He let the question trickle through his body, feeling how it flowed from his fingers to her mind. The black girl she talked about was the Nubian he'd seen earlier. The Watch looked like thugs everywhere.

"Witchcraft," Rosalyn said, stepping back.

Pietro raised his brick and Josh reached for a dagger in his belt.

Tycho might have had to fight them, maybe kill one, but the moon stopped the fight before it began. Sliding from behind cloud, it lit the door of his ruined wooden warehouse. It also lit his face, although Tycho only realised this when Rosalyn's own softened and she shifted, almost unknowingly, to put herself between Josh and Tycho.

"Wait," she said.

They stood as they were. Pietro with his raised brick, Josh scowling and Tycho swaying on his feet. Rosalyn looked into the bleakness in his eyes. "Are you a slave?" she demanded. "Is that why they're hunting you?"

"I was," he admitted. "But that was before here."

"And I suppose your mother was a princess?" Josh said spitefully. "Your father was captured in battle? No doubt your grandfather lived in a palace." He rolled his eyes derisively. "Never met an escaped slave who didn't claim he was a prince."

Tycho wondered how many he'd talked to. And then, wondered how many escaped slaves there were in Venice. A dozen, a hundred, more? What happened when they were caught?

"Were you a prince?"

"*Rosalyn* . . ." Josh sounded exasperated.

"Just asking. *Did* you have a palace? *Was* your mother a princess?"

"My mother died when I was born. She was a slave before that. I don't know, maybe she was a princess before she was a slave. No one ever said. The woman who brought me up called her, *Lady* . . ."

Rosalyn tipped her head to one side. "Maybe that's the truth," she said. "Otherwise he'd say his palace was huge."

"And perhaps he's just being clever," Josh said flatly. "He looks clever. Maybe he's a Jew. His hair is strange enough."

"Jews aren't slaves."

Josh spat. "They should be."

Rosalyn flushed, her face darkened and she bit her lip, hugging herself. This only made her small breasts jut. And that only made Josh smirk. There was a tension and strangeness to the night. A chill wind holding scents that demanded Tycho find their origin even as they told Rosalyn to flee.

"You hungry?" she asked him.

Tycho shook his head.

"*Rosalyn.*"

"What?" The girl looked nervously at . . .

Who? Tycho wondered. *Her brother? Her lover?*

Strays, thrown together by chance? He looked more closely, seeing if he could guess which. Siblings, perhaps. There was a family likeness. Unless that was simply the hunger in their eyes and the dirt.

As if hearing his thought, Rosalyn said, "Josh is my boss. Pietro my brother. We're going to San Michele. You should come."

"It's an island," Pietro added.

"He knows that . . ."

"How would he?" Josh demanded. "He's foreign. He doesn't know anything." Jerking his head at Tycho, he said, "I say we leave him."

Tycho thought of telling them that crossing water made him feel sick. That even crossing bridges made him uneasy. But he didn't want them to know that. So he watched them go instead, seeing Josh snarl when Rosalyn looked back.

The sacking of the sultan's *fondak* lasted until daybreak. A stranger would have thought one house on a canal was attacked by all the others. That was wrong. The area inside the walls was

Mamluk. As foreign as France or Byzantium itself. Just easier to sack, with less distance to carry the spoils.

Screaming told Tycho he was near.

He could feel lightning in the air. Looking up, he expected thunderclouds, but found a sliver of moon that tugged at his mind.

Hunger was the missing fact of his life.

Around Tycho, Venetians slurped stolen pomegranates, licked their lips and looked satisfied. Beggars hunched over dried figs like misers over gold. Dogs fought for pastries looters had taken, half eaten and discarded as too strange for their tastes. It made Tycho certain something was missing in himself.

He could no longer distinguish flavours. Eating or not eating made little difference to his happiness. It didn't even seem necessary to keep him alive. And yet, he'd lied to Rosalyn about not being hungry. He had a hunger no food could fill. A hunger he dragged after him like a shadow, always half seen and oblique to the world in which he lived.

The dead were dead to him now. Either they'd abandoned him or he'd abandoned them. The empty city, below this one, he tried to avoid revisiting. It was too strange, too lonely, too much like him. The beasts roaming it terrified him. He was beyond being able to meet his fears in its distorting mirror.

The empty city called him, of course.

But not as fiercely as the women's screams from up ahead. He was almost at their source when a Nubian with silver-tipped braids stopped him. "So are you going to kiss me this time . . . ?" She smiled. "I didn't think so."

He flinched as she reached for him, scared of the silver thimbles glittering in the moonlight. "Don't reveal your weaknesses," she said. "Only your strengths. And if you don't yet know what those are, keep silent."

Tycho tried to say he was silence's closest friend, but she hadn't finished. "Change is painful," she told him. "But not to change is . . ."

"To die?"

"You don't have that option. The longer you fight against who you are the harder your transformation will be. Believe me," she said. "We are different enough to be alike." The closer she stood the more scents Tycho recognised. Sweat and shit and garlic and cloves, and something else.

The Nubian laughed softly. "What drives your hunger?"

"I don't know."

"Most boys want this." Slipping her hand under her skirt, she touched herself. Smearing her finger across his face, she laughed. "Trust you to be different."

"I'm not," Tycho lied.

"You want . . . *What?*" Looking up, she found the moon. "Not the Goddess exactly. Although your hunger grows as she does. But her blood tides are not the blood you need . . ." Her voice sounded as if it belonged to someone older. And there was a strangeness in her eyes that made him shiver.

"You will feed," she said.

"I've tried eating . . ."

Her slap snapped his head sideways. "Listen to me," she hissed. "Twice I've helped you now. Once kindly, this time not. When we meet again it will be as strangers. Understand me?"

Tycho didn't. "Where am I?"

"Here," she said. "As opposed to there. *Dust and ashes, dead and done with. Bjornvin spent what Bjornvin earned.* You will never go back. No one does. No one can. There is nothing to go back to. Go now, feed."

23

Had there not been snow, and had the *fontego* been built around a proper courtyard it might have held out for longer. But the Canalasso side made it vulnerable to attack from water as well as land. And three luggers filled with Castellani bobbed offshore to make certain no Mamluk barges tried to escape. The barges were burning, and the screams from inside said their crews burnt too. The snows simply meant no one watching this happen worried about accidental fires starting elsewhere, since the embers from the barges landed in the water or sizzled out on slush.

The building itself was intact. Sacked and savaged, shit-smeared and pissed in, but still standing and unburnt. It would be sold by the city to the highest bidder and the buyer could hire men to clean up what this night had done.

In the central courtyard, overlooked by the colonnades of its three sides, a young woman was backlit by burning barges. She looked to Tycho the same age as the girl in the basilica, but there the likeness ended. This girl had dark skin, and hair cut from the night, perfectly black and waterfall straight. Where the earlier girl had been thin this one was not. Her hips were full, her breasts fuller. The anger in her eyes was as fierce as any Tycho had seen.

"*Little bitch*," a man said. Wiping spittle from his cheek, he flicked it to the ground. "Have your men hold her, Roderigo. And make sure they bend her right over. We'll see how she likes this."

Two guards grabbed the girl, who visibly flinched when the man with the steel breastplate began untying the laces to his codpiece.

"Strip her, then."

A squat man stepped forward.

The same man who'd helped free Tycho from the ship, only to make him a prisoner again. Pulling down his cap, Tycho wrapped a filthy scarf around his neck and backed into the crowd.

"Hurry it up . . ."

Grabbing her collar, the squat man yanked so hard he pulled the young woman free from the two holding her. As the guards reached for her, she spun round and spat full into the face of the man in the breastplate. This time her spittle hit his lips and he didn't flick it nonchalantly away; he scrubbed his lips with the back of his hand instead. And Tycho watched the smoky evil he felt around him enter the man's eyes. Pointing at Roderigo, the man snarled, "Nail her to that tree. Flay her."

"My lord?"

"You heard me, Roderigo."

"She's barely a child, my lord. And the building is yours. Cut her throat and be done with it. Take her first if you must."

"Kindness is a weakness. Tell your man to flay her and do it fast. I'm due at prayers in an hour. You'll be coming with me."

As one guard went to fetch nails and a hammer, another disappeared looking for a kitchen knife and steel. His face relaxed when Roderigo ordered him to give both to Sergeant Temujin. The sergeant swore.

"What did he say?"

Roderigo looked uneasy.

"What did your man just mutter?"

"If it takes a Mongol to do the job, my lord. He's happy to serve."

Tycho doubted these were the exact words. So did Roderigo's master, from his scowl. Although the words obviously hit home, because he shot the sergeant a glare and stared round the mob-filled courtyard, his gaze alighting on Tycho. "You," he said. "Come here."

The man behind pushed Tycho forward.

"I'm Prince Alonzo, Regent of this city. You hear me?"

Tycho nodded slowly.

"Typical," the Regent muttered. "The village idiot. Give him the knife, explain what he's to do. And hurry it up."

It had been dark in the boat and Tycho's face was now filthy, framed by a stolen cap and what showed of his hair was matted and greasy. All the same, the sergeant stood on the edge of recognition.

"*Buonasera*," said Tycho, sounding like the Nicoletti's son the dead printer had been. Temujin shrugged.

"Cut her a bit. Kill her soon after. Only not too soon . . ." Jerking his head towards Prince Alonzo, he added. "He needs to hear her scream. His type always does. Right, you two, wrap her arms around that tree."

Temujin's knuckles were white as he put a nail to her wrist, drew back his hammer and slammed it down so hard its crash almost drowned her cry. She howled again when the second nail went in. Thrashing as Tycho stepped up behind her with his knife.

"Please," she begged. Her voice guttural, her Italian so thick he barely recognised the words. "Don't."

She knew he was there to hurt her.

Into Tycho's mind came memories of a flaying. *Bloody Boot* stripped the ankles, *Red Gauntlets* the hands and wrists. *Raw Saddle* flayed the . . .

"Get on with it," Temujin hissed.

Slicing fast, he outlined her spine, adding a second cut beside the first, slashing a third at the top and scooping under to give him something to grip. It was over in a second, maybe less. When he ripped, the young woman screamed so hard her voice broke. Behind Tycho someone vomited.

"*Please . . .*" The word was in his head.

A child's whisper behind her animal howl. Pain spread like angel's wings from her body, feathered and bright. Brighter than his eyes could stand.

"*Please,*" she begged. "*Make it stop . . .*"

He did as she asked, taking the brightness into himself. Feeling her shock as her mind abandoned the bleeding meat nailed to the tree. She was two people now. One silent, inside him. The other loud and bestial.

Such as it was her life lay open. The taste of food he'd never eaten, and memories of a rambling family home in Egypt, seen through her eyes as a child. Snatches of her language. Memories of a happy childhood turning sour as a father's love hardened to anxiety. And the *fontego* that had been her world became her prison.

Tycho felt his dog teeth extend.

The night was his. The night, the city, the world . . . Everything was his and he moved freely through it. The water under the bridges barely troubled him as he flowed through the city at impossible speeds, streets unravelling as he printed them on his memory. Giving names to places he knew, learning locations for which he'd only known names. Behind him he left a crowd shocked into silence. Stunned guards and a prince open-mouthed with horror.

Tycho's body hummed with power, his hearing was so sharp he surprised a hunting tom before the cat was aware of him. Time stretched and twisted and became malleable. Eventually moving so slowly he owned the spaces between seconds as well as the seconds themselves. He knew the stars for tiny suns lighting a night sky to the brightness of day. Except this sky was red.

As was the rest of his world.

Red walls and water held within red canal banks. The underworld and the overworld and the world of the dead were finally one. To look at somewhere was to be there. He could kill, he could observe, he could touch. Drunken couples fucked in doorways, feet slipping on slush and snow. Masked thieves waited to rob elegant *cittadini*. Old men staggered halfway across the city with goods from the sacked building that they didn't really want anyway. And light to their darkness, children played marbles by candlelight on dusty floors. A boy stroked the face of a girl and ventured a kiss, feeling daring. Little knowing how long she'd been waiting for him to make this move. The air stank of sweetness. It smelt sweetly of dung. He was God and the Devil in one.

It was close to dawn before his euphoria faded. Dangerously close.

Too late to return to his lair, he found an empty attic above a goldsmith, with tiles new enough to keep out sunlight and settled himself into one corner, folding one arm under his head to make a pillow and folding his knees to steady himself.

He felt stronger than before, no longer hungry. But he also remembered how he'd earned this God-like happiness. Opening his mouth, Tycho ran a finger across his teeth, finding them normal. The creature that moved so confidently through the night was gone. But memories of the creature's power, speed and glory remained. He'd thought his greatest challenge was to remember who he was. And had been wrong, almost childishly so. Who he was paled before tonight's slaughter. What he was . . . That was the real question.

24

The carved face of a lion between bat's wings decorated the keystone of an arch over an old palace door. On the left bank of the Canalasso, below la Volta, to the left of San Gregal, the palace was being restored. Its position almost opposite the sacked Mamluk warehouse was a coincidence.

The bat-winged face was carved into a roundel.

A patera, of which there were several thousand in Venice, featuring hundreds of separate insignia. Everyone in the city could identify the lion reading a book. The lion was Venice, the book Saint Mark's gospel. San Marco being their patron saint. So the patera *was* Venice, which was why it could be seen everywhere.

It marked the Dogana di Mar, the Palazzo Reale on one side of Piazza San Marco, where the city authorities gathered, and the Orseolo Hospice opposite. It marked the Zecca, which minted ducats, and the campanile, which doubled as a lighthouse, and a place from which traitors' bodies could hang.

It practically smothered the *bucintoro*, Marco IV's ceremonial barge. A vessel so impractical it could barely navigate the Grand Canal and so top heavy it could not survive open sea.

Palaces sported the badges of their owners.

The almshouses and guild schools had symbols of their own. As did the Arsenalotti, and even the Nicoletti and Castellani, whose patera became accepted simply through frequency of use. In a world where few could read, and churches used murals to tell improving tales, most Venetians could identify at least a dozen patera. Slightly fewer could identify two or three dozen. A handful of scholars could identify sixty or so without effort.

In the Street of Scribes, where Jewish letter writers mixed ink and sharpened quills and kept secret the letters they read in whispers for a single grosso, was a rabbi who could identify at least two hundred. But there were patera—flaking and rotted by wind, rain and sea salt—which remained obscure because the last scholar to know the answer was dust.

The bat-winged mask was one of these, supposedly.

The Moor who waited for his *gondolino* that Friday afternoon in January knew what it represented, and was glad others didn't. He'd purchased the palace, which was near the Dogana, because it amused him that the house now called Ca' il Mauros exhibited one of only two examples of the Assassini's patera. At least, examples that could be publicly seen. The Assassini master who'd had that patera carved was long dead, and his descendants had struggled down the generations, without knowing what it represented. Only selling up, reluctantly and with bad grace, when repairs became too expensive for their pocket.

"You'll be safe?"

"My dear . . ." Gathering his robes, Atilo kissed his beloved on both cheeks and smiled. "I'll be fine." When Desdaio raised her face, he let his lips touch hers before stepping back. "I'm going to the palace for a few hours. Nothing important."

"You're Ten, now . . ."

Atilo regarded his victory over the German fleet as far more important than anything that might come from talking with nine other men. But this was Venice. Although Duke Marco IV owned the Istrian coast from Austria to Byzantium, his court looked inwards instinctively, being interested in their own reflection. The briefest glimpse of lovers, seen through the window of a candlelit room overlooking the Grand Canal, carried more interest than princes murdered on Venetian orders miles away. The world outside existed only as a place from which the city could make money. If a deal was good, that was enough. The circumstances, Venice regarded with mild curiosity at best, maybe not even that.

"I'll be back for Compline."

"You'll eat then?"

Atilo sighed. There would be food at Ca' Ducale should he be hungry, but Desdaio obviously wanted them to eat together. "Something light."

"I'll make something."

"Desdaio. We have a cook."

"It's not the same . . ." Lord Bribanzo's daughter had discovered the joy of dressing herself, brushing her own hair, washing her face and preparing food. Chores that had plagued Atilo's mother, the unlucky bride of a star-gazing poet who wasted his money on instruments while his children ran wild and his estate ran to ruin.

Atilo found it strange and oddly touching. "Eggs, then."

Despite the January cold she remained on the steps, splashed by spray, and with the occasional rough wave soaking her shoes, while Atilo settled back and Iacopo bowed low to Desdaio, his eyes sweeping her body. Then he grabbed his oar with a flourish, untied the ropes holding the *gondolino* steady, and pushed off into those tides that made steering difficult in the mouth of the Grand Canal. Those young man appeared to have focused on crossing the choppy water as swiftly as possible, but Desdaio couldn't shake the thought he was still watching her.

If Iaco continued to make her uneasy, she'd ask Atilo to find him another job. Either that, or get rid of him altogether. Amelia, however, she liked. Not beautiful but striking. That black skin, lean figure and braided hair with silver thimbles. She wondered if Atilo had . . . Feeling her stomach knot, Desdaio refused to finish the thought. Her future husband was known to have lived like a monk before he courted her. Everyone said so. She was sure they were right.

"Amelia, I need your help in the kitchen."

"My lady?"

"Chopping things."

The young Nubian's eyes flicked to the window, where late afternoon had turned to early evening and the outlines of a dozen *gondolini* had blended so far into darkness as to become almost invisible. All she said was, "I thought you told me Lord Atilo wanted eggs, my lady."

"I'll include eggs."

"If you make me chop things . . ." The girl hesitated, and then turned away, deciding her words best left unspoken.

They hadn't really talked, Desdaio realised. A few hellos, the occasional good morning, and pretence at a curtsy from Amelia. Desdaio had no idea where her slave was born. Not even if she was Christian.

"Where are your parents?"

Amelia's mouth shut with a snap. Muttering an apology, she turned away . . . And Desdaio grabbed her, feeling Amelia struggle, only to fall still when Desdaio pushed her cheek against the other girl's face and refused to let go.

"Stupid," Desdaio said. "That's me. I'm sorry."

Amelia laughed through her tears. "My lady. Iacopo and I . . . We're orphans. All of the Admiral's servants are."

"Even Francesca the cook?"

"Yes, my lady," Amelia nodded.

"What were you going to say? About chopping things?"

"Francesca lets you in the kitchen, because . . ."

"She can't refuse?"

"Yes, my lady. You are the mistress of this house. Me, I'm not welcome in her kitchen. No one is. Francesca's been with Lord Atilo for a long time. Even he knocks before he enters."

"Then we'll knock too," Desdaio said brightly.

25

For the second time in days Giulietta felt smothered by the Persian rug in which she'd been rolled. She'd never felt so helpless. Not even when the *abadessa* held her wrists, Dr. Crow froze her tongue and Mistress Scarlett forced her knees apart . . .

Hot tears filled her throat. All that did was make it hard to breathe when her nose started running. And it was hard enough to breathe wrapped in a carpet anyway. She tried to concentrate on what was happening outside. She was in a boat of some kind. But whether it was a small boat or a large galley . . .

How would she know?

When she heard the keel grate on gravel she realised they'd reached land and she had her answer. A small boat and a short ride. Having been carried ashore, her smothering prison was tossed down and picked up just as quickly when someone hissed with anger. "It's Persian. I'm not paying you to get shit on it."

The men answering sounded Schiavoni.

Hoisting the carpet on to their shoulders, they began to carry her up a slight incline. While inside, now gagged, and with her hands trapped by the carpet's tightness, Giulietta heard the curses of men struggling through mudflats. Her journeys had been so brief she suspected she was back where she had started. In Venice, or on the Venetian mainland. But not, it seemed, near the Riva degli Schiavoni.

Uncle Alonzo? Aunt Alexa? Patriarch Theodore?

Who would do this to her and why?

Were the men who stole her from the basilica the ones who delivered her to the little temple in the walled garden? If so, who were these? And why were they in league with *krieghund*?

Lady Giulietta had wanted excitement her entire life. She'd wanted it through Fra Diomedes's lessons, Sunday services in San Marco, formal meals with her family. Something more real than ritual and gossip. Now that she had it, she wanted her own boring life back.

Somewhere behind her . . . In the ruined furniture of a little temple's hallway, on a leather divan in the Sala de Tortura, on a stinking road through Cannaregio, in a throwaway comment that she'd kill her husband if not allowed to kill herself, were the pieces of her broken childhood.

Unable to help herself, Giulietta started sobbing.

The old man had died instantly. His throat torn out in a sweep of claws from the monster in the doorway. The *krieghund*'s second blow removed his head, the squelch of it landing still sounded in her ears. The old woman had clapped hand to her own mouth, looking hideously sick. Then turned abruptly to Lady Giulietta.

"*Hide* . . ." The word was silent. When she didn't move, the old woman pushed Giulietta towards her bedroom.

You can survive rape.

You can't survive what krieghund *do to you.*

The old man's death, Atilo's brutal words and her own terror made her scrabble as she grabbed the key from the lock, slammed her bedroom door behind her and locked and bolted it from inside. She dragged a chest in front of the door, then her bed in front of that. And, finally, she looked round her.

She had her bed, her blanket, her mattress. A bowl of water

to wash her face, which would do for drinking. A bucket for pissing. And a thick door between her and the danger beyond. Nothing she could use as a weapon.

Hammering began at the door.

"Go away," she shouted. "Go away . . ."

By then there was no one left to hear but the monster outside.

A night of sobbing, raging and promises to God on Lady Giulietta's part gave way in the morning to surprise when, after an hour or so's silence, someone knocked softly at her bedroom door. The voice accompanying the knock was also soft, and very human. The man on the other side offered her safety. All she had to do was turn the key and undo her bolts, lie face down on the floor and shut her eyes.

"What about the monster?"

The silence was eloquent, followed by a deep sigh. "What choice do you have?"

"And if I don't trust you?"

"The *monster* will be back."

He was right, of course. What choice did she have? What choice had she ever had? Lady Giulietta's whole life was one of duty and demands. Why should today be any different? On the plus side, she was alive, which was surprising. And she wasn't on her way to marry King Janus . . . Patriarch Theodore always said concentrate on life's goodness. And being alive after being abducted was good, wasn't it?

So Giulietta unblocked her door, half expecting the monster to burst in immediately. And then she lay face down and closed her eyes, keeping them tightly shut when the door began to open. The man who came in, gagged her, blindfolded her and used the rug from the sacristy to roll her tight.

And, following a short boat trip, she found herself here. Wherever that was. "My lord," she heard a Schiavoni whisper.

"Not far now," someone whispered in return. "Not far at all.

26

"Wait here," Atilo ordered.

Iacopo bowed, checked the knots holding the *gondolino* were secure enough to defeat the waves washing over the Molo, and glanced longingly towards the food stalls lining the muddy start of the Riva degli Schiavoni.

Darkness came early in winter. But the city still ate late.

The Riva looked crowded; with sailors seeking employment most likely, and captains seeking new crews. A tenth of the hiring was paid in advance and went just as fast on one of the whores plying their trade along its length. Another fifth was collected on boarding, and the rest paid at the journey's end.

"I mean it," Atilo said.

Iacopo looked up, surprised.

"Wait *here*. Buy yourself a pie if you want." Atilo tossed a coin, watching in amusement as Iacopo checked if it was bronze or silver. "But no taverns and no brothels. I expect to find you here when I get back."

Iacopo's bow was even lower. So low Atilo didn't see his face.

Leaving his servant beside the black *gondolino*, Atilo stepped between a captain and an Arab who was insisting he knew every sandbank in the mouth of the Nile. When he looked back, Iacopo was staring longingly at three nuns leaving a convent where the novices were known to be young, beautiful and friendly.

Sucking his teeth, but not crossly, Atilo changed direction.

A guard stepped aside at that night's password, and the Moor swept through an open door, turned right immediately and negotiated the benches of an empty audience room. Well, its lobby. That particular audience room was now locked for the day. Checking the corridor beyond was empty, he slid behind a tapestry. The ducal palace was riddled with secret doors. Listening posts, too, recesses hidden by panels or wall hangings where spies could note what was said that shouldn't be said. Most secret doors led from one floor to another, as hiding a spiral of stairs was easier than building a passage down which a man might walk.

Such passages existed, however.

It was along one of these that Atilo strode, his outstretched fingers dusting cobwebs from brickwork. Touch told him how far he'd gone, since every ten paces or so the walls were marked with the bat-winged patera. If only two patera were visible in Venice, there were ten hidden in this corridor alone.

Behind him Atilo dragged five centuries of history, the names of the twenty-seven previous Assassini masters, and the worry he could offer no name to follow his. Every master proposed his successor. The final choice was the duke's, but in five hundred years no recommendation had been refused.

Iacopo hid ambition behind a smiling face. Some masters believed this was an essential quality. An assassin with a smile could open doors shut to those who frowned. Atilo was unconvinced. To his eyes — old as they were — the essential quality was an ability never to reveal your calling.

On the Canalasso this night, the old-House patricians — those whose families had graced the Golden Book five centuries before Ca' Dolphini was built — would flatter their host, whose grandfather bribed his way on to their company. The Dolphini fortune was one reason. The other, that Lord Dolphino—by nudges and winks, sly boasts and strategic silences—claimed, without claiming, to be the duke's Blade. His son Nicolò had bedded more than one virgin from a family in trouble enough to believe the Assassini could help.

Since the new duke could not give orders, the real Blade obeyed instructions from both Alexa and Alonzo. The ground rules were simple. Neither would order the other's murder, nor a murder within the other's immediate entourage. Their individual orders would remain secret from each other. Atilo's duty was to say if this agreement was broken. A responsibility he could do without.

He was getting old. Well, older.

Old enough to know the Angel of Death was watching and would add tonight's business to the scroll. Atilo wondered if those he killed in battle would count against him in the final weighing. Or only those murdered in cold blood on his master's orders. He also wondered, and despised himself for this, if the old duke had already taken some of that weight on himself.

It would have been quicker to reach where he wanted to go by walking through the small garden behind Ca' Ducale, which each new duke threatened to destroy by extending the Rio di Palazzo side of the palace, and no duke had yet been able to bring himself to do.

Cutting through the first, to a second garden beyond belonging to the Patriarch's city residence would have been simpler. But then he might have been seen entering the Patriarch's little study, and that was not Atilo's plan.

A city limited to sandbanks, surrounded by sea and supported on thousands of piles driven into the underlying sand and clay could not afford the waste of space that large gardens represented. A single poplar in a private *cortile* might form a patrician's entire garden. Three trees in a *campo* were as close as many Venetians got to nature. At least at ground level. Many houses had *altane*, roof gardens decorated with flowerpots where women could sit and sun-bleach their hair.

For the Ca' Ducale to have gardens was a matter of pride. Although the patriarch only had one because Marco I's respect for the Church made him divide the strip along Rio di Palazzo in two, and give the smaller section to the Church.

The fact Patriarch Theodore had been called from his sickbed in San Pietro di Castello by a message from the Regent made the night's work easier, sparing Atilo the burden of having to visit the eastern edges of the city.

"My old friend." Laying down a tiny pair of pliers, the patriarch started to stand, then sat down again. "You know I've been ill?"

"Nothing serious, I hope?"

"Old age. A sickness of the heart. You know how it is."

Atilo did. Picking up the ball hammer, he examined it. The hammer was too small to use on nails, even small ones.

"For beating metal," Theodore said, although this was obvious. The top of a hollow censer was crushed out of shape, the fili-gree twisted. "The provost says my altar boy dropped it. The boy denies it."

"If it had been dropped it would be crushed at the base."

"That's what the boy says. The provost whipped him. I wish he wouldn't. It'll only make him more nervous. But, of course, I can't really . . ."

"Of course not."

To treat this altar boy differently was to recognise him as the Patriarch's bastard. A brief moment of loneliness, several years ago. When the palace at San Pietro was cold and the Patriarch's bed had looked warm to a novice newly arrived from the main-land. Not Theodore's only moment of loneliness. Although his other bastards had reached maturity without their father having to protect them.

Theodore had several nephews and nieces. Most bishops did.

Looking round the small room, with its old manuscripts, most in Latin and Greek, the patriarch said, "I'm not sure he's suited for the Church. I was wondering. If anything were to happen to me. Perhaps you . . . ?"

Atilo looked at him.

"I'm not saying it will," Theodore said sadly. "Just, if it does. You're known for your kindness to orphans. I've always wondered," he added, "if that was penance of some kind. If you were, perhaps . . ." He looked embarrassed. "We're all atoning for something."

Did he know? Atilo wondered.

"Have a look at this," said the patriarch. He lifted a lamp so its light fell across the table, before removing a cloth with a slight flourish. Under it was the chalice the duke used to marry the sea.

"Damaged?"

"Yes," Theodore said. "So much is these days."

The rim was dented, two precious stones missing from the base. A third stone cracked across its surface. A scratch on the bowl looked deep enough to need filling rather than simply polishing out.

"You know I trained as a jeweller?"

Yes, Atilo knew. The story was famous. As a young man, the patriarch heard God's call while helping repair the rood screen in front of San Marco's altar. He threw away the money his father had spent buying an apprenticeship. Entering the White Crucifers, he found himself making swords instead. When not giving last rites to those who died of fever and battle.

Theodore tapped the damaged censer.

"This, my old friend, I can mend. A little hammering, some soldering, not difficult, even with these old hands. That, however . . . needs someone better than me. Someone better than I would have been had I stayed a jeweller."

"What's so difficult?"

The patriarch had Atilo stand behind him, then adjusted the

lamp so it threw more light. "See?" A bas-relief of vine leaves and grapes in gold and rubies circled the base, and Atilo realised they were cracked where three stems wove an intricate plait. "You think I should try," said Theodore. "Or leave it for someone else?"

"Someone else."

He nodded sadly. "You don't mind if I say something?"

"No," Atilo said.

"You should ask yourself why the chalice was left. If her abductors took the ring and took her why did they leave this?"

"The Mamluks?"

"If it was them."

"What have you heard?" Atilo's voice was sharp.

"I've heard nothing," said Patriarch Theodore gently. "And what I suspect cannot be revealed without breaking the seal of confession. You would not expect me . . ." Turning down the lamp slightly, Theodore suggested they take the night air and talk further, if talking was why Atilo was here. He made no attempt to take his lamp with him, and Atilo didn't suggest it. When he knelt on damp grass to tie his laces, holding the position longer than necessary, Atilo knew Theodore knew. Whatever had happened, Alonzo could not allow him to live.

He cut the man's throat fast, yanking back his head and dragging a blade through gristle until it hit bone. And in the final moment, Atilo could swear the patriarch smiled.

"Thank you, my dear . . ."

Atilo finished washing his hands in a bowl and took the towel Desdaio offered, drying his fingers carefully. Like everyone in Venice, he washed his hands before and after every meal. As surely as he washed his face each morning and before going to bed each night. As surely as he'd washed his hands before returning to Ca' il Mauros.

His thoughts were on what came after the murder.

A noise . . . ? That must be what made him go back. Mostly

likely he'd heard a noise without realising it. He'd just entered Theodore's study, with the study's owner lying in the damp garden behind him, when he stopped, turned and hurried back. Taking the handful of steps that would change his life.

Complimenting Desdaio on a dish involving eggs, noodles and salted mutton, Atilo took another glass of wine, and wished the storm in his head would subside; only then would be able to unpick what mattered from the rest. He'd turned back. And a boy was there.

That was the nub of it.

A boy had knelt over Theodore, cradling him.

For a moment Atilo thought the figure listened to some final words. But dying men don't speak with their voice boxes cut. They gasp air, bleed to death, and die. That didn't stop the boy asking his question. "Tell me where she is."

Theodore gurgled.

"In the basilica," the boy hissed. "That girl. Where is she?"

When Theodore still didn't answer, the boy bent his head and bit, adding another wound to the ruined flesh of the Patriarch's throat. Although Atilo drew his knife, he never came close to frightening the unwelcome witness.

Instead, the moon slipped from behind cloud to light a creature with the face of an angel and the eyes of a demon. Its hair was silver-grey, braided into snakes. Blood dripped from its open mouth. Its dog teeth were unnaturally long.

Instinct made Atilo flip his dagger so he held it by the point. And he threw hard, allowing for where the creature would be when he realised a blade was coming. The blade still passed through empty air.

"Fine," the creature said. "I'll find her myself."

It sounded like a boy and it looked almost like a boy, but nothing human moved that fast. Flicking its gaze from Atilo to the wall, from the garden wall to the Patriarch's little palace. Its calculations were swift. Its answer unexpected.

One second it stood there.

The next? Atilo looked round. A scraping behind him made him look back, and the creature was halfway up the Patriarch's palace, clinging to the carved balustrade of a balcony. The wall was too smooth to be climbed. The balcony far too high to reach by any other means.

As Atilo watched, the creature rolled itself on to the balcony, jumped up on to the balustrade, crouched like the wild animal it was and unleashed a bound that carried it to the roof's edge above. Finding an impossible foothold, it disappeared.

Fifty years as a soldier. Twenty-six as the duke's Blade. A lifetime staying alive against the odds. Not a single missed kill. In less than twenty seconds Atilo had been bested by *what*? An angel-faced thing that made impossible jumps. A creature, God help Atilo, who fed on the dying.

So be it.

Atilo had made his choice. That creature would be the next master of the Assassini. But first it must become an apprentice. Atilo just needed to hunt it down.

27

The Moors, Mamluks and Seljuks make their first call to prayer in the moment a single black thread can be distinguished from pre-dawn darkness. It had a name few Venetians knew. Anyone looking out of their window on the second to last Sunday in January, in the fourth year of Marco IV's reign, would have assumed it was still night. Yet day and night balanced on the cusp. And though the moon, two days from being full, was cloud-shrouded, and the sun still to rise, the nature of the darkness changed. In this black-thread moment three things happened.

The least of these was that a silver-haired boy discarded his Arsenalotti tunic and cap and wound himself in rags, like a leper. Protection against the city, other beggars and the coming sun. Had he known better, he would have protected himself from the moon, because it was the moon that drove his hunger, and his hunger that drove him to trace a scent on the wind to a square south of San Polo, where the alleys led nowhere and the only way out was back the way he'd come.

The second thing, more important by far, was that Atilo dragged himself from his knees, having spent the night praying for Archbishop Theodore, whose murder had so shocked the city.

After five days of masses and mourning, the patriarch was to be buried that day in the nave of San Pietro. Newly elected to the Ten, his election unopposed following Duchess Alexa's nomination, Atilo was expected to attend. But then, as an old friend of Theodore, he'd have been there anyway.

Iacopo and Amelia were out scouring the city for the boy Atilo had seen in the Patriarch's garden. Amelia's final test before ending her apprenticeship. So she negotiated unnamed streets, arm in arm with Iacopo, dressed as Arsenalotti or Nicoletti or Schiavoni from Dalmatia. Whatever it took to enter the areas they were searching. Another half-dozen of Atilo's orphaned ex-apprentices, now found safe jobs as cooks, stallholders and fishermen, had orders to report what they saw.

One of these, Junot, who fished off della Misericordia, that square-shaped bite out of the northern shore, sent news of the third, most important event of that morning. Junot's brother-in-law had a good night's fishing. Or so he thought, until he drew his net higher and found his catch human.

Catching one bloated corpse was unlucky. Two was simply life being cruel. Junot's brother-in-law knew he could not simply return them to the tides. At least, he knew that once he saw the bodies wore sleeveless mail under Mamluk robes. Had he known the mail was Milanese, he might have tipped them back anyway.

As it was, he brought them ashore and sent word for the Watch, whose captain went cap in hand to the duchess later that morning. By noon the following day Archbishop Theodore was buried. Tycho was safely back under his *sottoportego*, having survived another round of fever. And Junot's brother-in-law confessed, under torture, to killing two soldiers and dumping their bodies in the sea. For which he was swiftly executed. The Captain of the Watch, being of use to the city, was simply ordered to forget everything he'd seen.

The fisherman had *not* found Milanese mercenaries dressed in Mamluk clothes, possibly similar to those worn by Lady Giulietta's captors. There was *no* suggestion that anyone other than Mamluks was behind her disappearance.

The Watch captain took those words away with him. It was, he told his men, a misunderstanding. They valued their lives enough to nod.

The fourth and final thing was that, a few nights later, having listened to his Nubian slave's report, Atilo decided to use the street children who told Amelia where the boy was as bait. So, as night fell, he and Roderigo headed for an underpass south of Campo San Polo; one of his bait boastful, one silent, one in tears.

"Told you," Josh said. "Didn't I? He's hunting for someone. He stands and sniffs the night wind like some dog. Said I knew. Here is where he comes most nights. Would I lie?" He turned to Rosalyn. "Would I lie to them?"

She turned her head away.

Josh scowled. "You'll keep your promise?"

"Not to kill you?"

The youth glared. He knew, from that night in Cannaregio, this was a great lord, and so he had to tread carefully. But he was still alive, which was more than he'd expected that night last year. And much more than he'd expected when the old man appeared, just before tonight's sunset, and reintroduced himself by putting the edge of his dagger to Josh's throat, wrapping his fingers into Josh's hair and dragged him from between Rosalyn's sullen thighs.

"To let us go," Josh said. "That's what you promised." In the moonlight, the boy looked slightly younger than Atilo remembered. Small, narrow-faced and tricky, with a thin nose. His shoulders hunched round some slight he employed to justify using the other two as he wanted. The hierarchy of the dirt poor.

"You three stay quiet, right? Otherwise . . ." Temujin mimed cutting their throats. "And don't run, little rat." He grinned at Pietro, and lifted his bow slightly. "Cos no one outruns this."

"Sergeant."

"It's true," Temujin told Atilo. "A galloping horse can't outrun this. How do you think my people conquered half the world?"

"And lost it again."

That wasn't strictly true. The Golden Horde *had* conquered lands stretching from China to Western Europe, including India. They still owned much of their empire. But until recently it had been divided between the Great Khan's descendants, who fought each other as bitterly as they fought outsiders. Now Tīmūr, known as Tamberlaine, at most a bastard of a minor branch, for all he claimed the heritage, was busy being Khan of Khans.

"Down here, you say?"

Josh nodded.

"Go ahead," Roderigo told Temujin, having checked that this met with Atilo's approval. He followed after, leaving Atilo where he was. The Moor's gaze never leaving the roof line above.

"Shoot to wound," Atilo said. "I want him alive."

A flick of Roderigo's hand in darkness acknowledged this order. All might have gone well if not for Rosalyn; who took a deep breath as Roderigo and Temujin headed towards the *sottoportego*, opened her mouth and screamed words guaranteed to wake the entire area. "Fire. Fire. Fire . . ."

"Shit," Roderigo said.

Flipping his knife, the old man hammered its hilt into her head. "Stop him," he snapped.

Stop who?

And then Temujin and Roderigo knew.

In the mouth of the underpass stood a gaunt silhouette, lit by pale moonlight and framed against the blackness of the passage behind. The figure glanced from Temujin to Atilo and grinned. Then it saw Rosalyn in the dirt.

And stopped grinning. He'd hunted the scent this far. A faint trace on the night wind that pulled him here, and then left him here, unable to trace the scent further. He was stupid to have stayed in one area for so long. Tycho had known that, even as he found himself unable to leave. And now his nightmares had caught up with him.

The old man from the garden. The soldier who cut him free. And the squat Mongol who ordered him to flay the dark-skinned girl, whose memories still haunted his head. To make it worse, at the old man's feet lay the girl who'd dragged Tycho from the canal, the one who'd smiled at him in the night alleyways.

He could run, of course.

The ruined *corte*, with its broken well and collapsed buildings, was behind him. Its walls were unsafe, its floors unsteady. He could climb faster than them, jump further. "He's going to run," the sergeant said.

"Where?" The one they called Roderigo was contemptuous.

Raising his bow, the sergeant said, "Straight through us. If I don't get the order to fire."

"*Temujin.*"

"You know I'm right, boss."

People in this city used their real names, not knowing the danger they put themselves in. To know a real name was to own a sliver of that person. All the great shamans used this knowledge in their magic. Tycho couldn't believe people would waste their strength so freely.

"My lord Atilo?" Roderigo said.

Tycho moved.

"Boss . . ."

Ducking a grab, Tycho elbowed Temujin hard, fast and brutally, finding himself facing Atilo a second later. Atilo dropped to a fighting crouch and lifted his knife. Did the old man think him a fool? That order to take Tycho alive was Atilo's mistake, his weakness. He should want Tycho dead.

Spinning round Atilo, Tycho stopped in front of Josh.

"I had no choice," Josh's voice was desperate. "He made me."

And Bjornvin made me, Tycho thought; and look what it made

me into. Grabbing the back of Josh's head, he put his other hand to Josh's chin and twisted savagely. A sudden shit stink rose from his falling body.

"Impressive," Atilo said.

Tycho had the old man, his other hand reaching for his neck when Roderigo threw. Dodging cost Tycho his kill and almost his life. Because Atilo jabbed at Tycho's throat. If he hadn't ducked fast enough for the blow to pass through air he'd be dead.

"You're enjoying this," Atilo growled. "Aren't you?"

Someone was.

Tycho just wasn't sure it was him.

He had the *sottoportego* behind him now. Atilo still holding a dagger. Roderigo undecided. Temujin climbing to his feet. Of the other three players, Josh was dead, Pietro standing petrified in a puddle of his own piss, and Rosalyn . . .

Moving.

"She dies," the old man said. "If you don't surrender."

How had the old man identified her as his weakness? Was it even true . . . ? Atilo looked cool now, almost amused as Temujin notched an arrow to his bow and aimed at the girl on the ground.

"All it takes is my order."

What should Tycho do? Let her be killed? Let himself be captured? The triumph in the old man's eyes decided him. Grabbing Atilo's wrist, not to snap, but to freeze his dagger and put the old man in the way of Temujin's bow, Tycho brought their foreheads so close he and Atilo touched.

Kill Rosalyn, he thought. *And I flay your woman.*

Shock and fear. The last quickly brought under control. Unease that Tycho might actually harm the soft-faced girl he'd sensed earlier. The one the old man had yet to bed. The inside of Atilo's mind was a charnel house of whispering secrets. Bat's wings and lion's faces. A thousand corpses silhouetted in almost military neatness against a horizon that went back years.

And three girls. Two dead, Tycho knew immediately.

The other waiting at home, not knowing why he wouldn't come to her. Didn't simply marry her and take her to his bed as she expected the man who loved her to do.

Ask the Mongol. He's seen me do it already.

The wind was in his face, the city's scents intense and cloying, disgusting and exhilarating at the same time. Someone shouted in an attic below, but he was gone before they could open their shutters. A shadow among shadows, faster than thin clouds scudding across a night sky.

He leapt without looking; laughing as he dropped two floors and rolled to his feet, his sinews stretching with the shock. His fever was gone, unless it was simply lost beneath his exhilaration. Jumping another canal, he landed at ground level, looked around him and decided he preferred the roofs. So he scrabbled the wall of a palace, leapt an alley and climbed higher. Until he stood on the very top of a bronze cupola, with Venice spread below him and an unclaimed night ahead.

Atilo would come looking.

As would Roderigo and his Mongol sergeant. They would not forget and they would not forgive. He held their secrets, and knew their failures. Maybe he should be worried. But worried about what? He was here, with the night creatures. They were down there in the dirt.

28

Everyone in the palace slept except the night guard, and those
in beds not belonging to them, who'd creep back to the stillness
and silence of pretend slumber before next morning. Alexa was
alone, her bed unoccupied behind her. She was less cross than
Atilo expected about being woken. Maybe it was the fact he
couldn't stop his hands shaking.

"So, did you find him?"

"We did, my lady."

Duchess Alexa put down her tea, pushing the tiny porcelain
cup away from her. Sitting back, she said. "I'm not going to like
this, am I?"

"We lost him."

"You woke me to tell me this?" Amusement lightened her
voice, as if the guard's shock, and her lady-in-waiting's outrage
at his arrival, requesting an audience, was an elegant joke.

"It's the nature of our loss."

"The nature of our loss." She smiled. "You would have made
a poet. They say the Maghreb is a land of poets. Of fountains
and palaces, stark mountains and lush orange groves . . ."

"And beggars," said Atilo. "Braggarts, brothers who kiss publicly and hate in private. Much like everywhere else. Except," he hesitated. "Maybe more beautiful."

"Why leave?"

"I had no choice." Atilo waited for her to nod before realising she didn't know his early history. "I always assumed you . . ."

"My husband was discreet. Sometimes I suspect no one in his council knew all there was to know. He arranged matters to make this so."

Their discussion about the escaped boy was suspended, apparently. Since Alexa did little from chance she would have her reasons. They would involve thwarting her brother-in-law or protecting her own son, which often turned out to be the same thing. And if not these directly, then increasing her own power or binding Atilo to her camp to balance Roderigo's decision to support the Regent; a blow, since the Captain of the Dogana controlled the money coming into Venice, theoretically at least. Clearly, Atilo already belonged to her, since he was her choice for the Council. Whichever mix of these, it would boil down to the same thing. She would move heaven and earth to protect Marco, since the young duke could not protect himself.

"What drove you out of your homeland?"

Taking the tiny porcelain cup she offered him, Atilo sipped fermented leaves soaked in boiling water. The duchess drank the mixture several times a day, her cups so fine candlelight shone through them. They had been part of her dower. As had the first crate of fermented tea. When the crate was half empty, Marco III sent orders for another. This arrived the month the first crate ran out.

Duchess Alexa cried at his kindness. So it was said, anyway.

"Well? A love affair gone wrong? Gambling debts? A wish to explore the world? An overbearing wife . . . ?"

Giving up his battle to like tea, Atilo put his cup down carefully. "Those are very Venetian reasons," he said lightly.

"A matter of honour then?"

Atilo smiled. Without saying it, the duchess was admitting non-Venetians thought Venice a city without morals. But then you didn't become the Middle Sea's richest city by behaving nicely. "My father remarried."

"You hated your stepmother?"

"I liked the first. I mistrusted the second."

"The second?"

"The first died shortly after the second arrived as her lady-in-waiting. We lived in glorious squalor while my father searched the heavens for new stars. Emirs came to ask their futures. Princes sent gifts from Frankish lands. It would have made more sense to send us food."

"He was a scholar?"

"A hoarder of knowledge. Perhaps it's the same."

The duchess greeted this with a nod. Candlelight softened her nightgown, and though its shadows shifted in the night wind, it couldn't reveal her face behind the veil. Mostly, Atilo had to guess her thoughts from gestures. The fact her head was slightly to one side said she listened intently.

"You were afraid?"

Atilo considered denying it. "Yes," he admitted finally. "I was thirteen. A bitter, unruly child. My half-brother eleven. The grain house rats started dying shortly after she became my new stepmother. The cats came next. Then my hunting dog. I fell ill that winter and she insisted on nursing me. I knew then it was time to leave. So I crawled from my bed, and hid in a culvert until night."

"Poison, cruelty, betrayal. Sounds pretty Venetian to me."

"You're probably right."

"So why did you wake me at this hour?"

"You said you wanted to know about the Patriarch's murderer. That you were to be the first to know if I captured him." Did she tense suddenly, Atilo wondered. As if sensing he'd lied? *Or is that me?*

"But you didn't capture him."

"No, my lady. I failed."

"Ahh . . ." The duchess clapped her hands to summon a girl with a silver jug of boiling water, and a squat iron teapot, already warmed. As Atilo watched, the duchess sprinkled leaves into the pot and added water. "You don't like my tea?"

"I've drunk it half a dozen times. Always in your company. I'm sure I'll learn to appreciate it eventually."

"Bring Lord Atilo wine."

He nodded gratefully.

"So," she said, when they had the room to themselves again. "It is how he escaped that will interest me."

"My lady . . ."

"I know you, Atilo. When they fail most men hide the fact. You drag me from my bed to tell me you failed. I should be cross. But something tells me you believe his escaping is more important than your failure. Am I right?"

"As ever, my lady."

"Don't try to flatter me." Her voice was sharp, the atmosphere between them suddenly colder.

"I'm not," Atilo said simply. "And I need your advice."

"About this?"

"Which would be easier to control? An angel fallen to earth? Or a demon escaped from hell? Because that boy isn't human."

"*Krieghund?*"

Atilo shook his head. "Not *were*, not a night walker." Finishing his wine, he sat back in his seat, feeling every one of his years. "My lady, what else is there?"

Duchess Alexa took longer than usual over her next sip. She considered her answer as carefully as Atilo had considered his. And this, he knew, as she knew, was answer enough.

"You ask me why?"

"Captain Roderigo of the Dogana di Mar has . . ." Atilo shrugged, apologetically. "A half-Mongol sergeant who was with us when the creature escaped. He fired an arrow . . ."

"That fell magically to the ground?"

"No, my lady. He plucked it from the air, flipped it round and threw it back."

"And this sergeant?"

"Would be dead. If not for a boiled-leather tunic with buffalo-horn scales. The arrow hit his chest."

"My father had such a tunic," said the duchess, sounding almost wistful. "He had another made for my brother. Although riveted mail was common by then. A tunic and a laminate bow. This sergeant, he uses a proper bow?"

Atilo described Temujin's weapon.

"That's the one," she said. "So, this *thing* caught an arrow, and returned it hard enough to split horn scales. It did split the scales, didn't it?"

"Yes, my lady."

"Tell me more . . . No." She shook her head crossly. "Tell me everything. Especially the things you don't think important."

So Atilo did, from beginning to end, admitting finally that the boy, the creature, whatever this thing was, might not have killed the patriarch after all. He might simply have seen the murder. At which, Alexa said she could see how that might make Atilo want to find him. A point to which he had no answer.

"And it killed the beggar who led you there?"

"Broke his neck. Almost broke mine."

The duchess looked thoughtful. "To kill without spilling blood even when the moon is fat, while sparing the beggar's girl and her brother. That shows . . ."

"What, my lady?"

"Self-control."

"It twisted the boy's head half round."

"Believe me, it could easily have ripped his head right off."

"You know what it is . . . ?" *Stupid comment*, Atilo told himself. Her words made it obvious she did.

"It's our answer to the *krieghund*."

Alexa laughed at Atilo's shock.

"We've been losing the secret war for too long. It's about time we found a way to fight back. You think I didn't notice when you changed *killed Archbishop Theodore* to *might have witnessed his murder*? You hate my brother-in-law . . . No, don't bother denying it. Yet you let his captain help your search. Admittedly, Theodore was a friend of yours. But you're not sentimental. Certainly not enough to hunt down this boy for him. I doubt you're sentimental about anything. Except, perhaps, that little chit you plan to marry."

Atilo shivered, remembering the boy's threats.

"So why all this effort? The answer is you think this creature useful. Am I right?"

"He's my heir."

Duchess Alexa froze. "Everyone desires old magic. No one really knows what it will do when it arrives. Catch it, train it. We can talk about it being your heir later. Meanwhile, I'll write to my nephew . . ." She meant Tīmūr, newly created Great Khan of Khans and conqueror of China.

"I'll ask what his librarians know of creatures like this. It will take a year for my request to arrive, be deciphered and his answer to return."

Duchess Alexa hesitated. Whatever doubts she had about what she wanted to say, they lasted long enough for Atilo to fill a glass of wine and empty it in slow sips, while looking around at her room. It was small, but its paintings, statues and tapestries would buy a city. He'd just realised every single thing here once belonged to her husband when Alexa leant forward, her decision made.

"Once upon a time," she said, "angels fought. They fought high up in the wastes of space, where the stars are. This was long ago. When the gods still walked the earth openly and the oldest of the old kings ruled. When power meets power terrible things happen. The gods died, the kings died, the angels died . . . Whole forests burnt in the blink of an eye."

Atilo stared at her.

"This is a tale from my childhood. How the gods became the sky god, who watches everything but interferes little. A handful of angels escaped to wander, bitter and alone, in the wilderness. They moved like lightning. Killed without thought. Regarding us as we regard the animals."

"As food?"

"Among other things. But the last of them died in the year Kublai Khan was born. My nephew's librarians will know if it is otherwise. That's why I will write to him. You have the year it takes."

"To capture this creature?"

"No, Lord Atilo. To capture it, break its spirit, and make it our answer to the *krieghund*. If that can't be done, kill it. However, I would regard that as failure."

Discovering her water jug was empty, the duchess reached for a bell to summon a servant, then changed her mind. "Marco, my husband, believed talking of demons brought bad luck. That evil comes at the sound of its own name. He was wrong. It enters when invited. So, the real question is . . . Who invited it?"

Atilo had never heard her talk like this.

He had never heard her refer to the late duke by his first name or call him simply *my husband*. And he had never, in the times they'd met in public or private, heard her talk about her childhood, about being Mongol, about being foreign in how she thought. It made him uneasy.

"Come here," she said, patting her seat.

He could obey, or find a reason to leave. The first might make her an enemy, eventually. The second would make her one now. When Duchess Alexa lifted her veil she was smiling. And, Atilo couldn't answer anyway. Her face's beauty stole his breath away. *Words for a poet*, he told himself crossly. *I'm not one of those.* But it was the face of a girl a quarter her real age. Bright-eyed and innocent, knowing and inviting. Atilo shivered.

"Come on," she ordered.

He did.

If her face was flawless and her eyes undimmed, her body belonged to the daughter she never had, if not that daughter's daughter. Alexa di Millioni's skin was the yellow of fresh velum and soft as Moroccan leather. With her head thrown back and her face safely veiled she rode him to some place he could never reach. And Atilo realised there *were* more things in heaven and earth than dreamt of in anyone's philosophy, and he was looking at one of them. "Your turn," she said.

Feeling every ache in his spine, Atilo wrapped one arm about her waist and twisted them both round, so she lay flat and he rested above.

"You've done that before."

"My lady, I'm sixty-five. I've done everything before."

"I'd tell you my age," she said lightly, "but you wouldn't believe it. And I'd tell you what I've done. But it's best you don't believe that either."

Then she said nothing much, because Atilo shifted his position and she gasped and grabbed his hips, forcing herself against him savagely. He ploughed her with an intensity that surprised him, collapsing on top of her when it was over. But felt his pleasure was more ordinary, less unknown.

"I take it you haven't bedded that chit of yours yet."

Raising himself on to his elbows, Atilo glared at the woman sprawled naked beneath him. Her voice was mocking enough to make him grab her upper arms. He rode her harder this time. Knocking gasps from her body. Until he collapsed breathless across her, his forehead pressed into the pillow.

"I guess not," she said.

In the early hours, after a maid arrived to take that day's orders, replace the tea and trim the wick, without once appearing to notice anyone else slept in her mistress's bed, Alexa woke Atilo with the sound of pissing in a pot.

"Have you met my *stregoi*?" she asked, dropping her gown.

He shook his head groggily. Alexa had a *stregoi*?

A wild witch child . . .

"You should," Duchess Alexa said. "In fact, you must. Send word to Desdaio that you've been detained by Council matters. And order your household to continue as normal. It's time we came up with a plan."

"For tonight?"

"No," said Duchess Alexa, kissing Atilo's cheek lightly. "We have a month to lay our trap. Requisition silver from the treasury and have it made into wire. Send the wire to the rope walk at Arzanale. I'll give orders that it be woven into a net. You can leave the rest to me."

Atilo tried not to shiver.

29

Velvet soiled. How easily Giulietta never realised, not having had to wear any garment for more than one day at a time. Locked in a cold attic, she still wore the red *houppelande* gown and fine woollen chemise she'd worn the night she was abducted. Which was, it happened, what she'd worn that time with the boy in the cathedral.

A tiny slit in the *houppelande* showed where she'd put the dagger to her chest, unwittingly ruining embroidery her mother had sewn. And she could still remember her trembling hands undoing mother-of-pearl buttons and slipping aside her chemise to put the point to her skin. Giulietta blushed.

The memory of that silver-haired boy refused to leave her. It left her troubled, sleeping badly and waking early. Part of her had always believed he was searching for her. There had been other fondnesses, of course. Other crushes. No matter what her aunt and uncle thought. A lute player, chestnut-haired and slight, with soft brown eyes that captured everything in their gaze. His fingers held her shoulders as he kissed her lightly on the lips. A sweet sin that would have seen them both whipped had she told anyone. Which she hadn't, except Eleanor, who could keep a secret.

The eyes she thought of now were not soft. Their owner not slight . . . Wiry, maybe. She could imagine his fingers on her shoulders. Elsewhere too.

A single look, and his memory burned.

Giulietta shook herself crossly. Of all things to think about, a boy had to be the most stupid. So she thought of her mother instead. More stupid still, since her eyes backed up with tears, overflowed against her will and kept falling long, long after she willed them to stop. Her mother was even less able to help her than a stranger seen across a darkened nave.

Wishes granted kill you. Her mother had whispered that.

Curling up on the floor, Giulietta tried to sleep; but the memories of her mother were too strong. She'd been assassinated three days after that whisper, at the age of thirty-six. Her marriage to a Visconti had been unhappy.

Her death a release.

The old duchy included Venice itself, and the towns, villages and estates on the mainland inland for a day's ride on a fast horse. The estates boasted fortified houses, built of brick and limed with stucco. Those towns not built with limestone-faced defensive walls had made good their lack in the last few generations.

By accident, long before returning merchants brought Chinese cannon to Serenissima, the creators of the first town walls provided protection against not-yet invented weapons. The stone-faced walls split, but the compacted earth inside withstood the impact of a cannonball.

The young woman curled on the attic floor — hips stiff, swelling breasts pressed against cold boards — owned two estates, three towns and more villages than she'd bothered to count. She could recall, if she tried, the names of the ones she'd ridden through as a child, when they still belonged to her mother.

At dawn, she gave up trying to sleep and went as close as she dared to her only window. It was locked and shuttered and, from what she could see, looked out on broken roofs and a part of the city she didn't recognise. A church tower in the distance looked ready to topple. The houses opposite were ruined, or near-ruined. None of them seemed occupied.

Unbuttoning her gown, the girl weighed one breast as a cook might examine a plump capon. It was definitely bigger. This would have delighted her a year ago. Now she was simply scared. Her nipples, usually pale, were puppy-tongue pink and hurt to touch. She prodded one all the same.

"You're safe," said the note she'd found on waking.

She didn't feel safe, and she didn't understand the bit about not stepping outside the circle until she realised it meant an oval of salt trickled round the edges of the room. That amount of pure salt was expensive. So she obeyed, being as yet too afraid of what might happen if she broke the command.

Her breasts ached, her flux had stopped its tides and her belly, she could swear it was swelling. Added to which, she'd worn the same gown for days. In a world where poor women wore rags that rotted with sweat under the arms, beneath the breasts or across their buttocks that would be unremarkable. But Giulietta changed her dress regularly, washed daily and bathed weekly.

At least she had, until that night in the cathedral.

Now she stank like a servant. And her food would disgrace an almshouse. Bread so stale it needed soaking. Rancid cheese that clogged her nails as she picked free the mites. Always served on a filthy pewter plate.

In one corner a bucket was hidden under her discarded chemise. She could wear the chemise and suffer the stink of her own shit. Or cover her bucket and freeze. From the scratches on the wall, she'd covered the bucket and been frozen for the best part of six weeks.

"You're a fool," she told herself.

It made a change from her uncle being the one to tell her. So many memories and so few of them good. "You have your health,"

Giulietta snapped. Something her nurse used to say. It made little enough sense then. She had her health, and her life.

Didn't expect that, did you?

She'd taken to talking to herself. There being no one else to talk to. This made her think of Lady Eleanor, her long-suffering lady-in-waiting . . .

Well, Giulietta didn't think she was long-suffering. But she'd heard it said, more than once, and been so offended she slapped Eleanor next time they met, and demanded to know what she'd been saying. The memory made her ashamed. At least, she assumed that was the feeling. It made a change from rage, and fear and despair. These being her usual responses to waking in this attic.

She never saw who collected her bucket. She never saw who delivered her food. The one time she stayed awake to find out, her slop bucket went unemptied and her plate unfilled. No one arrived to clean the mess when she kicked her bucket over in fury. Only the memory of cleaning it herself stopped her from doing so again.

Damn it . . .

She could scream and shout for help. But what was the point? The last time she tried she screamed herself to a frog's croak and damaged her throat so badly it hurt to swallow. Her nails not encrusted with rancid cheese she'd broken scraping mortar from around the door that kept her prisoner. Someone had thought about this. Her prison was filthy, its floor splattered with pigeon shit, its ceiling sticky with cobwebs, in which dead flies and desiccated spiders mixed equally.

Only the door was new, its hinges freshly oiled. When she woke, still rolled in the carpet, it was the hinges she noticed after struggling free. Now she wondered if the carpet was more significant. Still here, looking rich and out of place.

Like me, Giulietta thought.

Except she and squalor were proving to be closer bedfellows

than she liked. The dirt troubled her less than it did. Her bucket's stink was bad, but she was close to choosing warmth over her sensibilities. And she was regarded as having delicate sensibilities indeed. She was changing, and that scared her too. Because the change that scared her most was the one she didn't dare think about.

A vicious wave of fear broke over her, tumbling her emotions in its wake, and then swept back, threatening to drown her altogether. *What*, she wondered, feeling tears fill her eyes again. *What if it was even worse than she thought?* People said Dr. Crow called up demons, captured djinn in bottles.

What if she carried a monster?

30

Men were watching for Tycho's return. A collection of restless Dogana guards, changing every few hours and all grateful to be relieved. Who knew what the captain told them? That they faced a demon, probably.

On the wind was the scent he hunted.

So slight and fragile he heard it as a perfect chord, a single bell-like note in the silence of his mind. He could not ignore its call. He could not stay away. Nothing in his life came close to how the scent made him feel. Hollowness and hunger ate away at him, bringing him to the edge of despair.

Above him, the sky was piled high with cloud. The full moon a sullen circle behind this masking. A fact for which he felt grateful. The sunlight burnt him, but the full moon hurt in other ways. So he stood in the squalid cave of an upper room, staring at the *campo* floor through broken shutters, and tried to master his emotions as he sought the scent he was tracking.

Red hair, blue eyes and a defiant glare. He could smell her, only too aware her scent might be in his head, with no right to compete with the stink of this world.

Eyes glared from under rotting floorboards and Tycho glared back.

The cat blinked first. Tycho wasn't the only predator in these ruins, simply the largest. The tom was sandy, little more than skin over bone. An Egyptian desert cat, from a ship that abandoned it by accident. The home-grown Venetian ignored them both. The lesser animals stayed away. When mice scattered below him, Tycho knew people were coming.

Few people were stupid enough to wander this way by accident. And fewer still came to ruined squares like this one by choice. So he knew the hesitant steps belonged to someone who had none.

Sharpening his senses, Tycho let go the scent that brought him back here and concentrated instead on who was approaching. He did this from instinct. Unaware he had until the rotten doors and broken shutters of the square became so clear he could see beetles scurrying, and hear the nervous breath of a girl entering the square, loud as shingle on a beach.

She was naked. A black tangle of hair between her thighs.

Rosalyn, shivering with fear. Her emotion so extreme fear barely began to describe it. Instantly he could taste her terror. Like the promise of rain before a thunderstorm.

Up here, Tycho thought, stepping from the shadows.

As she looked for him, something clattered from her fingers to the *campo* floor. Its loss dragging a swallowed sob from her throat. Falling to her knees, she scrabbled with her fingers, searching frantically.

She's blind in the dark.

Of course she is. How could he forget that being blind in the dark was normal . . . ? It had been normal for him too once. Now he had trouble knowing the normal from the passing strange.

Let me help you.

Dropping three flights, Tycho landed on heaped rubble, sliding the final stage to stop a dozen paces from the girl. She was sobbing openly now. Her shoulders quivering and her face twisted in misery.

"I won't hurt you."

You will. Tycho heard the words clearly in his head. He was trying to pin down how that worked when her fingers found the dagger and she stood, facing him as heavy clouds finally parted and moonbeams lanced down.

"Don't," he said.

But she did it anyway.

Raising her blade, Rosalyn put its point to her shoulder. And before he could stop her, hacked diagonally across herself from collarbone to hip, the blade negotiating the valley of her breasts. Skin peeled, blood flowed.

Hunger hit.

So hard Tycho rocked on his heels.

Narrowing his eyes against the moon's flaring brightness he closed the gap in a blur, ending on his knees in front of her. All thoughts of being able to control his hunger forgotten. His dog teeth sharp as he bit into the wound and her body went rigid with shock. Grabbing her hips, he held her in place. She moaned and he fed, blood dripping down his face until the red mist faded and the ruined courtyard around them lost its hard edges and the sky paled to a watery pink.

Lifting his head, Tycho took another look at Rosalyn and discovered her mouth wasn't twisted in misery. It was sewn shut.

Scrambling up, he slashed it open. His fingernail growing from nothing. The action leaving her lips untouched.

"Behind you," Rosalyn whispered.

Every strand of the net burnt, searing his skin as silver weights fixed to its corners wrapped round his body, trapping him in its agonising embrace. His scream made rats scatter and sleeping pigeons swirl into the air from their roosts on the ledges. He fought the mesh, burning himself with every move he made, as he searched for the net's edges and tried to free himself from pain. He might have made it too. So desperate he was to escape. But the blood in his mouth soured, and the pink sky swirled and he felt himself fall, wrapped in fire and still screaming.

Within a minute his screams had turned to whimpers, turning to silence shortly afterwards. No Nicoletti came to see what was happening. The *campo* was ruined and unsafe, and no one they knew lived there. Some of them had seen a veiled chair being carried by guards from their windows. The rest simply had more sense.

"Wash him well," Duchess Alexa said.

A'rial scowled.

As the red-haired little witch broke the seal on a bottle and splashed purple liquid over weeping burns that stopped oozing and began healing before she had time to find a stopper, Duchess Alexa unwound a strand of horsehair and threaded a needle, the one she'd used to guarantee the beggar girl's silence.

"Stand up," she barked crossly.

The beggar girl continued to crouch, in blood and piss, swaying backwards and forwards, until the duchess grabbed her hair and dragged her up.

"It's not deep," she said. "At least you got that right. But it'll heal faster if you stand still yourself and we do this properly. What's your name?"

"Rosalyn, lady . . ."

"Jewish?" Duchess Alexa sighed. "Not sure why I'd expect you to know. It's like expecting you to know your age or your father's name. Your mother's too, probably."

"She was called Maria."

"Of course she was," Alexa said. "Mother of God. The inviolate. Amazing how many whores have her name in this city."

"*She wasn't a whore.*"

A'rial looked round, grinning.

Then hastily went back to dressing Tycho's wounds when her mistress raised her veil to give her a look anyone watching would have thought mild.

"And you," Alexa said. "Are you a whore?"

Rosalyn shook her head indignantly.

"So, little not-a-whore, what are you?"

"I'm Rosalyn," she said, trying not to cry as the duchess dug a needle into her shoulder, hooked it through flesh and tied off the knot with the ease of someone who'd done the job before. The pain from the stitching was worse than the pain when Rosalyn cut herself, unless one had simply caught up with the other.

She looked to where the red-haired child had Tycho laid out like a corpse, stripped of his clothes as she finished wiping his face and moved on to cleaning the rest of his body. "He's dead?" Rosalyn asked, her bottom lip quivering.

A'rial grinned.

"He's drunk," the duchess said. "On blood and opium, moonshine, a little antinomy, some henbane." She sounded amused. "And mandrake, obviously. To muddle his wits. Not that his wits needed muddling. Sadly . . ."

"Lady?"

"You're not the one."

"I'm not the one what?" asked Rosalyn, unconsciously mirroring the thoughtful tilt of Duchess Alexa's head.

Tying off the final knot, the duchess leant back to examine her handiwork. Her nod was satisfied. She was happy with the result. Pulling a tiny jar from her pocket, Duchess Alexa prised off its lid and stopper.

Rosalyn was staring at it transfixed.

"Would you like a look?"

"Please, lady."

The duchess scooped up a little ointment, then replaced the

lid and handed the jar to Rosalyn, while she smoothed the odd-smelling mix along the stitches. "Camphor," she told Rosalyn. "That's what you can smell."

But Rosalyn was turning the jar in her hand. Her fear, the pain and her stitches forgotten as she traced the path of a twisting, seven-toed dragon that chased itself around the rim. "*It's beautiful.*"

"From my grandfather's grandfather's days. It belonged to a Ming empress. And was found in the ruined gardens at Chang gan . . ."

That was when Rosalyn realised she should know who this woman was. She was rich, obviously. Rich enough to be carried in a chair and have guards. Powerful enough to talk openly about her witch when witches were to be executed. And foreign enough to go veiled and talk with an accent Rosalyn didn't recognise.

"Lady. Who are you? Can I ask?"

The woman smiled beneath her veil. "I am the weeds in the rubble. The bricks in that . . ." She nodded at a ruined warehouse. "The women bedded and children born in those broken tenements behind you. I am the hammering in Cannaregio's forges. The sweat of artisans boiling hides for cheap armour."

"Lady?"

"Call me *my* lady," she said, almost kindly.

The woman traced the stitching down Rosalyn's chest and sighed. Then she pulled back her veil to show her face in the moonlight. "I am Alexa di Millioni, and my son should be those things, not me. Be faithful and my favour is yours. Betray me and you will wish you died here tonight."

Looking into her cold eyes, Rosalyn believed her.

In the days when Venetians wore rags and Venice was a collection of fishermen's huts on stilts in the middle of a muddy lagoon, where inhabitants worried more about staying alive than building palaces, invaders threatened and the last imperial fragments of

Western Rome broke up around them, salt and fish were what they traded. Back then, salt was scraped from the rocks. Now the sprawl of low-walled tidal pools beyond Cannaregio produced salt for export in industrial quantities. Which was just as well, as a month's production of a single pool seemed to have been used to redraw the oval around the edge of Giulietta's attic.

If she hadn't been upset enough to kick it away to see what happened—the answer being nothing—she would never have seen tonight's gruesome little moonlit masque. And her dull despair at imprisonment, and her fear of what might happen, if she stepped over the salt circle would never have been burnt away in her anger that the silver-haired boy had come so close to finding her. Only to be stopped by the very aunt who had promised to protect Giulietta after her mother died.

It look Lady Giulietta forty minutes to climb down from the roof. And before she could do that, she had to cut her way through bottle glass. The house she was in was a ruin, but once it had been rich enough to have glazed windows.

The actors in that night's masque were gone.

She was grateful for that.

Using the stairs at first, she navigated in darkness, feeling her way from rotten step to rotten step, each slimy with frost and wood canker. She'd believed exiting her attic window was hard, as was crawling over tiles and tumbling through a skylight to hit the floor below. That was not the hard part.

Finding the second set of stairs broken and the floor so soft one heel tore wood as if it was paper was not the hard part. Not even doing this while shaking with fear and struggling to stop her teeth chattering in case anyone heard. (Since her bucket had still to be emptied and her platter refilled.) The hard part, she realised, was what came after she escaped.

Her uncle had betrayed her and so had her aunt. Even if her aunt had not, what could Giulietta say? Nothing, since she could barely form the words in her head to describe what Dr. Crow had done to her and forcing them from her mouth was impossible. Giulietta knew. She'd tried . . .

I can't go to a physician, she realised in horror. He'd examine her, find her maidenhead intact, and proclaim a miracle, or damn her as bewitched. A wise woman? Mistress Scarlet was one of those. What if wise women talked to each other? They were out, priests were out, Dr. Crow was definitely out. Uncle Alonzo would kill her before she could betray him.

And the woman she'd always turned to . . . ?

On whose lap she'd rested her head and poured out childish woes. Giulietta barely recognised Aunt Alexa in the terrifying being who stalked after that naked girl, and later sewed the girl's wounds shut. Her face, when she pulled back her veil. So beautiful lit by moonlight. So unbelievably cold.

It took Giulietta twenty minutes to crawl through a jagged hole in the floor, hang by her hands from splintery boards and drop on to rubble, twisting her ankle in the fall. Nineteen of those were spent summoning her courage. Unless, she thought bitterly, it was desperation that finally forced her through.

The blood on the *campo* where the girl cut herself had frosted like expensive icing. A scuff showed where the silver-haired boy had fallen to his knees, and buried his face in the naked girl's stomach. Of all the things she should be thinking, Giulietta was certain jealousy shouldn't top the list.

31

A thousand events happened next morning. Fishing boats docked on Venice's northern edge, their nets safely reset. That day's catch would go to feed the city, since it was Friday and eating meat that day invited the fires of hell.

Since none of the three corpses caught in the nets belonged to anyone who mattered, no fisherman was dragged to the leads, made to confess sins belonging to someone else and executed.

Master shipwrights scrambled from their mattresses, having bedded their wives for warmth in the minutes before the Arzanale bell rang. Apprentices and journeymen tumbled their women and left them with half promises of marriage, and a newly made brat to widen their wombs, as like as not.

The rope walkways, dry docks and shipyards of Arzanale were the source of Venice's power. The older men still called it Darsina, from the Arabic *Dar-al-sina*, and a few even called it that. Across the city, foreigners — including those from the countries that gave the city that word — finished their prayers and rose to stock their stalls or unload boats or carry goods through alleys more complex than any minotaur's maze. White men, black men, yellow men. A dozen face shapes and twice as many languages. Their laws did not require Friday fish but most ate it out of expediency. Although they called it politeness.

Night soil men carried waste to barges bound for the mainland. Butchers slaughtered pigs, working under canvas to protect them from the drizzle. The Church might forbid eating pork on Friday, but it allowed the butchering of swine and the preparation of tomorrow's meat. Awnings or not, the dirt beneath the butchers' feet still turned to slop from the blood, guts and excrement that spilled from the swine, along with their lives.

Whores swore, splashing water between sore thighs as brothels closed or shifts changed. Losers staggered from gaming houses, having mortgaged already mortgaged houses, as card sharps shook aces from their sleeves, and rolled loaded dice for that day's luck, knowing that it was already secure.

Hearths were swept. Kindling chopped.

In the hours either side of the black thread moment Venice changed her masks like a gambler hoping to avoid his creditors as he heads for a new *casa chiusa*.

The sun rose cold and pale over the lagoon's edge, where the first villages stood. A starving memory of the previous summer's sun, which had glowed like slowly falling iron shot. And along the Riva degli Schiavoni, fighting memories of that summer sun, walked a young woman in a half-mask of her own.

The mask was cracked, found in the mud a minute earlier. Her shoes were filthy. Her velvet *houppelande* gown squalid enough to suggest she earned her living on her back. Lady Giulietta di Millioni was used to seeing Venice from the canals. Her Venice was ornamental and gilded, and glimpsed through the fringes of her gondola's scarlet curtains. The rare times she'd left Ca' Ducale, it was to walk Piazza San Marco. This Venice was unknown to her.

Stinking and strange and badly dressed. It didn't help that her gown, as well as being filthy, was cut lower than it need be. A dozen men mistook her for a whore between the Rialto and the start of Riva degli Schiavoni. And Moorish sailors leered openly as she dodged between carts, calling out offers for her service she wouldn't toss to a beggar. The sailors guarded women chained at the ankle. *Criminals*, Giulietta decided, then noticed their cheekbones and dark hair. Captured on the wild plains beyond Dalmatia, they were headed for slave markets in the Levant.

Fifteen ships lay close to shore between Ponte della Paglia, just beyond Ca' Ducale and the bridge before Arzanale. French, Tedeschi, Byzantine, Andalusian and English . . . Lady Giulietta identified as many of the eagles, lions, fleur-de-lys and leopards as she could. Maybe, if she'd been looking where she was going, instead of playing herald, she wouldn't have walked into a French officer, negotiating for a dozen large barrels of fresh water.

He swung round, hand on his sword hilt.

The Schiavoni laughed as Giulietta jumped back. And the French officer's face darkened, thinking she mocked him. There was little doubt the merchant was. The Schiavoni were the largest group in the city after the Venetians. When Serenissima claimed the Dalmatian coast it gave the inhabitants trading rights. The new stone quay along the city's southern edge became home to Slav traders. They built churches, *scuole* and hospitals, founded charities and supported monasteries with their tithes. They also built the largest water cistern in the city. It gave them, their competitors claimed, unfair advantage. But then Venetians widely believed anyone who came between them and a greater profit had to have an unfair advantage one way or another.

"Look where you're going . . ."

Lady Giulietta glared back. When the young Frenchman scowled deeper, she made to walk round him and froze in shock when he thrust his arm out to stop her. He caught her wrist just ahead of her slapping him. Gripping it, he slapped her arse hard. "Sauce for the goose," he said.

"*How dare you?*"

"Dare I what?" he asked, grinning. "Object to you slapping

me. Or object to you trying to walk off without apologising?" He realised he still held her wrist when she did. Stepping back, he let his eyes flick to the Schiavoni, and Giulietta realised, belatedly, he was simply trying to regain his pride.

Men was her first thought. Her second was to say sorry. So she did, realising that was probably the first time she'd said it. *Do I mean it?* Giulietta ran back through not looking where she was going, running into him, and being cross. "Yes," she added. "I mean it."

Uncertain how to answer, the Frenchman turned to the Schiavoni merchant instead. "We have a deal, right?" Taking five grosso and two ducats from his belt pocket, he double-counted them, tipping the gold and silver into the man's hand. "Deliver them there." He pointed to a tired-looking lugger.

Surely he knew enough to make sure the casks were full? And was he really going to walk away without checking his supplier delivered the number of casks just paid for? How did she, who'd never paid for anything in her life, know he should do when the Frenchmen didn't? Because she was Venetian, and he wasn't, obviously enough. Nor was the water seller, but a hundred years of Venetian rule rubbed off on people. There was a joke about Schiavoni men. How can you profit from one? Buy him for what he's actually worth. Sell him for what he says he's worth. Buy a house with the difference . . .

"You," she said.

The Schiavoni looked at her strangely.

"Deliver the right number of barrels. And make sure they're full." His scowl said he'd been planning to do neither.

She walked on. Head up, shoulders back. Doing her best to hold her misery at arm's length. Squeezing between carts carrying swine, Giulietta stepped under a hoist lifting pigs into a boat, and only just missed being showered with the terrified animal's excrement. Someone laughed. Laughing louder when Giulietta turned her head aside to hide her tears.

Beyond the Riva degli Schiavoni and Arzanale gates was San
Pietro di Castello, the island housing Venice's main cathedral. It
was here Giulietta was headed, because when she'd summoned her
courage to try the Patriarch's little palace by San Marco, announcing
she was a friend of his, she'd been sworn at, called a grasping little
whore and damned for her impiety. When she insisted she needed
to see him, she'd been told with a sneer to try San Pietro.

Despite taking her two hours to walk there, this being further
than she'd ever walked before—certainly alone—and discovering
an unknown city in the space occupied by one she knew; even
though she crossed a rickety bridge to discover her confessor was
dead, his body having lain in state in San Pietro, before being buried
under the nave; and a sour-faced, wimpled nun, looking too much
like another sour-face wimpled nun, had rolled her eyes at Giulietta's
sudden sobs, and sent her packing, with threats of a whipping, this
was not the important part of Giulietta's story that day.

This came shortly afterwards.

Her return from San Pietro di Castello was quicker, in the
way such walks always are. On a mudbank before Arzanale two
vessels rested on their sides; one was being caulked with twists
of rope dipped in tar. The other had a hole in its side large
enough to ride a horse through. Two men stood beneath, arguing.

By skirting the shipyard's gate, Giulietta avoided being whistled at a second time. She avoided hoists lifting hog-tied swine,
although excrement still splattered her as she waded, ankle-deep,
through Judas-soft mud.

"My lady . . ."

She turned, surprised.

Her admirer was broad, high-cheeked and darkly bearded.
Dressed in a scarlet doublet, tight black hose and a floppy hat.
His codpiece was more prominent and more highly decorated
than she'd seen. Eyeing the sailors watching her, he smiled lazily.
"*Eggs,*" he said. "*Have no business dancing with stones.*"

"You know me?"

"I know quality."

Her eyes tightened at his mockery.

"Believe me," he said. "I mean no insult."

And then, strangely, he leant close and inhaled her scent, as if smelling new-mown grass or some expensive perfume. And taking her hand, he opened her fingers to reveal a ring turned so its stone was hidden from view. The stone was priceless. The setting so old that much of its decoration had worn away.

He smiled and shrugged. His smile was easy and the shrug elegant. "I have . . . a certain *facility* for reading situations. And you, being beautiful, caught my eye. A second glance and I knew . . ."

"What?" she demanded.

He pointed to the chaos of the quayside. The penned pigs and sullen slaves. The whores stumbling from doors and blinking at the sunlight. The Schiavoni, the Mamluks, the Greeks. "That you don't belong here. You belong in a palace."

Maybe bursting into tears wasn't her wisest reaction. Alternatively, it was exactly what was needed. Either way, she found herself in his arms, held tightly until the crying fit passed.

"Prince Leopold zum Bas Friedland," he said, introducing himself. "The German emperor's envoy to Serenissima."

"Sigismund's . . . ?"

"Yes," he said. "The emperor's bastard." Leaning forward, he kissed her carefully on the brow and she felt herself shiver. A part of her did more than shiver. It began to melt.

"I'm Lady Giulietta San Felice di Millioni."

"I know," he said. "All things come to those who wait."

It was later, walking north, through alleys that Giulietta barely knew existed but which Prince Leopold seemed to navigate as if he'd lived his entire life in the city rather than it being the other way round, that she vomited. She did it guiltily. Turning aside and spewing against a wall, kicking dirt over her mess.

"Are you sick?" Prince Leopold asked.

She shook her head, face miserable and mouth turned down. Tears began to back up behind her eyes and she turned away again, unable to stop their fall and not wanting him to see her cry twice.

"What is it then?"

Maybe he read the answer in her silence, because he stepped forward to put his hand softly on her lower gut, feeling Giulietta freeze at his touch. And then, she felt a flutter beneath his fingers and his face turned white.

32

Situated in Dorsoduro, between the Grand canal to the north and the wide expanse of the Giudecca Canal to the south, Atilo's palace occupied half of what was once a small mudflat before it was reclaimed from the lagoon. The ankle-deep channel between it and the next mudflat had been dug out to make a usable canal. The edges staked with oak pilings, lined with stone and turned into *fondamente*, those inland quays that ran along many canals. Although the house was brick it was faced in stone. Elegantly open galleries overlooked a red marble fountain dominating its central *cortile*, the private courtyard beloved by patrician families. Fretted boxwork balconies hid its public windows from the world.

Marble columns, supporting arches carved with flowers and plants and animal faces, ran around the *cortile*. A narrower row supported the trefoil windows of the floor above. The whole effect was of an elegant lace knit from stone.

There were two *porte d'acqua*. An ornate one on the Grand Canal and a slightly less grand, but more often used, one on Rio della Fornace. While the land door was close enough to Dogana to be walked in minutes. Of course, everywhere in the city was within walking distance of everywhere else.

Since Atilo didn't trade, which made him rare in Venice, his colonnaded *cortile* was empty and his servants few. He entertained in the piano nobile, a wood-panelled first-floor reception room with alternating black and white tiles, huge fireplace and long windows stretching from floor to high ceiling. Furniture was sparse but the walls had Murano mirrors. And a painting of Atilo as a young admiral, by Gentile da Fabriano, held pride of place among round-faced madonnas and anguished saints.

A huge Persian carpet covered much of the tiling.

Directly above one corner of the piano nobile were the separate chambers where Atilo and Desdaio slept. A strongroom and chambers for guests took up the rest of that floor. In one of these, Desdaio's possessions waited to be unboxed.

On the floor above was the kitchen, with an iron range venting to the sky. That floor also had servants' quarters, additional storage rooms and attic space never used by anything other than pigeons, mice and rats. When Atilo summoned labourers to dig a cellar in the weeks before Tycho joined his household, Desdaio was puzzled. No one had cellars. In a city like Venice they were an absurdity.

But the labourers arrived towards the end of spring.

They dug where Atilo ordered, and an intense young Sicilian with greasy hair, sucked his teeth and talked to himself, before sketching plans that he scrawled over and crossed out and scrawled over again. And though the men mocked his twitch and his accent behind his back, and sometimes to his face, they dug where he told them, dug as deep as he demanded, and built a double-skinned cellar without windows. The underfloor and the cavity between the first wall of brick and the second had to be filled with fiercely puddled clay to keep water from flooding the room.

In the Griffin and the Winged Lion and the Whore's Thighs, which is what the labourers called the Aphrodite, men drank and squabbled and talked of the strange strongroom Atilo il Mauros was building. It was agreed it must be to house Lady Desdaio's fortune. Since he'd never bothered with such a room to protect his own treasure. Had they looked closely, they might have noticed the clay they puddled with bare feet contained finely powdered silver. Enough of it to pay them all several times over. And they left before a door was installed at the bottom of a short run of steps leading from the *cortile*. Its handles, hinges and locks were also silver.

"Why keep him in a cellar?" Desdaio asked.

"For his own good."

"In the darkness?" she said. "Locked in."

Atilo took a deep breath, wondering what reason would convince her. He could say his new slave was so dangerous it was for her own good. But then she'd want to know why he'd brought Tycho into his household.

"It's only temporary. Until he gets over his fear of daylight."

Desdaio looked doubtful. "You're not punishing him?"

"I'm helping him," Atilo promised. And he was, in his way. The alternative to Atilo's training was death. Duchess Alexa had made her position clear. Atilo had wanted this boy, not just as his apprentice but as his heir. It was up to Atilo to make him fit for both positions.

He had a year.

Atilo suspected the time limit was arbitrary. A way of reminding him he might share her bed but she still held his life in her hands. With Alexa it was almost impossible to know. "What are you thinking," Desdaio suddenly demanded.

"Nothing," Atilo assured her, wishing his thoughts had been about something else. She'd heard the rumours. The whole city had heard the rumours.

There was a distance growing with every conversation he refused to have. Already he could see unhappiness in Desdaio's eyes. This was why he'd long avoided remarriage, bedding only women he would never love. Now he had a lover who haunted his dreams, and a wife-to-be who haunted his daylight thoughts.

"My father used to lock me in the dark."

He looked at her, wondering. All he remembered was how cosseted she'd been. How surrounded with servants and toys and nurses.

"He's not who you think," she said. "He's vain and ambitious and a coward . . ."

A dangerous mixture. The fact she could say it made Atilo take another look at the young woman he'd asked to marry him. She was as clear-eyed, attentive and gentle as ever. But he couldn't shake his feeling that her wits were sharper than he first thought.

"We live in dangerous times."

As they stood in the piano nobile, looking down from an arched window on to the *cortile*, where the artisan who fitted the cellar door was packing his work tools, Desdaio nodded to show she was listening.

"Sometimes it's necessary to make difficult alliances."

She went very still and he watched her glance from the corner of her eye. Her hand shifted and one finger touched his as if by accident, remaining there. Although she gave no hint that she was aware of this. "Alliances you might not make in other circumstances?"

"Yes," Atilo said.

"I see," she said. "I think."

Picking up a small wooden box, Atilo opened it. Watching as she shook out an ornate collar and held it up, letting the last rays of that day's light play across overlapping scales of filigreed silver tied with twists of gold wire. At the bottom, a heavy pear-shaped pendant was set with rubies, pearls and squares of mutton-fat jade.

"Silver?" Desdaio sounded surprised.

"I have one too." Atilo opened his cloak to show a new chain where his gold one usually hung. "I know silver's for *cittadini* here but in my country it's lucky. And it suits you better than gold. Silver sets off your eyes and hair."

Desdaio smiled. "I'll put my gold away."

"No," said Atilo. "Wear it. But wear this as well."

When he looked, her eyes were bright and her chin trembled with unspilt tears and unexpressed emotion. Taking her hand, he kissed it. Seeing tears spill down her cheeks as she turned away from him. A rustle of silks, and the click of a door handle said she was returning to her chamber.

She did so in silence.

Unquestionably more intelligent than people supposed. She'd understood instantly his comment about alliances, and believed his answer about their being necessary. Whether he believed it was another matter.

33

The craft Atilo arrived home in that evening was larger than a *vipera* and smaller than a *sandolino*. It had been designed to Dr. Crow's specifications and built in half a day by a master shipbuilder and his apprentices. The fact the shipbuilder had been given his orders by Duchess Alexa ensured the man worked hard and asked no questions.

The vessel featured a small cabin, no windows.

Atilo was uncertain what brief Dr. Crow had given the master of the Arzanale. As a member of the Ten he could find out. As head of the Assassini he should probably know already. To say Atilo lived between those two roles was simplistic. His fame as Venice's old Lord Admiral, his new position with the Ten, and his duties as head of the Assassini were three strands of poison ivy strangling each other. How he could support a fourth as Duchess Alexa's lover was beyond him.

"Ready that rope."

The mage's vessel powered itself. Although Dr. Crow claimed a dwarf hid in a compartment at the rear, turning a handle to drive infinitely complex gears that drove a screw that forced the craft through the waves.

Atilo thought that unlikely.

Twisting the rope back on itself, Iacopo dropped the noose he'd made over a bollard, holding the rope's free end while the vessel's forward momentum narrowed the gap and brought the strange craft to rest.

"Neatly done, Iacopo."

Iacopo lost his smile as the cabin creaked open, revealing darkness.

Eyes shielded behind smoked glass peeked through a narrow gap and vanished just as quickly. Hightown Crow had told Tycho daylight was now safe for short periods. He obviously doubted it. Braided to snakes, even the boy's hair was oiled against sunlight. His braids being all Atilo could see above the arms Tycho had crossed over his face to protect him from the day.

"It's safe," Atilo said gruffly. "Now hurry it up."

He'd asked for this *thing* as his heir. Now he had to train it. Atilo's job was to make sure Tycho didn't disappoint. *Be careful what you wish for.* The old man's guts twisted with doubts he couldn't risk showing, least of all to Duchess Alexa.

Moonstruck poets were the mainstay of fable.

But a moonstruck assassin? One the duchess half believed a fallen angel? Assuming Atilo had the point of her wilfully oblique fairy story. Stepping on to dry land, Duchess Alexa's protégé sniffed the air, his shoulders sagging a second later. Whatever scent he was after he'd failed to find it.

The boy was dressed in a flowing leather coat over a doublet of silk, both black and both oiled. His hose was also silk, also oiled. Boots and gloves matched. Cut from black Moroccan leather so fine it stretched like skin. He was undoubtedly the most expensively dressed slave in the city.

Hightown Crow's choice.

From his belt hung a pocket. Inside it, a purple-glazed ceramic dragon curled around a pot of ointment mixed by Hightown Crow himself. Duchess Alexa defined what it should do. He chose the zinc-white, camphor, pounded silica and grape-seed oil needed to achieve that. The mixture stopped the sun from burning Tycho for up to an hour at a time. The alchemist was proud of this. Proud enough to tell Atilo twice what the mixture did. The leather coat and oiled silk might protect Tycho's body, the gloves his hands.

But the ointment was Tycho's mask.

"Shall I tell Lady Desdaio we have a new member of the family?" Iacopo asked, stepping back at a growl from Atilo.

"He's a slave."

Iacopo bowed deeply, and then turned to enter the *porta d'acqua* to Ca' il Mauros, leaving his master with the newcomer still peering at the ghostlike sun hiding on the far side of drizzling clouds.

"I own you," Atilo said. "Do you understand that? Whatever you are, wherever you come from doesn't matter now. You live and die by my rules."

Tycho shrugged.

"Do you understand?"

The boy's shoulders straightened at Atilo's tone. *He's taken orders before*, Atilo thought. *That's good.* Also bad. Most of those who passed through Ca' il Mauros arrived young and unformed. Eleven or twelve, homeless, unprotected and hungry.

Their gratitude carried them through early weeks of brutal training. The girls, less likely to be vicious, let their gratitude overwhelm their scruples about violence. Dragged from the streets to the palace of a strange patrician, one obviously rich and powerful, most girls thought they knew what awaited them. That Atilo proved them wrong bound them tight. The boys had less awareness of their possible fate.

Atilo put that down to lack of imagination. "Well?" he said.

"I understand." Something about the boy's tone worried his new master.

"What do you understand?"

"That you believe what you say."

Atilo stared at him. "Tomorrow we begin training," he said. "It will be brutal. You will be punished if you fail." The Moor kept his sentences simple, still not certain how much of what was said Tycho understood. He expected the boy to nod his agreement, to show some gratitude. Gratitude and respect. If needed, gratitude, respect and fear. Those bound an apprentice to his master.

Instead Tycho shook his head. "Tonight would be better."

"What?"

Touching his glasses, the boy said, "I see best in the dark." He weighed his words and obviously found them wanting, because he added, "Probably kill better too. If that's what this is about."

34

"He's a strange one," Desdaio said.

Taking another spoonful of venison from the pie in front of him, Atilo felt rather than saw her smile. She'd trimmed the meat herself, chopped root vegetables, ground Indian pepper and cut stale bread to serve as plates. He had a cook to do all that. Just as he had a serving woman to stand behind his chair and top up the glass Desdaio refilled from a jug.

He sat at the head of his long oak table in the piano nobile, with Desdaio at his right. Although light from a candelabrum made his glass sparkle, it barely reached the high-beamed ceiling overhead, and he sat with her in a puddle of brightness surrounded by shifting shadows. Both of them ate using forks. A habit Byzantium had adopted from the Saracens, its enemies. A princess brought the fashion to Venice two centuries before when she married the doge.

"Maybe three," Atilo admitted.

Desdaio nodded to indicate she was listening.

The rest of Italy still ate with knives and their fingers and regarded Serenissima's use of the two-pronged forks as proof the city was corrupted by its links with the Levant. As Gian

Maria of Milan jeered, "What needs man with a fork when God gave him hands?" He would have been even less impressed to know the implement's heathen origins.

"I have to go out later," said Atilo, putting down his silver fork and wiping his mouth with his hand. Desdaio would be disappointed. She'd found a harpist from Brittany. On the run from something, Atilo imagined. He was to play for them that evening. It was meant to be a surprise.

"Can't it wait?"

"Probably not," Atilo said. "Council business."

Desdaio's face fell. Nothing came before the Ten. The daughter of a Venetian lord, the great-granddaughter of a rich *cittadino*, she understood that.

"You're taking Iacopo?"

"Tycho," Atilo said. "I'll be taking Tycho."

"He's a strange one," Desdaio said. As before, Atilo said nothing, simply waited for Desdaio to put her thoughts in some sort of order. People thought her beautiful but simple. She was not. She simply thought slowly. "He scares me," she admitted finally.

"Why?" Atilo was interested.

"Something about him." Desdaio bit her lip. She hesitated, considering her words. "He could be a prince," she said finally. "When he's not sulking in corners like a beggar. I'm not saying he is. Just sometimes, when he looks at us . . ."

"He seems . . . princely?"

"Don't laugh at me. He eats *castradina* with his fingers, but stands up when I enter a room. And he watches always. I find him in rooms and don't know how he got there. He's like a shadow. Always there, except when he's not."

"And Iacopo doesn't scare you?"

"That's different."

"In what way?"

Desdaio blushed, looking towards the fire as if shifting logs had suddenly caught her attention. All men looked at her, Atilo knew that was what she wanted to say. Iacopo was simply one of those.

"Should he scare me?" she asked instead.

He's knifed a dozen men and cut a child's throat without hesitation, simply because those were my orders. He uses his fists freely on whores, and more often than not takes them and forgets to pay. When he thinks I'm not looking, he leers at you as if he would deflower you on the spot if not for me.

And, God forbid I was to order it. But if I did, he would knife you now, weight the sack containing your body with stones and row it beyond the Giudecca himself, returning for breakfast with his appetite intact.

"That was just an example."

"Something about Tycho is wrong."

"He's been living on the streets," Atilo said. "We don't know what's been done to him."

"It's what he's done to others that worries me. Oh, I don't *know* he's done anything. It's just . . . The way he barely speaks."

"Give me a month," Atilo said. "If he still worries you the Black Crucifers can have him." It was a lie, of course. He could no more give him to the Crucifers than he could tell Duchess Alexa he'd changed his mind and he no longer wanted the boy as his heir. And that would be a lie in its turn. He wanted the boy, just on his own terms.

"You'd let Crucifers torture him?"

"My dear," Atilo began, and changed his mind. Let her think that was what he meant, rather than what he *had* meant. That Tycho could join the Order, being darker in temperament than even them.

She'd let him stay now. She'd probably have let him stay if the alternative was Tycho being accepted as an order acolyte. Desdaio hated the Black, not understanding the purpose they served. The White Order protected Cyprus and guarded caravans in the Middle East. The Black extracted every last sin with torture, before forgiving the lot. The Black Order's purpose was to ensure no prisoner faced God with crimes on his conscience.

"Can you row?" Atilo asked, when he and Tycho stepped on to the landing beyond the watergate of Ca' il Mauros.

No, of course I can't . . . The boy shook his head.

"Then learn quickly," Atilo growled, settling himself into a *vipera* and sitting back. The night was clear and full of stars, an old moon hung above the city, already tired in that way fading quarter moons are. "And when I ask you a question you answer. And you call me *my lord*. Understand?"

Tycho nodded, too nauseous to speak.

Atilo hissed in irritation.

Their trip across the mouth of the Grand Canal was a vomit-inducing nightmare. One that took five times longer than necessary according to Atilo. Glowering at his master, Tycho wondered if he knew the only thing standing between him and drowning was Tycho's fear of being left alone on the water. Although he had been told what would happen if he rebelled. He would be given to the Black Crucifers. An order so fearful Desdaio crossed herself when he asked what they did.

Jumping from the *vipera*, Tycho slipped and fell, hitting his face on the slippery boards of the new jetty. Dark water taunted him through its gaps. So he rolled sideways a couple of times to reach land, lying there gasping, while stars left trails in a spinning sky.

Having tied the boat for himself, Atilo stamped over to Tycho and kicked him. "You're afraid of *water*?" Tycho's reply that water made him sick earned another kick. "This is ridiculous."

"Not at all." Stepping out of the shadows, Hightown Crow yanked Tycho upright before swinging round to face Atilo. "Did I or did I not fashion boots he was to wear? And did I or did I not ship him to you in a cabin floored with earth?"

The fat little man with his absurd beard and wire spectacles glared at the Moor who towered over him like a wooden carving of a hard eyed god. And all the while Tycho knelt by the jetty, hands pressed to the dirt as he willed the sky to stop spinning. A dozen late-night revellers staggered by, ignoring the little tableau as if such things happened every night.

"We train in bare feet."

"He wears what I provide. Unless you want this to happen every time you take him across the lagoon? God knows, he gets sick simply crossing the Rialto bridge. How can you be so stupid?"

Atilo glowered. "Why are you here?"

"To watch him train."

Atilo wanted to say no one watched. But since the only other person to know where Tycho trained tonight was Alexa, Dr. Crow's presence meant she'd sent him. Which meant he stayed. Atilo was wise enough not push the point.

They woke a cobbler at random in a tiny alley to the west of Piazzetta San Marco, a stone's throw before la Volta. Once he recovered from his fright, and realised he'd been selected not for his sins, such as they were, but because his was the first sign they'd seen, he vanished into his shop and returned with second-hand boots and shoes. Many were simply heels designed to be sewn to leggings. More than a few were designed for women. It looked as if the man had simply obeyed Dr. Crow and brought every piece of footwear in his shop.

"Try these ones," Dr. Crow suggested.

Having selected the softest and most worn pair, these being the ones least likely to rub, Dr. Crow ordered the cobbler to rip free their soles and heels. Then he went into a nearby *campo*'s church, unlocked the crypt by passing his hand over the key plate and scraped dirt from the lid of an old coffin.

The cobbler was ordered to trim a new sole from the best leather he had, cut away its centre and sew what remained to the boot. He was to fill the cutaway space with the dirt before fixing the original sole over it.

"My lord . . ."

Taking the shoes, Dr. Crow gave them to Tycho, saying, "These will also make it easier to cross bridges." To the cobbler, he said. "This never happened. Understand?"

"I understand, my lord."

"Good," said Dr. Crow, tossing him silver.

They were fifty paces beyond the shop when Atilo vanished. A few minutes later he caught them up again, tossing the alchemist his coins. "There are better ways to buy silence," he said, wiping his blade on a scrap of leather.

35

Tycho recognised the place immediately. The Patriarch's little gardens, adjoining the gardens of the ducal palace. Ca' Ducale showed lights. The Patriarch's palace, however, was in darkness. According to Atilo, Gregory XII, the new Pope in Rome, was too busy trying to negotiate a union of the two papacies with his rival, anti-Pope Benedict XIII, to appoint a new Venetian archbishop, and, besides, he didn't like the Venetians, few people on the mainland did, so he felt they could wait . . .

A very slight wind rustled the branches of the poplars; bushes looked uncared for. But staff had taken the trouble to scatter earth across any stains that might remain from Archbishop Theodore's murder. Unless that was simply the rain, sleet and snow that had filled the last few weeks.

A girl, a young boy and a dead-eyed man stood beneath the garden's single oak. Their hands were tied, and a noosed rope around each neck threaded over the lowest branch and was pegged into the dirt behind. Tycho recognised two of the three immediately. Rosalyn and Pietro, last seen the night he was captured. The third was a broken-faced man who watched Atilo approach with the stare of someone who's seen violence before, much of it of his own making. Anger burnt off him like steam.

Did the others know how dangerous he was? Tycho wondered briefly. He imagined they must. As he moved forward, Tycho felt fingers on his shoulder lock him to the spot. Whatever nerve Atilo squeezed cost Tycho his ability to move.

"Look around you. Always look around you."

An archer with a three-quarter bow stood behind another tree. An arrow already notched, his bow drawn and his fingers curled around the string.

"Poisoned," Atilo warned.

Where Rosalyn's hands were secured with a single rope, the man's were double tied, his ankle fixed to an iron ball by a fat chain. If he tried to run, unwise as that seemed, a second archer waited to make sure he didn't get far.

"The garden is secure?"

"Yes, my lord." A sergeant nodded.

"Then give me the key," Atilo said. "And go."

If the sergeant's gaze stopped on Atilo's apprentice it was simply his strangeness. From the speed at which the man hurried off he had little stomach for what was about to happen. Letting go of Tycho, Atilo said, "Lesson one. You have no friends." He jerked his head towards Rosalyn. "Punch her."

"No," Tycho said.

"You refuse to punch her?"

"Yes, I refuse."

Atilo pulled a dagger from his belt and reversed it across his wrist. "Then you cut her face," he said. "And if you won't do that, you'll take an eye. If you won't take an eye, then you'll take both ears and her nose. If you won't do that, the archer will shoot you . . ."

"Please," Rosalyn said. "Do what he says."

"Never." Tycho shook his head.

"More fool you," Dr. Crow muttered.

Atilo's dagger slashed once and the ropes binding the wrists of the broken-faced man fell away. A second slash severed his overhead rope, leaving its noose dangling like a scarf. Lobbing him a key, Atilo said, "Free your feet . . . Right, now we trade." He caught the key and tossed the man a blade in return.

"You know what to do?"

The man's eyes slid to Rosalyn. And Tycho saw her skull beneath the skin. Her eyes hopeless in hollow sockets.

"Don't," he yelled. As he lunged for Atilo something hit the side of his head. Turning, he saw Hightown Crow raise his walking stick. It came down a second time so hard the boy fell. When he tried to stand, Dr. Crow hit him again.

"Stay there, damn you."

"Make it fast," Atilo told the freed prisoner.

Without needing to be told again, the man grabbed Rosalyn by her throat, rammed Atilo's blade between her ribs. Her little brother's scream ended when Atilo punched him in the stomach.

"Slow is better," the flat-eyed man said.

"How many women now?"

"Eight, my lord."

"Our friend tortured the last he killed. Slit her from sex to throat. The Watch captain said it took her an hour to die."

"Longer," the man insisted. "Much longer."

Standing over Tycho, Atilo said, "Punching her would have saved her. Cutting her face would have saved her. *You* could have saved her. *You didn't.* Learn from your mistakes."

Ignoring him, Tycho crawled to where Rosalyn lay dying.

And, blood falling from his wounded scalp across her face like tears, he watched life leave her eyes. Bile filled his mouth. The smell of her blood made his jaws ache so badly he felt punched on both sides at the same time.

Above him the moon's normal hue was gone, replaced by a blood-red filter between the world and his anger. And something else . . . For the first time Tycho *felt* his body begin to change.

Something black slithered inside him, strengthening his muscles, heightening his senses.

Dragging Tycho to his feet, Atilo said, "Are you listening?"

"No," Tycho said.

His entire anger went into the blow that crushed her killer's voice box. Lacking a blade, Tycho dug his thumbs into the man's eyes until yolk ran down his wrists. When Atilo reached for his dagger, Tycho went for his eyes instead. He missed because Atilo blocked with the speed of a man half his age.

"Don't," Hightown Crow ordered.

And Tycho felt the point of a blade burn his neck. It felt colder that the coldest ice. Dr. Crow had drawn a sword from his stick.

"Silver. From the court of the Khan," he said. He was talking about the blade. "Not pure, of course. That's too soft to take an edge."

"*Dr. Crow.*"

"He must learn," Hightown Crow said, lowering his weapon.

"Metallurgy?"

"Everything. Those are Alexa's orders. Anything else she will regard as failure. *Your* failure," the alchemist added, in case this wasn't obvious. "So, now you've cleverly killed the only person he trusted, I suggest you work out other ways to influence our little friend."

36

Desdaio was the one who half tamed him, and asked diffidently if Atilo could stop referring to Tycho as *that creature*. She was the one to suggest, since daylight scared him, magic ointment or not, perhaps he should be reserved for duties that needed to be done at night.

And Atilo, who considered every word he spoke, and judged others by what they meant rather than what they said, weighed her words and realised she meant precisely what she said; astounded by how that realisation touched him.

Sentimentality and ruthlessness were the prerogative of old age. Sometimes he wondered if they were all he had left.

She would never have unlocked Tycho's door had she known he intended to kill her in revenge for Rosalyn's death. And Tycho would never have found himself with the opportunity. Only to discover he lacked the desire.

His war, Tycho's war, was with Atilo, who was away doing whatever he did when he locked Tycho in the cellar and left Desdaio alone with her tapestry.

"My lord Atilo says I should be wary of you . . ."

"Of me?" Tycho asked, bowing his way into the high-ceilinged piano nobile of Ca'il Mauros and realising she was the only other person there. Alone, defenceless, wearing a gown that barely covered her breasts. She sat near a huge fire, a scrap of embroidery on her lap. Wine, glasses, bread and cheese rested on a table next to her bench. Her face was flushed from the fire and too much red wine.

"And I am a little afraid," she said. "Is that silly of me?"

Tycho waited to discover what Desdaio wanted. It turned out she'd like to make friends. Since he was a slave and she was rich beyond his imagining, he wondered why he was the only one of them to see the stupidity of this.

"What did you do this morning?"

Stabbed corpses in a morgue until the knife was blunt and the corpses mince . . . Almost worth telling her to see how she'd react. Hours spent learning *where* to stab, followed by hours practising on the bodies of beggars, criminals and foreigners. People without friends.

"Well?" she asked.

"I studied with Lord Atilo."

Desdaio sighed. "I know that. What did you study?"

"Ask him, my lady."

"I'm asking you." It was rare for her to frown. So rare her face looked wrong. Her nostrils flared and her lips thinned, lines appearing at the side of her mouth.

"My lady," he said carefully. "I'm not allowed to tell you."

"My lord Atilo said that?"

"Yes, my lady." He'd told Tycho exactly what would happen if Desdaio discovered through him about the Assassini. Although that was something else Tycho was not allowed to say.

"Why are you here?" Desdaio asked.

Tycho was about to say, "You ordered me," when he realised this was not what she meant. "Because I can't leave."

"You could run away," she said, as if discussing a game. "Steal a boat and row to the mainland. Or escape on a ship." Glancing towards a window, she said, "There are always ships."

"Water hurts me."

"Hurts?"

"It tried to kill me once. And I have other reasons."

"Really," Desdaio said. "What are they?"

"I'm looking for a girl . . ."

Laughing, Desdaio reached to cut cheese and tear a loaf to pieces. When she filled two glasses with wine from a jug in front of her, Tycho realised she intended to feed him. "My lady, I've eaten already."

Her glance was sharp. "Amelia says not."

Ah yes, Amelia of the silver braids and the double life. They were strangers to each other these days, as Amelia had said they must be.

"I ate with Lord Atilo, my lady."

"Drink, then. Drink, and tell me your life. Who are your family? Where did you live before this? I want to know these things . . ."

"My lady, I'm a slave." Tycho wondered if she knew he'd used a whole fifth of his precious pot of Dr. Crow's ointment protecting himself from the weak sunset dribbling through her window. Of course not. And she knew next to nothing of her husband-to-be's life, even less about his training methods.

Masters beat servants, journeymen beat apprentices; such was the nature of training. Atilo had shown him the whip he used to beat Amelia and Iacopo. Then the whip he would use on Tycho. This was leather and silver wire. The single lash he'd slashed into Tycho's naked back that morning made Tycho piss himself with agony.

"I know all about Amelia," Desdaio said brightly.

What could she know? He wondered how close it was to the truth. Reaching absent-mindedly for a glass, he looked up to find Desdaio smiling. She tapped the double seat in which she sat.

"Come here. And tell me all."

The rule, *don't show what you feel*; had kept him alive. But with Desdaio the temptation to tell her how he found himself here was overwhelming. And she might know who the girl in the basilica was.

That would be worth discovering.

"I don't know my name," Tycho said. "Not my real name. And what I remember changes. But I know I was born in a rotting town. With little food in summer and less in winter. Beyond the walls lived demons. Inside, a crippled lord and his drunken brother, their guards, their women and us. Their slaves."

"You were a slave before?"

"I believe so . . . Until Duchess Alexa trapped me this may be the only time I've been free."

"What does Alexa have to do with this?" A sudden bleakness wintered in Desdaio's eyes.

"I was born a slave," Tycho said quickly. "And became a dog. That much I've remembered."

His words did what he wanted. The trouble fled her eyes. She smiled, laughed, wondered if he was serious and smiled again. "A dog?"

"A wolf dog . . . Wolf dogs kill wolves."

Desdaio leant closer. The fire was warm, her face flushed. Leaning forward shifted her breasts under silk. Tycho watched them try to overspill the embroidered scoop of her gown. "How many wolves did you kill?"

"It's hard to remember . . . I mean it," he added, when Desdaio rolled her eyes. "I was . . . ill, when I arrived here. Remembering is hard."

"Maybe you simply want to forget?"

"That's possible."

Atilo was away on Council business, Iacopo with him. Amelia? Who knew where she was? Fighting Nicoletti, probably. The cook was up in her kitchen, glad to have it to herself. There were only three people in the whole of Ca' il Mauros, and one of those was pounding dough a floor above.

"Tell me about the wolves," Desdaio said impatiently.

*

Lord Eric's wolf dog was old, its temper erratic. Tycho remembered that much. And in remembering this, remembered more . . .

Since there were no sheep left, owning a wolf dog was pointless. But the lords of Bjornvin arrived with wolf dogs and sheep, not to mention cattle, horses and slaves and their brats. All the things needed to settle a new land. Lessons had been learnt from earlier colonies. The lesson from Iceland was that, if you want families to come, don't name it after the cold. So Greenland, which had far more claim to be *Iceland* than that country ever did, was named to sound welcoming.

Vineland had vines. It had green fields and clear streams and less harsh winters than either Greenland or Iceland, for all its winters turned brutal in later years. But after Greenland no one trusted settlers. So the Vikings and their families who should have come never did. And the founding families slowly lost land and the will to fight the wilderness. Bjornvin was the last town. When it fell, and no one but Lord Eric and his cousin Leif doubted it would, Vineland would be no more.

This is what the thralls whispered.

Silent and watchful, silver-haired even as a child, Tycho grew up among truths that couldn't be said. Lord Eric was unable to father children but his bard still sang of glorious generations to come. Lord Leif fought drunk, because fear made him vomit when sober. But poems celebrated his battles with the Skaelingar . . .

"The wolves," Desdaio demanded.

"First the wolf dog. Which was old, its temper erratic . . ." Realising he should have started somewhere else, Tycho stopped. "First me. A thrall the others avoided. For the first seven years I ran naked. I did so because my mother hated me too much to clothe me. At least, I thought she was my mother. Maybe she hoped the cold would kill me."

It almost had. One winter he'd been saved by a drunken house carl who staggered from the great hall, found Tycho curled in a little ball by an outhouse door locked against him, and thought it funny to piss on a sleeping child. A dozen other house carls staggered out to join the fun. He woke crusted in yellow slush and heaped with snow where they'd buried him. But he woke. Having been saved by the casual contempt of others.

He was three at the time.

The memory hurt less now Tycho knew Withered Arm wasn't his mother. Back then, he believed if she hated him the fault was his. And his brothers followed her lead. Afrior, though, never hated him. She saved his life.

Half starved, his ribs sticks and hair so filthy house carls stopped calling him silver hair and simply started calling him *you*, *thing*, *shitface*, he'd been combing through a rubbish pile, searching for anything edible, food being scarcer than ever, when Afrior screamed his name. Looking up, he saw his brothers grinning.

The wolf dog's chain was fixed to its post. The collar was fixed to the chain. The wolf dog wasn't fixed to its collar. In that split second, Tycho understood what his brothers' look meant. He dropped as the beast leapt from behind him, splattered by the creature's drool as it passed overhead. Scrambling up, he ran. Cunning and hatred made him head straight for his brothers, who scattered. The wolf dog went after one of them instead.

Grabbing Afrior, he threw her through a gate.

The gate was huge, at least for him. But he pushed it shut anyway, heels dug into the dirt, expecting at any time to hear snarling behind him and feel jaws close on his hip. When he looked round, the dog had his eldest brother cornered by the log pile. The best anyone could say for what came next was that it was quick. Leaping, the beast bit the boy's neck to bring him down, and ripped out his throat.

Throwing a stone at the dog was stupid. His other brother did it anyway.

And the beast would probably have killed again if Tycho—

aged seven, and naked—hadn't grabbed a pottery shard from the rubbish and intercepted the beast. He didn't do it to save his brother. He did it because Lord Eric was back from hunting, and Afrior had entered the gate behind him.

Driving the shard between the beast's teeth, Tycho's blow cut into its jaws until his shard hit bone with a jolt. The dog tried to bite but its jaw muscles were severed and the shard stopped its teeth from closing.

"You, step back . . ." Lord Eric's shout brought all noise to a halt.

He should have obeyed. He should have let go of the shard, leaving it lodged in the dog's jaws, and stepped back. Instead, he pulled the shard free and slashed it hard across the beast's throat, feeling hair drag and flesh open. It was blind luck that he found an artery and bled the dog out.

Grabbing the boy's shard, Lord Eric looked at it.

It was a quarter of a broken bowl, with the bowl's rim making a handle and the break and glaze creating a razor edge. Even so, the shard had chipped where it crunched into the bones of the wolf dog's jaw. For a moment, it looked as if Lord Eric would use it on him. Instead, he pointed at the collar in the dirt.

"Fetch that," he ordered.

The boy did so.

"Who undid this?" Lord Eric demanded, his face hard and his eyes furious. Afrior glanced at her middle brother, and the boy saw Tycho notice.

"My brother did," the boy said, pointing to the corpse by the log pile.

Lord Eric grunted.

When Withered Arm arrived she began keening for her eldest son, until the master glared at her and she felling into hiccupping silence and swallowed sobs instead. The look she shot Tycho was brutal.

"This is your boy?" said Lord Eric, pointing at him.

She stayed silent until the Viking grabbed her and twisted her face to look into his. "When I ask you a question you answer." His voice was quiet and dangerous. "Is he your son?"

"Yes, my lord."

There was something unnerving in Lord Eric's gaze. When he released her face, Withered Arm stared at the ground.

"Well," Lord Eric said, buckling the collar round Tycho's neck. "Now he's my wolf dog . . ."

"And what happened to Afrior?" Desdaio asked.

She looked at Tycho's drained face and his barely drunk glass of wine. When she touched his hand, he flinched. "Another time," she agreed. "You can tell me about it another time." Hesitating on the edge of saying something, she shrugged. "I think you're better off here. Such things could never happen."

Remembering Atilo's silver whip, his warning of what would happen if Tycho was ever sent to a Venetian prison, and the Mamluk girl nailed to a tree in the *fondak* garden, Tycho kept his silence. On the way out, he suggested Desdaio lock him back in and not tell Atilo they'd talked. It would upset him.

Tycho took back to his cellar the thought that Atilo now owed him two lives: Rosalyn's, and the one he'd just refused to take.

37

There were a dozen pig shambles in Venice. The one Tycho was delivered to by Amelia on a hot summer night was on the city's northern edge; ten minutes west of della Misericordia and almost opposite the island of San Michele. Like all slaughterhouses it was as far away from human habitation as possible. Which translated as far away as possible from anyone rich.

So it stood on the lagoon's edge, with a gently sloping floor that let the bricks be sluiced and the filth be washed into the sea. Although little was left after butchering. Outside, in a stinking pen, pigs milled and snuffled and slopped up to their knees in their own dirt, or the dirt of meat before them. They were jointed according to Guild rules; not to be sold within twenty-four hours of slaughter or longer than ten days after. Their blood, guts and viscera made sausages. The skin became leather, and the hooves and long bones, once split for their marrow, boiled down to glue.

Even individual vertebra provided soup. The method used by Master Robusta involving two cuts, one either side of the backbone, instead of the more common single cut that split the spine down the middle.

Most of the pork was salted and sold to ships moored in the

Bacino di San Marco, since they needed to revictua for their journeys south. The better cuts ended up on stalls in the Rialto market, and pork sausages fed the poor across the city. Master Robusta's place stank. It was a shambles after all. But it stank no worse than other slaughterhouses and smelt far better than the tanneries. And, unlike the iron foundries to the west, it was unlikely to kill you with air poison while you slept.

"What brings you back here . . . ?"

Amelia jerked her thumb at Tycho, scowling as Master Robusta grinned at his silvery braids and white skin. "Don't say it."

"You have a letter?"

She gave him Atilo's note, waiting while he broke its seal, read the contents and held the single sheet of paper over a flame, letting it burn to his fingers before letting go and watching embers dance away.

"Every month?"

Amelia shrugged. "I don't read. Anyway, it wasn't shown me." Glancing at Master Robusta, she added, "I'll be accompanying him." Her tone said how much she liked that idea.

"We kill, gut and joint every minute of every day, except those forbidden by the Church. These days we use cleavers. Your master has asked you be taught the old ways first." Walking to the back, Master Robusta chose a knife from a rack. "Use this," he said. "It's too old to damage."

It might be old but it was sharp. The edge so honed it curved like a sickle moon. That upset the balance.

"Good enough for you?" Master Roberto and Amelia were watching him. The butcher's look was half amused. Amelia's harder to read.

"May I?" Tycho nodded to a sharpening wheel.

"It's sharp already."

That was when Tycho knew he was expected. The business with the sealed letter was play-acting. At least on the butcher's part. Amelia had probably been told after Tycho, which was less than an hour before. Walking to the wheel, he set it spinning and ground wood and slivers of tang from the handle, until the knife balanced properly.

"Where did you learn to do that?" The first words Amelia had spoken to him since they left Ca' il Mauros. Since he could hardly say, *Watching Lord Eric's armourer*, he shrugged her question away, watching her mouth tighten.

"Through here," Master Robusta said.

A dozen men looked up but it was Amelia they watched as she moved among them like a black lynx jostling a herd of something too stupid to know just how dangerous the newcomer was.

"Take a bench each."

Amelia shook her head. "I'm just here to watch."

The master butcher looked as if he might disagree. Instead he shrugged and told her to keep out of the way if she couldn't be useful. Point made, he nodded to an oak frame hung with two pulleys. "I'll show you once only."

A small boy dragged in a pig, which he trapped between his knees, before fixing two slipknots round its hind legs and yanking on a rope that ran between three pulleys. In no time at all he had his victim hanging upside down.

Kicking a tub into place, Master Robusta took the knife, yanked back the squealing pig's head and slit its throat. He began cutting immediately, ripping down the animal's belly to drop pulsing guts into the tub. They landed with a splash he ignored. The butchering was brief and brutal, two slashes down the spine, forelegs, shoulders, flanks, saddle . . . He stripped meat from bone and severed joints with a ruthless efficiency that spoke of thousands and thousands of animals before this one. When he looked up, he found Tycho watching with a fierce intensity.

"Think you can do that?"

Tycho nodded.

"Then show me."

A boy dragged in a second pig and looped its legs, hoisting

the shrieking beast into the air and wrapping its rope briskly around a hook. Then he vanished, one of a dozen junior apprentices, to do the same for another butcher.

Gripping the animal's snout, Tycho slashed.

He expected red mist and shifting shadows. A fear his dog teeth would descend had travelled with him across the Rialto bridge to the doors of the shambles. He felt nothing. Without considering, he dipped his hand into the blood flowing from the animal's slit throat and drank. It tasted mud-like and flat. The fierce flame that heightened every sense was missing.

In the moments following he repeated Master Robusta's movements exactly. Splashing viscera in the blood-filled tub, slashing parallel lines either side of the spine, and butchering the animal with cold efficiency that left him time to think about the slaughterhouse around him.

Amelia was scowling. Master Robusta's gaze was keen.

Other butchers stopped to watch until Master Robusta's glare returned them to their duties. Fresh pigs were dragged in and hoisted, gutted and killed, often in that order. The shrieking was hideous, sometimes unbearable. And the iron stink of blood, and the smell of shit, and the heat released from the butchered pigs, joined to that of the summer night outside, filled Tycho's hairline with sweat.

"You've done this before."

Tycho shook his head.

"But you've killed?"

"Wolves," Tycho said. "People." He looked at the one-sided battle around him, the slick of spilt blood and the twitching bodies. "Although killing pigs doesn't seem that different."

38

A roof tile slid beneath his feet, skating towards the roof's lip, and Tycho followed it over the edge, pushing off from the overhang and catching it on the way down, to land silently in the tiny garden of an insignificant palace in San Polo.

A scrap of black leather followed him.

He ignored the scrap. Since magic was best ignored in his opinion.

A leap for the garden wall, a roll over the top and he was in a private alley, with a wrought-iron gate at one end. Beyond the alley was an underpass. And since he couldn't leap over the iron gate he lifted it off its hinges, as silently as rust and age allowed, then replaced it.

Unless the palace's owners looked carefully for prints in their overflowing flower bed they would never know he'd passed through there.

Two down, three to go.

He scrabbled to the top of the first church he found beyond the *sottoportego* and found the scrap of black leather already waiting. It stared at him with amber eyes. "Are you going to follow me all night?"

It opened its mouth, displaying tiny needle-like teeth.

So Tycho ignored it again, inhaled the wind, and searched for the scent he was after. In there, like a missing note, was a gap where the scent he'd been hunting the night Duchess Alexa trapped him should be. He missed finding it, but ignored the hollowness this opened in his belly. The hardest lesson in a hard year of training. One that had seen spring turn to summer and leaves finally begin to fall.

This test mattered, which was not to say others didn't. Simply that Atilo placed a greater value on this one. He'd tried not to let Tycho know, but the youth had become expert at reading the emotional currents swirling through Ca' il Mauros. So he breathed deep, filtering out bass notes of sewage and tanneries.

Five prisoners from the pit released, one deserving to die. The others mere prisoners. Kill the right one and the others went free. Kill the wrong one and everyone died. That was meant to be his incentive. A call on his sympathy. But up here in the wind, on the tower of a San Polo church, Tycho had no sympathy for those sleeping below while the night crawled around them.

He wanted to get it right because he wanted to get it right.

Quickly, in the early days he'd reached a point where he judged himself only against what Atilo could do. Even Amelia, better than Iacopo, couldn't move as silently as Tycho could. And a handful of months after that, he'd stopped judging himself against Atilo and started judging himself only against himself.

He was his own competition. The only person he was interested in beating was himself. It made the world a private place and most of Tycho's life was lived inside his head. This, he suspected, suited everyone just fine.

Atilo, he knew, expected him to try to escape. That he didn't worried the old man far more than Tycho trying to escape would have done. Another reason he kept his own company, retired to his cellar and sat out the full moons to keep his hunger manageable. Rosalyn's murder was walled around with ice; Afrior's death; his other fragments of memory from Bjornvin. He could consider his losses. Examine them without feeling the hurt that should go with them. His was a life of stale pig's blood, and an iron control that filed each new skill he learnt as he waited for Atilo to admit what Tycho already knew.

He was the old man's heir.

A slave would become the duke's Blade. Chances were, he'd be freed first, but even that wasn't necessary. The Seljuks had generals who were born and died slaves, the property of their sultan. It made no difference to him. Maybe he could, as Desdaio once suggested, escape the city. But why would he bother?

When the only life he wanted was closed to him?

Venice was as good as anywhere in this world. Maybe better. Since it sat in the middle of its richest trade routes. And a job was waiting for which he was suited. For which his nature could have been . . .

He caught it then.

A scent of fear, an echo of feet as they left dirt and hit herring-bone brick in a street three blocks beyond. He caught it, and he followed it. If he was those he hunted he'd use canals, take to the water and rely on it to hide his stink. They'd been ordered to keep to dry land. One reason to do the opposite.

A skinny whore of fifteen, maybe younger. Dressed in rags and with a desperate look in her haunted eyes. Even beggars had more sense than to push through a late-night crowd around the Rialto bridge. A *cittadino* turned on her, expecting a clumsy pickpocket. And met fear and a gabble of prayers.

The Rialto bridge was not yet closed for the night.

On the bank she'd abandoned, porters sluiced the floor of the covered fish market and the guard changed shift outside the state prison. On the one she wanted, stevedores emptied ore from Tedeschi barges along the Riva del Ferro, despite the lateness of the hour. The ore was loaded on to carts headed for the foundries.

Tycho let her begin to cross. Watching from his fish market roof.

Only to beat her to the other side. Having run fleet-footed over the bridge's wooden roof, jumped the gap where drawbridges raised to let masts through, and leapt from the bridge beyond into the mouth of a passageway she entered, thinking it empty. Her scream died beneath his fingers as he brought his forehead close to hers.

A theft, a little whoring, a murder not reported. Her sins were minor in a city where most people like her would have regarded that as innocence. He could see her face but not the skull beneath.

"Make it to the end," Tycho said. "Stay safe."

The whore gaped at him. "I'm not the one?" she asked. He knew then she knew the rules but not the reasons.

"Go. Before I change my mind."

It was enough. She vanished into the darkness.

A hired thug; a discarded catamite; a little part-time whore, who did no more or less than half the patrician women he'd come across in his year in the city, but paid a price no one demanded of them. In the Corte Seconda Millioni, Tycho stopped to gaze at the house where Marco Polo was born. It was grand, but not that grand. If it had belonged to a *cittadino* he wouldn't have been surprised. No one lived there now, although the Millioni still owned it. Marco III brought his mistress there. Duchess Alexa accepting a duke must have mistresses, while refusing to have them in the palace.

Its walls were old, mortar crumbling beneath Tycho's fingers as he climbed. In the distance, beyond the dry docks, walkways and factories of Arzanale, was the squat cathedral tower of San Pietro di Castello. It was here the prisoners must reach.

Two more to go.

He ran the roofs, barely entering Sestiere di San Marco before leaving it for Sestiere di Castello, avoiding loose tiles, skirting *campi* and jumping canals rather than cross bridges at ground level, which, more often than not, were guarded by informal militias or taxed by local thieves who regarded whichever parish as their own. Only once did he hesitate.

On a roof in Santa Maria dei Miracoli a clawed and shaggy figure was changing against the half-moon. As Tycho approached, the creature twisted, moaning softly as its limbs straightened, joints shifted and flesh remade itself, leaving a naked man in the creature's place. He turned to watch Tycho approach, dipping to wrench free lead piping at his feet. Nothing in his expression suggested he intended to offer a reason for being there.

Tycho hesitated. Shocked to find this creature from the silent city so at home in the noisy one above. Tycho had settled into this world, the one around him. Although it made sense the dead should seem real on his arrival and fade first. And the silent city fade next. At least, he supposed it did.

"Think you can take me?" The man's accent was strange.

Tycho nodded.

"Then do it."

Atilo's orders were firm. Tycho must kill his target before the first prisoner reached San Pietro di Castello. "I don't have time."

He watched the man's eyes narrow. The mouth that had been mocking settled to a thin line and his stance became less easy. Anger was always a waste of emotion unless converted to something useful. Maybe he intended to fight. Tycho couldn't afford time to find out.

"Later," he promised.

The *krieghund* followed, his breath animal and rasping. And then Tycho was gone, in a leap that crossed both the Fondamenta di San Lorenzo and the *rio* beyond, landing him on the flagstones of Corte Maltese, where a crumbling palazzo slipped by beneath his fingers as easily as if someone had fixed handles to its walls.

The meeting with the *krieghund* sharpened his senses.

So when Tycho stopped, a few minutes later, to check the

krieghund wasn't following, he'd found both his targets by the time he spotted the naked man watching from inside a bell tower three or four minutes away.

Two prisoners, one little more than a youth.

Both better fed and healthier-looking than the others. This suggested families rich enough to bribe prison guards or have food sent in. Maybe even money enough to guarantee a daylight cell. Since it hadn't been one of the first three, his target had to be one of these. Tycho wondered how apprentices without his abilities made the call. By seeing who panicked? By who blustered or begged?

Atilo had taught him to read men's faces for lies. How to listen for telltale weakness in their words. How to count the pulsing of blood in a guilty man's temple, wrist or throat. He hardly needed to tell Tycho to watch for this. There were times when he found it hard to watch anything else.

To go through Arzanale would be stupidity for the prisoners.

The great dockyard worked day and night and was guarded by Arsenalotti militias who assumed, probably rightly, that anyone found in the dockyard who didn't belong was a thief. The prisoners he chased would go south of Arzanale's walls. This meant navigating a strip barely three houses deep, between the dockyard walls and the lagoon's edge.

Tycho let the first three through the strip without stopping them.

They skulked so obviously when they were forced briefly on to the open quayside of Riva Ca' di Dio that lookouts on ships half a mile away would have been able to spot them. Should the lookouts be able to see in the dark.

The last two came together.

They had a dagger, at least one did. Since it looked new and lacked a sheath they must have robbed a drunk. Weapons were forbidden, like entering the water. But the smugness on their faces said rules were not for them.

"*Stop*," he said, dropping from a window ledge. A scrap of black leather remained behind. The two men looked at each other, then rushed him at once. Their blade flashed and Tycho dropped under it, his movement a blur as he grabbed the knifeman's wrist and twisted, breaking half a dozen bones.

Tycho caught the knife before it hit brick. His victim would have screamed but the dagger to his throat persuaded him otherwise. Abandoning his friend, the other man made a run for San Pietro di Castello, hoping for sanctuary. Not knowing Atilo, Iacopo and Amelia waited at the church door. So accurate was Tycho's throw that it cut the tendon in the running man's heel.

"I'll give you money," he promised. "More than you can imagine. You name it, I'll give it to you." His voice was raw, his fear real. But his eyes betrayed him as they focused beyond Tycho, who ducked as a stone hissed past where his skull had been.

He stabbed the runner in the leg and twisted the blade. Not caring if the man's yell brought the Watch. And then Tycho returned his attention to the stone thrower and knew suddenly why he should die.

"God's name," Iacopo said. "What happened to you . . . ?"

Blood dripped from Tycho's mouth. He was shaking, his whole body humming with energy, as if it was fighting itself. He had taken his reward for success and taken it without thought.

"I was attacked."

"And your attacker?" demanded Atilo, his voice flat.

"Is dead." Tycho shrugged. "And his friend. I was forced to bite out the first's throat. And break the neck of the second."

Having laughed, Amelia apologised.

Atilo waving her apology away as he told Tycho to clean his face. In the time it took the boy to swill lagoon water around his mouth and spit, his breathing steadied and the shakes subsided. So he knew what to say when he got back. Although first Atilo had to say what Atilo needed to say.

"You failed." The words brought glee to Iacopo's eyes.

"No," Tycho said. "I didn't."

"You killed two when you should have killed one. And you didn't even kill the one you should have killed. You had a one in five chance of getting it right by luck. And even taking two chances you failed."

"You think it should have been the girl?"

Atilo's face went still.

"Do you? Because of what she saw?"

"Who told you of that?" Atilo's voice was dark and dangerous. Coming from a cold and distant place. And his own hands twitched towards his dagger before he brought his reactions under control.

"She doesn't even understand what she saw."

"You know this?"

"Yes," Tycho said. "I know this."

"And why did you kill the others instead?"

"Because they ordered the murder she saw. You said the Blade was justice in action. Where would be the justice in killing the innocent?"

The old man wondered if he was being mocked.

39

Looking up from her pillow, Lady Giulietta asked the question that had been troubling her for months. Certainly since Prince Leopold had moved her into a house on a small estate on the mainland. "Will you kill me when my baby's born?"

Prince Leopold wiped sweat from her brow with a vinegar-soaked rag and wrinkled his nose at the smell. "Why would I do that?"

"That's not an answer."

Taking her hand, Prince Leopold waited until she looked him in the eyes. "I won't," he said. "I can't believe you'd think I would."

"You hate Venetians. Remember?"

He looked apologetic.

And then she swore. "Shit. Shit, shit, shit . . ."

"*I'll get the midwife.*"

Face screwed in agony, her hands gripping her gut, Giulietta cursed as a second contraction hit. And then she drew breath, air rushing into her lungs as the muscles in her abdomen unlocked. It was an hour since Leopold had arrived. Five hours since this torture began.

"Answer my question first."

Watching him look around her room, an upper chamber in a near-ruined farmhouse near Ravenna, she wondered what Leopold saw.

A sweating prisoner with distended stomach and swollen and aching breasts, screaming in pain? A young woman terrified of what came next? A child who'd already caused him endless problems?

She should never have sent for him.

In dismissing the midwife and demanding they let Leo in, she'd doubled the rumours. The guards below already said he was the father of her child. This would simply confirm it for them.

"My love," said Leopold.

She felt tears fill her eyes, and was too exhausted to stop sadness spilling over and running down her cheeks. Instead, she turned away.

"What?" he said, turning her face back.

"You called me . . . You've never called me . . ."

As he stroked her face, she felt him scoop up a tear and trace it back to the corner of her eyelashes. He was smiling. "I never dared."

She looked at him. "You're scared of nothing."

"I'm scared of losing you."

"Why would that happen?"

"Because you love that boy you talk about."

"*Leopold!*"

"It's true," he said. She was still crying when her maid, his doctor and the midwife returned.

In the hours that followed, the pain became so fierce that Giulietta barely stopped screaming. She had never imagined, had never dared imagine, such pain existed outside a torture chamber. Each contraction was fiercer than the one before. But the baby inside her showed no sign of being born. When she begged for the shutters to be opened to cool her room they were for a while. Until the doctor ordered them shut again. Giulietta thought stuffiness was part of her treatment. Then she realised the shutters were kept closed to keep in her cries.

She pushed until she could push no more.

As the afternoon wore on the encouragements of the midwife and the platitudes of the doctor faltered and finally faded. When Leo's doctor went to the door, shouted for Giulietta's maid, and told her to find the master and tell him to come at once, Giulietta realised he thought she could no longer hear them. And inside the tight red swirl of her pain there were times when she couldn't. Although this wasn't one of them. And then it was, and she was lost in memories.

Leopold's words hurt.

His sadness that she had loved someone before him, and better. She wanted to say . . . If she lived through this, she would say, it was untrue. And it was, she told herself, even as she knew it wasn't. The fierce-faced boy in the basilica had set his hooks in her flesh with a single touch and his was the scowl she now saw.

Silver-grey hair. Amber-flecked eyes that looked right through her. Shivering, Lady Giulietta felt a little warmth leave her body.

"She's going," the midwife said.

"Why hasn't someone found the prince yet!"

"He's outside, sir."

"Gods, woman. Ask him to come in."

"I was riding," Prince Leopold said, shutting the door behind him. "I couldn't stand . . ." His voice was a whisper that Giulietta heard from miles away. The rustle of wind through the grass. She was beyond pain now. Floating in a red warmth far removed from her body.

"You have a choice," the doctor said.

"What choice?" Leopold said.

"I can try to save my lady but you will lose her child for certain. Or I can save her child, and you will lose her. If it's a boy, God willing he will live. My lady's ability to live is less certain . . ." To Giulietta, it sounded as if the doctor had already made his own choice.

"Save both," Prince Leopold said.

"Your highness. That's not possible."

"You don't have the skill?"

"No, sir. No one could . . ."

"Then find someone who can," Leopold said, not letting the man finish his protest. "*And do it now.* I will not accept the death of either." His voice held an anger that threatened bloodshed if he was disobeyed. Even Giulietta, cocooned in her red warmth, and wondering if it wouldn't simply be best to let sleep take her, flinched at his fury.

"Highness," the doctor said, his voice tight from the fear of being asked to do the impossible. "I beg you to . . ."

"There's a man in the next town," the midwife interrupted. "He cut a baby from a slave, and a pup from a hunting dog. All lived."

"He's a heathen." The doctor sounded outraged.

"Yes," she said. "A heathen who dislikes losing his slaves."

"The man's a Jew?" Prince Leopold asked.

"Calls himself a Saracen, my lord." The midwife sound scared to be addressing the prince directly.

"Send for him."

"Your highness, consider . . ."

"You know who this is?" Prince Leopold asked the doctor.

"No, my lord. They said she was . . ."

"My woman?"

The doctor nodded.

"God willing she'll be my wife. If she dies I will have you hanged."

The Saracen was sent for.

Having cleared the little room of people, he opened the shutters and announced that if the screams of a birthing woman were bad luck then people should go elsewhere. Since it was the nature of women in childbirth to scream. Even Christians should be able to accept that.

Water was brought.

Cold water for drinking. Warm water for washing. And boiling water for cleaning his implements. And having sharpened his knives, and knelt at Lady Giulietta's side and whispered his apologies, the doctor removed her sweat-soaked sheet and washed between her legs before feeling for the child.

"As I thought," he said. "The baby has turned."

Since she hovered on the edge of the red darkness, and the room was empty apart from the two of them, he had to be talking to himself.

"It cannot be turned back. So it is best if you sleep. Either you will wake or you will not. Mostly that is in God's hands. And a little bit in mine."

Opening a wooden box, he found black paste wrapped in oiled silk, and unstoppered a small bottle of spirits, the only spirits he ever let himself touch. Mixing the paste with the spirits he dribbled the mixture between Lady Giulietta's lips and waited for her to settle. Once she had, he began to cut open her abdomen.

The newborn boy issued his first cry ten minutes later.

Although it was a day and a half before Lady Giulietta was awake enough to realise she lived and her child already suckled for milk, his face against the ring she kept on a chain between her breasts. By then, Prince Leopold had named the boy Leo, claiming him as a son.

PART 2

"May the winds blow till they have waken'd death!"

Othello, William Shakespeare

40

Easter 1408

"If an angel can fall a demon can rise . . ."

Nothing in the books Desdaio used to teach Tycho to read suggested this was true. But she said it the evening he told her about the Skaelingar attack, Bjornvin burning and Withered Arm ordering him to make a fire circle. An evening when the waxing moon above Venice was near enough full to fire his hunger.

He'd told her about elk horns over the great doors. About red-painted naked Skaelingar flinging themselves on to sharpened palisades so that those behind could climb over. Red bodies and red weapons and a red world. Everything the Skaelingar owned was painted with ochre and oil, even their canoes.

Desdaio had been seated on a bench in the piano nobile, talking about the winter just gone, about the snows that had fallen, the fires that had warmed them. That was how their conversation started.

With snow and fire.

Iacopo was with Atilo, Amelia in bed, monthlies so fierce Desdaio fed her poppy seeds in wine. The cook was making pies for a party, and her scowl said no interruptions.

Tycho was there because Desdaio had summoned him.

She was lonely and cold and scared, her happiness draining day by day as her husband-to-be spent ever more time with his duchess. She didn't say this. Desdaio didn't need to. Tycho could feel her sadness. She was wondering if those who shunned her were right. She'd made a mistake.

Her grief was revealed in talk of flowers, and memories of summer barley on the mainland, the counterpoint to her forced brightness. A shadow to the wideness of her smile. "Aren't you cold?" she asked suddenly.

Tycho shook his head.

Somehow this led to him talking about Bjornvin and the snows he remembered from childhood.

"Bjornvin?" said Desdaio, tasting the name.

Then she shuffled up on her bench and patted the cushion beside her. Frowning when Tycho didn't immediately abandon his place to join her. He could smell oil in her hair, the orange-blossom scent she often wore, and the gunpowder she was using for toothache. And beneath these a smell that hooked him brutally. So that his jaws throbbed, his throat dried and he couldn't keep his eyes from her when she adjusted her shawl, her breasts spilling against her gown's low front.

"Tell me about Afrior," she demanded.

So he did. Talking fast and desperately. Aware of the tightness behind his eyes and a growing ache in his groin he hunched to hide. He talked of the Skaelingar, of Bjornvin, Lord Eric and Withered Arm. Of the day he took Afrior swimming. He told Desdaio everything he remembered. And in telling her he came face to face with the shame and regret he'd spent so long denying. From which he'd been running so unsuccessfully for what seemed like so long . . .

Afrior of the golden hair, sweet smile and soft curves was Bjornvin's most beautiful girl. She was also a slave and the youngest of

Withered Arm's children. Peering from under her long eyelashes, she'd smiled, her modesty at war with her lips.

To Tycho, her blue eyes held the sky and her smile his heart.

"See," he said. "I came after all."

"I thought . . ." She stopped, not wanting to finish.

People said Afrior was simple. That she had to be to befriend him.

If Lord Eric discovered them together, he'd beat them. Tycho was meant to be guarding goats against the wolves, Afrior grinding rye. But it was nothing to what their mother would do. Withered Arm might be old, but she was vicious with it.

"Come here," Tycho said, grounding his spear.

She stepped away. "We're . . ."

"No," he said. "*We're not.*"

No brother could want his sister the way he wanted her.

Wanting Afrior was more important to Tycho than hunting. More important than his mother's lack of love. More important than Lord Eric's hatred. And Tycho and Afrior *did* look different. Her impossibly blue eyes against his own's amber-flecked darkness. Her hair sun-yellow. His wolf-silver, as if he'd been born old. He had sharp cheeks and not a sliver of fat. She was all curves.

For a second Afrior fought him, and then her mouth opened and his tongue touched hers. She was shaking when he pulled back.

"This is wrong."

"It's not," he said.

But her gaze was firm. "We can't. You know that." Lord Eric would expect her untouched and know if her maidenhead was gone.

Afrior was thirteen. Maybe fourteen.

Her mother said thirteen, but Lord Eric and his warriors had been away fighting red-painted Skaelingar when she was born. Whispers said she lied to allow her daughter a few months' extra happiness. Given Lord Eric's temperament, it was a miracle he hadn't taken Afrior already.

"He'd know," Afrior said.

Tycho had tried not to let glee show in his eyes. Until that moment she'd never admitted she wanted to. *He'd know* was close to admitting she might if not for that.

"Let's swim."

Her scowl said she suspected a trick. All the same, she followed him through the speckled alder and showy mountain ash, using a path the deer cut back when they still came this way. The herd was gone these days, eaten or too sensible to venture closer. Finding a dip in the river bank hidden by wild roses, he told Afrior to turn her back and stripped off his rags. The day was hot, the sun bright on his skin and the air rich with scents of roses and grass, life's freshness and tumbling water.

"And you," he said, not giving her time to argue.

He went into the water fast, fighting the shock that diving into icy currents tightened around his ribs. And Afrior was crouched naked in the shallows when he turned. Lord Eric, his warriors and body slaves were raiding a Skaelingar village. That was what they called it, *raiding*. Mostly it meant killing women while the savages were away fighting each other.

No women meant no babies, no babies meant fewer warriors in years to come. It was more effective to kill those who would deliver the unborn than fight those already living. "Come here," Tycho said.

"You think I'd trust you?"

There was humour in her voice, and enough truth to make him glance away. So he missed her edging closer.

"You really believe we're not kin?"

Feeling full breasts brush his chest like the touch of tiny fish, he nodded. "I'm sure," he said, banishing doubt from his voice. "We don't even look alike."

Kissing her deeply, he registered the moment she felt him go hard. The sudden wariness that had her stepping back. So he used the gap to cup one breast, finding her nipple already erect from the coldness of the river.

She let his hand wander until . . .

"No," she said, grabbing his wrist.

They wrestled, until she found his thumb and twisted.

He ignored the pain for as long as he could, then stopped fighting and dipped his head to recognise her victory. She was staring at him. "I thought you were going to let me break it."

"So did I," he said.

Afrior's face softened. Taking his hand, she kissed his thumb, which ached with a dull pain that would last for days. And, having kissed it, she replaced his fingers between her legs. Tycho knew then he would never understand women.

Her insides were more mysterious than he expected. Afrior moaned, her mouth nuzzling as her sounds got louder. When she froze, mid-moan, he thought he'd been too rough. But her eyes watched the bank behind him.

"Stop," she said.

Turning, he felt piss leave his body before his mind caught up with what he saw. A row of five Skaelingar warriors, bright red in their mixture of oil and ochre. They were naked, flint knives hanging on sinews from their shoulders. Some had sycamore bows already drawn. A sixth man stood between them. A half-Skaelingar slave who'd escaped Bjornvin the year before.

"How interesting," he said.

The Skaelingar chief snapped out a question, and the ex-slave's smirk closed down. His reply was humble. Whatever he said, it wasn't that this was a brother and sister. That would have earned more than the growl he got in return.

"You're to come here."

Afrior looked doubtful, but then she was a girl and naked. Looking at her, one man muttered and a second laughed. Both silenced by a snarl from their chief. At his command, they grabbed Afrior the moment she climbed from the water.

Tycho attacked on instinct.

And fell to a blow to his head. Having kicked the air from his lungs, and what was left of the piss from his bladder, the chief stopped when Tycho shat himself. It wasn't a serious beating. More a warning not to be stupid.

Then another Skaelingar picked him up and turned him to face Afrior, who was struggling with her own captors. When one dug his thumb into her elbow, she started to cry instead.

"I am to translate," the half-Skaelingar said. "Have you seen what we do to your women? Yes, or no?"

Tycho hadn't. But he'd heard it whispered.

"We take these," the translator said.

Their chief gripped Afrior's breasts, lifting slightly.

"Cutting like this."

The chief's hand traced a circle, sloping in so that Tycho understood they cored a pit to take what was behind as well. Afrior might have been an animal for all the attention the man paid her.

"And we take this."

She screamed when the chief dropped his hand. Tycho didn't think he hurt her; it was the shock of having him grip her there.

"And, finally, we slit from here to here." The chief traced from blonde body fur to the arch of Afrior's ribs. "And pull out what we find." He stepped back, offended, as she soiled herself.

"You understand?"

Tycho nodded dumbly.

"There is another choice," the chief said, his words translated through the half-Skaelingar. "Would you like to know it?"

"Yes," he said. "I would."

Having glared, to make sure Tycho paid attention, the chief unslung his flint knife, grabbed Afrior between her legs and cut. She jerked in her captor's hands. And then the chief scattered pale hair at her feet.

"This is all that will happen."

Tycho looked in disbelief at the man translating, then at the chief whose words these were. He wondered if the ex-slave translated right.

"No harm will come if you do what we ask." And then the Skaelingar told him what was wanted. Since it seemed the two Viking slaves should not be out together, their chief would not find it strange if one returned alone. Sometime tonight Tycho would unlock Bjornvin's gate. If it was not unlocked, his lover's mutilated body would be left at the gates at dawn. If it was, both would have safe passage through Skaelingar territory to the lands beyond.

"The next tribe will kill us."

"What you should consider," the chief said, "is that we will not."

Tycho could have let Afrior die. With her would have died the risk of anyone finding out what had happened. He could have return to his life as Lord Eric's wolf dog, continued to ignore the hard-faced bitch he called mother.

He was a slave. Lord Eric said *do this*, he did it.

Running faster than the others, jumping higher, hunting swiftly and silently didn't make him valuable. It simply made him hated. Most days, he got up at daybreak, obeyed orders till nightfall, then slept. Saving Afrior meant betraying everyone else. How could that be right?

He could tell Lord Eric what had happened.

The beating would be terrible but he'd survived others. But Afrior would die and Tycho wanted her. So he killed the gate guard instead. Hitting the man clumsily, clubbing him from behind. When the guard was dead, Tycho lifted the bar to Bjornvin's gate.

The first thing the Skaelingar chief did on entering Bjornvin was yank back the head of the naked, bound and gagged Viking girl in front of him, spit into her face and rip his blade across her throat.

Afrior bled out before she hit the dirt.

Tycho's attack would have made him a hero had any lived to sing of it. Grabbing the fallen gate guard's sword, he flung himself at the chief and plunged the blade in the man's guts, twisting in his fury.

Then Lord Eric was there, broad-shouldered, more grey than red in his beard. A bloody battle-axe in hand. He believed his slave was guarding Bjornvin's gate. In three blows Lord Eric killed another three Skaelingar. Then he turned, clapped Tycho on the shoulder. "Wake everyone," he ordered.

Tycho would have done.

But his mother grabbed him before he reached the great hall. The first thing she told him was that she wasn't his mother. The next, that he was neither Viking nor Skaelingar, but *Fallen*. She said this through gritted teeth, hatred in her face. "Where's my daughter?"

"Dead. The Skaelingar killed her."

Withered Arm slapped him. "*You* killed her. You think I didn't know?"

Her eyes were hard, her voice cold as winter. Tycho had no doubt she wanted him dead. Would like to kill him herself. Instead, with battle raging, she hurried him to her quarters, and told him to spread the straw from her mattress in a wide circle.

"Do it now," she ordered.

Outside the slaughter continued.

Individually, Lord Eric's warriors were better armed. Their swords, chain mail and the helmets brought from Greenland gave them an advantage. But they were outnumbered. The Skaelingar had been closing on the village for years. When Withered Arm returned it was with a flaming brand.

"My mistress told me how to do this before she died. Maybe she knew . . ." Withered Arm stopped, face bitter. "Oh, she knew all right. She died in birth so you could live. And I knew it for a bad bargain then. Now we die so you . . . Who knows what? Who will be left to even care?"

Pushing him into the middle of the circle, Withered Arm set

fire to the straw, stepping back as flames crackled around him. And then he felt ice instead of flames, and a rushing like wings, and a vicious wind as if he was falling from a great height. The last thing he saw was the hatred in her face.

"That's true?" Desdaio asked. She was blushing furiously. At the things he'd said about Afrior and the river, Tycho realised.

"It's what I remember."

"Does Atilo know?"

"No, my lady. He never asked."

"You stepped into the flames of where you came from. To find yourself in my world?"

Tycho nodded.

Crossing herself, Desdaio scrambled to her feet and returned staggering under the weight of a leather-bound Bible. "This was my mother's," she said. "Take it from me. Use both hands."

He did as she demanded. Watching her chew her lips.

"What did you think would happen?"

"I thought you'd go up in flames."

"Why would I . . . ?"

"If you were a demon you would catch fire. I thought . . ." She looked embarrassed. "It sounds as if you came from hell."

"I thought *this* was hell," Tycho told her truthfully. "When I first arrived. All these people crowded on to misty little islands. And the water here . . . In Bjornvin I'd swim when I could and it always made me happy. Here, simply crossing the canals sickens me. The air stinks of smoke and shit."

"But you were starving. You said so. We have food here."

"Some people have food here. And why shouldn't there be food in hell for some. Do you think Satan lives in squalor?"

They sat in silence on a bench after that. Desdaio fed him wine and cake, which he barely drank and didn't touch respectively. And, finally, she asked him where he went at night, on the occasions he accompanied my lord Atilo.

"Council meetings," Tycho lied.

Dog days, full moons, his training kills. Tall scratches for men, shorter ones for women. A single dot for an infant, all that stood between Venice and an estate on the mainland, a dying count's new grandson. The truth was scratched on his cellar wall. All of it, apart from Atilo's visits to Duchess Alexa.

There were too many of those.

Nine deaths in total. Fewer than he expected. Lord Eric had killed more than that in a single battle. A dozen Skaelingar, their guts steaming and their eyes fresh for the crows. Almost all of Tycho's kills had been clean. Atilo was impressed at first, worried later. More worried still when Tycho's final kill in San Pietro di Castello proved so much bloodier than his previous eight.

41

During the year that Tycho trained Iacopo grew a beard. A soldier's beard to make him look older, fiercer. He used masks less these days. No longer needing to hide his youthful softness in the company of others.

A tumbler of wine sat in front of him. The last of this year's wages glinted on his chest. A steel breastplate in the Aragonese style. A scratch below its left armhole suggested its previous owner died in battle or was knifed in his sleep.

Iacopo wasn't superstitious, and that sign of ill luck was enough to bring the armourer's price down to something he could almost afford. Although it had taken a dagger borrowed from Atilo's collection to seal the deal. The Schiavoni claimed the scratch was simply where the breastplate fell and the piece was worth double Iacopo's final offer. But he spat on his hand and shook on it just the same.

"New?" someone asked.

Looking up, Iacopo saw Captain Roderigo. So he smiled modestly, and let the captain believe that if he wished. The last year had seen Venice split between Prince Alonzo and Duchess Alexa's factions. Almost by accident, Roderigo found himself on one side. And Atilo found himself on the other. Positions worsened after last week's incident with Tīmūr bin Taragay's messenger.

A minor prince from Tīmūr's wife's family, the Mongol refused to deliver his message to the Ten, talking only to the duchess and leaving immediately. No one knew what Tīmūr's message said. The duchess simply burnt it after reading and refused to say. So now, Prince Alonzo found himself trapped between caution and fury. Never a good place for someone like him to be.

"Captain." Iacopo raised his glass. He saw no point in making unnecessary enemies. Life at Ca' il Mauros was complicated enough. Lord Atilo and his betrothed keeping separate quarters. Everyone knew they would marry. No one knew when. Some said not until Atilo left the duchess's bed. Others, that the Moor would be stupid to exchange vows if he had any chance of marrying Alexa instead.

And then there was the freak, with his strange spectacles, priest-coloured doublet and hateful silences. Tycho didn't talk to Iacopo, he didn't not talk to Iacopo. He barely noticed Iacopo's existence. Desdaio and Amelia, on the other hand . . .

Iacopo sucked his teeth.

"Problems?" Captain Roderigo asked.

"Such is life," Iacopo replied. Realising the captain was about to move on, he found his smile. "Let me buy you a drink, my lord."

"It must be my turn."

Iacopo looked surprised.

"After you won last year's race. We drank at the Griffin behind St Bartholomew, remember?"

"How could I forget, my lord. I'm simply surprised you remembered yourself." He'd overdone it. The captain was glancing round the tavern, not finding who he'd come to see, and framing reasons for refusing the offer. Iacopo could see it in his eyes. Although why a man like Captain Roderigo would bother to excuse himself to a servant like him . . .

Because that's what he was, Iacopo thought bitterly.

A servant, for all he owned a breastplate and greaves and a sword. His training was secret, the tasks he performed for his master equally so. No one knew the secrets he carried. No one was allowed to know. There were days he found this harder to bear than others. "An honour to buy you a drink," he said, forcing a smile. "An even bigger honour to leave you with a hangover."

Captain Roderigo laughed.

"Who were you looking for, my lord?"

"My sergeant. He's off duty but we have business tomorrow that needs discussing today."

Iacopo nodded sagely.

He had an idea what that business might be and had sense enough to say nothing. Today was Maundy Thursday, one reason the tavern was full. Obviously enough, tomorrow was Good Friday, when the devout flogged themselves through the streets, and the rest avoided sex and gambling, and a long list of other vices the new patriarch had recently read from the pulpits.

It was to be the day of Tycho's testing. Just as it had been the day of Iacopo's testing. And Amelia's, and all those who went before. All those who died nearly two years back in the slaughter at Cannaregio.

"Perhaps I will have a drink," Captain Roderigo said.

"This might even be the real thing," Iacopo said, wiping blood-like drops of wine from his beard. The tavern keeper claimed it was Barolo and it looked dark enough.

"I agree," Roderigo said.

Iacopo had never tasted Barolo in his life.

"So," Captain Roderigo said. "How are things with you?"

"Much the same. His lordship attends Council. Dotes on Lady Desdaio. Visits Duchess Alexa for advice."

The captain grinned.

Iacopo thought he might.

"And how is Lady Desdaio?" Even if Iacopo hadn't known the

captain for an ex-suitor, the careful nature of his question would have announced it.

"As sweet as ever."

Roderigo took a sip of wine. "It's none of my business, obviously. But what news of their marriage?"

"None I would know."

"No," Roderigo admitted. "I don't suppose you would." Holding his glass to the light, he examined the contents critically. "I'm not sure this is Barolo after all." But he emptied it quickly enough. And Iacopo was careful to demand Barolo when he bought the next jug.

"Yes, my lord."

Iacopo checked the tavern keeper wasn't mocking him, but the man seemed serious enough. "Open a tab," Atilo's servant ordered. "I'll send my man to settle tomorrow."

"That's Good Friday, my lord."

"Maybe so. You'll still want paying, won't you?"

The tavern keeper nodded and filled a jug to the brim from a barrel apart from the others. Even if it wasn't Barolo, it was obviously special enough for him not to want jugs given away by accident.

"What is it really?" Iacopo demanded.

The tavern keeper glanced round. "It really is Barolo," he whispered. "Just not a very good one."

Iacopo laughed loud enough to make the hazard players look over. He met their gaze and they saw a stranger with a sharp black beard, wearing a stylish breastplate, taking a jug of the best wine. A couple of them nodded, one even smiled.

"Friends of yours?" Roderigo asked.

"Not really," Iacopo answered, leaving it understood he knew them, just not very well. His embroidering was interrupted by the tavern keeper, who carried a bowl of stewed mutton, which he ladled in heaped spoonfuls on to thick slices of stale bread. The captain ate his mutton and left the bread. So Iacopo did the same.

"I should go," Roderigo said. "Temujin's probably drunk by now." He stood unsteadily, appeared on the edge of saying something about his own state and shrugged. "Bloody man," he muttered. "Always causing trouble."

Iacopo hoped he was talking about the sergeant.

"About Desdaio . . ." Roderigo said a few minutes later.

"My lord?"

"Is she happy?"

"Oh yes, she's . . ." Iacopo stopped. "Well, as happy as can be expected. It must be hard to be disowned. And she . . . My lord, may I speak plainly?"

"Feel free."

Roderigo waited.

"What," he asked finally, "did you have to say?"

Iacopo sucked his teeth. "Maybe she's not that happy," he said. "She expected to be wed by now. But my lord Atilo is always busy. And it must be a lonely life for a healthy young woman . . ."

"You have her confidence?"

"No, my lord. She confides in Amelia, her maid. And . . ." Iacopo hesitated again. "Atilo has a slave."

"The blind boy?"

"He's not blind, my lord. But light does hurt his eyes. So he wears strange spectacles and avoids daylight whenever he can."

"So I gather," Roderigo said shortly.

"My lord, if I've offended you . . ."

"I've had dealings with the boy."

Iacopo caught himself and kept drinking. Something in the captain's voice was too casual. If Iacopo hadn't known better, he'd say Captain Roderigo feared Tycho. "My master intends to release him."

"So soon?"

"Soon, my lord?"

"I heard Atilo kept his slaves and bondsmen for three to five years before releasing them. To release them at all is ridiculous. No offence, of course. But to get only one year's work." Captain Roderigo shrugged. "How long before he freed you?"

"I was not a slave or bondsman."

"Really? I thought . . ."

"I was an orphan, true enough. My father died on the galleys."

Iacopo had no proof of this, since his father was unknown. But Venice held a special place for freemen who died in battle protecting the city's trade routes or opening other avenues of trade. And Roderigo's approving nod said this mythical father counted in his favour.

"Why is Atilo freeing this one so soon?"

"He learns fast," Iacopo said flatly. "Table manners. Italian. All that Desdaio teaches him. He's even starting to learn to write."

"You don't like him." Captain Roderigo said this as a fact.

"I don't trust him, my lord. And Desdaio watches him," he said carefully. "I used to think she was afraid of him. Now I'm not sure. They spend a lot of time together."

"Desdaio and the slave?"

"Lady Desdaio, the slave, sometimes Amelia," said Iacopo, forcing a worried smile. "Hours alone in the piano nobile while Atilo is away. And the slave accompanies them on evening walks. Sometimes they go for hours. I'm sure nothing happens . . ."

"He's a slave."

"Indeed, my lord."

Captain Roderigo looked disgusted.

42

"Iacopo?" asked Tycho, hearing his door begin to open.

Desdaio peered into the cellar. "Are you expecting Iacopo? she asked, sounding surprised.

"He was moving about earlier."

Slipping inside, she left the door open and moonlight flooded in from above. The moon was full tonight, the sky bright with stars.

"My lady, shut the door."

"We can't all see in the dark."

More moonlight filled the room as Desdaio obstinately opened it a little wider. Turning, she found Tycho facing the wall. "Leave," he said. "Or close it."

"Tycho . . ."

"Do it now."

She shut the door with a bang.

"Go to that corner. Don't come any closer . . ."

Kicking a wooden wedge under the door, Tycho found a candle, kindling and flints. The kindling was rag, the flints dropped by a *cittadino* too spoilt to retrieve them. "Candles cost," said Desdaio, with the fervour of a rich woman who believes she is now poor.

"Moonlight hurts me," Tycho said.

"That's the sun."

"A different kind of pain."

Desdaio looked at him doubtfully. Moving closer, she seemed surprised he kept the candle between them. "I have things to tell you. And I want to sit."

"On my mattress?"

"Do you see a chair?"

She smelt of roses and sweet wine, an undertaste of sweat, and a musk Tycho loved, loathed and found addictive. Every woman in the city between fifteen and thirty smelt the same.

"Are you all right?"

"No," he said harshly. "I'm not."

Desdaio was so shocked she stepped back. And for that Tycho was grateful. Her body still called to him, the pulse in her throat the beat of a drum summoning him to disaster. The skin of her neck glowed with youth and candlelight.

"Leave," he told her. "Just go."

"I thought you were my friend," she said. "And then you talk to me like this." Her eyes were huge with unspilt tears. "You can't. It isn't allowed."

"Because I'm a slave?"

"It's rude."

"Some days," he said, "I hate you."

She sobbed. A single gulp in the back of her throat. "I thought if I was kind it might help. They say all slaves want to kill their owners. You're meant to be different. You have a good heart," Desdaio said fiercely. "Inside all your hate."

Tycho's smile made her shiver.

"You're wrong, my lady. I doubt I have a—"

The knock interrupting his boast was abrupt and Desdaio's eyes widened. Being found here was bad enough. To be found in her nightdress, a woollen shawl thrown over her shoulders and her feet bare . . .

"Maybe it's Amelia. I'll explain."

"It's Atilo," said Tycho, as the knock repeated.

It came again, angrily. Atilo now knew the door was jammed, from trying its handle when his second knock wasn't answered.

"How do you know?"

"His footsteps."

Pulling aside his mattress, Tycho revealed a hole in the floor. An early and abandoned attempt to tunnel out. When Desdaio hesitated, Tycho lifted her — one hand under her knees, the other round her ribs — and dropped her in, before dragging his mattress back into place. From the look on her face she'd felt his hand come to rest under her breast too.

"*Open this door.*"

"My lord, if you could stop pushing."

The pressure ceased and Tycho pulled away the wedge, moving just fast enough to avoid having his fingers crushed by Atilo's furious entry. The old man glanced at the offcut in Tycho's hands, then glared round the cellar, his eyes alighting on the candle. "Why do you need that?"

"My night sight's not perfect," Tycho lied.

"Where is she?" he demanded.

"Who, my lord?"

"Amelia."

"Asleep in her bed, I imagine."

The old man scowled. "She was meant to come to me tonight." He sucked his teeth, deciding he'd said too much. "Iacopo is also missing. If they're up to mischief together . . ."

"He returned a little earlier."

"How do you know?"

"I heard him, my lord. His new breastplate scraped the wall above and he swore loud enough for me to hear."

"Drunk, I imagine." Dark eyes above a sharp beard watched Tycho. "You don't miss much, do you?"

"I try not to, my lord."

"And your locked door?"

"You know there are no bolts inside. But I found this above." Holding up his offcut, Tycho said, "It keeps my door secure. You say we should secure our entries and exits. I'm simply obeying orders."

The old man snorted. "Get some sleep. Wake early, rested and ready, with your wits sharp. Much turns on tomorrow. Don't let me down."

"My lord?"

"Pray to your gods for success."

There are no gods, Tycho almost said. *Not for the likes of you and me.* "I will, my lord. Goodnight."

Kicking his door jamb back into place, Tycho dragged the mattress aside and hauled Desdaio from the hole beneath. She shook him off when he tried to brush earth from her gown. "That's what I came to tell you. Atilo has a special job for you tomorrow. And I should have known . . ."

She hiccuped.

"Known what?"

"Amelia goes to his bed. I thought . . ."

That he confined himself to the duchess? That he kept his whoring for brothels? She couldn't really believe that a man as powerful as Atilo il Mauros slept alone under his own roof? Even Desdaio wasn't that naive.

Holding her tight as she cried, Tycho folded her in his arms, feeling her breasts press against him and her nipples harden. Her eyes went wide when he kissed her and for a second she responded. Then he was blocking a slap.

"You kissed me back."

"I did not."

"My lady . . ."

"Enough." Her voice was furious. "We won't talk of this again."

43

"This had better be good . . ."

Atilo stood in his chamber door in a long-sleeved woollen robe, with scarlet slippers that curled at the toe. Even though Iacopo had given his name when knocking, the old man had a stiletto in one hand and a lamp in the other.

Oil thrown at an attacker was everyman's mage fire. Ten years earlier a patrician died after a lamp was hurled by a servant whose daughter he'd raped, with the girl tossing a flaming torch after. Duke Marco let the two hang. He forbade the slitting or castrating, gutting and burning tradition demanded. A popular decision with everyone except the noble's wife. And she was Genoese anyway.

"Well?" he demanded.

"May I enter, my lord?"

Atilo stepped aside grudgingly.

"Forgive my intrusion . . . You intend to test Tycho tomorrow?"

The old man's face hardened and he sat on a wooden stool without inviting Iacopo to do the same. His eyes fixed on Iacopo's face and held his gaze until the young man looked away. "Jealousy gets you killed."

"I'm not jealous, my lord." The young man shrugged. "Although I envy the speed with which he learns. And his night sight is useful. Guard dogs ignore him also. As if he wrapped himself in magic."

"It's not magic," said Atilo. "He has no smell."

Iacopo's mouth fell open.

"You should have worked that out. Whatever sickness makes him day-blind denies him a scent. That's why hounds never find his tracks. They've nothing to follow . . ."

A season's lessons in how to double back, lay false scents and hide in water had been abandoned after a week. Tycho couldn't hide in water even if he wanted to. And, since the dogs couldn't find his scent in the first place, the rest of the lessons were irrelevant.

"No smell," Iacopo said. "That must be useful."

Atilo looked on him more kindly. "You're drunk. Get some sleep and you'll feel better. And make friends with him . . ." Atilo held up his hand, admitting the obvious. "Not easy for you, I know. But make the effort. Because he will join us if he passes tomorrow's test."

"You're freeing him?"

"Separate the two," Atilo said. "Training takes five years. He's a slave. I free slaves when they complete training. If he succeeds tomorrow I free him. One follows the other."

"No one can train in a year."

"Are you saying I'm wrong? That I don't know when an apprentice is ready to become a journeyman?" There was ice in the old man's voice.

"No. Certainly not, my lord."

"What are you saying?"

"He was trained already . . ." Iacopo considered his suggestion, obviously liked it. "He must have been. He came here to kill someone. To betray us. He could be working for the emperor."

"Which one?"

"Either," Iacopo said, warming to his theme. "German or Byzantine, it doesn't matter. They both want Venice. How better to . . ."

"Iacopo!" Atilo's tone was sharp.

"Sir?"

"Why don't I let you street-brawl? Why aren't you allowed to compete in sword competitions? Because you'd pick up bad habits. If Tycho had trained do you think I wouldn't know? Every sword school boasts of a move—elegant or deadly—that only they teach. All lies, of course. Sword schools have styles. So do assassins. I'd *know* if Tycho had been trained. He has amazing reflexes and reactions. But he was untaught when I first met him . . ."

And there things might have remained if Atilo hadn't stood, patted Iacopo on the shoulder and said, "He's not here to betray us, my boy."

"Not me certainly," Iacopo agreed, turning for the door.

Fingers like claws locked him into place. He tried to twist free but he might as well have fought a gaff through his flesh. The old man's fingers were immoveable. The utter stillness Atilo exhibited before a kill was in place.

"Explain yourself."

"My lord . . ."

"Forget politeness."

That in itself was warning. Atilo believed in the art of manners, because manners opened more doors than a crowbar. Just as a smile could kill more easily than frontal attack. Although it might hurt less to begin with and take the victim longer to die. Atilo was smiling.

That was the second warning.

I should have stayed silent, thought Iacopo, the truest thought he'd had all day. *I should have stayed silent. I should have left when I could. Then I could have dealt with this in my own way.*

"My lord, I'm sorry. But I saw Lady Desdaio leave Tycho's cellar. She was dressed . . ." Iacopo bowed his head. "In nightclothes. A gown covered by a shawl. Her hair was down, my lord." As an unmarried woman, Desdaio was allowed her hair down. She'd taken to pinning it up, however, the morning she joined Atilo's household. None of his staff had seen her since with her hair untied.

"Really? When did you see this?"

"Just now, my lord. A few moments ago."

"You swear this?"

Iacopo gulped. "Yes, my lord."

Atilo moved so fast that no one, no matter how good, could have blocked him.

One second his stiletto was on a table beside him, the next its blade had slithered up Iacopo's nostril and a single drop of blood ran down its edge.

Iacopo could feel the knife *behind* his face. To move was to slice the cavities of his face open. If Atilo pushed further Iacopo was dead. It would take little pressure to ease a blade that thin into his brain.

"Then you're foresworn. A moment ago I was *in* Tycho's room and he was alone. If you'd said Amelia, an hour ago." When Atilo shrugged the trickle of blood from Iacopo's nose grew thicker. "I'd have had Tycho whipped. But that wasn't enough. You want me to sell him. And so you're prepared to *blacken* . . ."

Iacopo thought the old man would kill him.

"Take it back," Atilo snapped. "Withdraw your accusation. Admit you are foresworn and tried to blacken her name."

"I would never . . ."

"You just did," Atilo said coldly.

"My lord, I'm sorry. I must have misunderstood what I saw."

The blade edged higher. He was standing on tiptoe, Iacopo realised. Drunk, with a stiletto nestling in one nostril. As if standing on tiptoe could keep the blade from entering his skull.

"I lied," he said hastily. "I'm sorry."

Atilo withdrew his stiletto. The next moment saw him slash

it forward to open Iacopo's cheek. Scarring him for life. "Everytime you look in a glass, remember you risked a woman's good name to further your ambition."

Stumbling, Iacopo turned for the door.

"Iacopo . . ."

He turned back.

"You sew that yourself, understand? You don't wake Amelia. You do it yourself. And you will behave around Tycho."

A knock at her door woke Desdaio to shame and spring moonlight. A single knock, almost hesitant. Amelia was out of her truckle bed within seconds, pulling a shawl around her and looking sleepily for orders.

"I'll go," Desdaio said.

She approached slowly. Her anger bright and with it her shame. He'd told the truth, damn him. She, Desdaio Bribanzo, had melted in the arms of . . . a strange and beautiful slave admittedly. One who read her thoughts and seemed to know her mind and understand the nature of her unhappiness.

"My lady, would you prefer . . . ?"

"I said I'll go," Desdaio snapped. "*Who is it?*"

"Me," said a deep voice. "Atilo."

She opened her door slowly, knowing he'd never visited her chamber before. It was her demand that Amelia slept in a truckle at the end of her bed. A demand Desdaio made when she understood her wedding would not be immediate. A way of saying Atilo could not come to her bed without a marriage contract. Except he'd never even tried to come to her bed.

Amelia's late nights looked like the reason why.

"My lord?"

He looked like a man undecided what to say. One whose ideas and actions and words had fallen out of step with each other.

"Is there trouble?"

"That's it. I thought I heard someone on the stairs."

"Iacopo, perhaps?"

"No," said Atilo. "We've been talking."

"I heard nothing, my lord."

He was still apologising when Desdaio shut the door firmly.

Amelia had simply come in later than expected, Atilo decided, listening to bolts slide into place. Any suggestion Desdaio had been with Tycho was unworthy. Yet he was troubled by the anger in her eyes.

44

Tycho drank small beer for breakfast in a shuttered house in Cannaregio, in the hour before daylight. The last intoxicating drink he'd touch all day. Small beer was only intoxicating in the way a blunt knife was dangerous. You could do yourself damage if you tried hard enough. But everyone would think you a fool and it would take weeks to live down.

Cutting a small chunk of bread, he trimmed rind from a ewe's cheese before slicing himself a waxy sliver. It looked like wax, and smelt and tasted only marginally better. Hunger for food was not something he recognised any more.

A locally made candle burnt in front of him.

The buildings around here were greasy with smoke from tallow vats that boiled day and night, rendering fat for cheap candles. White candles, the expensive ones used in churches and the ducal palace, were made elsewhere. These were candles that cobblers used to do their work. Which burnt in brothels and taverns and the hovels of the almost poor.

Beer, cheese, bread, candle and flint . . .

All had been waiting in the upstairs room of a deserted leather boiler's shop north of the Grand Canal's upper entrance. A hundred paces from the church of Santa Lucia, patron saint of assassins and the blind. The table on which these sat was wooden and old. As were the floor, the shutters, the walls and the roof. All of them were old, and wooden. Except for two upstairs windows, which were both shuttered and lined with waxed paper. It was a while before Tycho realised how quickly the building would burn. Perhaps that was the point. A single flame to one of the waxed windows would reduce all this to ash.

His heart had sunk on entering. All this wood reminded him of Bjornvin.

Most buildings in Venice were brick or stone. Even huts with wooden frames or wattle and daub walls were plastered. This was bare wood, except for a chimney rising three floors to exit from a small *fumaiolo*, one of those conical flues common in this city. The chimney was brick. The fire in it had heated the shop's cauldron, the one used to boil and shape leather.

Over the fireplace a lion's face was flanked by bat's wings.

This said he'd come to the right place. If that wasn't enough, the weapons on the table told him anyway. A Florentine stiletto, thin enough to slide from armpit to heart, or enter the anus and destroy vital organs without leaving a mark. The sword Dr. Crow gave him, not seen since the day Tycho arrived at Ca' il Mauros.

Climbing hooks, which Tycho didn't bother to examine. He wouldn't be taking or needing those. Rope, which he also ignored. Focusing instead on the steel span, wooden stock and intricate trigger of a tiny hand-held crossbow.

Assembling it quickly, without mistake, he wished Atilo was there to see it. Time and again he'd fumbled slightly when watched by the man. Five silver-tipped arrows came with the bow and these made him shudder.

The silver would hurt if he touched it. Tycho knew that well enough. He also knew Atilo reserved this crossbow for *krieghund*. And most of those were meant to have been driven from the city. It made him wonder about that night's assignment.

The final gift was three throwing blades.

Lifting one, Tycho flicked his wrist and put the blade between the teeth of the lion mask across the room. Five other knives had found its mouth over the years. Several dozen had missed. He hoped this was a good omen, and forebore to throw again in case he risked his luck.

Tycho oiled the little bow, checked the edge of his sword, which was sharp enough to shave him, and carefully wrapped the silver arrows. The balance of the stiletto was faultless. Pivoting on his first finger at the point where the blade met the handle.

Having chosen his weapons for the evening, Tycho found the darkest corner of an already dark room and folded his cloak into a crude pillow, closing his eyes and imagining water flowing through him as Atilo had taught.

"Your face?"

"Attacked, my lady. Three robbers." Iacopo smiled modestly. "I managed to fight them off."

Desdaio looked at him. "I heard you were drunk."

"You heard?"

"I mean . . ." She blushed. "I heard you come in last night, and thought you were drunk. I didn't realise," she looked at the crude stitches on his cheek, "you'd been injured."

"It's a dangerous city, my lady. Particularly for those who wander where they shouldn't at night. No one remains lucky forever."

Nodding, Desdaio glanced at the cages making up the duke's zoo. The morning air was chill enough for her to see her breath, but warmed by the scent of caged animals. The smell reminded her of stables. Although it was obviously ranker. "You are clever. How did you get permission?"

Iacopo sketched a bow to acknowledge the compliment, and smiled for the first time that morning. "A friend's father."

The truth was he'd blackmailed the son of an official in the Office of the Duke's Animals, who couldn't afford to pay the sum

Iacopo won from him an hour earlier at breakfast. A game where Iacopo supplied the dice. That Desdaio Bribanzo was Iacopo's guest made the visit easier to arrange. And brought a warning. Don't let her near the tyger. Iacopo grinned when he learnt the reason why, almost hearing the final part of his revenge fall into place.

Three clerks from the zoo sat on a wall, smirking at the infamous heiress. Iacopo cursed them and himself. He should have insisted he, Desdaio and Amelia had the place to themselves. Preferably without Amelia, who was relieving herself after accompanying her mistress on the walk from Ca' il Mauros.

"Iacopo . . ." Amelia had just noticed his face. "What happened?

"Cutthroats. You know what this city is like."

"He fought them off," Desdaio said.

As Amelia tipped her head to one side the silver thimbles on her braids clattered. "Looks professional to me. Unlike the stitching."

"*Amelia* . . ."

"Not that I'd know, my lady."

"I was attacked," Iacopo said stiffly. His beloved beard was gone, with the lower end of the livid cut extending far below the shaving line to the edge of his jaw.

"And you fought them off?"

"Obviously," Desdaio said. "Since he's here. Now let's all look at the animals." She refused to think about bad things today. Sometimes she thought it was all Atilo could talk about. Politics, violence, old wars, and . . .

The duchess.

That was his other topic. Alexa's name slipped in and out of conversation like that of an old friend. Or an old lover, Desdaio thought bitterly. The rumours were impossible to miss, even for her. Old *friends* who hadn't talked to her in a year went out of their way to make sure she knew. And Amelia . . . Maybe Desdaio had misunderstood what Atilo meant. And maybe not.

"A tyger, you say?"

"Yes, my lady. To go with the camel bird."

"I thought Marco had a rhinoceros?"

"It died. They say it mourned the old duke's passing and refused to eat."

"Probably ill," Amelia said. "Ill and bored. It probably died of being ill and bored. If it didn't simply die of boredom."

"What's wrong with you today?" Desdaio's words were sharp.

"Look around you, my lady." She indicated the iron bars, the walls edging deep pits, the fishermen's mesh overhead that kept exotic birds from flight. "This place is a prison. It's loathsome," said Amelia, loudly enough to make Desdaio turn to see if anyone had heard. The only people who might were the clerks and they were too busy giggling.

"You can wait outside then."

"Thank you," Amelia said, although Desdaio meant this as punishment. Sneering at the clerks, Amelia nodded to a caged leopard as she passed. Its eyes followed her to the gate, and seemingly beyond.

"Really! I don't know what's got into her . . ."

"I'm glad we're alone," Iacopo said.

She blushed prettily. If he'd been Atilo he'd have taken her to bed a year ago. She was a rose, perfect in every way. But he'd have taken the bud before it had fully opened. Not waited 'til the bloom risked being blown. And that magnificent figure. There wasn't a woman in Venice half so fine. An opinion shared by the clerks, who keep staring. But it wouldn't last. Women's figures never did.

If she lived through childbirth, he could see her with half-Moorish brats, feeding and spanking and cajoling and spoiling. Employing a wet nurse and day nurse and then refusing to let them do the jobs they were paid to do. Iacopo had fantasised after the slaughter at Cannaregio of becoming the Blade. Maybe even becoming Atilo's adopted son. It would never happen. Desdaio would give him heirs. And if she didn't, the old man's favourite was now his white-haired freak.

"You're scowling, Iacopo."

"Thinking, my lady." He swept a low bow. "I'll try not to do it again."

Desdaio laughed. "Think away."

When he offered his elbow, Desdaio looked surprised, but threaded her arm through his all the same, and headed for the camel bird's cage. Passing an empty enclosure on the way.

"What lived here?"

"Duke Marco's unicorn, my lady. It was the last living example in existence. So I've heard said."

"Really?" said Desdaio, wide-eyed. "What happened?"

"Died of old age is one version."

"And the other?"

"Butchered and wind-dried on the new duke's orders. Marco wanted to know if unicorn tasted like horse. I'm sure that's a lie . . ."

So shocked was Desdaio, she let him wrap his arm round her for comfort, pulling away a few seconds later. As she did, his hand grazed her buttocks, which felt as plump as they looked. She flushed, and he said nothing.

Merely smiled.

The camel bird was huge and grey, with short body feathers and absurd little wings. Its feet were turkey-like but fifty times bigger. Its neck stretched so high its tiny head reared above them.

"It doesn't have a hump."

It did. Albeit a small one. But Iacopo had more sense than to point this out. "They live in the desert," he told her, having learnt this at breakfast that morning. "Hence the name. They can go for a month without water."

Desdaio was impressed.

"And the tyger's over here," said Iacopo, steering her to a brick hut where one wall was replaced by bars. A new ditch surrounded it. "Poor Marco," Desdaio said, as they were approaching.

Iacopo raised his eyebrows, languidly he hoped.

"I imagine that's to keep him away. He probably wants to feed the beast by hand."

"You've met the new duke?"

"Yes," said Desdaio, her voice neutral. "My father hoped . . ."

Of course he did. What Venetian father wouldn't want to marry his virgin heiress to a duke, insane or not? A small sacrifice, when the reward was birthing the next heir to the ducal throne. Access to the Millioni millions. Trade routes to the East. And Khan Tīmūr bin Taragay's protection to use them.

"You refused?"

He'd offended her. So much so, Desdaio stopped dead, twenty paces from the hut. Sweeping a low bow, Iacopo smiled his apologies. "Forgive me. I've upset you." Smiling hurt him, but he needed her favour.

"I'm a good daughter."

Really? Iacopo thought. Then why are you living with a Moor who isn't your husband? Why did your father disown you? And how come I have this . . . He touched his new scar, feeling its crude stitches. When all I did was tell the truth about seeing you leave Tycho's cellar?

"Let's see the tyger," he said brightly.

A scowling white face greeted them. The beast barely bothered to sneer as it turned tight circles, the straw beneath its feet marked by endless pacing. The stink was incredible for all that it was only spring, the sky was overcast, the sun on the far horizon and the air cold.

"I thought tygers had stripes."

"She's a snow tyger," Iacopo said. "The rarest type in the world. Even the Mamluk sultan doesn't have one."

Desdaio looked at the beast with new respect.

"Beautiful, isn't she? said Iacopo, as Desdaio edged closer. He stepped behind her, feeling her shift forward. Another tiny nudge put her nearer the bars.

"My god," Desdaio said. "She's magnificent."

Even away from her high mountains and the snows that gave her that colour, the tygress was impressive. Also unhappy and crowded. Turning, she lifted her tail, as Iacopo had been warned she might, and squirted rank-smelling urine across Desdaio's fur-edged cloak. A little hit Desdaio's hand.

"*My lady.*"

"Oh my God . . . Foul creature."

Desdaio was already wiping her fingers, tears of mortification filling her eyes. As she glanced back to check if the clerks had noticed it happen, Iacopo grinned.

"I want to go *now*."

"Of course, my lady. Let me take this." Unclipping her cloak, he folded it to hide stinking velvet and tucked it under her arm. "There's a trough by the gate where you can wash . . ."

The trough was stone. Used to water horses that brought food for the duke's animals from the Riva degli Schiavoni. Desdaio washed her hands so thoroughly in the freezing overspill that she made her fingers red.

As the late afternoon sky filled with clouds and the air prickled with unused lightning, Atilo retreated to his study with plans for the Rialto bridge. The old duke had wished to replace the existing wooden bridge with a stone one. His bridge was to have shops down both sides. Since Marco owned the bridge the rents would be his. More importantly, his new bridge would be defensible, with arrow slits, and floor gratings through which burning oil could be poured.

His plan called for ten thousand larch piles, cut by hand and hammered into the sand, clay and gravel to support the foundations at either end. The corpse of an entire forest would be compressed into a tiny area and covered with oak beams, on which rubble from Istrian stone would rest. Only then could the new bridge be built.

Three things worked against this.

Two solvable, one not. The current bridge was loved by all. This was solvable. The duke announced that San Domenico Contarini, one of Serenissima's greatest doges, came to him in a dream to say Venice deserved a stone bridge . . .

The changing of the date of the duke's marriage to the sea, from Epiphany to Easter, and the fact the dukedom should become hereditary, had both been announced to the Millioni in dreams, backed by saints. San Marco was always a good choice. Unfortunately, he'd approved the duke's previous plan.

But if San Domenico demanded a stone bridge, then the second problem could be solved. Houses both sides of the Canalasso would have to be pulled down for a hundred paces inland to allow those foundations to be built. There would be protests. It was hard to argue, however, with a saint.

The unsolvable problem was that Marco III joined San Domenico Contarini in Heaven before the old bridge could be ripped down and the new one begun. So the wooden bridge remained while the Ten argued about the cost of replacing it.

"Come," he said, hearing a knock at his door.

Iacopo opened it and waited until Atilo gestured him coldly inside. Iacopo's plan, Atilo decided sourly, was obviously to bow and apologise enough to irritate Atilo into forgiving him.

"What do you want?"

"I thought . . . perhaps . . ." Iacopo took a deep breath. "Perhaps I could take tonight's orders to Tycho? Then I could wish him luck." The young man's usual bravado was gone in the face of last night's tongue-lashing. His cheek was livid, his face raw from where his beloved beard had been hacked away.

"I've given the job to Tomas."

A quiet and unassuming man, quite unfit to lead, Tomas had trained with Atilo before Iacopo. He baked cakes, these days, in Campo dei Carmini, his bakery famous for pastries in the French style. His other skill, poisoning people, went unremarked upon and unadvertised. On the night of the *krieghund* he'd been in

Paris introducing a Valois prince to God with a succession of tartlets that, if eaten alone, had no effect whatever.

Atilo's troops might have been reduced to a shell, but Tomas's work in Paris had saved their reputation. He did more than kill a Valois. He gave Marco's enemies something to fear. None of them yet understood how weak this city was. The average training for a member of the Assassini was five years. No empire could afford to employ so few blades. And those still living, those away that night, were ragged from moving city to city enforcing the Ten's silent will.

Looking up, Atilo realised Iacopo still waited for an answer.

"Go," he said. "Make your peace. Never bring Lady Desdaio's name into your disputes again."

Spinning, knife in hand, Tycho found Iacopo behind him.

"Don't," Iacopo said.

Tempting, Tycho couldn't deny that. His rival framed in the open window of a room two floors up in a parish the Night Watch avoided. Who would know? Well, Atilo for a start. If his servant was found skewered in the dirt outside a house the Assassini owned.

"I could claim it was an accident."

Tycho didn't realise he'd said it aloud until Iacopo's eyes widened. And the man glanced down and behind him, judging the drop to a muddy alley below.

"I have your orders."

"Tomas was meant to bring those."

"Atilo asked me. He wants us friends." Iacopo's scarred face and twisted smile said he knew it wasn't that simple. But their master's name was enough. Tycho gestured him into the room.

"What have they told you?" Iacopo asked.

"Nothing." Surely that was the point? Orders were given and obeyed without notice. No one knew when an order would be passed or by whom. He was to wait in this room until told otherwise. Tycho guessed Iacopo was telling him now.

"Find the Golden Horse behind San Simeon Piccolo . . ."

That meant crossing the canal near its mouth.

"Buy a jug of wine and insist on Barolo." Iacopo placed two gold ducats, three silver grosso and five tornsello on the table, arranging them in piles. Nudging them slightly until they were neat.

"Il Magnifico died years ago," said Tycho. "But the ducats are new."

"Magnificos are still minted. The Moors and Mamluks won't take anything else. And Byzantines give a better rate for these than their own bezants."

"Why?"

"They're purer," Iacopo said as if it was obvious. "The emperor can cheapen bezants if he has to. Venice can't cheapen ducats. If we did, trade would fail."

"And what does a jug of Barolo cost?"

"A tornsello. A tornsello and a half at most."

Nodding to say he understood, Tycho scooped up the coins and thrust them into a leather pocket on his belt.

"Let me help you." Pulling a scrap of fur from his boot, Iacopo thrust it quickly into the pocket and folded the leather top. "It'll stop the coins from jangling," he said. "One of my own tricks."

Tycho nodded.

"I'll go now," Iacopo said. "You'll need time to prepare. But let me have some of that small beer first." Taking the jug, he began filling a rough-blown glass, his grip suddenly slipping and the glass crashing to the floor to roll away unbroken.

"Shit," he said. "I'm sorry."

"No matter. The glass isn't broken."

"That's not what I'm worried about." Producing a scrap of velvet, Iacopo wiped beer from the back of Tycho's boots. "That's more like it," he said.

45

The carving above the door of the Golden Horse, a narrow tavern between narrow houses in a street south of the Grand Canal's northern mouth, looked more like a donkey. Once cheaply gilded, it now peeled in patches. The bits not peeling were the hue of rancid fat. Tycho wasn't surprised to hear a man pissing outside call it the Mouldering Mule. The man stank, as did the tavern and the street in which he pissed. Anywhere near a tannery always stank.

Shit shovellers and tanners' boys bathed daily. Probably the only people in the city to do so. Except for the very rich, for whom bathing was an expression of power. The difference was that the rich bathed inside, sitting on huge sponges, their baths shrouded by tents to preserve the heat. While the shit shovellers and tanners boys bathed in canals that were frozen in winter and rancid in summer. So rancid that their sole virtue was that they stank less than those bathing.

The man leaving the Mouldering Mule worked a shit boat. From the smell of him he'd decided to have a drink or three before facing the waters of the canal.

"What are you looking at?"

Ignoring him, Tycho turned to go in. He wore his black leather coat, collar turned up. Black doublet, black codpiece, black hose, black boots. Maybe these made customers stare when he began to push his way through. Many glanced up, most glanced away. A human response to seeing someone pass.

A few kept staring.

He could stare back or look away. The first a challenge, the second surrender. So he glanced away, heard a snort and glanced straight back, hardening his gaze. It left his mocker uncertain. Shouldering him aside, Tycho found a table near the back. A one-eyed ex-soldier sat with a heavy glass in front of him.

"This stool free?"

The man spat into the sawdust. "What do you think?"

Tycho sat himself and smiled at the man's scowl. After a moment, the soldier went back to examining his mug of wine. The woman who came over to take Tycho's order was Schiavoni, large and busty. In a Venetian her tied-up hair would make her married. With the Schiavoni who knew?

Apart from another Schiavoni, obviously.

"Well?" she demanded.

"Barolo . . . A jug."

She scowled. "Red, white, strong beer, small beer. You want anything else go somewhere else."

"Barolo."

The soldier laughed. "Your red's shit," he told her. "Your white's worse. As for the beer, you should pay us to drink it. Tell Marco to give him a jug of the good stuff."

When she came back, she banged Tycho's jug down hard enough to make her breasts bounce and wine slop across the table. Running his finger through the puddle, Tycho licked it. When he looked up, she was blushing. He gave her a tornsello and a half coin and watched her flounce away. At the counter, she looked back and flounced some more.

"Too bad you'll never get to explore what's in that blouse . . ."

Pushing a folded note around the newly made wine puddle, the soldier said, "Can you read?"

"A bit." Tycho said.

"More than I can."

Along the Fondamenta delle Tette, the bare tits and rouged nipples that gave the brothel canal its name were on display. In a hundred and fifty pairs of chilly flesh, and an endless choice of shapes from barely there to pendulous. The patriarch owned this area. The Church having decided that making whores cheap, available and frequent would cut down on sodomy, at least between men.

"You're no fun . . ."

The half-naked girl in a tavern full of sailors and off-duty soldiers scowled at Tycho, who shrugged and didn't bother to disagree.

"I'm cheap," she said. "And good."

He could see why she might be proud of the second. But being proud of the first was odd. Unless he misunderstood her.

"And I'm here on business."

Turning away, she threw her arms around the neck of a passing Schiavoni bosun, who nodded at her whispered price and thrust his hand up her skirt; unable to wait until he reached the stalls before beginning to toy with his purchase.

Although Tycho drank as little as he could get away with at each stop his head was still spinning, and his thoughts wandering by the time he reached the Alexandrian, his fifth destination. A single-storey building leant against the side of a palace, with the fish market downstream on the Canalasso's far side. He approached it along a narrow alley, and found himself facing an original palace, which was halfway through being rebuilt. Bamboo scaffolding rose in the darkness.

Slick with rain, the rope lashing the lengths together was dark and swollen. A vicious-looking guard dog turned to watch Tycho approach. And for the first time since he'd arrived in Venice a dog raised his hackles and launched an attack. Only to be brought up short by its chain.

Picking itself up, it bared its fangs and tried again.

"Easy," said Tycho.

This only drove the beast into a frenzy of snapping teeth. Until saliva flew and the beast's eyes looked ready to roll in its head. *Dogs ignore me*, Tycho thought. It wasn't that they liked him or disliked him. They simply behaved as if he didn't exist, until now. He hoped it wasn't an omen.

The club's owner obviously had permission from the palace's new owner to keep trading, because nothing looked temporary. The Alexandrian was as far from the Mouldering Mule as two drinking dens could be. Far further than the thousand steps it would take to walk from one to the other. Above this door stood a gilded warrior, dressed in a battle skirt and holding a sword. "Iskander" said a carving on its base. "Conqueror of the Known World."

The room was narrow but deep, with a painted ceiling. The floor paved in Istrian stone that was almost clean. A carpet hung on one wall, its reds and browns matched by smaller carpets on other walls. Marble-topped tables matched stools that didn't wobble. Candles burnt in candelabra.

And the air stank of beeswax, incense, expensive wine and perfume so heavy Tycho thought he'd wandered into another brothel by mistake. According to Atilo, brothels existed in Venice for every taste. Young women, older women. Whores who would hurt you. Whores who liked to be hurt. Whores who didn't like to be hurt, but, for extra, you could hurt them anyway. The best provided food, usually at a loss. Food and drink and hazard tables and areas for conversations best not overheard. According to Atilo brothels were for more than fucking.

A dozen masks looked across. None looked away and Tycho could feel their hunger. Languidly pushing back his chair, a figure in a white mask, red silk gown and golden shawl came to drape one arm around Tycho's shoulders.

"First time?" Before Tycho could respond, a waddling doll propelled herself to her feet, and hurried over.

"He's with us."

"I saw him first."

"Allophone, you'd be wise . . ."

The first figure dropped his arm from around Tycho's neck and left hurriedly, muttering apologies and protests that he hadn't realised who he'd been talking to.

"He's a little idiot," Hightown Crow said, pushing back his gilded mask and smoothing the front of a purple gown. "But a *pretty* little idiot. Who will get himself into trouble. Probably serious trouble if we're lucky."

Tycho gaped at him.

"Welcome to the Alexandrian," said Dr. Crow. "I have two patrons who want to meet you." He pointed to a door at the back.

"You're grown," Duchess Alexa said. She looked at Tycho thoughtfully. "Into what is another question. In height, certainly. Atilo tells me you're ready for testing . . ."

"Yes, madame."

She laughed at his flatness of tone. "Still hate me, do you?"

"I'd kill you."

"What prevents you?"

Something did. His fury at seeing the woman who used Rosalyn as bait to catch him burnt like flame. And that Rosalyn had died that night should have . . . But the flame shrank and shrivelled, leaving only regret. Blinking, Tycho claimed back a little of his anger. "Magic."

Alexa smiled. "Close enough."

"I'll kill you though, eventually."

"When you're able to kill me you'll no longer want to . . ."

"Don't count on it."

"I won't," she promised. "You should know I count on

nothing." Tiny octopuses filled a plate on a table in front of her. They were dressed with oil, large flakes of pepper and sprigs of some dried herb. "Try one," Duchess Alexa said.

Tycho shook his head.

"I insist." Tycho popped a tiny octopus into his mouth, feeling it wriggle briefly as he crunched. "Did you taste it?"

He nodded, swallowing his mouthful.

"Now eat another."

This time he felt a tiny spark and watched the duchess smile at the surprise in his eyes.

"Finish the plate."

By the time he bit into the last wriggling morsel the spark was obvious. A flicker of tiny lightning as the creature died. Wiping the platter clean with a sliver of bread, Tycho was surprised to find himself happier.

"You know why you're here?"

"For the testing."

"In the old days my husband would give your master the name of someone he needed dead. A foreign prince. A troublesome priest. Your job would be to make that happen. Tell me what *deniability* is."

"I know you did it. You know you did it. I can't prove it."

She laughed. "The basis of a *perfect kill*. No one can prove a thing. A *trick kill* blames someone else. A *non-kill* looks like a suicide. A *possible kill* looks *almost* like an accident. That's its subtlety. Since doubt enters our enemies' hearts like a blade. I can see from your face Atilo has taught you this. So, another question. Why do we allow this club to exist?"

"It keeps Dr. Crow happy."

She clapped her hands. "Marco would have loved you," she said. "So young, so cynical. What else?"

"It gives you his friends to blackmail."

"So astute. If I told you to kill Dr. Crow, would you?"

"Happily, my lady."

"I almost want to make him your target. Sadly, this comes first." Unrolling a piece of paper, she revealed an ink drawing. Somewhat between man and wolf, with sharp ears, shaggy fur, pointed snout and long claws. Tycho felt his throat tighten.

"You recognise it?" Alexa asked.

"No, my lady."

"Would you lie?"

"Of course not, my lady." Tycho glanced round the room. A raised divan covered with a silk carpet was visible behind her chair. More carpets draped the walls. A tiny single window was leaded with small circles of glass. The room's only real oddity was its smell. A mix of smoke and something sharper. Tycho had been catching traces of the latter all night.

"Hashish," said Alexa, "the poor man's opium." She nodded to a fretted brass dish, which dribbled smoke. "Your nose wrinkled."

"And you read my thoughts?"

"Not easy. In fact, surprisingly hard. But tell me first how you got here . . ." She waited expectantly.

Tycho opened his mouth to say he walked from behind San Simeon Piccolo, along the edge of the Rio Marin, and Rio di San Polo, then cut between the churches of San Aponal and San Silvestro to the Rialto bridge. The way anyone Venetian would describe his walk. Only, he realised, as he prepared to answer, this was not what she meant. "I don't know."

His words tasted bitter as ink.

"Ragnarok," she said. "I see more than you think."

"Not my beliefs." He said it without thinking, but it was true. Lord Eric and his followers believed in flames and fire at the end of time. Tycho's mother was not Viking, nor Skaelingar. That much Withered Arm had told him.

Duchess Alexa seemed strangely pleased with his answer. "That's Prince Leopold zum Bas Friedland." She gestured at the drawing. "His father's emperor, his mother's French. He's a *krieghund*. As the German's bastard, a *krieghund* and the German envoy, Leopold is protected. In all senses . . ."

Tycho should ask what the duchess meant.

She sighed when he stayed silent. "Officially, we can't touch him. No matter what he does." Tycho *shouldn't* ask what that meant. This was not his to know. Assassini orders existed to be obeyed, without question and without thought. Thought limited action in the happening, according to Atilo, and destroyed the chance of rest afterwards.

"What's he done?"

"None of your business." Duchess Alexa tipped her head. "Surely you were told that?"

"It's almost the first lesson."

She laughed, reached for her glass of wine and sipped it, careful not to stain her gauze veil. "He murdered fifteen women over the course of five months. Well, his men did. Only three of the deaths mattered. The third, the seventh and the last. There's a subtlety in that. Killing at random so his target kills appeared also to be by chance. And then, to finish, he destroyed the Assassini. In a single night, a year and a half ago, his Wolf Brothers killed most of Atilo's men. They crippled Venice's reach and left us open to threats."

"Why not act before now?"

"So," she said. "You can think as well as look pretty. In which case, answer your own question . . ."

"The time wasn't right?"

"You weren't ready."

Tycho looked at her and knew his mouth hung open. So he shut it smartly and smoothed the shock from his face. More rested on tonight than he first thought.

"How could so many Assassini be killed?"

Duchess Alexa took a deep breath. Such a deep one that her breasts rose beneath her dress, and she saw him notice . . . "Concentrate," she snapped, and Tycho knew she intended to tell him.

Lady Giulietta had been abducted twice.

Most recently by the Mamluks. There was something about the way Duchess Alexa said this that troubled Tycho. But by then she'd returned to talking about Prince Leopold. He'd been behind the first abduction. And Alexa and the Regent hadn't even known about it until Atilo returned Giulietta, distraught and in tears, to the palace and reported his losses to . . .

"The Council," Prince Alonzo said, shutting a door crossly behind him. "You should have waited."

"I did . . ."

"And yet here the two of you are." His gaze swept the room, the carpeted bed and single glass of wine before finally reaching Tycho and dismissing him. "I guess I should be grateful talking's all I find you doing."

"Is there a point to this?" Duchess Alexa demanded, sliding the freshly rolled scroll discreetly into her pocket. The Regent and his sister-in-law faced each other, both on their feet and leaning forward. The difference was that Alonzo was blind drunk.

"We agreed to do this together."

"I was simply awaiting your arrival."

"Of course you were. You . . ." Alonzo glared at Tycho. "What do you know so far?"

"Nothing, my lord."

"Good. Your job is to kill a German princeling. He means nothing. It's a test. That's all you need to know." Leaning forward, he emptied Alexa's wine glass, either forgetting or not caring it wasn't his. "Kill the bastard, kill his sister, kill everyone in the house . . ."

"*Alonzo* . . ."

"You have a problem with that?"

"This isn't what we agreed."

"We didn't agree you'd see this brat first, either. Do you see me complaining? He kills Leopold, end of story. Let your Moor prove he hasn't lost his grip." Refilling Alexa's glass from a jug,

Alonzo emptied it again. Only to look up and appear surprised Tycho was still there. "You," he said. "Go make yourself useful."

At the door, Tycho was stopped by a question. "How old are you?" asked Duchess Alexa.

Prince Alonzo snorted.

"Seventeen winters. Maybe eighteen."

And maybe more, if the fact that Bjornvin burnt a century before meant anything. And there were his dreams of slaughter, of light and ice.

Ca' Friedland was ten minutes' walk from the Rialto bridge, north along the right bank of the Canalasso, at the corner with Rio di San Felice. A once unfashionable area that was obviously being redeveloped. Prince Leopold's palace was a huge waterside mansion in the old style, its grey façade black with age. A single lamp burnt in an upstairs window and an ordinary looking *gondolino* was moored by its watergate. Tycho had assumed a prince's *gondolino* would be grander.

Tycho would have liked a house like this. One that rose five storeys, with endless arched windows. A house with columns and statues, and probably carpets and tapestries.

"*No you don't*," said a voice.

A beggar squatted on the quayside. Rat eyes bright in the night as he curled a turd into the dirt. He was squinting to see more of Tycho than shadow.

"Fuck off now. This is my patch."

Closing the gap, Tycho killed. Simply shifting from there to here to break the man's neck and lower him silently, before life left his eyes. A splash, and the current carried a new corpse. The kill was instinctive, unpremeditated.

Tonight he'd discovered Atilo's truth. A truth Tycho doubted Amelia and Iacopo had worked out. The Assassini's greatest weapon was currently their name, backed up by the occasional murder, and the fact no one had yet discovered how weak they really were.

It would take years to rebuild the group. Atilo didn't have years. He was an old man busy making a fool of himself with a younger woman. And looked—more so every day—to be regretting it.

The Assassini were there for Tycho's taking.

Atilo insisted belief made fools of men. Tycho had started to wonder if lack of belief wasn't more crippling. Tycho didn't believe in anything. Not really. He might do if he knew how. But, most days, the hole where his heart should be felt too huge to fill. Being the duke's Blade might fill it.

Get to it, he told himself.

The walls were built from crudely cut Istrian stone, and rotting brick held by mortar that had soured years earlier. Cracks meant handholds were easy. All the same, Tycho made himself edge round to Rio di San Felice, and scale the side of Ca' Friedland that rose from the narrow canal, using the shadows to hide himself. Tycho had no wish to be spotted by the Watch, another beggar or some passing drunk.

Idle thoughts filled his climb.

Another handhold and he'd be outside the only lit window. A balcony called him from above and Tycho reached for it, hooking one hand over a decorative detail made from a single run of bricks, before stretching for the balcony's floor.

He should concentrate but the climb was easy. Not suspiciously so. Simply easy. A climb that would have left Iacopo exhausted barely troubled him. His heartbeat as slow as ever. His skin cool to the touch.

No sweat, no sign of fear.

Listen, he told himself sharply. *Do this properly.*

The problem was he *knew* three drunks were leaving a tavern in Campo San Felice. He'd *already noticed* the splash of oars from an unlit *vipera* in the *rio* below. The law forbade unlicensed movement on the side canals after dark, and sluice gates blocked many of the smaller intersections, but gates could be raised if smugglers offered enough.

A clipclop of hooves came from the street.

To ride like a Venetian was an insult. For all stables existed in the city, the standard of horsemanship was appalling, according to Atilo. Anyway, riders had to dismount before crossing the Rialto bridge, and horses couldn't be brought into Piazza San Marco, but had to be tethered next to the Mint. So the only point of owning one was show.

And from inside the Ca' Friedland?

The sound of a harpsichord. An instrument he recognised because Desdaio had one at Atilo's house. Hers was Flemish, as were most in Venice. Whoever was playing was good. Desdaio simply managed basic tunes.

See who was in there or keep climbing? The question answered itself when the music stopped, a stool scraped back and he heard a woman grunt gently as she lifted a heavy lamp. Behind the shutters the room dimmed to darkness.

Tycho kept climbing.

Grit rattled beneath his boots and fell with the sound of rats scuttling as it trickled down the wall to patter lightly on a balcony below. Too much noise, he thought, listening to falling dust settle and wondering why it didn't worry him.

Because he was drugged.

The twist of Iacopo's body as he picked the glass from the floor. Iacopo's sudden decision not to drink small beer after all. Tycho using the glass, to drink down the last of the water before leaving for the Mouldering Mule. It all made sense. He'd been feeling strangely relaxed since.

One chance, Atilo said.

That was what everyone got. No exceptions.

Failure would see him sold as a slave, supposedly. Although Tycho suspected, given his recently learnt skills, failure would see him dead. Which was fine, he didn't intend to fail. He intended to kill the German and return to Ca' il Mauros to rip out Iacopo's throat.

Levering himself over a parapet, Tycho dropped to a crouch and discovered he wasn't alone. A dark-haired man waited five or six paces away, lazily elegant in an open shirt; his crouch a mocking mirror of Tycho's own. He was grinning behind his beard. "I hope you realise you stink like a polecat? And—I have to admit—I thought you planned to hang on the edge of that balcony all night."

"Leopold Bas Friedland?"

"Prince Leopold zum Bas Friedland." His eyes slid over Tycho's costume. "Is that how Atilo dresses his bum boys these days? And that sword . . . I thought a dagger in the back was more the Venetian style?"

"You're not an assassin?"

The German flushed at Tycho's jibe. Much of the humour going out of his face. "I'm a soldier in a secret war. A peasant like you wouldn't understand what that means."

Tycho snorted.

"Took you long enough to get here."

"A few minutes to climb your crappy wall."

"Eighteen months to pluck up the courage." Prince Leopold saw Tycho's scowl. "Oh, not you. You're the disposable bit in this. The Regent, Duchess Alexa, that raddled Moor she's fucking. Perhaps you should tell me before you die . . . What took them so long?"

Tycho drew his sword.

In the muted light of a cloud-shrouded moon he saw Prince Leopold's eyes narrow. Tycho's blade glittered like water reflecting sunshine. And then Prince Leopold's gaze flicked upwards, and a patch of black detached itself from the night's upturned bowl with a creak like old leather.

"Six months to make the sword," it said. "A year to turn this boy into your death. Another five minutes for that to become a reality. Emperor's bastard or not, Prince Leopold, you've plagued this city too long."

"Alexa, and I thought you didn't care."

Rolling the sword across his hand, Tycho swept a figure of eight. It felt like any sword to him. For all that its blade . . . Stepping closer, Tycho saw the blade brighten. So he stepped back quickly and saw it dim.

"Well I never," the prince said. "A mage sword matched to a boy who doesn't quite know how to use it. This should be interesting."

He drew and lunged in the same second.

His lunge changing direction. Tycho was so busy blocking he almost missed the dagger in Leopold's other hand. It would have killed him had it pierced his side. Instead it ripped his doublet and drew blood.

Both men stepped back.

Your job is to kill a German princeling. He means nothing. That's all you need to know. The Regent's words rang sour in Tycho's memory.

In a year, Tycho had swapped a crude knowledge of axes for swordplay, knife work and unarmed combat. But he'd also half-learnt to read, studied poisons, and discussed politics. He felt spread thin in the face of a man who held a sword like an extension of his own arm.

"Ready to die?" Prince Leopold asked.

Dropping his dagger, the prince raised his sword. As if intentionally opening himself to attack. But he could sweep his weapon down to either side or straight ahead. He could block every stroke Tycho offered with a single move. So Tycho raised his blade in turn, and waited.

Overhead, cracking leather circled.

Dipping and swooping and offering dry clicks that sounded like falling dust. When it swooped close, Tycho realised it was large. As large as his doublet given the power to fly. Prince Leopold snorted, flicked his gaze at the clicking darkness, and struck as Tycho's gaze followed, swinging his blade in an arc brutal enough to lop a man off at the knees.

292 • *Jon Courtenay Grimwood*

Metal met metal. Sparks flying as shock numbed their arms.

Tycho had no idea how he blocked the blow. From the look on Prince Leopold's face he had no idea either. Sweeping the man's sword aside, Tycho went for his throat. Almost losing his own entrails as Leopold ducked beneath the strike and spun, his sword passing a hair's breadth from Tycho's belly.

The princeling changed styles three times in seven moves. Switching again for the three strikes after. Blocking a skull strike, Tycho jumped a Sicilian sweep, just avoiding a backslash to his Achilles heel. Tycho's arm was already dead to the shoulder. His fingers gripped his sword from instinct.

When he stepped back, Prince Leopold was also gasping, sweat running down his face. The veins in his neck standing out like hawsers. His scowl said Tycho shouldn't have been able to survive that rally.

His next attack came so fast it drove Tycho to the parapet.

Risking a glance, Tycho saw a low wall stretch away on both sides behind him. Beyond his attacker, a roof rose steadily. On that slope's far side would be another slope falling gently to a gutter cutting across the roof's middle. A second slope would rise and fall beyond that, ending above the land gate.

It was a traditional design.

Ducking a blow, Tycho tried to spin past Prince Leopold, risking death to reach the slope. Had he succeeded he'd have had the roof's height on his side and room to fight freely. But Prince Leopold's sword caught his above the hilt and took the blade from Tycho's hand.

The princeling's smile was gone.

Opening his mouth, he bared teeth in a grin that narrowed his eyes to slits. A trickle of drool ran down his beard and Tycho felt his stomach lurch. Lord Eric's brother had been berserker. They lived outside pain. Died outside it too. They'd crawl up a sword to gut the man who stabbed them.

As Tycho waited, night clouds parted.

A full moon nailed Tycho to the spot, fever waterfalling through his body as the sky went red around him and the city acquired hard edges and the water in its canals glowed like molten steel. For the first time ever, he let the moon's rays take him and felt his dog teeth descend.

Opposite him, Prince Leopold raised his face to the blood moon and howled, his body arching as his shriek split the air. Behind him the stars distorted, and the shimmering air ripped as worlds fought each other.

The stronger of the worlds won.

Peeling back, the skin of Prince Leopold's chest split to reveal blood, raw flesh and fur beneath. His ribcage cracked. Muscles tearing and ribs breaking as unseen hands racked him, dislocating his joints and twisting him to a newer shape. Prince Leopold's clothes tore too. Rags he ripped away to stand naked. His fingers turning to claws and black fur flowing in a wave across his reformed body. Blood dripped from his jaws where his teeth had extended.

Sex erect, head back, Prince Leopold screamed at the moon.

When his gaze flicked to Tycho it was animal.

The sword he'd been wielding fell from his claws and clattered to the lead of the roof. The prince barely noticed. He was too busy completing the changes that made him *krieghund*.

Tycho moved.

He moved so fast the roof blurred as he reached the sword he'd dropped, grabbed it up and adopted the stance Prince Leopold had used earlier. Legs apart, blade held high above his head.

"Ready to die?" he asked.

The *krieghund*'s eyes blazed as it dropped to a crouch and sprang. Leaping high over Tycho, it twisted on landing, claws raking down Tycho's spine. Blood rose black and sticky through torn leather, pain hitting Tycho a moment later. So shocking, he dropped to his knees.

The red sky faltered.

A second later, Tycho realised he'd dropped the sword.

The creature reached it before him.

It stood on Tycho's blade, jaws so wide its tongue lolled from one side. While Tycho stood in a puddle of his own blood watched by the grinning monster. Stepping sideways, Tycho saw the *krieghund* do the same.

So he did it again and again.

Always moving closer to Prince Leopold's own sword. Until he was close enough to grab it from lead flashing at his feet. And the creature howled with laughter as Tycho let go, clutching his fingers.

The sword was bewitched in some way.

Magic was all Tycho needed.

He reached for Prince Leopold's sword again, his fingers blistering. The prince was judging distances and Tycho only just ducked in time to avoid claws jagging for his throat. He was about to retreat, when crackling blackness eclipsed the moon and Prince Leopold leapt high, trying to hook the irritation from the air.

And in that moment the red sky steadied.

"Become yourself," the bat said.

To do so was to ignore every rule Atilo had taught him about remaining in control. But Tycho obeyed anyway, embracing the moonlight. Across his back cuts began to mend. The pain in his fingers vanished. The city became as clear as day. Stretching out around him with a shocking clarity. Light scribbled bright lines around the buildings. He had the secrets and the scents of the city in an instant

He discovered how both Leopold zum Bas Friedland and the guard dog from the Alexandrian knew he was coming. His boots stank. It should be unmissable. And then Tycho identified the drug in his blood dulling his senses, and felt the effects wither as whatever made him who he was swept it swiftly away.

Standing on Prince Leopold's blade, Tycho snapped it in two and hurled handle and hilt, seeing it scour a line in the wolfthing's cheek. His blade might be magic. The handle was common metal. Stepping back, Tycho swallowed the roof's layout in a single glance. He felt . . .

Good came in there somewhere.

Good, and *focused*. And *here*, and *now*. He belonged inside his own skin for the first time ever. Looking at his fingers, he realised they were longer. His skin whiter. When he raised a hand to his mouth his fingers came away bloody. His dog teeth had grown. Not like this creature's. His face hadn't twisted and become animal, it had refined.

This was what being *Fallen* meant.

His speed and strength were simply side effects. Good ones, but side effects as surely as his hatred of sunlight. "You die here," Tycho said.

And the *krieghund* feared him.

They met in the middle of a leap. Crashing into each other so hard a human's bones would have broken. Tycho landed three paces away, spinning sideways as the *krieghund* used the parapet for leverage and leapt straight back. Tycho swept one foot under the creature as it landed, sending it rolling towards a corner.

As he grabbed the creature's hips to hurl it to the canal below, it twisted and sank claws into his shoulders, dragging him close. Tycho could smell the *krieghund*'s fetid breath. Feel dog-like heat rise from its body.

Struggling would bury those claws in his flesh. Pulling away wouldn't free him. Going close put him within jaw reach. The *krieghund* was strong but Tycho was faster. That had to count for something.

He kneed the *krieghund* from instinct and heard the creature gasp. So he kneed it again, and as its grip faltered, put his elbow into its throat.

The beast stumbled. Clawed hands clutching for its neck as it fell to its knees, rocking backwards and forwards. As if keening in silence. Maybe it was, Tycho thought, not caring either way.

46

This time he could clearly see magic rippling along his sword blade. Flecks of fire brightening as he approached his target. Hightown Crow had designed the weapon for one purpose only. Killing *krieghund*.

"Any last words?" Tycho demanded.

Prince Leopold looked up dumbly.

"I guess not." Drawing back his sword, Tycho found its balance. "Quite sure about those last . . ."

"*Don't. Please don't.*"

The words came from behind him.

Tycho froze. He refused to turn. Refused to admit what his senses told him. Instead he watched the wolfthing's eyes focus beyond him and something human slip back into them. Prince Leopold shook his head very slightly.

"Anything," the voice promised, closer now. "We'll give you anything. Leopold has estates. He'll pay a ransom. Please."

Kill Friedland. Kill his *sister*. All Tycho had to do was obey those orders and the Assassini would be his eventually. He didn't dare turn around.

"I have my orders."

He could prove himself worthy to be Blade. Assassini killed with no more thought or conscience than a dagger. They existed to be wielded by the duke and his Council. Who they killed was not their concern.

"Stay back," he warned.

The young woman sobbed as Tycho's sword reached tipping point. Already the *krieghund* was changing. Its limbs straightening. Blood running down its face as its jaws retracted. A near-human head would roll across that roof.

He chose a point behind the prince's skull.

As his sword readied for the kill, a young woman flung herself across Prince Leopold's naked body. A black scrap of sky detached, falling fast. And Tycho only just managed to pull his blow, shredding the bat instead. Wheeling away, the dying animal tumbled dirtwards.

A tear-stained face looked at Tycho.

Huge eyes widening as she recognised him. He felt unable to breathe, unable to do anything but stare back. He had hunted for over a year to find her and now she had found him. It was the girl from the basilica.

"You won't kill Leopold?"

Tycho shook his head mutely.

Putting his sword down, he stepped back from temptation. How could he not let the prince go? The sight of Lady Giulietta stole his will to act. He could *feel* the hairs on her arm as they rippled in the wind. Her scent was a drug far stronger than whatever Iacopo used. A golden heat haze danced around her. He felt awe. An awe so absolute it left him barely able to function.

"Your price?" she whispered.

Touching her lips, he smoothed his fingers down her cheek and rested them lightly on her throat, feeling her pulse flutter. She blushed, and then caught herself. Making herself meet his eyes.

"Me?" she asked.

"Yes," he said. "You."

Lifting her to her feet, he looked deep into her eyes and saw himself silhouetted against a night sky. Her eyes were blue and he saw in them things no one would see. A thousand specks of light arranged around darkness. A flotilla of ships drawing in on an island.

"In the basilica," she whispered. "I almost . . ."

I know.

The memory of her, with a dagger to her breast, remained undimmed. The taste of a single drop of blood from the slightest of wounds had changed him forever. She had locked him to this absurd city.

"Will you let Leopold rise?"

He let her help the German princeling to his feet. If the man attacked Tycho would kill him. But Leopold simply stood there, swaying. His gaze met Tycho's own, and then Leopold zum Bas Friedland looked at Giulietta and tried to speak. No words came from his ruined throat.

"It's all right," she promised.

He was objecting to her offering herself. All three of them knew that from the anguish on his eyes.

Lady Giulietta had a chamber of her own. On the third storey, above the piano nobile and overlooking Rio di San Felice. It was ringed with salt, enough salt to leave a clear trail around the edge of the room. All the passages were lined with salt, even the stairs. Every room in Ca' Friedland had salt around it.

"Leopold's idea," she said. "It's there to keep me safe."

"From what?"

"You," she said, tears filling her eyes.

Shuttered windows led to a tall and narrow balcony with a tiled overhang supported by elegant pillars. Tycho opened the windows slowly, already knowing no enemy waited beyond. In time he would learn to trust his instincts. For now it felt arrogant simply to believe he was right.

Caution made him lock her chamber, sliding its bolts, before checking outside. If you wanted to reach her balcony you would have to climb from the canal, using cracks in the outside walls and the stone ribs of the window arches. Anyone trained by Atilo could do it. That was what made him nervous.

"What are you doing?"

Tycho stopped lugging an old iron chest by its handle. "Blocking that." He pointed at balcony doors. She nodded mutely, perched on her bed, its curtains down, except the side she'd tied back earlier.

"He won't try to come in."

"It's not Leopold I'm worried about."

Her eyes went huge in the darkness. She was the girl he'd seen in the basilica. And yet she looked different. As if life had not been kind. "He hurts you?"

She flushed angrily. "Never. Not once."

His fingers were steady as he slid her undergown over her shoulders, exposing her breasts. They were full, fuller than he expected. Tipped with dark nipples that looked engorged. He lowered her gown further, letting it drop and tugging her hand to show she should step out of it.

Small, but swollen breasts, narrow hips, and flame-red pubic hair.

"What's that?" A scar crossed her abdomen, and she shivered as he traced its length with one fingertip, halting at the end.

"You can see in the dark?"

He nodded, realised that wasn't much use, and said, "Yes, but not in the light. Tonight my sight's clearer than ever." Why did he tell her that?

"That scar," he said.

Instead of answering, she slid from his fingers, disappearing behind a curtained arch. When she returned it was with a baby swaddled in bandages so tight it could barely move. Tycho felt constricted just looking at it.

"Yours?"

She nodded defiantly.

"Someone cut a baby out of you?"

"A Saracen surgeon," she said. "Cut Leo free to save my life. He sewed me up with a tail hair from a white stallion. Said he always knew he'd need it one day." There was awe in Giulietta's voice. Women died in childbirth every day. Even a good birth held risks and offered pain.

"It's Prince Leopold's child?"

"Leo's not an it," she said crossly. "He's a he. My son . . . Our son." She stood naked. Slight hips and soft belly. Milk oozing from her nipples like tears, to trickle along the under slope of her breasts.

"Feed him."

"Now's not appropriate."

She tried to meet Tycho's eyes, but her room was in near darkness and he had the advantage. She reminded him of the stone mother in Pio Tera dei Assassini, his first night in this hellish city. The one the woman prayed to.

"Lie down," he told her. "And do it."

When she continued to stand there, he edged her towards her bed, pushed her on to her side, told her to stay there and took her child, unswaddling it before placing it at her breast. And then he stripped off his doublet, boots and hose. Most of his remaining weapons he put in one corner.

A single stiletto went under her pillow.

Lying behind her, he folded one arm across her stomach and shaped himself around her, feeling the curve of her buttocks, the line of her back and the slope of her shoulders. In the silence that followed he heard her crying.

"Is this so bad?" He knew it for a stupid question even as he asked it. She tensed, with him curled there. Although her child simply guzzled.

"You're young," she said eventually.

"You're younger."

"Only in years. You know he'll kill you afterwards?"

"Leopold?"

Lady Giulietta sighed. "My uncle."

"I'm not here to kill you. I'm here to kill your lover, surely you realise that? Anyway, why would I murder you? How would I even know you were here?"

She opened her mouth to say something, and closed it again.

"Leopold's *krieghund*," Tycho said. "You saw what he became."

"It's a curse," she protested. "You can't hold being cursed against him. And he told me about it, right at the beginning. He kept nothing back."

"Can I ask you something?"

"You half killed Leopold. You're naked in my bed. My baby lies defenceless beside me. Do you think I'd risk refusing?"

"I don't know. Would you?"

"Depends," she said.

"Why don't you go home?" It seemed an obvious question. At least, obvious to someone who didn't have a home. Who'd been born a slave, grown up a slave, and would likely die one now, probably soon.

"This is my home," Giulietta said. "Well, it was. The Ca' Ducale is simply where Uncle Alonzo and Aunt Alexa live. Plus, my cousin, of course. Poor Marco, always condemned to being mentioned last."

"He's mad?"

"They're all mad. I could join them. Or leave."

"You believe that?"

"Oh yes. Who knew being abducted from your abductors was lucky?" There was a mix of bitterness and resignation in Giulietta's voice. She understood the irony. "Let Leopold go and take the baby. Kill me, if someone has to die. It will be enough for my uncle."

"Go where?"

She shrugged. "France's out; he's not safe there. And the Byzantines would torture him both for every secret he knows."

"What about if it was all of you?"

"Cathay maybe. In the long term."

"And in the short term?"

"Cyprus. If Janus will take us."

"Won't he mind that you were meant to marry him?"

Lady Giulietta sighed. "Is this nerves? Do you always talk so much in . . . When forcing yourself on a woman."

"My first time."

"Your first rape. How sweet."

"My first anything."

"You're like Leopold," Giulietta said, turning to face him and using the baby to hide her breasts. "A beast inside a man. And a man inside the beast."

"No," Tycho warned her. "I'm nothing like him."

Wrapping one hand into her hair, he dragged back her head until her throat was exposed.

"You are," she whispered.

He bit her neck savagely, blood flowing into his mouth, across the baby and on to the sheets. As she screamed, and Prince Leopold began to hammer at the door, Tycho bit deeper, tasting the sweetness her life had to offer.

He'd done what he did. While the baby howled and Prince Leopold beat at the door, Tycho walked Giulietta to the very edge of death's precipice. The *krieghund* had known what Tycho's feeding meant even if Tycho hadn't.

When Tycho opened the door the German wanted to kill him. Only Leopold was weak and wounded, and Tycho was more alive than he'd ever been. Aware of every movement in the city outside. And there was another reason for Prince Leopold's fury. One Tycho learnt when the man's anger ebbed through livid recriminations to tears and guilt. He would rather have died on the roof himself . . .

Tycho's kind no longer . . . Nephilim were . . .

"Save her," he demanded.

"How?" Tycho asked.

"Don't mock me."

"I'm not."

Tears rolled down the *krieghund*'s face, his voice reduced to a grating whisper. "Your blood," he begged. "Smear it on her wounds. You can have this palace. My gold. Anything you want. Just save her."

Biting into his wrist—watched by Prince Leopold, whose gaze never left the child at his lover's breast—Tycho dripped blood into Giulietta's mouth and on to her ravaged neck, which began to heal, almost as if a saint touched her.

In place of Tycho's hunger came stillness. The wild fever that the full moon had summoned withdrew like surf on shingle now the storm was over. As Tycho stroked Giulietta's face, watching her cry wide-eyed and silent on the blood-soaked bed, he knew he loved her.

As did Leopold zum Bas Friedland, lord of the Wolf Brothers and the German emperor's envoy to Serenissima. Who loved so unwisely both her family and his would kill him without thought if they knew about it.

"Go," Tycho told her. "Get out of here. Take money, weapons, whatever your lover doesn't want found." Tycho stopped, remembering something. "Where's Leopold's sister? Atilo told me he lived with his sister."

"Atilo il Mauros?" Giulietta said. "What has he got to do with this?"

"I killed fifteen of his men." Prince Leopold's voice was flat. "About a year and a half ago. In Cannaregio. We were hunting someone and his men ended up hunting us. It was a bloodbath. He killed my men and I killed his."

"Leopold, that was . . ."

"Yes," he said. "We were hunting you."

"You wanted to kill me?" Lady Giulietta's voice was a whisper.

"Capture you. And I didn't know you then."

"That isn't an answer." Shrugging on to an elbow, she realised she was still half naked and wrapped her blanket more tightly around her, completely covering her child. "Throw me that," she ordered, pointing to a robe.

Both men stood. Prince Leopold fetched the blanket, letting his fingers brush hers as he handed it over. She appeared not to notice. Tomorrow would bring fear, anger and anxiety. For the present she seemed to take almost dying in her stride.

"Tell her why you fought."

Prince Leopold glared at him. He wanted to say this was none of Tycho's business. In the end he shrugged. "Atilo heads the Assassini."

"You're wrong. That's Lord Dolphino."

"No," Tycho said. "It's not."

"Duke Marco had my father assassinated," Prince Leopold said, his voice heavy.

"My cousin?"

"Your late uncle. When they offered me Venice, how could I refuse? The German emperor's envoy by day. Leader of the Wolf Brothers by night. We were to terrify you into loving us. Terrify you into signing a treaty of friendship." Leopold scowled. "I begged for the job."

"For the chance of capturing me?"

"I didn't know you," Prince Leopold said desperately. "When I received news you'd fled Ca' Ducale I couldn't believe my luck. Every Wolf Brother in the city was called to track you. When we realised Atilo had Assassini tracking us it was too late to back down. My friends died trying to reach you."

"To capture me?"

"Or kill you if we couldn't do that." Leopold looked ashen in the candlelight. "I'm glad we failed," he said. "I couldn't bear . . ."

"You'd never have met me. You would never have known."

"No," he said. "I never would."

47

Atilo stood in the silence of the early morning gloom trying not to let his gaze slide beyond the palace balcony to the mist on the lagoon. Today's mist was so thick he could barely see the monastery at San Giorgio.

"You failed . . ." The Regent's voice was icy and his face white with fury. The cold flame of his anger was far more dangerous than his usual red-faced bluster. Prince Alonzo was afraid.

He believed Prince Leopold was alive.

Krieghund healed quickly. Leopold zum Bas Friedland had been an implacable enemy before this. As the German emperor's envoy to Serenissima he'd been bound, at least in appearances, by diplomatic niceties. Any such restraint would now be gone.

"Do you have an excuse?"

In Atilo's head were Desdaio's words.

"*If you love me you'll save him.*" How much did Atilo love her? Enough to be cuckolded? Enough to live with the fact that Iacopo spoke the truth, later denied. Desdaio had been seen coming from Tycho's cellar.

That's what Atilo was starting to believe.

"Nothing to say?"

"My lord?"

"Don't you *my lord* me. You have told us *that* was ready. That it had the necessary skills to . . ." Prince Alonzo waved his hand dismissively. The Moor knew exactly what was wanted. That was what his wave meant.

"I was wrong, my lord."

"Yes, you were. Weren't you?"

That knelt silently at the feet of the throne. Blood glued his braids to his skull. Atilo's beating of the boy had been brutal, his most brutal yet. The old man couldn't work out if stupidity, ignorance or courage made the boy return to announce his failure. That was all Tycho said. He'd failed.

Behind the kneeling boy stood Captain Roderigo, looking bleary-eyed and furious. He'd been to Ca' Friedland and waited to make his report.

"We'll give him to Black Crucifers for public torture."

"Alonzo," said a voice from the doorway. Alexa's tone was surprisingly mild. Clearly, she realised how close the Regent was to doing something stupid.

"*What?*" Prince Alonzo demanded.

That Alexa let his rudeness pass said it all. Pointing out the obvious in front of servants to a drunken prince who should have realised it already was a delicate task. "Perhaps that's not fitting."

"Why not?"

"He's young."

"What's that got to do . . . ?"

Children were frequently tortured. Sons required to condemn their fathers. Daughters their mothers . . .

"Ahh," Alonzo said, stumbling over the answer for himself.

Tycho's age was an irrelevance. Alexa simply wanted him to pause long enough to think. The torturer would discover every detail of Tycho's training. He would know about Prince Leopold's true nature. Who knew the complications that would bring?

"Wine," the Regent demanded.

The steward's eyes flicked to Alexa. The little man wouldn't dare refuse Alonzo but he could have his staff dilute the wine. He'd served the old duke and served him well. He'd have done the same for the new duke, if the young man hadn't been sitting there watching mist slowly burn off the lagoon.

The duchess nodded. Alonzo tight was easier to handle.

"You said he was *ready*," the Regent insisted, grabbing a goblet and emptying it in one gulp. "You said he was up to the task."

As well Roderigo was loyal. In the old duke's day Assassini matters were not discussed openly. Then, in Marco III's day, all decisions were taken by the duke, who was not given to discussion. Except, occasionally, with his duchess. And Atilo only knew that because she'd told him. They'd been in bed at the time. Glancing across, he saw her watching him.

"Well?" Alonzo said. "Are you going to answer?"

"I'm sorry, my lord."

"Sorry isn't good enough. You should pick your people better."

"The mistake is mine."

"I'm glad you admit that. We wouldn't want you wriggling out of your responsibilities. Would we, Alexa? Roderigo, tell us what you found."

"Blood on the palace's roof, my lord. Discarded weapons. A broken blade." He opened his right hand, unfolding a cloth to reveal burns. "Enchanted. It took Dr. Crow to make it safe. A woman's chamber exists on the third floor."

"His sister?" Duchess Alexa's voice was tight.

Atilo hadn't even known Prince Leopold had a sister. And Alexa's voice was much too tight for a woman of her subtlety. Now that he thought of it, she seemed less shocked than Alonzo at Tycho's failure. Though she'd been careful to glare at the boy fiercely.

"I would imagine so, my lady," Roderigo said.

"What about servants?"

"No sign of servants, my lord."

"You checked?"

"Yes. I checked. The attics were derelict." Attics were where servants slept. Hot in summer and freezing in winter, they were shared with mice, rats, pigeons and old furniture.

"Leopold zum Bas Friedland and his sister, alone together. That sounds suspicious to me." Prince Alonzo's eyes gleamed at the thought. When he waved his goblet a woman hurried forward. His gaze as he watched her pour was hungry. "Describe the state of her chamber."

"The bed had been slept in, my lord. The sheets were . . . in need of laundering."

"You mean what I think?"

"Possibly, my lord."

"Then say it clearly," Prince Alonzo snapped.

"The sheets were stained, my lord. With blood, urine and shit. Either she was murdered there by . . ."

"Her brother?"

Captain Roderigo winced. "Or Atilo's apprentice violated her first."

Prince Alonzo looked at Tycho with new interest. His eyes glancing at Atilo's impassive face. "Roderigo. Do you believe they're dead?"

The captain shrugged. A mistake.

"The mattress was drenched with blood," he said hastily. "There were also splatters of blood on the roof, and signs of a struggle and the broken sword . . . But no bodies anywhere. They could have been removed." They could also be alive. The more he drank, the easier the Regent was to read, and Roderigo knew his master was scared, and furious.

"Death," Alonzo said. "That's my verdict." When Duchess Alexa opened her mouth, he snapped, "You disagree?"

"This needs discussion."

"No, it doesn't . . . Let the Black Master extract every last secret in private. Although I've a mind to do it myself." For a second it looked as if the Regent was serious. "Go," he said, glaring at Roderigo. "Take him away."

"Where, my lord?"

"The Crucifer pit, obviously."

48

"Strip him . . ."

Tycho struggled to locate the speaker. His gaolers had him blindfolded with his hands tied behind his back tight enough to make his fingers distant memories. Shackles locked his feet. He was ungagged. Perhaps they expected him to plead.

"Get on with it."

Rough hands yanked his doublet; when the buttons failed to rip free, someone punched him and Tycho fell to the floor.

"*That's enough.*"

A different voice this time. Behind him.

"Maybe you'd like to tell me what's going on?" There was a smoothness to the words that set Tycho's teeth on edge. A reasonableness that grated.

"Sir, we're preparing him."

"What day is it?"

"Saturday, sir." The man sounded afraid.

"And why is preparing him like this a bad idea?"

"We're not torturing him, sir. We just need to remove his clothes. It's not like . . ." The voice trailed into gurgling, followed by a thud. Pushing his foot to the side, as far as his shackles allowed, Tycho felt another body.

"Pick him up."

Hands hauled Tycho to his feet.

"Right," the voice said. "Free his hands, unbutton his doublet properly, throw him naked into the pit. Leave the shackles. I begin torturing him on Monday. Understood?"

"Yes, sir. Sorry, sir."

"My lord." Tycho's throat was dry. Partly fear, partly that he hadn't drunk anything since the previous night, and his head ached from Atilo's beating.

"You speak."

"Sunlight, my lord. It . . ."

"Burns you. So I've been told. An interesting fact, don't you think? What kind of sinner is burnt by God's own light? Only the worst, I suspect. The Regent has instructed me to question you myself. An unpleasant task, but one I shall undertake to the best of my abilities. And I wouldn't worry. Where you're going now has no sunlight, nor any other kind most of the time."

Footsteps climbed stairs.

"I can open it myself," he said.

A second later hinges creaked, then the door shut again. Every gaoler listened to check the man was gone. And then a punch to the kidney dropped Tycho to the floor. A vicious kick took air from his lungs and filled his throat with bile. "You cost me a man," a voice snarled.

"Boss . . ."

"*What?*"

"He comes back and sees this we're all in trouble."

"You afraid?"

"Of course I'm shitting afraid. I almost piss myself every time the Black Master enters a room. You want him angry, fine. I want to keep living." There was muttered agreement.

"Throw him in the pit then," the boss said.

The gaolers freed Tycho's hands but left him blindfold, his feet shackled by a short chain joining two crude iron fetters, with a single silver wire welded to the inside. The fetters tore at his ankles, which was the point. There was no space to run where he was going.

"Too pretty for his own good," a gaoler laughed. "Dee, then Blue. After that Federico. The others later."

"He's only there two days."

"Long enough," the voice said. A fist caught Tycho in the back and he stumbled, ankles burning as he took three quick steps to regain his balance.

"Here we go."

A clang told Tycho a hatch was opening.

"Don't fight it," a voice muttered in his ear, sounding almost sympathetic. "It's going to happen anyway. So soak it up, and work out who you can take your revenge on later."

"*What are you telling him?*"

"That he's going to get his good."

"Damn right. All that sweet flesh. Too bad I only like slit . . ."

"And this one's so pretty," said another voice. "Put him in a dress and you couldn't tell the difference." The man guffawed. "Like to try it. Dee would be good for gold." He stopped, realised what he'd said. Waited for the inevitable question.

"You saying Dee's still got coin?"

"He's got friends. They've got coin."

Hands gripped Tycho's shoulders and walked him to the edge. A gaoler dragged free his blindfold and Tycho twisted, avoiding a vicious jab to his side. He'd seen someone liver-punched. If all you did was vomit, shit yourself and black out briefly you were doing well.

"Slippery bastard, isn't he?"

"Yeah," said Tycho, juggling numbers. Three gaolers here, four guards at the top of the stairs, two levels and three doors between him and freedom. Acceptable odds, if he could change. Against that, he was shackled with silver wire, stark naked and it was daylight if he made it as far as outside.

And he deserved to be here. All the same, he planned on evening the odds. Grabbing a rusting dagger from a gaoler's belt, Tycho stepped backwards and dropped into hell, falling for two seconds before hitting something soft, which swore, and dislocated.

"Fuck," it snarled.

Tycho had landed in an oubliette.

Flooded, except for a tiny island on which three men huddled. Half of the remaining prisoners crouched in stinking water, some of them up to their waists, others to their necks. Against a wall, a huge treadwheel was turned by the rest, who swore and whimpered as they worked. A single torch lit the fetid pit from the far side of a grate high above. That was the trapdoor.

"Which one's Dee?" Tycho demanded.

"I am, you fuck. And you're going to die hideously."

If Prince Alonzo got his way Tycho's death would undoubtedly be hideous. Since he mended fast and died slowly it would be more hideous than the Regent realised. The man with the dislocated shoulder intended to get there first, however . . .

"And Blue?"

"What's it to you?" said a man behind Dee, answering Tycho's question anyway.

"I guess that makes you Federico?"

The third man scowled in the half darkness. Instinctively, he'd shifted into a street fighter's stance. He was younger than Dee and Blue, his muscles less wasted and his skin healthier.

"Keep the wheel turning, you bastards . . ."

Dee's order had the pump working again. Prisoners climbing from step to step, their chains clanking as the wheel kept the water from rising further and the small island from being drowned.

"I'll fix your shoulder, boss," Blue told Dee. "Then you should get some rest. Give your muscles a chance to mend."

"If you think," Dee said, "I'll fall for that. *You get some sleep and I'll just break him in for you.* You think I'm shitting stupid?"

"Don't think you're stupid at all, boss."

"No," Federico said. "We don't think that." The slipperiness in his voice suggested others did.

"Bugger this." Slamming his palm into his twisted shoulder, Dee grunted as his arm slid into its socket. "That's better. Now bring him here. I'll show you who's stupid."

The *bucintoro*, Marco's ceremonial barge, was scrubbed, painted and newly gilded. Its hull was free of barnacles, the caulking between its planks freshly tarred. New-woven ropes guided its triangular sail, and the lion flag of Serenissima flapped high above. The flag was the height of a man, with St Mark's winged lion picked out in gold on a white background.

When not flying above the *bucintoro*, the flag lived in a jewelled case behind the altar of San Marco. The duke's annual marriage to the sea, and his leading an army into battle, were the only reasons to remove it.

On the black throne of the Millioni, Duke Marco IV hummed softly, watching the seagulls that followed his barge. The gulls were hungry for the scraps and fish guts usually found in the wake of fleets this size.

For once the Regent was not centre stage.

He had no right to marry the sea. And Alexa, being a woman, could not. Marco IV would marry the sea for them, and for the whole city and its empire beyond. His mother doubted her son even realised the ring on his little finger, the one he would toss into the Adriatic at a nod from her, was fake.

A good fake, of course.

The lapis was real and the gold pure. The design exact. Even the scratches around the old-fashioned Byzantine setting and across the shank were lovingly recreated. Fake only in that it wasn't the original. Alexa regretted having to kill one of Venice's finest jewellers but regarded it as a price worth paying. Her only worry about offering the sea a perfect replica was that the sea might reject it.

The problem with Westerners was that they fulfilled their rituals carefully, without understanding the reasons behind them. Half of the nobles thought this day stupid superstition. The other half imagined it a gaudy display designed to overawe the *cittadini* and keep the Arsenalotti in their place. None considered what the sea's rejection of this marriage might mean ... Fierce storms at the very least. Ships lost at sea and fishermen returning with their nets empty.

At the lagoon's mouth, the surrounding flotilla slowed its pace and came to a halt, the oarsmen holding their place against the pull and push of the tide. Only the *bucintoro* went on.

"You have the list of prisoners?" Alonzo asked.

"Yes, my lord." Roderigo's voice rang clear across the deck. Tradition demanded Marco free one prisoner in honour of his marriage. Vast sums changed hands, with families desperate to buy freedom for one of their own. Sometimes the money went to someone who could actually influence the choice. More often than not, it made no difference.

"Read it, then."

The captain bowed. Being one of the Regent's favourites was a double-edged sword, and sometimes even the handle was too dangerous to hold.

"Federico, an expert forger and murderer. Who claims to have sometimes given aid to this city ..." As close as anyone would get to admitting he was a spy. "Giovanni Cisco, salt dealer. Murdered his wife, wrongly. She was not cuckolding him as he suspected. Lord Gandolfo, accused by his enemies of false witness."

Captain Roderigo's money was on Gandolfo.

Not literally. He was too close to the Regent to find anyone willing to take his bet. Even old friends assumed he knew something they didn't.

"Those are the names?"

Tradition demanded three. So three was what they got. Tradition also demanded that question. And that Captain Roderigo answer it. "Those are the names, my lords."

"Then let our duke show justice."

Roderigo was thinking how hard Alonzo found it to say those words, acknowledging his nephew's rule as they did. And wondering whether Marco would be able to repeat the name his mother had just whispered to him, when a sob broke the uneasy silence.

"You have something to say?"

Everyone looked at Duke Marco in shock. Their gazes flicking to the sobbing Desdaio a moment later. Every patrician there knew who she was. Not one had acknowledged her on arrival, although they'd all been careful to recognise Atilo. He was one of the Ten. And, quite possibly, Duchess Alexa's lover. A fact that might help explain the stiffness between Atilo and the woman beside him.

"Well?" Alexa said.

"Tycho should be included."

Prince Alonzo raised one eyebrow. "*Who?*" he said.

"The boy you sent to . . ."

"Do what? We sent where?" Duchess Alexa's gaze settled on Atilo. He shook his head slightly.

"I don't know."

"Atilo's slave is charged with treason." Alonzo's voice was firm. "The sentence for treason is death. It cannot be revoked."

"Slaves can't commit treason."

Someone gasped. Technically, it was true. Slaves could commit murder, rape and steal. All of these counted as treason against their master. But they could not commit treason against the state. This was the act of freemen. Such acts belonged to their masters.

"Do you understand what you're saying?" Alexa asked.

If treason was proved and the penalty was death, and Atilo's slave could not be held responsible, then the only person who could was Atilo.

"Yes," Desdaio said.

As Federico and Blue advanced, Tycho glanced behind to see a squat man reach for his ankle. Kicking back, he broke the dwarf's nose and heard a splash. Next time he risked a glance two boys were holding the dwarf underwater, while bubbles rippled the water's dark surface.

"Look," said Dee. "Fighting just makes it harder."

"Depends how well you fight." Whipping the blade from behind his back, Tycho slashed it across Blue's throat, stabbed Federico in the guts and threw it at Dee in a single moment. Dee had a hand to his eye, already sinking to his knees, when Tycho stepped forward and drove the dagger home.

He wiped his blade on Dee's face for effect, though he doubted many could see, the light being so bad. Hooking his toe under Dee's body, he rolled it into the water. The other two he simply picked up and threw. Those in the shallowest water were obviously stronger or meaner than those behind. So they were his greatest threat. Letting them see his contempt was simple common sense.

"Anyone else want to fight?"

There were growls of anger and snarled insults, but no one stepped up to the challenge.

"Well?" Tycho said.

In the shallows the dwarf stopped struggling. An old man who'd tried to save him was being shuffled into deeper water, while the boys moved forward to take his place. "Wait till you're hungry," someone muttered.

Tycho looked for the voice.

"And then?"

"We'll see how tough you are."

A bear of a Mamluk with a matted beard and a belly that

jutted like a boat's prow. He was chest deep in water, but only because he crouched down.

"Man's got a knife."

The Mamluk snorted. "He's gotta sleep sometime. We'd all be tough if we had a knife."

"He's tough without, believe me." A boy's voice came from deep water. "You ain't seen nothing like it. Moves like lightning. Kills just as fast."

"You," Tycho said. "Come here."

"He's just a kid," a voice hissed.

"Like that ever stopped Dee and Blue," someone else answered.

Hands bundled the boy towards the island. Where he stood naked, hands clenched into fists, his ribs thin as twigs. His eyes never left Tycho's face in the half-darkness. "It's you," Tycho said.

Pietro nodded.

"I'm sorry . . ." Tycho made himself say it. "I'm sorry about your sister."

"Not your fault," Pietro said flatly.

Tycho wished he could agree with him. "Here," he said. "Hold the knife for me."

The small boy gaped, then grabbed the dagger by its hilt and stepped back. He swung the blade at the first man to grab for it.

"Anyone tries to take that from Pietro they answer to me."

Heads turned to fix on Tycho in the darkness. He pointed to the barrel-chested Mamluk, gesturing him closer. "The island's his if he can take it."

The challenge was enough. The treadmill stopped. Only starting when people began shouting. "It's time to change shifts," whispered Pietro. "Only Dee's dead. Maybe you'd better tell them?" He made the last part a question. In case Tycho grew angry.

"Change shifts," Tycho ordered.

The wheel worked a pump that stopped the pit from drowning

its inhabitants. As long as people worked the wheel every hour of every day, the level stayed low. At least, low enough for the island to remain visible and the slopes to be shallow enough for most to stand and a few to kneel.

"Right," Tycho said. "Want to try your luck?"

"I'll be having that knife," the Mamluk warned Pietro. "If you've got any sense you'll give it up without fuss."

Stepping forward, Tycho kicked the man in the balls.

There was nothing subtle about his move. He waited until the Mamluk was ashore, stepped forward and kicked hard. The shackle around his ankle crushed the man's bollocks. Both of Tycho's ankles ripping as the linking chain snapped tight. His curse was lost under the Mamluk's scream.

Breaking the man's neck with a twist, Tycho kicked his body into the shallows. "The knife," someone begged. "Lend me your knife."

"Why?"

"So I can fillet him quickly. Please. In this heat he'll be rotting by tomorrow. Believe me, I know. I used to be a butcher."

"How long?" Tycho asked.

"Months," the man said. "Years, tens of years. How can one tell time in hell? Will you lend me your knife?"

"No," Tycho said.

The man sighed, dragged the Mamluk towards the shallows, and collected Dee, Blue and Federico as well. He left the dwarf floating. "We'd better eat what we can then."

Everyone fed.

The deck of the *bucintoro* remained in silence except for sails creaking, the hum of the hawsers and slap of the waves. Even Duke Marco stopped drumming his heels, mesmerised by the twisted expression on Atilo's face.

Lords who hadn't met her gaze in a year, their ladies, who'd spent time looking through her, stared openly at Desdaio. And the young woman stood there, wide-faced and innocent, her body soft, her breasts heavy and her smile gentle. But there was steel in her eyes.

Duchess Alexa was impressed.

"Let me get this right." The Regent's grin was that of a cat that had got both the cream and the canary, and had just discovered seconds. His hatred of Atilo was well known. "You're accusing your lover of treason?"

"He's not my lover," Desdaio snapped.

Atilo stared at his feet.

"Really?"

"We're to be married. Sometime." There was a world of bitterness in Desdaio's last word and her eyes filled. Raising her chin, she ignored them. "Until then I remain a virgin. I swear it."

The duchess smiled behind her veil. "If," she said, "you're accusing your beloved of treason I doubt there will be a wedding or a bedding."

"I'm not, my lady."

"That's what it sounds like to me."

"I'm not saying Lord Atilo is guilty. I'm saying his slave is innocent. Tycho wouldn't commit treason any more than my lord would. There must be a mistake. What can he have done that is so bad?"

The nobles began looking at their wives.

Everyone knew patrician women sometimes had affairs with servants. Young wives with old husbands had to find comfort somewhere. As did women married to men more interested in men. Sometimes the wives were simply bored, or married to weak men who accepted it. A few women ended poisoned, returned to their fathers or locked in their rooms. Mostly, the servants were found floating with their throats cut.

But this young woman had just publicly sworn herself a virgin.

"*You* don't believe he's guilty, do you?"

Iacopo shuffled his feet, obviously stunned to be thrown so

publicly to the lions by Desdaio's question. He was only there as Atilo's bodyguard. It might be Easter, a day of peace and celebration, but nobles still took sensible precautions.

"My lady," he said. "I'm hardly in a position . . ."

"Yes, you are." Atilo's voice deep and slow. He was, those who knew him realised, in battle mode. His face was stern, his eyes steady. "And I'm interested to know your answer. Tell me. Do you believe my slave guilty of any treason?"

Maybe Alexa imagined the stress on *any*.

"How can I . . ." Iacopo stumbled to a halt. "I'm a servant. If I say no the lords think I lie. If I say yes, the lords might think I lie anyway. These are matters far above . . ."

"Your highness." Desdaio's voice cut through the excuses. "May I have leave to talk privately with my lord Atilo?" It took Alexa a second to realise she was talking to the duke. Marco stopped looking at the seagulls.

"I don't see why not," he said.

Nicolò Dolphino gasped, and then flushed under Alexa's glare. It didn't matter that the duchess wore a veil, she was obviously glaring. And it didn't matter that most days Duke Marco could barely string two words together. Everyone was to pretend he ruled. Expressing surprise that he'd managed two sentences in one day slighted that.

Desdaio walked Atilo to the stern of the *bucintoro*. Ahead of her, podgy wooden cherubim, painted gold rather than gilded, gambolled and rolled and exposed tiny genitals and even more unlikely wings. She dismissed a year of a master carver's life with a single sniff.

"Do you love me?"

Hard eyes looked at her. She'd never seen his face so cold or severe. He wore his age and experience like armour. She felt stupidly young and not worthy of him.

"Answer me," she demanded crossly.

He let his silence stretch to the point of cruelty.

"I love you," she said, feeling her eyes fill. She was furious with herself, furious with him. Furious that fifty people who'd spent a year ignoring her were now openly staring. "I love you more than life."

"I'll ask you again," Atilo said. "Did you go to his room?"

"That's what this is about? You're accusing me of . . ." She glared at him. "What are you accusing me of?"

He just looked at her.

His answer was in his silence and the stillness of his stare. She knew he could outwait her. He'd done it before over lesser things. Things that didn't matter. Not in the way this mattered. Although they'd felt important at the time.

"Well?" he said.

"No," Desdaio said. "I didn't."

She saw doubt in his eyes, and grabbed his hand before it could grow greater. He was stronger than her, experienced in battle as well as the ways of the world. He could free himself easily. But she held his wrist so tight, and looked so frightened at where she found herself, he didn't break her grasp.

Instead he waited for her to say more.

Desdaio breathed a sigh of relief. She couldn't say why but he smiled slightly, and some of the warmth came back into his eyes. "A little guilt," he said. "But only a little. I've judged people," he added, as if she didn't know. "People have hung on my assessment of their innocence or guilt."

That she didn't know.

She wanted to tell him the truth, and she wanted him to respect her. She couldn't have both, and she was a coward. Desdaio knew that. To risk everything on a simple statement of the truth. *I went, nothing happened.* She lacked the courage, the certainty he loved her enough to believe and forgive. Her life was full of the little truths she'd never managed to say. How could she start with a truth so big?

Atilo was staring at her, she realised.

"Tell me what happened."

"I entered his room. Nothing happened."

Atilo's gaze sharpened. "Why?" he demanded.

"I asked Amelia if you'd free him. She said maybe. Some you did. Others you sold. It depended on a test . . . No," Desdaio said, seeing him frown. "She didn't say what the test was. I asked, she refused."

"We come back to, *Why?*"

"I like him." Desdaio said, risking a little truth. Maybe she shouldn't have said that. But Atilo simply nodded.

"Do you like Iacopo equally?"

"No." Desdaio shook her head. "I don't trust him," she said. "Iacopo gives me the creeps. Always watching. Always so polite it feels like mockery. And he . . . he lusts after Amelia." She blushed at her own words.

Then blushed again at what she saw in Atilo's eyes.

He wanted to tell her everyone lusted after Amelia. With her long legs and narrow hips and black skin she was an exotic gazelle. Maybe even a tyger. As fierce as anything in the duke's zoo. If Amelia was a tyger, Desdaio didn't want to think what animal that made her.

"I swear on my life nothing happened."

"Should I be worried that you like him?"

Desdaio hesitated. "I know what he is," she said. "He's never said. But I've worked it out. And it must be so sad . . ." Stepping close, she whispered in Atilo's ear. Hearing his hiss of surprise.

"Desdaio."

"What?" she asked. "Am I wrong?"

"A fallen angel exiled from hell . . . Because his enemies paint themselves red? And his house burnt down? And he fears daylight?"

"Don't laugh at me."

"I'm not." Atilo cupped her chin in his hands and raised her face to smile at her. "You're beautiful," he said. "Rarer than gold.

Far sweeter than honey. I'm sorry things have been," he glanced towards Alexa, "complicated . . . We'll marry this summer, I swear it."

"You'll save him then?"

Atilo's smile faded slightly.

"You believe me? That I'm not wicked? That nothing happened. That I would never do that to you?"

"Yes," Atilo said. "I think so."

"Then prove it. Save Tycho."

Atilo's face set hard. It was the face of a general weighing his choices before battle. Considering what price he was prepared to pay for victory. And as Desdaio decided she'd asked too much, that she should take her words back, he nodded . . .

"This should be interesting," Alexa said.

49

Steam from the heat of a hundred bodies sweated the dungeon's stone walls and rose from the water's filthy surface in a parody of lagoon mist. It swirled through rotting tread steps, disturbed by the wheel's movement. Settling only when a shift changed, breaking into fresh flurries as soon as the wheel resumed turning.

The faces around him were also parodies. Deprived of light, bleached by the mist. Skin withered and puckered and rotten from years of immersion.

Sometime later, the flickering torch visible through the grating burnt out to leave the pit in darkness. It had to be late, because the gaolers barely bothered to rattle the grating as they passed. Contenting themselves with pissing through the grill, or defecating and kicking their shit on to the prisoners below.

Tycho slept in shallow five-minute naps.

A skill he'd developed in childhood, when not rushing to answer Lord Eric's call meant a beating and even less food. He could flash from slumber to fully awake in an instant.

"Why did they put you in here?" Tycho asked Pietro.

"Didn't want me to talk about that night, did they?" he replied with the certainty of an eight-year-old who'd thought it through.

"When Rosalyn died?"

Tycho held Pietro by his shoulders while the small boy fought bitter sobs and won. He felt embarrassed comforting the boy. When Tycho held it was to kill, or take. But the boy mourned his sister. And Tycho having killed Rosalyn's murderer was not enough to make that good. Not even close.

"Found yourself a friend?"

Spinning, Tycho saw a red-headed girl in rags.

A'rial was older than Pietro by a few years. Her hair tied up in a clumsy knot and fixed with a raven's bone. She stank like a fox. A purple light shimmered around her. When Pietro crossed himself, she grinned, her teeth glowing white.

"No one else can see us," she said.

Sure enough, a translucent haze enclosed the three of them and the pump's noise had faded.

"I've come with an offer."

"For me or him?" Tycho said, nodding towards the boy.

"You, *obviously* . . . The duchess knows."

He'd upset A'rial with his flippancy. Because she stopped there, leaving him to imagine what Alexa knew. That Prince Leopold was alive? That Tycho let him get away. That Lady Giulietta also lived . . . ?

"Yes," A'rial said. "That one."

Pietro was staring at the oubliette beyond the edge of A'rial's magic. He'd moved as far from her as he could without actually touching the shimmering bubble that contained them.

"Go," A'rial told him, tearing a gap in the haze.

Tycho grabbed the boy. "He stays."

"Collecting pets?"

"Is that what the duchess does?"

Tycho's blow struck home, because flint entered A'rial's eyes. Thinning the haze, she pointed to the relentless wheel and the oubliette's dripping walls. "You want to stay here?"

Even inside her magic the air was fetid, hot and stinking.

"Except you can't, can you?" she said. "At one minute after midnight the Black Master arrives to question you himself."

Pietro gasped. "Kill yourself while you can. Use the knife."

"What knife?" A'rial's gaze sharpened.

"This one," said Tycho, putting his blade to her throat. What Pietro saw was Tycho face one direction, then suddenly face another. But Tycho knew he'd moved the way a normal person moves, simply faster. Much faster. A'rial's fingertips lit and Tycho twitched his hand. "I can strike faster than you."

"Impossible."

"You willing to risk being wrong?"

Tension drained from A'rial's body and she smiled. He waited for her to try to trick him but she kept smiling. Looking for all the world like an eleven-year-old told to deliver a message by her mother or mistress.

"The duchess watched you fight Prince Leopold. She says you were magnificent. But you can be more. Embrace your nature. Complete the . . ."

Tycho wasn't listening. He was more concerned with another question. How could she have watched? His guts churned. What had she seen? The start of the battle? He could handle that. Giulietta's sudden appearance? The girl offering herself in return for Prince Leopold's life?

"Yes," A'rial said.

"Stop that." Tycho raised his blade.

A'rial shrugged. "I'll try, but it takes effort. And you do the same, don't you? You do it all the time."

"I need touch to sense thoughts."

"No. You just think you do," she said crossly. "You're your own worst enemy. My mistress can save your life."

"And in return?"

The small girl sighed. Reaching for Pietro, she wrapped her arm round his shoulder, and drew him close. For a second, the small boy rested his head against her, believing the embrace genuine. But the face she showed Tycho was distant and strange. "Make Alexa an army of immortals."

"No," Tycho said, stepping back.

Pietro looked between them, his face puzzled.

"He's going to die anyway. After you've gone, they'll kill him simply because you favoured him. So what difference does it make? Come to that, why this fuss about feeding. You've done it before. And beggar children? A dozen die every week of cold or hunger. Do you try to save them?"

"That's different."

"No," A'rial said. "It isn't. Claim him. Save yourself."

The calm of feeding on Giulietta was beginning to fade, and Tycho's hunger was tiny threads of twisting smoke looking for a way into his mind. With A'rial's words came knowledge that there was a step beyond where he was. There would always be another step until he was no longer human.

If he'd ever been human.

Remembering Prince Leopold's agony as his muscles ripped and tendons broke, and his body became wolf, Tycho said, "I won't."

If he closed his eyes he could see it happen. Skin splitting, flesh tearing and bones being twisted into new shapes by invisible hands. Bad enough the Black Crucifers would torture him. Why would Tycho do it to himself?

"That's twice," A'rial said. "I won't offer a third time. But you call, I'll come to you then."

"Never." Tycho was firm.

"Don't count on it," A'rial said.

There were two tides a day. A low and a high. The first mattered neither here nor there to those in the pit, who were removed from the festering mud banks of Venice's edges, and the stink of sour water, as backstreet canals revealed rubbish, puddles and the occasional corpse with every ebbing tide.

The second did concern them.

At high tide, lagoon water flowed along ditches, for a few minutes to as much as an hour, and splashed into the oubliette below. One day's tide left half the central island still exposed. Two days' drowned it, but left prisoners able to stand. Three days' killed those unable to swim. Only by constantly working the pump could everyone stay alive. Exquisite cruelty. Hard work for the sake of it. More than this, it stopped prisoners trying to escape. You worked the wheel; slept, woke and worked again. No one was allowed to slack. The oubliette was self-controlling, self-containing.

In it, Tycho saw Serenissima.

The varied councils, the courts within courts, the Arsenalotti at war with the Nicoletti, the *cittadini* jealous of the patricians, the patricians divided into old house and new, rich and poor. No one in Venice got off the wheel.

Beyond the city, Serenissima's colonies fed the capital, the Venetian navy fought the Mamluk pirates; the Moors allied themselves with whoever the Mamluks opposed. The Germans offered support, claiming Byzantium was Serenissima's greatest threat. The Byzantines claimed the German emperor's ambition was a greater threat and offered support in turn. Tīmūr's Mongols conquered ever larger slices of the world, threatening to recreate the sprawling empire of his hero Genghis Khan.

And the wheel went round and round and round . . .

"What did she mean *save yourself*?" Pietro said. The first words he'd spoken since A'rial vanished.

"It doesn't matter."

The boy looked embarrassed to be caught asking. But he continued watching Tycho with concern. High above them guards arrived, bringing fresh torches. "If you can save yourself, you should." Pietro sounded far older than his age.

"How did you first get involved in this anyway?"

Pietro told him.

Being hunted by Wolf Brothers sounded terrifying. And listening to the boy's tale of street rumours and outright lies, Tycho realised this was an old battle, one begun long before he reached the city. Maybe before Atilo even controlled the Assassini.

"We should have hidden," Pietro admitted.

That was what he'd been told to do. And that's what he'd done, as had his friends, until the battle was almost over. They had seen only the end. Admitting it, after Tycho had been captured, was their mistake.

"*Tycho* . . ." a guard yelled.

Pietro grabbed him. "It's the Black Master," he whispered. "Into the water. Hide now."

The grate clattered as it was thrown back. Crossbowmen pointed their weapons into the pit and a long wooden ladder dropped, squelched into the mud and sank several inches. This was enough to stop those on the wheel. For a second, total silence filled the pit, then a voice shouted, "Tycho, move yourself." Captain Roderigo stood lit by torchlight. He had his hand to his nose to shield himself from a rising stink Tycho had already forgotten existed.

"I said no," Tycho protested.

"No what?" Roderigo shouted down.

Tycho couldn't remember the *stregoi*'s name. He knew it once but he'd forgotten; perhaps that was part of her magic.

"The duchess's . . . girl," he finished lamely. "That red-headed one. She asked . . . She said . . ." He didn't know how to finish that sentence.

"Up here now," Roderigo barked. "Stop wasting my time."

Tycho pushed Pietro ahead of him, jeers and sneers following after. Pietro refused to climb. Tycho made him. And faced with Tycho armed here, and crossbowmen above, Pietro chose to avoid the here and now. Atilo would cure him of that weakness, Tycho was sure.

Roderigo stood beside the Black Master, who wore nightclothes.

His lips were thinned to a slash of fury. Behind him waited a gaoler and a turnkey, in a uniform of filthy silk with a tatty and sad-faced winged lion embroidered on his chest.

"Who's this?" Roderigo demanded.

"Atilo's new apprentice."

"My lord ..." The turnkey said. "Your order specifies one only."

Until then, Roderigo intended to toss the boy back. Now his pride refused. The turnkey opened his mouth to insist and shut it at a snarl from the Black Master.

"The *duke* is waiting."

50

Marco IV sat on his black throne gripping its arms like a sailor holding a rail in fear of being thrown overboard in a storm. His grip was hard enough to turn his knuckles white. Ignoring the unshackled child who shuffled ahead of Tycho, Duke Marco said, "Behold, the Grievous Angel."

Shackles made Tycho's answering bow clumsy.

Standing to one side, Atilo saw the duchess smile at her son. The Regent simply sighed. "Didn't it occur to you to wash him first?" he demanded of Roderigo, finding somewhere to aim his anger.

"My orders said bring him straight here, my lord."

"You always obey to the letter?"

The captain nodded.

"How admirable." The bite in Alonzo's voice ensured everyone knew he meant the opposite. "You," the Regent said. "Step forward."

Tycho did. A second later, Pietro did the same.

Atilo stood to one side of the throne. Desdaio's father and a handful of other inner council members stood to the other. Lamps flared and guttered, the night air was heavy with burning fish oil, and most of those in the chamber looked surprised, irritated or slightly scared to be dragged from their beds.

This was the Ten, Tycho realised.

He counted off those either side of the throne, realised that Hightown Crow was amongst them, and wondered who outside the Ten knew an alchemist was a member of the inner council. A small girl half hid behind Alexa's chair. When she met Tycho's gaze, she smiled. A cold and cruel and brilliant smile.

"You know why you're here?" Alonzo asked.

"No, my lord."

"Nor do I," the Regent said.

"Alonzo . . ." Duchess Alexa's rebuke was gentle.

"This is ridiculous," he said. "The Ten called for a matter that should be decided in private."

Alexa's voice hardened slightly. "My lord Atilo has a right to be heard . . . So," she said, looking at Atilo, "say your piece."

Stepping forward, Atilo dropped to his knees in front of the throne. "The city has proclaimed me *fidelis noster civis*. A faithful servant of Venice. Grant me a life," he said. "For the services I have done."

Marco IV picked his nose.

"I counted your father as my friend . . ."

Atilo's words were measured, his voice deep and serious. No one listening could doubt the thought he'd put into his plea. "I have served Venice well. Been both Admiral and commanded your land forces. And I have," he hesitated, "performed other tasks to keep this city safe."

"What do you actually want?" Marco asked.

Atilo blinked.

Alexa and Alonzo usually decided affairs between them. But no one could speak when the duke spoke, and his decisions were law. Those were the foundations on which his mother and uncle built their power. The duke's outbreak of sanity upset the balance.

"Well?" he demanded.

"Give me the prisoner's life. Please."

"There are two of them," Duke Marco pointed out reasonably. "You mean the one who scares you? The one you fear fucked your beloved? Or the one who knows you lied about Lady Giulietta's abduction?"

The chamber was already quiet. But in the seconds following the duke's question it was utterly silent. And then Desdaio stepped forward, her face red and tears of frustration welling in her eyes.

"I would never . . ."

"You would," Marco said. "You simply don't know it. He scares you too. That's why you like him."

"What's this about Lady Giulietta?"

The duke turned to face his uncle, who blushed and found himself apologising for his interruption. So the duke told him it was all right, just not to do it again. "Tell them the truth," Duke Marco ordered Atilo.

"That first time. She simply ran away."

"And you simply returned her?" Alonzo asked. "And forgot to mention the circumstances?"

"Yes, my lord."

"That was the night . . ."

"Alonzo," Duchess Alexa said.

"The Regent is right," said Marco, smiling sweetly. "That was the night the Blade was broken." Seeing the blood drain from Atilo's face, he smiled. "Well, cracked certainly. You admit it's cracked?"

The kneeling man nodded.

"And my mother is right. *Krieghund*, mages, death walkers, now this." Marco IV, Prince of Serenissima, stared round the chamber, nodding to each of the Ten in turn, before finally blowing Desdaio a kiss. "It's best to be discreet. We have so many enemies one can never tell who's listening."

Standing up, he descended the steps in front of his throne and dragged Atilo from his knees. Standing him straight. "You know what saves him?"

"No, your highness."

"I will not offend heaven. And I will not risk offending hell. Tycho's life is spared. So is that of your next apprentice. Though I'm not sure my uncle will let you keep the demon."

These were the last coherent words Duke Marco IV was to say for three months. No one knew that then, obviously. Except, perhaps, Hightown Crow, who hurried forward to help the duke back to his seat.

Gripping its arms, Marco clung tight as if his life depended on it. Relaxing seconds later, and kicking his heels against its base. A little while after that, he became lost in watching a moth circle a lamp. When Atilo was certain the duke's attention was elsewhere, he glanced from Alonzo to Alexa.

"Do I have the throne's permission to withdraw?"

"No," Alonzo said. "You don't."

Alexa looked across. "Marco has given him their lives."

"Their lives," the Regent said heavily. "He said nothing about the slave's freedom. The beggar brat means nothing. Atilo can keep him. But the other *is* a slave. He now belongs to the city. The city will dispose of him."

"Let me buy him," Desdaio said.

The Regent grinned. "I'm sure your beloved would love that. No, the slave will be sent south and sold. With those looks . . ."

With those looks he'd command a premium in the slave markets of Constantinople, Alexandria or Cyprus. The matter of his clothes, his fear of daylight, and the whiteness of his skin would merely add to his exoticism and increase his price. If he died there who could blame Venice? And if he didn't, well, he'd probably come to wish he had, given time.

"How many galleys leave harbour tomorrow?"

"A dozen, my lord."

"And where's the first headed?"

"Dalmatia, Sicily and then Cyprus."

"Make sure he's on it. As a galley slave. Give orders he's to be sold at the journey's end and any money sent to our agents. He may wear his ridiculous clothes. Be coated with whatever repellent unguent our alchemist recommends. And an awning can be used to stop our merchandise being damaged. Other than that, he's to be treated like any other slave."

51

A knock at the door made Giulietta look up from the baby at her breast.

When she didn't answer, the door opened slowly and Prince Leopold put his head round. "May I come in, my lady?"

"I've told you," she said. "You don't need to knock."

"You might have been feeding Leo."

"I was," she said. Smiling, she folded back her gown and stroked her child's cheek until his mouth opened and he returned to his hungry nuzzling. When Giulietta returned her gaze to Leopold, he was staring pointedly through a window at red-earthed Cypriot fields outside.

"Something interesting?"

"Farmers cutting barley on the upper slopes."

Their friendship was sometimes fragile. So much now unspoken.

Leopold and she shared a bed, sleeping together when the baby let either of them sleep, which was more often now than in the first few months following his birth. She could have had a wet nurse; in fact, Leopold offered to have one found for her. He seemed resigned to the fact she refused. Yet he knocked at the door before entering and looked away when she fed her child.

Such delicacy was at odds with the cursed thing he'd become on the roof of Ca' Friedland. And at odds with the savagery of the battle she'd witnessed in Cannaregio.

The fight against the Assassini was more than a year gone, but its memory still made her shiver.

"What are you thinking?"

"Nothing," she promised.

"About that boy," Leopold said sadly.

"Leopold . . . I swear. He doesn't even enter my head."

It was a lie. There were moments, usually on the far side of midnight, when she woke certain the silver-haired boy from the basilica was in her room, watching her as she slept. He never was, of course.

"I saw how you looked at him."

"That's not true."

"Yes," Leopold said. "It is. And I saw how he looked at you. You think he let us go because of me? If you hadn't appeared I'd be dead. He let *you* go, and he let me go with you."

"I love you."

Tears were building in Giulietta's eyes.

"And I love you," he said. "In my way. But you dream of him. It's as if you had one soul between you, and someone cut it down the middle. Remember, you told me how the child wasn't Marco's . . ."

"Leo, please stop."

"Is the baby his?"

Giulietta's mouth shut in misery.

Prince Leopold returned that evening carrying a Maltese lace shawl, half a dozen early figs and a bowl of sorbet—white wine mixed with lemon juice and crushed ice—as peace offering and apology. "I'm sorry," he said, placing his presents on a table and turning to go.

"You can stay."

"I'll only say something else stupid."

"All the same . . ." Giulietta patted the seat beside her. "You know," she said, "at the court in Venice they talked of your silver tongue. My aunt was furious at the number of her ladies-in-waiting . . ."

"Whose heads I'd turned?" Leo said, offering her a fig.

"Although maybe she was cross about other things," Giulietta admitted. "But I didn't know about you being *krieghund* then. But your reputation . . ."

"Around you, my tongue turns to lead."

She smiled. "Not always." Leaning her head against his shoulder, she let him fold his arm around her. Their companionable silence lasted for the time it took a candle to burn out. And then, when Leopold stood to light another from the guttering wick of the first, Giulietta rearranged her gown. "So it's true about the Mamluk sultan gathering a fleet?"

"What makes you say that?"

"The barley. They're gathering it against a coming siege."

"Possibly."

"Leopold, where did you get the ice for the sorbet?"

"From the last of the king's own supply."

"Exactly," Giulietta said. "I hear he's also drinking his best wine and sharing out the pickles the kitchens usually keep for banquets."

"What are you saying?" Leopold asked, fixing the candle into a holder and turning to face her.

"What will happen if the sultan does attack?"

"We'll fight."

"And will we win?"

When he came to sit beside her, wrapped his arm round her shoulder and kissed her gently on the forehead, she knew the answer was no. Instead of protesting or asking Leopold to lie, she snuggled against him and tried to frame the question she wanted to ask. The fact he said nothing meant he knew . . . If not that she was wondering about a question, then that she was thinking.

Thinking time when you had a new baby was rare.

Well, it was if you insisted on feeding the child yourself and letting it sleep in the same room. A decision so odd, Giulietta knew she'd become a talking point among the ladies of the court. If she hadn't been one already.

"Leopold."

"Yes?" he said, sounding ready for whatever she wanted say.

He really did know her, Giulietta realised. Their shared time here meant he knew her better than any man had. Maybe better than any other would. Leopold knew her weaknesses. These, he insisted, were fewer than she imagined. And her strengths, which, he told her she underestimated daily. He knew her so well she wondered if he knew what was on her mind.

"If we lose . . ."

"Yes," he said. "I promise."

She kissed him on the cheek. Not knowing the right response to a man you've just asked to kill you rather than let you be taken prisoner. When the man promising loves you, despite the fact, if you're honest, you dream of someone else.

52

Thunderclouds filled the far horizon. The light was a sullen grey, as if malign angels flew between the setting sun and the swollen sea, casting shadows over everything below. Tycho would vomit, but had nothing to throw up.

So, he hunched in his oil-silk doublet on a dirt-filled bag and hoped the rotten canvas of a makeshift awning would protect him while he waited for orders.

Everyone was waiting for orders.

The *Seahorse* was a small galley. One captain, the owner's son, one drummer, one slave master and fourteen rows of slaves. Tycho wasn't sure what she carried. Nothing heavy from the way she tossed on the swell.

The wind was rising. Ominously cool.

In other circumstances he might have welcomed it and been refreshed. But he learnt what it brought when Adif, the Mamluk next to him, began to count the gaps between lightning and thunder. The strikes were close and coming closer.

A wall of rain headed for them, hiding the distant lines between sea, land and sky. Behind them, night had arrived already, constellations visible and the ocean dark and flat where it met the night's edge.

"We must go north."

"Sir, that's impossible."

The galley owner's son stamped his foot. He was young, rich and afraid. If his father had been there to control him it might have been different. The boy wanted to be on land. In storms, orders said head for the nearest port.

But it was the storm that stood between them and the Dalmatian coast, with its cliffs, endless small islands and rocky shoals. Italy's own coast was a day in the other direction given wind and luck, much longer if luck was bad and the wind against them.

Captain Malo had offered two alternatives.

Hack down the mast and ride out the storm or run before it. That had been before he took another look at the wall of rain and declared he now lacked enough time for the first. So he suggested the second.

Fat-bellied, old and tired, the Greek was resigned to lugging his ship up and down sea lanes that faster vessels used daily. The *Seahorse* had been modern once. Now she was a patchwork of replaced planks. Her caulking needed redoing and she required new tree nails, those thin lengths of dowel holding her sides in place. Most days it a miracle she still floated.

He'd like to keep it that way.

Ruined galleys were found after every storm. So were dead slaves. Chained to their oars and floating or washed up on beaches among driftwood and splintered planks from the ships they'd served.

Running from the Dalmatian coast meant trying to outrun the storm, and widening the violent and nasty seas between the *Seahorse* and those cliffs. The odds weren't great. But they were better than trying for port.

"Find land," the boy said. "That's an order."

"I'm captain."

"Not much longer if you don't do as I say." The boy's words carried over a lull in the wind. "We return to port now."

Beside Tycho, the Mamluk hawked on the deck and spat words in his own language. Tycho didn't need a translator to know it was a curse.

"That's bad?"

"He's going to get us killed, snow djin."

Adif had taken to calling him that on the first day. After Tycho unhooked his makeshift awning as night fell, and let the doublet drop from his shoulders to reveal snow-white skin.

"If they unchain us, grab an oar and kick for land."

"Water will kill me."

The Mamluk hissed and then nodded. Cross with himself for expecting anything else. "Then I wish you a quick death."

Tycho and Adif sat either side of an aisle on the last bench of all. Ahead of them sat the other slaves. Immediately behind, an open-fronted shelter of canvas over wooden hoops was were Captain Malo and the owner's son slept.

Like everyone else on the ship, they shat over the side.

The difference was they did so at will. Adif and Tycho were restricted to pissing themselves where they sat, and shitting each morning, when their hands were briefly unchained. Not all of the slaves could wait that long.

"Arnaud, make him."

The slave master was midway in age between the boy and the captain. His face once handsome but his eyes hard and his temper brutal.

"You heard the boss," he said.

"He's not the boss," Captain Malo said. "I am."

The whip cracked and Tycho heard the captain stagger back, hissing in pain and outrage. "Return to harbour," the slave master ordered.

"If we try, we'll die."

"What's your plan then?" the boy demanded.

"Outrun it," Captain Malo said. "While we can. If we can." He spat, angrily. "Which I now doubt. We could head south, maybe. See if we can edge past it. But in the dark . . ."

"The storm's too big," said Tycho, without thinking.

"Who asked you?"

He heard a whip crack a split second after pain ripped across his shoulders, tearing oiled silk and skin. And then Arnaud was on the raised walkway that ran along the aisle. His boot scraping down the side of Tycho's cheek.

A slave on the row ahead turned round to see what was happening and took the rest of the slave master's anger.

"Enough," Captain Malo snapped.

The slave master raised his whip, and gasped as Adif suddenly slammed his unchained hand into Arnaud's knee. An awkward blow, but it struck lucky, dropping the man to his knees. When he came upright he was holding a knife.

"This is where you die."

There was a dignity to Adif's face as he braced himself to face the blade. And Tycho suddenly understood that the man had forced the quarrel, seeking a quick death instead of drowning. "Good choice," he said.

"*Wait.*"

Anger fought obedience as Arnaud hesitated at the boy's order.

"We've had nothing but shit since we took that thing on board." The owner's son meant Tycho. "Kill him after that one."

The slave master was readying his blade, Adif still waited, refusing to show fear. Captain Malo's face said he knew it ended here.

"Die well," Adif said.

"No," said Tycho. "It doesn't work like that."

Gripping silver-topped spike that nailed him to his oar, he screamed as he ripped it out, feeling flesh sizzle. And then standing, he blocked Arnaud's dagger with his forearm, and jammed the nail under the man's chin. Slamming it into his skull with a slap of his burning hand.

The slave master tumbled sideways.

As the slave opposite grabbed the owner's son by one ankle, Captain Malo elbowed the boy hard in the throat, ordered the slave to let go, and flung the boy overboard to drown. "Idiot," he said.

"*Right*," shouted Tycho. "*Turn her to the storm.*"

"Reckon you're a sailor now?" Captain Malo snarled.

"I intend to live," Tycho said, surprising himself when he realised it was true. "At least, I don't intend to die drowning. Tried it once. Never again."

"He's a djinn. Listen to him."

"Well," Captain Malo said, "he's sure as shit not human. My lord Atilo warned me of that."

Tycho felt his guts knot. He'd hoped Atilo felt some affection. Something behind the coldness in his face as he'd hammered the silver-topped spike in place himself.

"*Turn her. Then lose the oars.*"

"What?"

"Lose them."

"We can stow them," Captain Malo protested. Iron rests either side let the oars be lifted when the galley was under sail.

"It won't be enough."

The sea terrified Tycho. The thought of being swallowed was unbearable. He'd died, and still survived the canal in Venice. What if he sank, died and lived now? Water took his strength. Only the earth bag beneath him kept him sane. He'd be trapped in a watery half-life forever.

"You want to die?" he shouted. The silver-topped spike still jutted from Arnaud's skull, but Tycho had the man's dagger.

Captain Malo shook his head. "I'll get the key."

"No time."

Oars were removed in harbour to stop slaves rowing away when the crew were ashore. At sea, oars were chained in place. "Turn into the storm," Tycho ordered.

"Do it," Captain Malo shouted.

Slaves churned oars in the gravid waves. Those on one side rowing forward. Those on the other rowing back, until the *Seahorse* turned into the wind just as the rain arrived in a rushing wall.

"Hold her steady . . ."

Grabbed Adif's oar chain, Tycho snapped it and pushed the oar through the galley's side. He managed to clear two thirds the *Seahorse*'s length before a huge wave struck, breaking over them. It hit straight on, half lifting the galley, but catching the still-chained oars of those at the front.

The *Seahorse* screamed, wooden ribs twisting and dowels shrieking as they were dragged from their holes. Oak splintered and split. The noise as she fought the sea for the right to stay in one piece was unbearable.

It was a battle between shipwrights now dead and the sea, who wanted their handiwork to join them. Mixed in with the rage of the ship, the howl of the wind and the drumming of the rain were the screams of slaves nursing broken limbs or shouting prayers.

No god would lower his hand to pluck them from the storm. Endless promises might be made. Debts racked up. They meant nothing. The only thing that could save the *Seahorse* was blind luck and the skill of those long dead.

"I'll take it," Tycho said.

Captain Malo glanced from the tiller to the strange youth in front of him.

Rain glued Tycho's braids to his skull. His ghostlike flesh glowed every time lightning flickered. His eyes . . . Tycho could see from the captain's face that something about his eyes terrified the man.

He hadn't time to work out what.

Stepping forward, Tycho grabbed the rudder bar.

Fighting it, he kept the *Seahorse* into the wind. Muscles locked, sinews popping. It was touch and go if the tiller or his wrists broke first. He felt sicker than ever, numb with shock as a wall of water the height of San Marco raced towards him. And then the second wave struck.

53

"You've heard the news from Cyprus?"

"How could I . . ." When the news is so fresh a scroll lies curling in your desk and the wax from its broken seal still sticks to your gloves? "No, my lord," Atilo said. "I haven't."

Alonzo sighed, more heavily than he needed. "You're our spymaster within the city. Our Blade within and without. We should be able to rely on you for knowledge like this."

"My apologies."

"I know," said Alonzo, "life has been tricky for you recently. That failure with your apprentice. The disappearance of Prince Leopold's body. Those men you lost last year. Unless it was the year before. If you feel the burden of your job is too heavy. That perhaps old age is . . ."

"My lord."

The Regent paused expectantly.

"I work for this city day and night. All my energy goes tracking its enemies; recording what happens on the streets; gathering information on those who pretend to be one thing but are another . . ."

Atilo stopped, cursing that he'd walked straight into that one.

"And you must be tired," Alonzo said. "Rightfully exhausted by your burden. This is why important news slipped past you. As I said, if you wish for the freedom to take life more easily at your advancing age . . ."

"All I wish, my lord, is to be allowed to continue."

He could remember what his own father, the idiot astronomer, said. Young men fantasise about death and fear life. Old men fear death and fantasise about youth. Atilo had dismissed it fiercely, then not so fiercely, right up to the day he discovered it to be true. He sighed.

"You're certain? That you simply wish to do your duty?"

"Absolutely certain."

The Regent smiled happily. "I can't tell you," he said, "how glad I am to hear it. That new boy of yours settling in all right?"

A little dig. Just enough to let Atilo know Alonzo had no plans to let Tycho's reprieve go without mention.

"He has potential."

"That's what you said about the last one."

"My lord, whatever I failed in, I stand by my claim he had potential."

"To be the greatest assassin of all time? To be your chosen successor as the duke's Blade itself. Yes, I've heard of your plans for that troublesome young man. I must admit to being surprised.

Heard from whom? From the duchess . . . ?

Surely not. Alexa might have banished Atilo from her bed, but not so far from her favour that she'd share secrets with her hated brother-in-law. There had to be a spy in Atilo's household. Amelia was possible. Iacopo? He wouldn't want to think that likely.

"My lord, may I ask how you know?"

"Of course you may," Alonzo answered. Obviously delighted at the thought of Atilo, Serenissima's spymaster and chief assassin, asking him how he'd discovered such secrets. "Lady Desdaio told me."

"She . . . ?"

Atilo shut his mouth, wondering where Alexa was and why he was alone with the Regent, without even the duke swinging his feet and humming to provide legitimacy for this meeting.

"Not in so many words," Alonzo added. "She said you seemed surprisingly fond of him for you. I simply read between her words. Although your response confirms it." The Regent beamed, pleased with his cunning.

"My lord . . . The reason I'm here?"

"All in good time," Alonzo said, picking a honey-glazed almond from a Murano glass salver and sucking off its sweetness. "The duchess would be upset if I started without her."

As if on cue, halberds slammed on the marble outside as guards came to attention and a door swung open. Duchess Alexa took one look at Alonzo behind the table and Atilo standing there in front of it and scowled.

"I thought the meeting was at six."

"Did we say that?" The Regent sounded surprised. "I confess, I thought it was half an hour earlier. That was the time my lord Atilo arrived."

"Having been called by your guards."

Prince Alonzo smiled. "Perhaps we should start," he said. "Now that you are here at last."

The Regent pretended not to notice the tightness of Alexa's shoulders, or her awareness that, in choosing the desk, he'd left her to stand or take one of the lesser chairs. "My lady."

Alexa took the chair he suggested.

There were servants there, of course. There were always servants. As tradition demanded, they were treated as invisible, only obeying or reacting if spoken to directly. Nothing said here would be repeated. They had families: wives, children, parents . . . Silence was assured.

"Atilo has been telling me he's keen to help any way he can. He has no intention of refusing any task we'd like him to undertake."

The duchess relaxed. "Atilo?"

The Regent was luring him into a trap. No, Atilo shook his head. Far worse. He'd trapped himself already and left no retreat. All he could do was discover how serious it was and what room he had left for manoeuvre.

Easy to forget Alonzo had been a *condottiero*. No, even that was wrong. It was easy to remember, since he mentioned the fact constantly. What was easy to forget was that his fame was deserved. In the days before Alonzo became a drunk he was the best strategist in Italy. Atilo should have realised the Regent's current sobriety was significant.

"Obviously," Atilo said, "I will do what you command. Although my lord Alonzo expressed worries about my age . . ." He knew the Regent wouldn't let him get away with that and he was right.

"Worries now assuaged," Alonzo said smoothly. "Atilo is firm in his belief he's the best man for this."

Best man for what, damn it?

Unrolling a map of the Middle Sea, with red crosses against three Mamluk ports, Alonzo added another at the mouth of the Nile, near Alexandria, and a final cross halfway along the African coast to indicate Tunis or Tripoli. Quickly sketched arrows followed, converging on Cyprus.

Atilo's heart sank. "The sultan?"

"His fleets launched over a week ago." For once Alonzo's voice was flat, his tone matter-of-fact. "He accuses us of burning a Mamluk ship in the lagoon. He refuses to believe otherwise. If he takes Cyprus . . ."

The Regent didn't need to finish that sentence.

If the Sultan took Cyprus, Venice would lose a major ally, a way station between the Nile and Europe, and be disgraced. More than this, if Cyprus fell the Order of Crucifers would be root-less. Bad enough having their embassy in Venice. The idea that the whole Order might need a new base . . .

"Cyprus must be saved." Alexa's voice was brittle.

"My lady?"

"My favour depends on this. What we have in Cyprus is . . ." If Atilo didn't know better, he'd swear she cried beneath her veil. "It's priceless. It must be defended to the death."

Alonzo looked surprised.

"You don't agree?" she demanded.

He shrugged. "I didn't realise you felt so strongly."

"My lord, my lady . . . can we put a fleet together in time?"

"It's done," Alonzo said. "Such as it is. All ships have been ordered to gather at Cyprus. And we've kept a small fleet there since the new year. We simply didn't expect the sultan's own fleet to be this size."

"How many does he have?"

"Two hundred war galleys."

"And how many are we?" Atilo wasn't sure he wanted the answer. Two hundred galleys was a major force. More than the sultan had gathered before. Atilo was surprised that many Mamluk galleys existed in the world.

"Fifty," Prince Alonzo said.

A respectable fleet. An entirely respectable fleet, just outnum-bered four to one by its enemy. Atilo expected little of the Regent, not being in his confidence. But he was shocked Alexa had not told him of this before. "Did we know a fleet was gathering?"

"A fleet, yes," Alonzo said. "Two hundred war galleys, including hardened corsairs from Alexandria and Tunis, and an elite force of ghilman, all converging on Cyprus, no . . ."

"Ambassador Dolphino has failed," said Alexa. "Our spies in North Africa have failed. These are matters for later. I need you to leave immediately." She glanced at Alonzo, nodded slightly. "Janus has agreed you should lead his fleet."

"How?" asked Atilo. No messenger could reach Cyprus and return in the time available.

"That need not concern you."

Atilo's lips tightened. Hightown Crow, then. Unless Crucifers could talk across distances. That was possible. One Black Crucifer to another? If so, could Byzantine mages listen to the ethereal whispers? And if they could, would their emperor help or hinder Venice's ambitions? Byzantium hated the Mamluks. But it didn't love Serenissima either.

"Where does the southern emperor stand?"

A scowl crossed Alonzo's face. "Manuel Palaiologos stands with the winner. So Duchess Alexa believes. I find it hard to believe he'd support heathens."

"You're heathens to him," Alexa said.

Shrugging, the Regent smiled at Atilo. "We have our fastest galley waiting. Draw gold from the treasury. Select your staff, say your goodbyes, send Desdaio back to her father . . ."

"My lord."

"She can't stay at Ca' il Mauros alone."

"She won't go, my lord. They're estranged."

When a smirk twisted Prince Alonzo's lips, Atilo realised he'd walked straight into another trap. That made two in the same hour. The Regent was toying with him. Maybe the man was right. Atilo was getting old.

"Well," Alonzo said, "she can't stay where she is. And it seems she can't return home." He glanced at the duchess. "I guess she'll just have to come here."

"She could join my ladies-in-waiting," Alexa agreed reluctantly.

"Oh, I don't think she needs an official position. At least not yet. Let's see how it goes."

The Regent didn't expect Atilo to return. Whether he hoped he'd fail and die, win and die or simply just die was not obvious. What Atilo knew for certain was that Alonzo had just publicly staked his claim to the richest woman in Venice. In front of the man who was meant to marry her.

In front of the current duke's mother, too.

And Marco would be deposed for sure. If Alonzo got his hands on Lady Desdaio Bribanzo's fortune he'd be ruler of Venice before the year was out. An ex-*condottiero* could buy a very large army indeed with that kind of money.

54

Adif could taste the salt spray, as the wind and tides fought each other. He could feel the *Seahorse* shudder under his bare feet as her keel scraped rocks. Wince at the shriek from her already battered frame. The Mamluk could hear, taste and fear. But he couldn't see the Sicilian cliffs or the narrow gap between them.

Tycho could.

"Grip tight," Tycho said.

Dizzy from water sickness and barely supported by the rope he gripped, Tycho knew his strength was draining like sand in a timer. The power and certainty that feeding on Giulietta had brought him was almost gone. Gone already were his makeshift awning and his earth-filled bag. But he could see a gap between headlands leading to a bay beyond.

And that gave him a strength he didn't expect.

What showed above the gap scared him. A thin line where darkness was turning pale. It edged the cliffs as if an artist had mixed dark and lapis blue and added a tiny trace of imperial purple.

His death written in the sky.

Grabbing the rudder from Adif, he wrenched the bar towards him, feeling crosscurrents try to kick the *Seahorse* out of true.

"We should pray," Captain Malo suggested.

Adif nodded.

"Personally," Tycho spat, "I'd hang on."

Both the men gripped a rail. The captain appeared resigned to losing control of his galley to slaves. The way he kept glancing at a sodden but ornate strapped-down bedroll suggested other worries. Although, if the inrushing tide did carry his ship on to the headland rocks, how to explain the disappearance of the owner's son would be the least of them.

Adif had experience of steering galleys.

Ten years as a sailor had been followed by three as a bosun and two as captain. He had five years as a slave after that, having been captured. Five years was a long time for a galley slave to survive. Most died in their first year. A good number of those left in the year following. He allowed their captain wasn't bad as filthy infidels went.

"The boy died in the storm," Tycho said.

"What?" Captain Malo looked surprised.

"Why not? Your ship's near collapse. It's a miracle we survived."

Pointing to its broken mast, Tycho remembered Captain Malo couldn't see the full horror of what lightning had done. Nor the number of dead slaves still to be tossed overboard. The other slaves huddled, sodden, angry and injured.

"Believe me," he said. "It's nasty."

Close up, the gap between rocks was wider than it looked.

A minute before Tycho had been wondering if the *Seahorse* would fit, now he knew two ships could pass if they didn't mind being lashed together and having their sides scraped. "Hold tight," he shouted.

Seawater heaved as it lifted the galley, carrying her with a rush across the bulging water and down to calm conditions beyond. Behind her, the sea still fought for entry. Ahead lay a low beach on which a fire burnt in front of half a dozen huts. A ramshackle jetty sank into the sea.

"It's a fishing village."

The Mamluk clapped Tycho on the shoulder.

"He can see in the dark? That's how he got us here?"

"Yes," Adif admitted.

"Get me on to dry land," Tycho said. "Cover me before daylight arrives."

"*What?*" Captain Malo demanded.

"That's my price for saving you."

"He'll give you freedom," Adif said. "You saved the *Seahorse*, you saved our lives. We'd be dead if not for you. He'll give you freedom."

"No. He won't."

And looking at the captain's face Tycho knew he was right. The owner's son was dead. Captain Malo's ship needed repairs. Captain Malo could no more risk offending Venice by freeing Tycho than Tycho could fly. He would be taken to the slave market in Cyprus and sold as Alonzo ordered.

55

Limassol's slave market was open on all four sides, roofed in crumbling clay tiles, and supported on misshapen sandstone pillars. The steps to the selling plinth were worn and dipped from years of merchandise being led before buyers.

The platform could take five at a time. Outstanding offerings were sold individually. Brothers and sisters were usually sold in pairs. The rest in bundles of three or five. No one could remember a sale to sell a single slave before.

Certainly not a sale that started at midnight.

Maybe it was the strange hour, or the fact that only one slave was on offer, that drew a huge crowd to a district most patricians tried to avoid. Mind you, most patricians, including the king, tried to avoid Limassol altogether. Squalid by day, noisy by night, stinking of animals and slaves, it was fit only for merchants.

And maybe, Sir Richard Glanville thought, the rumours of an invasion had led to the party atmosphere. A reaction to everyone's natural worry. Since returning from Venice and his time as the king's envoy he'd found himself second in command of the White Crucifers. Sometimes a tricky place to be.

Sir Richard didn't relish taking the slave to market.

The boy was filthy, dressed in a squalid doublet, with his hair braided, and swaying drunkenly as he stumbled and muttered, trying not to trip over his fetters. Sir Richard would have thought this task beneath him if the prior had not suggested it.

The price Sir Richard received was irrelevant.

What mattered was that the slave be sold within a day of arriving. And so, having been delivered last night to the Priory of the White Crucifers, the boy had been locked in a dungeon for the day, slopped down from a bucket at nightfall, and delivered to Limassol in an ox cart guarded by five men at arms.

Sir Richard would have felt better if the boy tried to escape.

"We're here," his sergeant said.

"I can see that."

The man's face tightened.

They should be preparing Cyprus against the Mamluks. Goat herds needed driving into the mountains, or slaughtering and salting against the coming siege. Swords required sharpening. Damn it, they needed making. Sir Richard commanded five hundred soldiers. What was he doing at midnight with some pretty boy slave who'd end up a merchant's catamite?

Unless the king wanted him.

Sir Richard hadn't considered that. King Janus's tastes were complicated. There was a rumour, probably false, involving the Grand Prior when both were much younger. If Janus wanted this boy that changed things.

How subtle was Venice?

Subtle enough to send an assassin disguised as a pretty slave to attract the attention of the prince he intended to kill. Sir Richard wouldn't put it past them. But why would Venice weaken Cyprus at a time like this? He took another look at the boy with the silver-grey hair.

"You," he said.

The slave turned as Sir Richard punched.

A soldier swore, Sir Richard's sergeant dropped his hand to his dagger, wondering what he'd missed, but Sir Richard's attention was on the boy. Who blocked his blow without even thinking about it and settled into a rear-foot stance, readying but not throwing an answering blow.

Looking round, Sir Richard realised enough of the crowd had seen it for rumours to raise the boy's price still further.

"No," the boy said. "I'm not."

Sir Richard's blue eyes narrowed.

"I'm not here to kill anybody. That's what you're thinking, isn't it? That I'm here to murder someone?" The boy's voice was strained. His eyes sweeping the crowd as if looking for faces he recognised.

"Let's get this over with," Sir Richard said.

Leading the slave to the steps, he passed him to the slave master.

A fat Nubian with gold earrings, proudly protruding belly and a tatty gold waistcoat that barely covered his chest, Isak collected old manuscripts, carved ivory, read three languages and spoke five. His hooped gold earrings only came out on market day, like his waistcoat and oiled belly.

"It's a good crowd," Isak said.

"Given your advertising I'm not surprised."

Proclamations had appeared on doors for those who could read. Everyone else had the words read to them or picked up the gossip in taverns. "A male slave of unsurpassing beauty, so rare his milk-white skin cannot stand sunlight, to be sold at midnight this coming Tuesday. The only sale of the day. No credit will be given."

"You know he's trained to kill?"

Isak grimaced. "Really? That'll double his price with half tonight's bidders and halve it with the rest. I need to decide what to say about that."

In the event, Isak didn't mention it.

He simply took the youth from Sir Richard, walked him to the top of the sandstone block and cut away the tatty doublet covering him. "You know what you're buying," he said. "Here he is."

Turning the half-naked boy to face the crowd hemming in all four sides of the standing stone, Isak held a lamp close to the slave's body, so they could see the whiteness of his skin, the fineness of his features, the strange silver-grey hair.

"The bidding starts at five hundred gold ducats."

A stunned silence greeted the starting price, with some bidders mentally upping the level they'd set for their final bid, and others realising the auction was too rich for them but deciding to stay, anyway, to watch.

"Here," a man said, raising his hand slightly.

Exactly who Isak expected to make the first bid. A silk merchant from Alexandria. He couldn't afford the boy but was now known to have been in the bidding war. "Any advance on five hundred?"

A hand rose, a man nodded, a second hand twitched, and then a third and a fourth; someone scratched their nose near the back. When the frenzy stopped, the bidding stood at fifteen hundred gold ducats and the Alexandria merchant was shaking his head regretfully. Hangers-on were commiserating and telling him he was wise to stop there.

The man had money worries and trouble extending his line of credit. Having been seen to bid gold on a single slave he'd find credit easier. A man with money worries wouldn't bid so highly, would he?

Isak smiled at the ways of the world.

"Any advance on fifteen hundred?"

A merchant bid an enemy up to two thousand and then dropped out, leaving his enemy to drop out two hundred ducats later. A Crucifer knight twitched his hand, and at the rear a young woman raised her whole arm, ignoring rules that suggested bidding be discreet. She was newly arrived and newly bidding.

Isak had memorised those who had bid already. And had identified a handful of those waiting for the auction to be reduced to serious bids only.

With her curling chestnut-dark hair, sweetly round face and ample bosom he would have remembered her anyway.

Glancing behind him, the previous bidder tried to discover who he was bidding against. But the woman now had her hand to her side. Obviously embarrassed to be the centre of attention of those around her.

"Your bid, my lord."

The man was a simple knight, but Isak always found it helped inflate the bids if he inflated the bidder's importance. This man, however, was not bidding for himself. No Crucifer, bound to chastity, poverty and charity, had that kind of money. Or, if they did, they were taking their vows laxly.

"Three thousand gold ducats."

The crowd gasped in admiration at the way he'd cut straight from two thousand five hundred ducats to three without bothering to hit the hundreds between. You could fit out a galley for that money. Fit out a galley, or fill a brothel with the most beautiful slaves, even buy a small palace.

"Four thousand," the young woman said.

The Crucifer knight turned to stare. She blushed, but didn't take back her bid, although she looked at the ground, before raising her eyes to meet the scowling knight's gaze, then blushed all over again.

"My lord, the bid is yours."

Around the knight the crowd held its breath.

Why would anyone pay this for a single slave? Isak knew it stopped here. He could see that in the knight's face. Either he'd reached the maximum he was ordered to bid; or he was buying for himself, which, given the fury in his eyes, seemed possible. If so, he'd reached what his forbidden purse would stand.

"*Four thousand five hundred ducats.*"

Isak wondered if the young woman pushing frantically through the crowd knew she was bidding against herself. He looked at the knight, who shook his head. The slave was doing the same. Staring at the young woman and shaking his head as she edged towards the sandstone block and her purchase.

Pushing past Isak, the woman grabbed a blanket from the dirt and wrapped it round the slave's shoulders, covering his bare torso. The slave master noticed she was careful not to look at his body as she did so.

"My lady," the boy said. "Does Lord Atilo know?"

The woman shook her head.

"Why are you even here?" he demanded. "Why aren't you home?"

"Where's home?" she said, tears in her eyes. "With my father, who won't talk to me? Or at the Ca' Ducale, my body and fortune at the Regent's mercy, because staying alone at Ca' il Mauros isn't allowed?"

"And Pietro?" the boy asked.

The woman looked puzzled.

"The new apprentice?"

"Safe in Venice, with Iacopo and Amelia. They're allowed to stay at Ca' il Mauros, apparently." Her complaint was loud enough to carry. Those who heard it would tell those who hadn't. By morning, all Limassol would know. Although what they'd know would bear little resemblance to any truth. Isak had no idea who she was, but she worried him.

"My lady, you might want to have this conversation somewhere private. Let us settle, and you can take your purchase." He scanned the crowd for her retinue. Looking for her major domo or whoever kept her purse.

"I'm alone," she said.

Isak's smile froze. His rules were money on the nail, no credit and no taking the goods without payment. The knight's three thousand coins were better, paid now, than substantially more, paid sometime in the future, if at all . . .

"I'm Desdaio Bribanzo," she said. "This is Tycho."

The slave nodded ruefully.

Dragging a jewelled bracelet from her arm, she said. "Take this as payment. It cost five thousand ducats."

Very fine indeed. Filigree gold inlaid with cameos, carnelians, pearls, emeralds and rubies. Its weight alone made Isak wonder she didn't tire wearing the thing. "Venetian made?"

"Milanese. A present from the duke."

"Of Milan?" Isak asked, keeping his face impassive.

"As opposed to Venice, you mean?"

Isak turned the gold bracelet over in his hand, and nodded. Yes, that was exactly what he meant. And it really was very beautiful indeed. He wondered what she would have to do to earn this.

"Marco wanted to marry me too. But Alexa wouldn't let him. Well, I was told he wanted to marry me. I suspect it was Alonzo's idea."

That was the point Isak decided he needed to bring this conversation to a swift close. The bracelet had quality and was made for a duke. That would add value when it sold. All the same, the rules existed. If he broke them this time . . .

Mind you, with a Mamluk fleet approaching who knew what would happen? Mamluks needed slaves as much as the next lot. But they distrusted Nubians, and Isak had heard Byzantium was a fine place to sell slaves. Maybe even a fine place to retire. And her bracelet was portable. Useful should he need to leave in a hurry. In the time it took Isak to think this, Desdaio dragged free her earrings.

"Take these as well . . ."

And then she added a brooch to the collection. At first Isak thought the earrings were amethyst. Then he realised they were pale and flawless rubies. "Also from the Duke of Milan?"

"From Lord Dolphino."

Isak blinked.

He wanted to be away from this young woman with her impressive breasts and huge eyes, and seemingly inexhaustible supply of priceless jewellery. A woman who tossed around the names of admirals, and *condottieri*, and dukes and princes as if they were her closest neighbours.

"You should take your slave and flee."

"Why?" Desdaio asked.

"The Mamluks will be here within the week."

"Tomorrow, probably. Maybe the day after. But Cyprus is safe."

"How can it be?" asked Isak, stunned by her certainty.

"Because my future husband, Lord Atilo il Mauros, leads the fleet against them."

56

"You gave your mother's brooch? Dolphino's earrings. The bracelet Gian Maria sent you . . . ?" Atilo's mouth was a tight line. He put one hand to his dagger, although that was for Tycho, who stood to one side.

They were in an upper chamber of the Priory.

A stark and coldly decorated room, made hot by Atilo's anger and a night wind smelling of smoke and herbs. Sheep were roasting over pits outside. Food for the Crucifers who would fight tomorrow's battle.

Every ship in the Cypriot fleet would carry a mix of galley slaves and free sailors. Also Crucifer knights, crossbowmen, soldiers and pikemen. Those vessels carrying mage fire needed masters to fire the flame, work the bellows and keep the deadly mixture from killing those it should protect.

Mage fire won battles.

Stealing its secret from Byzantium had been the Crucifers' making. It also explained the hatred existing between them. Mage fire won battles and it lost them. Ships had been destroyed by the fire they carried before. They would be again.

None of that concerned Atilo now.

"How could you?" The pain in his voice was so raw that Desdaio blinked, tears filling her eyes and her bottom lip quivering. Atilo barely noticed. "I said I'd deal with it. After I talked to King Janus."

"They were selling him . . ."

"I'd have bought him back. You went *alone* to a slave market. You gave your own jewels for a disgraced slave." He shot a vicious glance at Tycho, who stayed silent.

"*You have no idea.*"

"No idea what?"

"What it feels like to be for sale."

"And you have?"

"Of course I have." Desdaio was furious. For a second, Atilo feared she would hit him. Should he let her? Or catch her wrist? How hard should he grip?

"Listen to me," she shouted. "Don't do that with your face. I don't want to know you're *thinking*. I want to know you're *listening* to me . . ."

Tears rolled down her cheeks.

"You went into his room," Atilo said, a statement of fact.

"*Yes*," she said. "*I went into his room*. To warn him about the test. *Nothing happened*. He told me to leave."

"Why didn't you tell me?"

"Look at yourself," she said. "Standing there with your hand on your dagger. Why do you think I didn't tell you?"

Tycho caught the moment the Moor's gaze shifted from Desdaio to where he stood a couple of paces behind her. Barefoot, half-starved, draped in the discarded blanket with which she'd wrapped him at the market.

"Is that all you're good for?" Atilo hissed. "Hiding behind a girl?"

"Give me a knife, old man. We'll see."

Atilo's mouth fell open.

"Even weak like this," said Tycho. "I can kill you."

"You dare . . . ?"

"You're past it." Tycho's voice was cold. "You've lost your strength, your nerve, your reflexes. All you've got left are your skills and they're not what they were, are they?" He could see the truth in Atilo's eyes. The man didn't believe all that was true. But he was worried it might be.

"Not yet ready for your grave?"

Turning his back on his old master, Tycho glanced at the darkness outside. Past midnight by an hour or so. He had two hours, maybe three, before he needed to protect himself against daylight.

And the sad thing, the thing that twisted Tycho up inside, was that he missed the sun. Missed its warmth and its brightness, its warmth on water and the smell it gave to bare skin. Memories of sunlight reminded him of the boy he used to be . . . Every time he changed the sun scared him a little more. Without his doublet and without Dr. Crow's ointment he had no choice but to hide.

"Face me," Atilo said.

"Why would I bother?"

Closing the gap in three steps, Atilo slapped him.

Tycho laughed. So Atilo backhanded him hard, obviously expecting the boy to go down. But Tycho stood his ground, grinning through bloody lips. "Is that the best you can do?"

The third time Atilo struck, Tycho caught his hand, held it briefly and then tossed it away, as if discarding rubbish.

"Don't you mock me," Atilo hissed.

"Someone has to."

Drawing his dagger in a single sweep, Atilo put its point to Tycho's chin, where a blade can pass through muscle, tongue and palate, entering the cavities behind the nose to pierce the brain.

"I let you do that."

The dagger's point jabbed tighter. "No, you didn't."

"Are you sure?" The question earned Tycho the dagger point digging through skin until blood ran sluggish and black down the outside of his throat.

"Feel that?" Tycho asked.

And Atilo did. Tycho could see that from the old man's stillness and his widening eyes. Atilo's spare dagger was at his own balls. Tycho had removed it from his belt without the old man even noticing.

"Do they still work?"

"Stop it," Desdaio shouted.

Tycho had no idea which of them she was talking to. Nor did Atilo from his face. That thought only made the man angrier. The Moor's eyes were cold, his mouth above his sharp beard set hard. He wanted to hurt Tycho. Wanted to punch his blade into Tycho's brain. But the dagger at his groin froze his courage. And Desdaio's presence prevented him.

"Am I interrupting something?" said a voice from the doorway.

"*You . . . Here?*"

Tycho could have killed Atilo then. Instead, he stepped back, shooting the newcomer a twisted grin. While Atilo was still staring, Tycho returned the spare dagger to Atilo's belt with a flourish and gave their guest a bow.

Prince Leopold laughed.

"You must be Lady Desdaio. As beautiful as rumour says . . ."

She was staring from Tycho to Atilo, and then at the elegantly dressed stranger, wondering who he was and why the man she hoped to marry hated him even more than the boy he'd just wanted to kill.

"Tell me what's going on," Desdaio demanded.

Sweeping her a bow, Prince Leopold zum Bas Friedland introduced himself by name, late of Venice and recently of Cyprus. "Three killers, one innocent. Unless there are things about you I don't know . . . ?"

Prince Leopold smiled.

"No? Thought not."

"Atilo's a soldier," Desdaio protested.

"Some wars are honourable," said Prince Leopold. "Others less so. He fights a darker war. As do I. If we fight the other type it's by accident. As for him . . ." He nodded towards Tycho. "His war's so dark he barely knows what it is."

"He's my slave," Atilo said dismissively.

Prince Leopold raised his eyebrows. His gaze slid to Desdaio, who'd gone tight-lipped. "I think your beloved might disagree. I hear she gave her mother's jewellery to buy him."

"Among other things," Atilo said. "I'll buy it back."

On Desdaio's face was an expression Tycho hadn't seen before. Somewhere between anger, stubbornness and irritation. Although her stance, feet planted as if she'd just stepped up to the mark on a *punta di Puglia*, suggested determination too. Meeting her eyes, Prince Leopold grinned.

"Tycho's nobody's," she said crossly. "I bought him. I freed him."

"We'll discuss this later."

Nobody saw Tycho move. One second he faced Atilo, the next he was stood behind the man, his finger drawing a line across Atilo's throat. Smiling, he stepped back and sketched another bow.

"You lose," he said.

"No," Leopold said. "He wins. He told Alonzo you had potential. Told Alexa too . . ." The prince shrugged apologetically. For mentioning Atilo's lover in front of his beloved probably.

57

A night of clarity and wonder. The kind that only comes before a major battle or the start of a siege. When everyone knows plague, fire and famine are saddling their horses and life's rules no longer apply. The end of the world will probably feel like this.

Although Bjornvin's burning, which ended his last world, felt different, Tycho hadn't known what was coming then until it did. He was someone different now. Now he could taste blood on the wind before it was spilt. Blood, and his own longing. If Prince Leopold was in Cyprus then so was Lady Giulietta. The thought made Tycho shiver.

He'd thought he'd never see her again. So the need had become a dull ache, a frostbite of the mind that ate his hope little by little, turning everything to ice. Until the hope of seeing her cracked it open.

The first surprise was King Janus sending for him.

Janus, also called John, stood in a hastily arranged chamber that had been a tower room until given grander duties. A wooden chair with a tapestry over it made do for a throne. Beside him stood the Prior of the White Crucifers. The king was thin and clean shaven, Prior Ignacio taller and even thinner, dressed in white robes. Both men had once been handsome. Having returned Desdaio's jewellery, King Janus confirmed Tycho's freedom, commended his courage and ordered him to kneel, drawing his sword to dub him a knight.

"Your majesty!" Atilo protested.

"He will save Cyprus," Prior Ignacio explained.

Atilo looked troubled. "You've seen this, my lord?"

"We detest predivination, as we detest all forms of magic," the Prior said firmly. Which wasn't answering the question. Everyone in the tower room knew this was his stated position. No one believed it for a minute. The rumours of Crucifer power were too open and too commonplace.

"I told them," Prince Leopold said.

"Then it's a trap," Atilo's voice rose. "My slave betrayed me because of this man. The prince killed a dozen of . . . my servants," he ended, realising *followers* might invite awkward questions.

"And you a dozen of his," King Janus said.

"Oh yes," said the Prior. "We know all about that. Prince Leopold is here at the king's invitation. And under Crucifer protection." Anyone who didn't know this had just been warned. The sour expression on Atilo's face said he understood this. And knew the person being warned was him.

"This boy," King Janus said, "has done me service already."

Catching Tycho's gaze, Prince Leopold smiled, his eyes flicking to the gallery above where women watched discreetly from behind a fretworked screen.

"What is your real name?" Janus asked.

"I don't know, majesty."

"You are a Venetian foundling?" Several of the court raised their eyebrows at this question. King Janus was notorious for how little he cared about the rules governing nobility. All the same . . .

"Far from Venice. My true name was scratched on a stone thrown into Bjornvin's deepest lake to keep it hidden."

"Bjornvin?" King Janus asked.

"My home."

"You've heard of it?"

Prior Ignacio shook his head. "Never, majesty."

"And where is this home?" the king asked. "How did you reach Serenissima? By ship? Overland from the north? In a caravan across Turcoman deserts?"

"Through fire."

The Prior blanched. He glanced at Janus, who looked round the tower room, considering. A handful of knights, a German prince, Atilo il Mauros. Women on the balcony above and Desdaio standing below. And, finally, the ex-slave kneeling at his feet. The story was containable if necessary.

King Janus tightened his grip on his sword.

"Through fire?" he said lightly.

Tycho nodded. "Bjornvin burnt. I was there, then not. I fell through flames and remember nothing after that . . ."

"Nothing at all?"

"My waking memory is of being bound. Walled up in a Mamluk ship's hull and starving in the darkness until Captain Roderigo cut me free and his sergeant and men set the ship on fire."

"Is this true?" King Janus demanded.

Atilo's mouth opened, but no words emerged.

"Well?" the king demanded.

"Majesty, I know nothing of this."

"Why didn't this captain tell anyone? Surely, he would have told . . ."

"He couldn't," Tycho lied. "I bewitched him to silence."

One of the Crucifers crossed himself. *Now, Roderigo owes me*, Tycho thought. Although he doubted if he would ever collect on the debt. On King Janus's face surprise was replaced by a realisation that the Mamluks had justice on their side.

"This is not good," Janus said.

"That ship?" asked the Prior.

It seemed the sultan had every right to accuse Venice of burning one of his ships, but knowing it changed nothing. An accept-ance he'd been wronged wouldn't turn back the Mamluk fleet.

"You were a prince in Bjornvin?"

"I was a slave."

King Janus laughed. "You're meant to say you're royal. At least claim nobility. It's compulsory."

"I was a slave," Tycho repeated. "My mother was an exile."

"What were her people?"

"The Fallen."

"Majesty." Prince Leopold stepped forward. Standing close to the king and the Prior, he spoke so softly that only those two men and Tycho would hear him, and Tycho shouldn't have been able to do so. "This is not something to be talked about openly. I vouch for his blood line. I owe him a life."

"As I owe you a life," King Janus said. "If you hadn't abducted Giulietta we would be married and I would be poisoned if her story is true."

"I believe it," Prince Leopold said.

"Yes," King Janus said. "So do I."

Having knighted Tycho, the king dragged him to his feet, ordered a chamberlain to find the startled youth a doublet more fitting to his new status. Janus was about to withdraw when Prince Leopold made a request of his own.

Tycho stood to one side, Desdaio to the other. In the middle was Prince Leopold, and, next to him, his bride. Lady Giulietta and Tycho had yet to look at each other.

Atilo's shock at seeing Lady Giulietta was nothing to his shock when he realised why she was there. The marriage of a Millioni to a German prince went against everything Venice stood for. He *knew* what Prince Leopold was. In a short, brutal but whis-pered exchange Giulietta told Atilo she did too.

And she knew Leopold had tried to abduct her that summer. But this was different. He'd saved her.

It took a direct order from King Janus for Atilo to stay in the room. And a second order to make him accept Desdaio as Lady Giulietta's maid of honour. That she chose a fellow Venetian as her maid surprised no one. That Prince Leopold zum Bas Friedland chose a newly made knight offended everybody inclined to be offended and shocked the rest.

"I do . . ."

Lady Giulietta's happiness filled the Lady chapel. Her wry smile when she looked at the stone mother was almost as sweet as her glance to the infant at her breast. Baby and bosom were shrouded by a Maltese shawl. Feeding him proved the only way to keep Leo quiet long enough to let the couple exchange vows.

"I do too," said Prince Leopold.

Then had to stand, red-faced, while Prior Ignacio insisted on asking the question which had just been answered precipitously.

The Prior's voice rolling out across the room. He was a man used to public speaking and his was a voice used to command. At the start, the congregation had been ordered to think of nothing but the wedding couple.

The Mamluk fleet did not exist.

No peasants herded sheep and goats for slaughter. No foot soldiers strengthened walls and prepared faggots of wood for burning or melting pitch to be poured from the battlements. No smiths forged new swords, no shipwrights made Cyprus's galleys seaworthy. No Crucifer knights sharpened their battle-axes.

None of these things existed.

Tycho wondered how many of the congregation realised they'd just been told exactly what was coming. What the Crucifers were doing to fight it. All under the pretence of being told not to pay it attention at all.

"Now can I say it . . . ?"

Prior Ignacio allowed himself a smile at Prince Leopold's

fervour, and the fact this was the second time he'd made his vow in less than a minute. He spoke the words, then said, "There's something else."

Prior Ignacio frowned. Wondering what came next.

"I acknowledge this child as mine." He indicated the baby. "I want him made legitimate."

"*Leopold . . .*"

"*Let me speak.*"

Giulietta shut her mouth. Not something that came naturally, and stared at the man beside her, tears in her eyes.

"This is my heir."

Prince Leopold drew back Maltese lace. As Giulietta hastily covered her breast her new husband lifted the baby from her, stared significantly at Tycho, and opened the baby's gown, exposing a scratch to its chest.

"My heir in all things."

"This is unusual," Atilo protested.

"These are unusual times." The king's voice was mild, his smile warm. But there was a rebuke in his voice.

"Yes, majesty."

Taking the baby, Prior Ignacio held it up. Maybe there was a ceremony legitimising bastards. Although Tycho suspected he was making it up as he went along. "You claim this boy as your lawful heir?"

"I do," Leopold said firmly.

"You are this boy's mother? As Prince Leopold zum Bas Friedland is his father?"

Lady Giulietta bit her lip.

"My child. We need your answer."

"The boy is mine. I went to my husband's bed a virgin. Nobody had bedded me before." Her eyes slid to Tycho. "No man has shared my bed since."

"Tell me if this is true," Janus said.

Taking the child from Leopold, the Prior stared into the

distance. The old man's face, initially blank, became increasingly puzzled.

"Well?" the king demanded.

"I sense Millioni blood in his veins."

King Janus waited impatiently for what came next. Before realising that nothing did. The Prior could sense Millioni blood. That was it. The king looked at Leopold with new interest.

"I swear I tell the truth," Giulietta said hastily.

In a handful of Latin, which was enough for the surrounding knights, Prior Ignacio named the boy Leopold's heir, confirmed the marriage of his parents, named him Leo di Millioni de zum Bas Friedland, and offered a prayer for his future.

58

"You knew?" Atilo demanded.

An hour before dawn. To the others it was still dark. For Tycho it had long since become light. He'd watched the horizon change colour. Mountains edge through shades of black. Windmills standing stark on the plain. This was a country of squat stone towers with wide sails, on slopes so barren there was as much dirt as scrub. He could have liked it here.

It obviously hurt Atilo to approach his last apprentice.

The old man's voice was as stiff as his shoulders, his question as cropped as his hair. He knew half the court watched them from a distance.

"I knew," Tycho said.

"She was there in Ca' Friedland?"

"In his bed, suckling his child." The last was a lie; she'd been in her own chamber until the battle above disturbed her. But there was no need for the old man to know that.

"Why didn't you tell me?"

"And get my throat cut? A Millioni princess in bed with the bastard of her family's enemy? You sent me to kill the prince.

Chances were, you'd kill me for failing. But returning to say that? I might as well stand naked in the sun . . ."

"You think that idea didn't cross my mind?"

"Maybe, but you'd be doing it to me. Telling you about Lady Giulietta and Leopold was doing it to myself."

"*Leopold* . . . ? He's really a friend?"

In as much as anyone could be. Tycho didn't bother to explain that bit of it. Besides, in any sensible world, Leopold and he would be enemies. Giulietta loved her husband. Tycho loved Giulietta. What better reason to hate a man than the very thought of his wife made your guts knot with longing?

"Where does that leave us?" Atilo said.

"There is no us. I could kill you but Janus wouldn't approve. So I'm going to let the Mamluks do it instead. That way you die a hero . . ."

Turning his back, Tycho threaded his way between Crucifer knights and Cypriot courtiers. Finally reaching an alcove where Prince Leopold stood with his arm round his new wife.

"Look after Leopold," she said.

"My lady . . ."

"I mean it. Protect him if you can."

"Two things," Tycho said, smiling. "One, does Leopold look like a man who lets others look after him? And two . . ." He indicated the coming dawn. "The battle will be over before I join it."

"Your eyes get no better?"

"They get worse," Tycho said.

"You're changing," Prince Leopold said. "Now, if you'd excuse us . . ."

Lady Giulietta pulled a face, but she let herself be steered towards the door, courtiers moving aside and bowing as she passed. As she disappeared under an arch, Leopold slapped her buttocks and laughed at her protest.

"The best of his family."

Turning, Tycho found King Janus at his side.

"I wouldn't know, majesty."

"Take it from me. You fight beside him?"

"With luck."

"If the battle lasts until dark?"

"You know about that?"

Janus shrugged. "Too delicate to face daylight. That's what Isak boasted on his posters. Delicate isn't the word I'd choose." His grey eyes searched Tycho's face. "Magically unable to face daylight, maybe. How did you and Leopold meet?"

"In battle, majesty."

"You've fought together before?"

"I was sent to kill him. Giulietta asked for his life. I gave it."

Glancing round, King Janus checked who might have heard the answer. His courtiers had dropped back. The Prior of the White was watching, his expression unreadable behind his beard.

"Walk with me."

The battlements were overcrowded, The air still cold, but ready to warm with the approaching day. A sergeant, in rusting breast-plate, turned to curse their pushing past and stopped, suddenly apologetic. He was old, one-eyed and crooked where his leg had once been badly broken.

Janus clapped him on the shoulder and kept walking towards a corner turret. A huge catapult had been dragged into position, and its plaited ropes were being tied to huge steel rings on the turret floor.

"The plaiting takes the shock?"

King Janus nodded his appreciation of Tycho's guess.

"You beat Prince Leopold. A famous duellist. Then gave him his life because a woman asked you. And were, it seems, banished for so doing."

Maybe the king was talking to Tycho. Maybe to himself. When Janus nodded, then nodded again, Tycho knew his second guess was correct and he'd been right to remain silent. "Tomorrow," said the king, "decides everything."

"Everything, majesty?"

"Until the next time. Of course, if tomorrow goes badly there will be no next time. No Cyprus. No Crucifer stronghold. No me, probably. No Giulietta or Desdaio except as slaves."

"Leopold will take Giulietta. I imagine Atilo intends to do the same . . ."

"Into battle?" King Janus looked aghast.

"Would you leave your woman to be defiled? If you knew defeat made that certain? Leopold won't. I doubt Atilo will either."

"My wife was poisoned."

"Majesty?"

"She died a year ago. No, two years now."

The king's gaze unfocused. Such bleakness flooded his face it was like looking at a Greek mask, right down to the hollow space behind the eyes and the drag of his mouth. A single tear said this mask belonged to a man.

"It feels like yesterday."

They stood in the near-dawn. On hastily fortified battlements. With a Mamluk fleet somewhere over the dark horizon. The men at arms had fallen back, unsure if the king's grief involved Tycho or just the situation in general. Few of those in the castle expected to be alive next month.

The peasants would change sides.

Why not? No one asked them if they wanted to be ruled over. And the cost to them was much the same whoever did. Taxes and tithes, daughters taken, sons drafted into militias. A ruler who was strong but harsh was better than one who was kind but weak. Strong rulers gave stability.

"Can you really make a difference tomorrow?"

"I have a question of my own."

King Janus sucked his teeth. "Maybe the Prior is right. I should have executed you and be done with it."

"Answering my question might be simpler."

"So like Atilo," the king said. "Perhaps that's the problem.

The Moor trained you too well. So now he has no reason to exist."

"He tried to kill me earlier."

"If he wanted to kill you, then you'd be dead." Janus caught Tycho's expression. "And so would he, perhaps. So maybe he didn't think his own life was a price worth paying to take yours. What's your question?"

"Why were you troubled when I mentioned fire?"

"Ah, yes," said King Janus, "the reason Prior Ignacio thinks I should execute you. Part of me fears he is right."

It was, Janus told him, how Charlemagne, the greatest of the Frankish emperors, sent reinforcements from the Rhine to Roncevaux. Though his loup garou arrived too late to save Count Roland. And Prior Ignacio had told King Janus the Four Horsemen of the Apocalypse would arrive through just such a circle. Tycho could see how the Prior might be worried.

"This is instant?" Tycho asked.

"I'm not sure I understand your question."

"You step into a fire in one place and arrive instantly in the other?"

The king scratched his stubble and sighed. "We're talking heresy," he said. "Dangerous heresy at that. But, yes, I imagine it's quick. Why?"

"I was wondering if it might take longer in some cases."

"How much longer?"

"A hundred years," Tycho said, and then shrugged at the king's expression. "It was just an idea."

59

"Prince Leopold says now would be a good time, Sir Tycho."

Knuckles tapped at a box lid, then a soldier apologised roughly for his rudeness, cursed himself for cowardice and rapped harder.

"If you're done sleeping, Prince Leopold says . . ." Atilo led the fleet, but Prince Leopold represented the king. From the bitterness in the soldier's voice, Tycho took it the battle went badly. How badly he discovered when he reached deck and found himself surrounded by a broken fleet under a darkening sky.

Sailors were lashing Leopold's ship, the *Lionheart*, to Atilo's own.

Grinding into her sides, a Mamluk galley had buckled the *Lionheart*'s planks and widened her seams enough to flood the bilges. Archers who should be fighting were bailing. Just not fast enough to keep her afloat unless tied to another.

The sullen sun sinking into the far horizon was mirrored and mimicked by two dozen fires dotting the wine-dark sea around them. Mamluk ships burnt, but so did Cypriot and Venetian ones. The screams of shackled slaves could be heard across the water.

"Enjoy your sleep?"

There was strain in Leopold's voice.

His jest was forced, almost insulting. His expression grim, and his face grimed with soot and his beard with blood. More blood oozed from an arrow's gash on his arm, which had been tied above the elbow. The dark eyes that had melted Giulietta's heart looked desperate. "Where is she?" Tycho demanded.

"You love her, don't you?"

"Yes," he said simply.

"She's below. I should probably kill you, but . . ." Prince Leopold indicated the smoke and flames, the sinking ships being slowly swallowed by the sea's flat surface. "There doesn't seem much point. But I still want an honest answer."

"To what?"

"My question. You knew Giulietta before that night, didn't you? On the roof at Ca' Friedland, you recognised her from somewhere else . . ."

Tycho nodded.

"Is the child yours?"

"*What?*"

Answer enough. Simply asking obviously left a taste in Leopold's mouth because he turned his attention back to the burning wrecks around them. "Suggest something," he said. "Suggest it quick. We can't afford losses like this."

The numbers were brutal. The Mamluks needed Atilo's ship, the *San Marco*, sunk or captured. The Great Lion flying from her mast was prize enough to make a pauper rich, a soldier an officer, an officer a noble of rank.

The Mamluk's pennant held the same value.

Sultans feared their sons, generals feared their staff. Their admiral's second in command would be good at provisioning but useless in battle. His third in command would be a fighter, hated by his immediate boss, viewed with suspicion by his admiral. Hindered from treason by the fact he was the admiral's nephew, second cousin or bastard son.

Although bastards were risky.

They hated their fathers as much as their legitimate brothers.

To destroy the Mamluk admiral's flagship would weaken his fleet.

News of his death would strengthen those Crucifers remaining on Cyprus to defend it. Knights, should they survive, would gain titles, captains become knights, sergeants become captains if they fought well. Four to one at the battle's start. The odds against Atilo now stood at six to one. Both sides having lost twenty vessels.

The odds could only get worse.

"Here they come again." Prince Leopold's voice was weary.

A huge Mamluk galley, its prow a castle, its copper-bound ram snaking a wake through dark water, was turning towards them, the oars along its side rising and falling in time to the beat of a drum.

"Their admiral." Tycho pointed.

An ornate galley waited on their far side.

The Mamluk admiral's aim was to crush the *Lionheart* and *San Marco*—one already damaged and lashed to the other—with one of his far larger galleys. There was a risk, obviously. That the Mamluk galley would become trapped. But if the enemy aimed right, it would smash Sir Leopold's ships to tinder, without destroying itself. Fine for mage fire.

At Prince Leopold's nod, a thickset man cuffed a boy, sending him towards a huge bellows. Another leather-aproned boy followed quickly after. The two apprentices worked a handle to pump air into a copper cylinder, where a return valve stopped it escaping. When the pressure was high enough, the firemaster stepped forward as Prince Leopold moved back.

"Try it and hide it," the prince ordered.

"Yes, sir."

Arcing over the *Seahorse*'s stern, a thin jet of fire sizzled as it hit the waves, breaking into sticky globules of flame. Although the Mamluk admiral on Atilo's far side could see this, the mage fire was hidden from the galley bearing down on Prince Leopold's own vessel.

"Fire ready, sir."

"Hold . . . Hold . . . Hold."

The enemy's prow was a wall hurtling towards them.

As the drumbeat drove faster, the ship's ram cut more water. A white wake high and visible to Tycho in the cloud-shrouded night.

"Sir . . ."

"*Wait*," Leopold barked.

The firemaster waited, brass nozzle in gloved hand, his head helmeted, his torso protected by a hog-hide jerkin. Below this, a singed and tar-stained apron told of near misses and lessons learnt. There were old firemasters and bad firemasters; there were no old bad firemasters.

"Fast, wide and high. *Now*."

Sweeping his flame up and over, the man undid his valve and fire whooshed into the air, blossoming into rain that soaked the enemy. Nothing would stop the Mamluk ship, but in that mo- ment — as mage fire fell — its slaves panicked, and their oars lost their rhythm and the screaming began.

"Sweet gods." Wrapped in a cloak, Lady Giulietta stood next to Tycho. She was clutching a dagger in one hand.

"Where did you get that?"

"From Leopold." She glanced from her weapon to where her husband stood, his whole attention fixed on the galley bearing down on them.

Her pride was almost painful to see.

"*Brace*," Prince Leopold shouted.

Time slowed. Inside the stretched seconds Tycho turned, took the blade from Giulietta's hand, discarded it, and moved to take her fall.

Tumbling hard, she drove the breath from her body. Too stunned to be embarrassed at finding him under her. Not aware yet she'd pissed herself with shock. Barely aware his arms held her and his face inhaled her scent.

As timbers ripped, the Mamluk ram skewered the *Lionheart*, smashing emptied rowing benches and tearing the deck above. The trick now was to stop it escaping.

"Grapple hooks," Leopold ordered.

Two land anchors curved towards the Mamluk prow, the first catching fast, the second falling back. Grabbing the rope of the first, sailors flung the rope's end round the *Lionheart*'s main mast and tied it tight.

"Your highness."

The grappling irons had chains spliced to their ropes to make them hard to cut free from the enemy side. High above, Mamluk axemen were hacking at the point where the rope joined chain.

"Deal with it," Leopold ordered.

A Cypriot archer shot and missed.

Grabbing his bow, Tycho saw the man's shock turn to anger, then caution as he registered the richness of Tycho's new doublet.

"He'll give it back," Giulietta promised.

Pulling an arrow from the man's quiver, Tycho shot a Mamluk through the eye slits of his helmet and heard him tumble. The second joined the first moments later, followed by a third.

In answer, iron bars thrown by Mamluks on a walkway behind their prow came raining down. One killed a firemaster's apprentice, another injured an archer, several cracked the deck when they landed.

"*Tycho, where's Giulietta?*"

"With me. Safe enough."

Leopold laughed. His laugh deep and loud.

"Take her somewhere safer," he said. "Understand me?" The prince had promised his wife he'd keep her at his side. Now he was breaking his promise and only Tycho knew it.

"That's an order, Sir Tycho."

Prince Leopold grinned in the darkness, his teeth white and his beard lit crimson by the flames around them. His gaze swept the deck, finding Giulietta. When she looked at him he blew her a kiss.

The man expected to die.

Before he did he would pass responsibility for his wife to a man who'd beaten him in battle, savaged his woman and driven him into exile . . . Tycho wondered if Giulietta understood what was happening.

"And take the child," Leopold shouted.

"I'll get him," Tycho told Giulietta. "You give Leopold courage."

"How could he think I'd leave my . . . ?"

"He didn't, his words were for me. He's saying keep you and Leo safe until after the battle." *And beyond*, Tycho thought grimly.

The iron bars had stopped raining down, flame licked up the Mamluk prow and the grappling hooks still held. Around him, knights and men at arms were holding their breath, preparing for the real battle. What came next would be worse.

"Go," Tycho ordered, pushing her.

He realised his mistake when she swung round, and a group of archers stared. "Please," he said. "Let Prince Leopold know you love him beyond anyone else. That you'll never love another like him."

Lady Giulietta covered her mouth with her hand.

Mounting the steps from below two at a time, Tycho hit the main deck in time to see Giulietta throw her arms round Leopold and whisper something. Then she headed towards Tycho, her mouth twisted in grief, tears streaming down her face.

When Tycho tried to comfort her, she yanked free, anger replacing her misery. "You'll never be the man he is."

"I know," Tycho said.

"Leopold's going to die."

"Gloriously."

"That's meant to make a difference?"

"It will to him. He's fighting for you. For your baby. Whosever it is."

"*He told you?*"

"He wanted to know if it was mine."

"I didn't even kn-know you before . . ." Her words were fierce, her face set in fury, but there was a stumble, a looking away. That night in the basilica remained with them both.

"Turn," Tycho said. "Wave to him."

Giulietta did.

60

"Your orders, highness?"

Prince Leopold looked at the Crucifer knight. Sir Richard was no fool. In his pale blue eyes, and lined, sun-battered English face the answer to his question was already written. He simply wanted it confirmed.

"Die well."

Sir Richard grinned, hefted his hand-and-a-half sword, checked the war hammer at his hip and looked up at the unbroken wall of the Mamluk ship's prow. "When do we start?"

"Impatient to die?"

"If we're going to do it," Sir Richard said, "we might as well do it while our courage is up and our strength still holds."

Half his men would lose control of their bladders or bowels. Not through fear, but because bodies could only handle so much at once. A man in half-armour can fight full pitch for five minutes before exhaustion sets in. Staying alive and blocking blows comes well ahead of natural functions.

Clapping Sir Richard on his shoulder, Prince Leopold made his round of the others, joking with some, clasping the hands of others, gripping one apprentice by the shoulders, telling him he'd find courage when the moment came.

The boy was in tears but stood straighter when Leopold stopped to talk to his master. Their talk was short and intense. There was no disagreement. Master Theobald simply wanted to check he understood what the prince required.

At an order from Master Theobald, his apprentices began rolling red-painted barrels across the deck, stacking them below the enemy ship's prow. They did so in the face of a shower of arrows, loosed up and over from the enemy side. Luckily, gusting night winds and the Mamluk archers' own fear protected them.

As the apprentices worked, Prince Leopold's archers kept loosing their own arrows to stop Mamluk axemen cutting the grapple free. And the ship's carpenter, a balding man, bad-tempered and stout, but good at what he did and not one to suffer fools, began to hammer a nail into the Mamluk ship.

He worked quickly, ignoring those around him. Ignoring everyone. Even Sir Richard, who went to see what he was doing.

"Ask the prince."

Sir Richard decided he'd wait and see.

Once the nail was fixed, the carpenter forced it free with a long, split-tongued pry bar, working it so hard muscles ridged across the man's back, his face turned red and sweat broke out across his forehead. "Done," he said. Into the hole he fixed a hook, using his pry bar to twist it tight. "Time for another, my lord?"

The prince shook his head. So the carpenter fixed a chain to the single hook and began to wrap it round the mast.

"Help him," Leopold ordered.

Once the chain was locked in place, Leopold nodded to Master Theobald, who widened his valve nozzle, and swept flame up the Mamluk bow.

"And beyond."

The last of the mage fire fell on to their enemy.

Men screamed, axe-wielding Mamluks tried to cut the grapple, not knowing they'd been chained to their doom. They died bathed in the flames, turned to arrow-stuck candles, filling the air with the stink of meat burning.

"Now," said Leopold.

Stepping forward, Master Theobald smashed a red-painted barrel and thick sticky black tar oozed around his boots. He smashed another, then another, until the deck became slick. Slivers of silvery metal in the mix began to smoke, gently at first.

"Out of my way . . ."

When Prince Leopold began to push towards Atilo's ship, Sir Richard looked appalled, then met his gaze and felt shamed instead. It went without saying the prince would stay with those about to die. But someone had to cut the *Lionheart* free from the *San Marco*. Old enemies looked at each other.

"Help me, and hurry."

"No," Atilo said. "Move your men to my ship."

"They stay," Leopold said. "It's the only way to stop the Mamluks freeing themselves. I'm not losing the *Lionheart* without reason . . . Help keep my wife safe. And trust Sir Tycho's instincts."

He grinned at the youth next to Atilo. "We'll never get that rematch."

"Be grateful," said Tycho.

Prince Leopold laughed, and jumped on to the rail of his ship, raising his sword to begin cutting the ropes that lashed their galleys together. After a second, Tycho joined him.

61

Around Tycho the ocean was dotted with burning ships. The fleet King Janus and Venice had provided Atilo burnt, listed and sank. As for their crews, the lucky ones were dragged down by armour or the whirlpool around their dying vessels, the unlucky drowned more slowly.

The Mamluk galleys stood off in a ring,

Only the *San Marco*, Atilo's own ship, remained. The Mamluks were waiting, Tycho was unsure for what. A whole day's worth of hard-fought battle had passed. Steady attrition wearing down the Christian fleet, although they died one for one, sometimes better, the result was always going to be the same.

And Giulietta and Tycho watched it all from under the shadow of an awning. It had been a day of thunderclouds and hidden sun, and for that Tycho had been grateful. Even wearing smoked glass spectacles his eyes had burnt at the brightness. Even coated with ointment, belatedly provided by Atilo. (Dr. Crow had given both to the old man. *Just in case you meet that pretty boy again.* Not daring to risk the alchemist's anger by throwing them away, Atilo had still been slow to offer Tycho this protection.)

Now the thick clouds that provided shelter had thinned to

reveal the last rays of the setting sun. From his place under the awning, Tycho examined the wreckage of Atilo's fleet, which carried in its burning hulks the ruin of the old man's reputation. It was hard to separate the Atilos he knew.

The man betrothed to Desdaio. The *magister militorum* who carried a history of battles won. The head of the Assassini. He might understand the old man better if he could work out where his loyalties really lay.

With his adopted city?

With the duchess he'd taken as a lover?

To the rules of the Assassini? Rules so rigid they begged for abuse from the likes of Prince Alonzo. The Regent would greet the news of this defeat with public fury and private ambivalence. The duchess's lover dead, her faction at court suffering humiliation, the youth he'd wanted executed also dead. Only Giulietta would be denied to him. And she'd be dead too.

"Tycho," Giulietta said.

He glanced back at her.

"You're crying." She sounded surprised. Leaning forward, she touched her fingertip to his face, examining the proof glistening on her finger like oil.

"Everyone has to die," she said.

Away to one side stood Desdaio, her head bowed and shoulders shaking with fright. She was fighting not to let fear engulf her body. Being killed would be better than being captured. At best being captured meant slavery, probably in some Mamluk's harem. At worst, torture and a slow death.

"You made Leopold a promise."

"What of it?" asked Tycho, already knowing the answer and wondering why he made her put it into words. Because he didn't want what came next on his conscience, probably. Assuming someone like him, some *thing* like him had a conscience.

"When the time comes . . ."

"What?" he demanded. "When the time comes *what?*"

"You're going to make me say it?"

Tycho nodded.

"Kill me. Promise?"

"I promise." And then he realised Desdaio had come to join them, because she was there in front of him, shaking her head fiercely.

"You can't," she said desperately. "What about her baby?"

Turning to Giulietta, she said, "Do you want him to kill your baby too? It's wrong. You'll go to hell."

"We're here already," Tycho said.

Giulietta slapped him so hard it shocked all three of them into silence, and make Atilo glance back from where he stood on the prow. "That's heresy," she hissed. "Cathars have burnt for saying that."

"You think hell is worse than this?"

She opened her mouth to say yes, then shut it again. Grief filled her eyes, for the man who abducted, married and then abandoned her, all for the best of reasons. But abandoned her all the same.

"He knows," Desdaio said.

Giulietta looked at her.

"About hell. Tycho's been there."

The Mamluk admiral's own ship turned slowly. There were other galleys closer to the *San Marco*, but a message must have gone out to hold off. The sultan's admiral wanted the honour of destroying Atilo for himself. Atilo was a Moorish traitor and turncoat, after all. If it took time to turn the admiral's galley so be it. This was a waiting game. And the Mamluks had time on their side.

"You love her, don't you?" Atilo said.

The second time in twenty-four hours Tycho had been asked that question. Glancing to where Lady Giulietta stood, her back turned and the baby at her breast, he answered, "From the moment I saw her."

"At Ca' Friedland?"

"Long before that. In the basilica."

Atilo looked at him. "You love Desdaio also?"

"I like her. She makes me . . . feel easy. But there it ends."

"*I cannot do it.*"

Such was the anguish in Atilo's voice, Tycho's guts tightened. "Nor can I," he said. "Giulietta is my responsibility, however much you hate that fact. And she has asked me to take her life already. Desdaio is your responsibility. And she has not."

"Desdaio mustn't fall into Mamluk hands."

"They might ransom her," said Tycho. "If she says she's Lord Bribanzo's daughter. He'd pay extra to get her back untouched."

"And I would be dead." Atilo's voice was dry. "In time, I would be forgotten, and other suitors would appear. Ones Bribanzo likes better. But, still . . . I would give anything. Surrender this ship if I thought it would guarantee her safety."

"My lord . . ."

"*I meant it, Tycho.* Have you never loved like that?"

The question jolted Tycho's memory. And the coldness inside his mind, and the flames eating the hulks on the ocean around him, and his residual fear of the sinking sun's crimson ball were not enough to banish it. He could taste Atilo's anguish, Lady Giulietta's unnatural calmness, Desdaio's despair. Try as he might, he could not keep their pain from mocking his refusal to act.

"How long do we have?"

"How long?"

"Before that reaches us." The Mamluk galley had finished turning. Both banks of oarsmen now working together, no longer fighting the deep keel's drag, and the strong currents that swept this part of the Middle Sea.

"A few minutes at most."

On the Mamluk galley's prow, boys were filling braziers and oil jars so archers could dip their rag-wrapped arrows when the time came.

"I'm going to tell Giulietta that I love her."

Atilo's shoulders stiffened at Tycho's words. "She's a Millioni princess."

"And I'm a knight, albeit a poor and new one. I need the courage that saying this will give me."

"To do what?"

"Become something else," Tycho said sadly.

Giulietta looked at him, her eyes wide. At her side, Desdaio stood frozen in shock, the hurt in her eyes as extreme as the shock in those of the Millioni princess.

"You loved Leopold," Tycho said. "This I know."

The young woman nodded slightly, her gaze rising to his face. "Why tell me you love me now?"

"Because," Tycho said, knowing that was no answer to anything.

And he turned away from Giulietta's scowl and the barely hidden hurt in Desdaio's eyes. Walking to the prow, he ignored the oncoming ship and spoke the words he'd told A'rial he'd never say.

"Help me."

For a few seconds nothing happened.

Then the air rippled, and static flowed around him, touching his body with intimate fingers, only to vanish. He heard mocking laughter in his head, then a bulkhead door opened behind him and he heard Atilo swear.

"I thought using a door might be more discreet."

Grinning, A'rial climbed a short ladder to stand beside him. Her shoulders, seen through rips in her dress, were as scrawny as ever. Her hair was filthy. Her toes black with dirt. But her green eyes, when they examined him, looked as old as the ocean, and more dangerous than anything found in its depths.

"Ask," she demanded.

"Save us from that." Tycho nodded to the admiral's ship and the ring of Mamluk vessels around them, beyond arrow's distance. As if Atilo's crew had any arrows left or the strength to fire them.

"You think it's that simple?"

"Isn't it? You said I'd call. You were right."

"You're saying it took a reputation in ruins, a victory for the Mamluks, soldiers preparing to die, a dead friend, and your loved ones preparing to be raped or killed, and not knowing which to hope for, before you'd accept help?" Her voice was mocking. "Tell me exactly what you want."

"Giulietta saved."

"Who knows what that means? Giulietta safely back in Venice? Ensconced as the chief wife to the sultan, bearing his heir and commanding his seraglio? Cleanly dead, and removed from the coming horror? What do you *want?*"

"I've told you."

"No," she hissed, voice hard. "You haven't. So I'm going to ask one final time. *What do you want?*"

"The Mamluk fleet destroyed," Tycho answered without thought. "The Mamluk ship destroyed and our ship safe. With all in her," he added, suspecting the *stregoi* would trick him if he worded his wish badly.

"What will you pay?"

"Anything," Tycho said.

A'rial grinned. "Right answer."

62

As the Mamluk kettledrum grew louder, and their galley slaves worked the oars to its rhythm, A'rial grabbed Tycho's hand, holding it in a vice-like grip. Her nails were black, her knees scraped and bare. Around her neck hung a yellowing bird's skull, with large eyeholes and a dagger-sharp beak.

"You pay the price freely? This you must state."

"I'm still waiting for you to tell me what it is," he said, flinching as the red-haired child turned on him, her eyes sharp as broken glass.

"You know my price," she hissed. "Pay it, or not."

Tycho looked at her.

"State you pay it, or let me return home. You cannot summon me, and then quibble." There was a fury to her words far more dangerous than shouting. He wondered, not for the first time, how old A'rial really was.

Whether she was human.

But who was he to ask those questions? And she was right. He knew her price. Although he imagined it was Alexa who really wanted it, and A'rial was simply her instrument.

"Take my life instead," he begged.

A'rial shook her head dismissively.

"My soul then."

Pushing her face close to his, she mocked, "What makes you think you have one? Or ever had one? Swear it by the goddess or Giulietta dies . . ."

He should have remembered there would be a full moon.

Pale as his skin, huge and poised just above the horizon. The sun might be sunk in its glory, firing a final sliver of horizon with sullen flames, but the moon had a whole night ahead of her, and a red-haired acolyte on the deck of a losing ship, taking promises in both her mistresses' names.

"I will make Alexa an army," Tycho said. "I will embrace who I am."

Stepping on to the prow of Atilo's ship, A'rial stood tall, brought her clenched fists to her forehead in a strange salute, then flung them back, with her fingers still clenched, her arms angled back and down like the wings of a bird.

Winds whistled around her.

Lightning cracked from an unbroken sky.

The storm began instantly. Clouds gathering on the dark horizon, banking and racing at impossible speeds towards the Mamluk armada like heavenly cavalry. Mamluk archers blinked to find spray in their faces. The crescent pennant above their admiral's galley flapped so hard it sounded like cannon fire. Beneath Tycho's feet, he felt the *San Marco* lurch as wind filled her sails and she listed dangerously.

"Lower the sails," he shouted.

Atilo stared at him.

"My lord, drop the sails. Hack down the masts if you must. But get the canvas down and get Giulietta and Desdaio below . . . Please." Maybe the final word helped. Because Atilo snapped out orders to cut the sails free, and hurried the women towards a hatch. Only returning to his post when they were below.

"What have you done?"

Thunder rolled across the sky, lightning lanced seawards. A Mamluk ship in the ring around them lost its mainmast as jagged fire split the wood, and sails tumbled before anyone had time to lower them.

"My lord, go below."

"Tycho . . ."

"I must do this."

"*What have you done?*"

"Paid the price demanded to save those I love."

Tears rolled down Tycho's face, harried by the wind. He could taste their sourness in his throat, and feel emptiness under his ribs where someone had cut open his chest and was replacing his heart with ice.

"Go," he ordered.

Atilo looked shocked.

"Or stay," Tycho growled. "And die. Those are your choices."

"Those are my . . . ?"

"You think we will distinguish between friend and enemy when the killing grows fierce?" He indicated A'rial in the prow; fierce winds gusting away the arrows aimed at her, her arms stretched back, her face raised to the sky.

She was mouthing incantations. Her fingers dancing as she pulled clouds across the sky and split ships in two with strikes of lightning. A lift of her chin produced a cliff-sized wave that crushed three ships, and faded just as quickly. In a flurry of waves and thunder she'd set about reducing the Mamluk fleet to a single vessel. There had never been a storm like it. And right in the middle, red hair streaming, stood the little *stregoi*, her face running with rain that filled her mouth and dashed from her chin like a million tears. She was laughing.

When he looked back, Atilo had gone.

Tycho wanted to be there, on the Mamluk galley, facing his enemy, ripping out the bastard's guts. To think it was to be there.

Stumbling, he glanced down, seeing the waves behind him. Fear filled his throat as he fought to balance on the rail.

How he got there didn't matter.

"*Over there . . .*" A Mamluk archer shouted warning.

And Tycho stopped his arrow in mid-air, wrapped his fingers around it before the arrow could fall, and stabbed hard and fast into the neck of a man-at-arms who was advancing, short sword in hand. Twisting, Tycho felt barbs turn before he ripped the arrow free, tossed the dying man aside and hurled the arrow at the chest of the archer who'd fired it.

The arrow flew so fast it disappeared.

And then the archer was staring in shock at the shaft jutting from his mail coat. Tycho killed him, almost as an afterthought. The crack of the archer's neck lost under the howl of the wind, the crash of the waves and the roar of blood in Tycho's head.

He could feel hunger inside him. It stared through his eyes. Filled his mind. Its vision sharpening as the western horizon darkened, the final traces of daylight drowning below the waves. The Mamluk ship with its galley slaves, slave master and admiral became a frieze of red. Frozen, as time hiccuped and the sea slowed to a sullen roil, and the beast tested the bars of its cage.

"*Do it,*" said a voice in his head.

A'rial, Tycho decided. Unless he was talking to himself.

So many people to kill. So many throats to tear out, so much blood. He could drown himself in the red he'd spill on this one ship. They were firing arrows at him. The wind took most of them. The few that came close he swatted away, not even bothering to return them.

"*I said do it.*" Definitely A'rial. She sounded crosser this time.

Should he? Could he, and remain who he was? He knew the answer to that. The few times he'd embraced the moon's rays he'd felt a sliver of ice enter his heart. Enough of those slivers and his heart would freeze. He couldn't unlearn the lessons that changing taught him. And after he became himself again, the memories of what he'd been remained. But how could he save Giulietta without changing? He would have to accept his destiny.

Become the last of the Fallen. The last of his line.

Or perhaps the first . . .

Raising his face to the full moon, Tycho let its rays wash over him and felt his dog teeth descend. Sinews tightened, bones twisted, muscles tore, his throat filling with his own blood. Touching fingers to his face, he found his ears had shrunk away and left knotted holes in their place. His nose was flatter, his nostrils wide like a hunting animal. However bad the *krieghund* looked, he looked far worse.

Inside Tycho's chest his heart froze, locking him into panic. Its beat was gone, his lungs were static, his breath disappearing. Only fear kept him upright. He was alive and dead in the same second.

"Sweet gods . . ."

Changing hurt more than he could imagine. A remorseless shriek of pain washing away his last dregs of being human.

This monstrous creature was what he'd become eventually. Tycho knew that for a fact. In the end, no matter how many times he reverted, this was how he would end. Monstrous and ugly. The world he'd been born into long dead. A new world in its place he could hardly bear.

His price for finally letting the beast free was that he'd spare the slaves. Because sparing them would prove to himself something human remained somewhere. And then Tycho stopped pretending he didn't want what came next and—as A'rial let her storm subside—became himself.

The Mamluk galley had double rows of benches on both sides. The top row open to the sky, with a raised walkway used by the whip master. Tycho swallowed this information in a single second.

"Die, demon."

You had to give the Mamluk sergeant credit for courage. He must have known he was about to perish. Lobbing his head over the side, Tycho kicked his body into the slave well, and faced the soldier beyond. Spiked helmet, chain mail, a wickedly curved scimitar. Tycho noted and dismissed his armour and weaponry.

The man's first blow almost landed. His second one did, slicing Tycho's lower arm to the bone and sticking fast. Grabbing the man, Tycho squeezed; throat armour buckling as Tycho crushed his voice box.

Shock, then pain. Tycho knew the sequence.

Ripping free the scimitar, he hurled it at the next man and watched him stagger back, the weapon protruding from his chest. The cut on Tycho's arm was a memory. So he gave it to a man with a spear instead. The spear man gasping as Tycho touched a hand to his face. Staggering back, he clutched his healthy arm, screaming loudly. Tycho threw him over the side. The kettle drummer died as simply.

Tycho kept moving.

It was a whip that stopped him eventually.

An iron-tipped lash spun out of nowhere and slashed his face, blood dripping into his mouth. Sword deep, he could feel his teeth where his cheek should be. Turning swiftly, to protect himself from a second blow, he held his cheek's upper and lower edges together and jagged flesh begin to mend.

The third blow he was ready for.

Catching the weighted end, he wrapped the thong around his fist and yanked, dragging the whip master to his knees on the walkway in front of him. The Mamluk never stood a chance. As Tycho moved for the kill, a slave grabbed the whip master's ankle from below. Another hand snaked upwards, chains clanking.

The slaves held the man in place while Tycho popped his eyes with taloned thumbs and tossed him sideways into the slave pit.

He tossed the whip after.

Behind Tycho were archers he didn't remember killing. Mamluk sailors, their heads twisted so far they stared in the wrong direction. A ship's mate dead on the walkway, his throat torn out, eyes missing, his guts in a pile between his knees. Tycho's thumbs dripped blood, his doublet was sticky. At no point did it occur to him to use a dagger. At no point had there been a need.

The red edges of the world faded with that realisation.

And inside Tycho's chest his heart started beating, and his lungs shuddered and drew breath. Bones twisted and muscles contracted. As stars lost their brightness in the sky, the full moon changed from scarlet to a rose-pink, and the waves began to ebb and flow at close to their normal speed.

Tycho checked behind him.

Atilo's ship stood there. A'rial still on the prow. But her arms were no longer flung back and her face no longer turned to the sky. She was staring between ships, and Tycho saw her smile as their gazes locked.

Around them lay wreckage. Broken masts and spars, vast canvas jellyfish made from sails that held pockets of air. A rudder floated with a man at arms slumped across it, an arrow in his neck. Bodies bobbed like stunned fish, rising and falling with the swell. Most were ordinary sailors, Mamluk, Cypriot or Venetian. Those rich enough to own mail were on the seabed already.

Apart from Tycho, only one free man remained alive on the ship.

And maybe he was the only one really. Because Tycho doubted he was human, and was certainly not free. A slave to his hunger if nothing else.

The Mamluk admiral was young, tall, thin and brave.

He had to be brave to stand in the door of his tiny cabin. Elegant riveted mail glinted silvery gold in the moonshine, the brand he clutched highlighted the gold-filled etching of his helmet. He wore a rich helm with a jutting nose-piece, steel cheek protectors and a gilded spike at the top. A silver crescent arched up over his eyes. It was the armour of a Mamluk prince.

"Demon," the man said.

Firelight from his flaming brand rippled along the sharpened edge of his sword, revealing tightly hammered damascene. Steel had entered the young man's soul and stiffened his spine. It was revealed in his steady gaze. Tycho was impressed.

"What are you?"

The changes Tycho had fought against became less savage as his face finished shifting shape, his ears regrew, his nostrils closing. His teeth were the last to go, retreating into his upper jaw. They hurt as viciously as ever, but this time it was less frightening. Taking a step back, the Mamluk appeared more terrified by the man than he had been by Tycho's shifting shape only moments earlier.

"*It can't be you,*" he protested.

In that second Tycho decided to spare him. At least for a while. "You know me?" he said. "You know who I am?"

A brief nod was his answer.

"Then you know more than I do," Tycho said. "Because I don't know you." Slowly the Mamluk undid his helmet.

And it was Tycho's turn to step back. Because the last time he'd seen that face, Sergeant Temujin was cutting its throat before burning an entire ship. At the start of Tycho's time in Venice, with no moon over the lagoon, and a Mamluk vessel freshly boarded by Dogana guards.

"You recognise me now?"

"I watched you die," Tycho said. "Saw your ship go up in flames."

The Mamluk closed his eyes, and his lips opened in prayer. He touched his hands to his heart, his mouth and his forehead in turn; in formal goodbye to someone. And then told Tycho who.

"My twin," he said. "She insisted."

"Insisted on what?"

"Accompanying your ship. It was stupid. But she was my father's favourite and he indulged her. Until you spoke, no one knew for certain she was dead. I could feel an emptiness in my heart but

I couldn't lose hope. My father will be upset." From the way the young man said those words, much went unspoken.

Unbuckling his armour, the Mamluk dropped it at his feet, barely noticing it clatter down steps to fall into the slave well where oarsmen watched in silence. A single tug pulled fine mail over his head and he let that drop too. Reversing his scimitar, he offered it hilt first with a slight bow.

"Make it clean," he said. "And when I reach paradise I will beg for your release from the curse that afflicts you."

Tycho swung the scimitar experimentally.

A beautiful weapon, with its handle wrapped in a strand of gold wire, and a blade weighted so it carried on the down stroke, whistling as it cut through the air.

"My curse is forever," he said, lowering the blade.

"Forever?"

"Anyway, you must live."

"*Why?*"

"So you can take news of this defeat to the sultan. So I can discover why your sister was on that ship. Because enough brave men have died . . ."

Tycho felt so tired his bones ached at the thought of it. Atilo had once spoken of sadness after battle being like the sadness that comes after sex, only bleaker. Tycho had not dared say he had no knowledge of either. This was worse than he feared. A desolation that carried the taste of carrion.

In disgust, he rolled a dead archer into the well with the scimitar's tip. The following thud made him feel sadder still. Where was the elation? Atilo said some men felt that.

"I am Sir Tycho. Once an apprentice blade."

The Mamluk bowed slightly. "I am Osman. My father is the sultan. My sister, nicknamed Jasmine, was his favourite. But I am his heir."

Tycho bowed in return.

"You can kill me," said Prince Osman. "Keep me for ransom

or free me. Even, it seems, send me as a messenger to announce my own defeat to my father if that is the load you put on me. Although he will not believe my tale."

"Why not . . . ?"

"A storm-summoning witch? A ravening, shape-shifting demon? My fleet destroyed by waves, wind and lightning? My archers' arrows swatted aside? The Venetians do not have that kind of power. My father would believe I made excuses."

"So what will you say?"

"My slaves refused to row. That I commanded poorly. The bowstrings of my archers were wet. That I surrender my command and accept my fate."

Prince Osman's eyes were bleak. His father had a reputation for cruelty. He also had enough sons, by both wives and favoured concubines, to sacrifice one if an example need be made.

"Stay here," Tycho ordered.

As if the Mamluk prince had anywhere else to go.

Atilo crossed himself when Tycho appeared from the door behind him. He opened his mouth to say something and left his mouth open as Tycho stalked past, only stopping when he reached A'rial. "I need something."

"Favours cost." Her green eyes were sharp. "You know that."

"Name your price."

"One kill. At my choosing."

"Your mistress's choosing?"

"Mine," the little *stregoi* said, her voice hard. "One time, when the hunger is on you I will ask for a kill. You will grant it without question."

"Not Giulietta, not Desdaio, not Pietro."

A'rial's smile was sour. "You're not in a position to bargain. But all the same, I agree. None of those three."

Tycho told her what he required.

A few dozen people were to forget what they'd seen and

remember what they believed they saw. As Tycho stepped back, A'rial drew herself upright and a shimmering wrapped itself around her. Once the space between her hands shone bright enough she began to chant the true history of the battle. The one the Mamluk slaves would remember.

"*Tycho* . . ."

"We'll talk later," Tycho said.

Atilo il Mauros opened his mouth and closed it once again. He was a man fond of saying the world held more than one could know. He just hadn't expected to come face to face with its strangeness that night.

"The duchess knows?" he managed finally.

Knows what? Tycho wondered. *About my hunger? About the changes that come with it?*

"Yes," he said. "Undoubtedly."

Tycho took the smoky brand from Prince Osman's hand and thrust it close to the face of a red-bearded slave, who recoiled from its flame. "No one's going to hurt you," the prince promised. Although the whip scars on the man's shoulders said he'd been hurt already, many times and brutally.

"What did you see?" Tycho asked.

The slave looked at him.

"During the battle. What did you see?"

A nod from Osman told the man he could answer.

"The Venetian fleet. It was vast. Masts like a forest circling us. So many ships, my lord, I've never seen so many. I thought we'd never escape."

Tycho could see bodies and broken spars, upturned ships and bobbing flotsam, the spreading aftermath of a naval battle. The slave could not. But when the man shivered Tycho knew he realised what was out there.

"What happened?"

For all the man had been Western once, a northerner to judge from his hair and the red in his beard, he answered as if the Mamluk fleet's fate and his were inextricably entwined.

As they were, of course.

"We were encircled. Their archers slaughtered our sailors. They had mage fire. It spread across our decks, burning everything it touched." The man's eyes were bleak as he remembered what never happened. "It was only his highness's skill that saved us. In the middle of a terrible storm he fought the Venetians to a standstill. Their entire fleet destroyed at a terrible cost."

Prince Osman's eyes were saucers. His glaze flicked between Tycho and the slave, unable to believe what he was hearing.

"Ask any of them," Tycho said.

"What will he say?" asked Prince Osman, jerking his head towards Atilo's flagship.

"That you lie. What do you expect him to say?"

"And I say he lies?" Prince Osman nodded. He was beginning to understand how this worked.

Tycho smiled.

"Your price is I tell you how I know you?"

"And a favour given without hesitation. Not involving a death in your family," said Tycho, remembering the price A'rial had extracted in her turn. "Beyond that I can't say, because I don't know."

The prince looked up sharply.

"Start with how you know me . . ."

63

In the far shallows of the night, with the darkest hours long behind him and the moon a low ghost on the horizon awaiting the sun's exorcism, Tycho crawled from his pallet to wash himself in buckets of water Giulietta had earlier ordered drawn for him. He carried the weight of Osman's answer in his heart.

Although his skin was now clean, he washed himself one final time, rinsing his mouth and spitting salty water back into a bucket, before tipping the lot over the deck. His torn doublet was over a rope in the hot pre-dawn breeze. It was now almost dry enough to wear.

Atilo slept in the captain's cabin.

Ladies Giulietta and Desdaio had the other. Denied his own bed, the *San Marco*'s original captain was at the rudder. He refused to meet Tycho's gaze. There was nothing strange about that. Everyone refused to meet Tycho's gaze, finding reasons to be somewhere else.

A'rial was gone. Already forgotten.

A storm had come from nowhere. A miracle from God, heavenly proof that San Marco, Venice's patron saint, had the ear of the divine. The only strangeness was Tycho's single-handed battle against Osman's ship.

A mighty leap, the sailors were saying. Heroic bravery, a madman's luck, sheer stupidity. Few admitted seeing anything. And those who had kept their thoughts to themselves. The newly made knight had leapt a near-impossible distance and been lucky. Everyone knew why Prince Osman had been allowed to leave. Atilo had told them it was to take news of his defeat to his father.

"Are you all right?"

Turning, Tycho found Giulietta behind him. She was dressed as no widowed woman should be, in a thin undersmock, which clung damply to her body. The garment was laced at her neck with a ribbon; loosely closed and loosely tied. "I could hear you prowling the decks."

"How did you know it was me?"

Lady Giulietta flushed.

The absolute clarity of his night vision was a secret from her, Tycho realised. A secret from everyone except Dr. Crow, and perhaps Prior Ignacio of the White Crucifers. Although Atilo must be close to guessing by now.

"Just guessed," she said brightly.

"Right."

"It's hot down there."

"And up here," Tycho said.

"At least there's breeze here," said Giulietta, facing the night wind. All it did was paste her undergown more tightly to her body. She must have known, because she turned to tug discreetly at the neck.

"I'm sorry," Tycho said, looking away. "About Leopold. I would like to have known him properly."

"We can talk about him later. Right now . . ." Her voice broke. "I can't bear to think about . . . I thought you were going to die too."

"So did I."

"Really?" She sounded thoughtful.

No, not really. The thought never occurred to him. From the

moment he appeared on the deck of Osman's ship he'd known he was the strongest and fastest and most deadly creature aboard. Until now, he hadn't really thought about how intoxicating that was. How it would be to let that go.

"Yes," he lied. "Really."

Lady Giulietta rested her head against his shoulder.

Somehow his hand came up to stroke her hair and he felt her melt into him, then pull away. "Leo's asleep. Desdaio also. Atilo too, I imagine."

"The wind's best higher up."

She smiled sadly.

All war galleys were built to an old design. Some said the Romans invented them. Others that it was the Greeks before them. In the old days galleys had two, sometimes three rows of oars, one above the other. Tradition gave Venetian galleys a single row. Although that could change.

The cabins on this were at the stern, with a space below for the tiller, and steps up to a small deck, made from the roof of the cabins fenced in for safety. It was here a huge arbalest could be fitted, one of those vast crossbows with arrows that would pierce an enemy's sides. And it was here Tycho led Giulietta. Although she seemed uncertain why they were there when she reached the top.

"What are you thinking?" she demanded. Only to grab for a rail as the *San Marco* shifted on the swell beneath them. He saw her hit the rail and caught her before she could stumble. "How come you can balance?"

"Sheer skill," Tycho said.

Giulietta stepped away from him. "You haven't answered my question."

"Just did."

"No. About what you were thinking."

"A'rial," he said. "She's . . ." Tycho hesitated. "One of your aunt's ladies-in-waiting, I suppose." From her scowl, Giulietta thought his hesitation was about more than how to describe her. "A'rial is eleven. She looks like a starved cat."

"Some men like . . ."

"Well, I don't."

"So why think about her now?"

There was a question. The kind he should expect from a Millioni princess, who kept a good head behind those watchful eyes. "Because I owe her a debt," Tycho said. "One I will need to repay."

"What?" she said.

"Nothing important. Why?"

"You shivered." Giulietta leant her head against his shoulder. After a moment, when he said nothing, she wrapped her arms tight around him, and he found himself stroking her hair as she clung to him. "This means nothing," she muttered.

"You're upset," he agreed. And felt her freeze. "I mean it," he said hastily. "This means nothing and you're upset about . . ."

"Don't you dare say his name."

Her face was wet beneath his fingers. Her thoughts a jumble of fears, sadness and anger he tasted and then let go. So much desperation. So much emptiness. These were what had brought her up here. "You know things," he said, tugging the ribbon at the neck of her undergown. "What lies beyond Al Andalus?"

"A great sea," she whispered. "Stretching further than any ship can sail. Everyone knows that. Filled with monsters."

"And beyond that?"

His fingers caressed her throat, opened her gown and smoothed down her warm skin until he felt her nipple harden as he cupped her breast in his hand. "Some say a void," she said, her voice shaky. "That the world ends like a cliff, with the ocean spilling into nothing. If you draw too close the current sweeps you over."

Kneeling like a knight at her feet, he opened her gown further and bit softly into the underside of one breast, hearing her whimper.

"Then how do the seas refill?"

She frowned down as if he was a child.

"Rivers, of course. The way a fountain bowl refills from the water spilling into it. I'm not sure it's true about the cliff. Aunt Alexa says the world is round. You start there," she nodded towards the prow, and you finish here . . ." The *San Marco*'s foaming wake stretched behind her.

Lifting her gown to her hips, Tycho kissed the darkness between her thighs, feeling her shiver and tasting wetness as salt as any ocean. They stayed that way for a long time. When Giulietta finally took her fingers from his hair, she was sobbing, tears for her dead lover rolling down her face, and Tycho had another question.

"What does Aunt Alexa say is beyond this sea?"

"The far edge of the Khan's empire."

Tycho nodded sadly. He'd thought maybe Bjornvin was there.

Epilogue

Tycho woke abruptly. Aware the sun was about to break over the horizon and Dr. Crow's ointment was in Atilo's cabin below. Ever since Tycho had been freed from behind the *Quaja's* bulkhead, he'd been tortured by ignorance of why he was a prisoner in the first place. No memories existed between Withered Arm's fire circle and being walled up in a ship, where waves sickened him and silver shackles burnt his wrists.

All he'd wanted was to know who he was.

That was all anyone wanted. Why shouldn't he know? And now he did. At least, he knew part of it, and the knowledge drove all happiness from his body. He would not rest easy until he'd told the girl asleep beside him.

Reaching over, he drew the neck of Giulietta's gown together to hide her pale breasts, and gently tied its ribbon, smoothing straggles of hair from her face. She looked strange asleep, younger and less tough. Her red hair spread in a flaming halo around her. Had Leopold looked at her like this? If so, Tycho wondered what he had seen that Tycho missed.

They were not lovers, Giulietta said. Never lovers.

At least not like that. Prince Leopold zum Bas Friedland had protected her. He had snatched her from those who first abducted her, keeping her secure without her knowing, and, when she escaped, hunted her down again and introduced himself.

They were *friends*, she told Tycho fiercely.

You were allowed to cry for friends, to miss them and love them and wish everything could have been different. As to who fathered Leo, she was unable to answer that. Literally unable.

Anyway, she was intact.

Lady Giulietta had to touch his finger to a scar on her abdomen before he understood what she meant. She had *never*, and she told him this with brutal fierceness, lain with a man. And she would not lie with him now. The only man she might have lain with was dead . . .

And Tycho had held her, and dried her tears, letting her settle when crying for Leopold, the lover who wasn't, finally exhausted her enough for sleep to rescue her from sadness. Now Tycho had something to tell her of his own.

The question was how much truth could she stand?

And how much truth could he stand to tell her? The full truth? That he'd been a ragged, wizened, nameless creature, never sleeping, little more than a living skeleton when he was hunted down in the Eastern deserts? That he still had no memory of how he got there, how long he'd been in the desert or who he was before?

The bleakness of Osman's description weighed on Tycho.

To the hideousness of what Tycho could make himself become had been added the monstrousness of what he'd once been. He had speed, strength and courage. All of these came at a price. And Tycho knew, because he knew himself better now, it was a price he would pay.

This too he needed to tell her.

If Osman spoke the truth, Tycho had been almost animal when trapped by Tīmūrid mercenaries on the borders of the Mamluk empire. He'd been sold to the sultan's vizier, in a trade that saw one old enemy deal with another on behalf of Venice, a third. The sultan's mages had emptied Tycho's head of nightmares, dreams and memories. They'd emptied it of everything except a need to carry out one single task. If he hadn't drowned in Venice's lagoon — or almost drowned, whichever it was — Bjornvin's memories would never have crept back.

The bribes must have been huge and the promised rewards enormous. Prince Osman's sister had held words of power. Words designed to bind Tycho to carry out her order. He was to kill Duchess Alexa. And the man who asked for this death, offering to deliver gold and territories to the Mamluks when he finally became duke, was Alexa's brother-in-law, Lady Giulietta's uncle, Prince Alonzo.

The Regent hadn't know when it would be done. Simply that it would be. When Alonzo discovered the plan had failed, his revenge on the Mamluk *fontego* had been terrible. Had he succeeded in killing Alexa, Duke Marco IV would have been next. Prince Osman had little doubt about that. Quite possibly Lady Giulietta after that. Unless the Regent had other plans for her.

Kneeling up, Tycho stroked the sleeping girl's face until she woke, looking puzzled and still sleepy. "You should return to your cabin," he said. "But first there's something I need to tell you . . ."

Look out for
Act Two of the Assassini:

THE OUTCAST BLADE

by Jon Courtenay Grimwood

Acknowledgments

You know where you are with a publisher who drags you off to the Porterhouse pub in London's Maiden Lane for a six hour editorial meeting—and waits with good grace while you go though the script page by page. So heads up to Darren Nash, lapsed Australian, Orbit UK editorial director and good friend...

And a big tip of the hat to Orbit supremo Tim Holman, who filled me with food and alcohol when I flew out to New York—running a temperature and fever—to pitch him *The Fallen Blade*. Having asked me to pass the one page synopsis to Devi Pillai, senior editor and Orbit US's self-styled Eye of Sauron, he waited while she read it. Devi nodded significantly and that was it. We were in business on both sides of the Atlantic.

To my agent Mic Cheetham for doing the real work that made this happen. Joanna Kramer for keeping me sane during the copyedit process. Darren Nash and Devi Pillai again for thoughtful and occasionally stern editorial notes (that's you, Devi).

As always the ex-lunchtime collective of, variously, Paul McAuley, Kim Newman, China Miéville, Chris Fowler, Barry Forshaw, Nick Harkaway, Pat Cadigan, for drinks, food, bitching sessions, general chat and sanity. If there was any justice, Rob Holdstock would still be on that list (and he is in spirit).

My son Jamie, who might have buggered off half way round the world but still calls regularly for all that he's rubbish at answering emails. Hearing from you always makes my day.

And finally, Sam Baker. Seventeen years married. More than twenty years together. Pretty good for what was meant to be a quick drink. Thank you.

extras

orbit

meet the author

Charlie Hopkinson

JON COURTENAY GRIMWOOD was born in Malta and christened in the upturned bell of a ship. He grew up in the Far East, Britain and Scandinavia. Apart from novels, he writes for magazines and newspapers. He travels extensively and undertakes a certain amount of consulting. Until recently he wrote a monthly review column for *The Guardian*.

Felaheen, the third of his novels featuring Asraf Bey, a half-Berber detective, won the BSFA Award for Best Novel. So did his book *End of the World Blues*, about a British sniper on the run from Iraq and running an Irish bar in Tokyo. He has just published *The Fallen Blade*, the first of three novels set in an alternate fifteenth-century Venice.

His work is published in French, German, Spanish, Polish,

Czech, Hungarian, Russian, Turkish, Japanese, Finnish and American, among others.

He is married to the journalist and novelist Sam Baker, currently editor in chief of *Red* magazine. They divide their time between London and Winchester.

Find out more about the author at www.j-cg.co.uk.

interview

Vampire novels are all the rage now. Did this help to inspire you, or did you imagine a different kind of vampire from the beginning?

I've been reading fantasy my entire life. I've always had a thing for historical fiction, particularly the kind where the heroine or hero is running round with a couple of daggers and something very nasty is going on in the background. And I terrified myself for weeks as a small child with an adult vampire novel, so I'm surprised I didn't write this sooner. But it took a while to nail the plot down.

Also, I wasn't even sure Tycho was a vampire when he swirled his way into my head, dressed entirely in black leather and velvet and carrying his daggers. All I knew was he lived for the dark, feared the moon and had lost his memories. And to be honest I'm still not sure he is a vampire. At least not in the *Twilight* sense.

What I wanted to do was a vampire ur-myth.

A story that explained how what we call vampires reached Europe, where they came from and what they really are. That's the backstory to Tycho's personal history. He's the first vampire in Europe. (The term wasn't in use in English before the 1700s.)

The Fallen Blade takes place around 1407, twenty-five

years before Dracula is born and fifty years before he ruled as prince of Walachia.

Obviously Tycho doesn't know what he is; just as he doesn't know yet what his powers are, or that he can transfer them to other people. He's simply him and not at all happy about that. What he really is becomes clear later. Although there are clues in the first book.

What would you do if you were invisible for a day?

One of those great barroom *what if*s. Most people say they'd rob a bank or empty the nearest jewelers, or hang out unseen in the dressing room of some incredibly hot Hollywood star, or go see what their friends and family really say about them when they're not around...

But realistically, they'd probably panic.

I'd spend the entire day worried I'd turned into a ghost, or was locked in some weird limbo where no one could see me or hear me and I would never escape. By the time I suddenly became visible again I'd either be totally insane or getting used to it and getting ready to have some fun. At least that was my reasoning when making Tycho come to terms with his new powers.

If weird powers came with an instruction manual, that would be different. Then, I'd probably rob the bank, and become an unseen assassin. Actually, I'd probably do all of the above. I guess most people would.

You grew up in the Far East, Britain and Scandinavia. Where did the idea to set a vampire novel in Italy come from? Did you travel there a lot before you came up with the idea or afterward to do research?

As a child I went to Venice a few times on holiday. (It was about three days' drive from where we lived in England, and my mother was born restless and liked museums.)

In my memory it's always hot, the sun blinding as it reflects on the wide expanse of the Grand Canal, the water in the little canals behind the big buildings is stinking and often green. There's also something creepy about the city. A really disconcerting feeling that I'm in one of the scariest places in the world...

And on a practical level I was certainly in one of the strangest.

Canals instead of streets. No cars; an entire city where everyone walks or takes boats. So layered with history that something has happened on every slab of every square. But it's more than that. When the winter fog fills saltwater lagoon around Venice, you can believe it's the only island in the world. The only city. That it is the world.

As a child—a strange one, admittedly—I decided that the water of the lagoon stopped the ghosts in Venice from escaping. That was why it felt so odd. In Venice ghosts had to outnumber the living by hundreds to one. When I walked through the city I was walking not just through history but ghosts everywhere.

I went back to Venice in my teens, and was shocked by how dark and tortured Venetian art was. At least the pictures in churches and the ducal palace. For every beautiful, redheaded Titian nude there were three paintings of saints being tortured, murdered, exiled...I began to see where the ghosts came from.

The Fallen Blade is not a ghost story. But that sheer sense of strangeness was in my head when I began thinking about

Tycho. And there seemed only one place I could set his story.

Obviously, researching the series is fantastic fun.

So far I've made three trips in the past two years. Walking the backstreets, using waterbuses to navigate from one part of Venice to another. A lot of my time is spent sitting in cafés with a notebook, thinking, "Ah, so that's what Lady Giulietta looks like," or, "That house there is obviously where Lord Atilo lives."

All of the locations are real.

I'm now halfway through writing the next part of Tycho's story, *The Outcast Blade,* so I'll be going back soon.

What do you do when you're not writing?

I'm always writing, in my head if I can't get to my laptop. Sometimes on my iPhone or on the nearest scrap of paper. I still have a novel outline I wrote on a restaurant napkin because it was the only thing I could find to write on.

I work in cafés and bars and on trains, in public parks and occasionally, if lucky, on planes and in airports. I'm writing this in a café in West London while waiting for a friend. When not at the keyboard I'm reading, walking or riding my motorbike. The bike's a Triumph Bonneville that I've had made all black, and I use it to belt round the winding back roads near my house in Winchester.

There's a certain purity and sanity that comes from riding a motorbike (at least there is for me). It locks you into a single moment. And you really know you're in that moment when you feel the bike stay still and the world flow around you. I always write better after riding. This is the other reason I do it.

I suppose if I'm not writing, reading or riding then I'm probably travelling or cooking, which is something else that works for me. Food tends to play a large part in my books. One of Tycho's great losses is nothing he eats tastes right to him.

Will the rest of the Assassini trilogy be set in Italy or will we be taken to other exciting locations?

The whole story arc is mostly set in Venice, which is a hundred or so little islands joined by bridges and divided by canals. When it's not there it's in one of the Venetian empire's colonies like Cyprus, or on the mainland of Italy. (Apart from all of Tycho's flashbacks to Bjornvin, which are set in North American in the last Viking stronghold, all that remains of the colonies of Vineland.)

It was said that the Venetians were more interested in lovers seen through a window of a palace on the Grand Canal than the murder of a prince five hundred miles away. (Even when they ordered the murder themselves.) Venice owned a huge empire, had one of the biggest and most powerful navies and the greatest shipyard in the world. But as long as the gold kept coming they kept looking inwards at themselves. Not for nothing is it a city of gilt and mirrors.

What film made you cry last?

It's well-known men don't cry. We choke up with emotion (yeah, right). The first ten or fifteen minutes of *Up* were devastating. And a really clever lesson in what you can do with any genre/form you like. The scene in *Gladiator* where the hero's dying and he sees his dead child waiting in the distance as he comes towards them is a killer. And I've known the video for Johnny Cash's version of "Hurt" reduce seriously hard men to tears. (Simply because it's impossible to watch without sensing the angel of Death hovering just off camera.) But what film made me cry last? A Studio Ghibli anime called *Only Yesterday,* right at the end, more or less after the credits, when a childhood version of the heroine appears in the train — like a cross between a ghost and a memory — and makes her adult self turn back to that place she's leaving.

It taps into that sense of, "If I only knew back then when what I know now . . ." But it's cleverer than that (it would be, it's by the guy who directed *Grave of the Fireflies*), so it also taps into a sense of, "If only I knew now what I knew then . . ."

Childhood and old age make for great characters, and I try to have a mix so all ages have their part in the book.

Your novel features a unique combination of pirates, assassins, vampires and Italian dukes. If you could be any one, which would you choose?

Vampire . . . Because a vampire can happily be any of those or, indeed, all of those over the course of a vampire lifetime, but the others can't necessarily be a vampire! The hook for me isn't just immortality, or near as, damn it, it's immortality with added powers and not that serious a trade-off. I'd happily function only at night if I could see in the dark and move faster than anything else around me!

I wonder sometimes if becoming a vampire isn't like growing up. You think you'll never be that age, you'll never do those things. And then experience creeps up on us in much the same way that I suspect vampireness creeps up on the undead.

At first they think they'll be just like humans but different; then discover that they're less and less like humans as years turn into centuries. Obviously, Tycho's right at the start of this. Well, he thinks he is.

extras

Do you have a favorite character?

I like all the characters in *The Fallen Blade*—even the wicked ones. But Lady Giulietta, red-haired and stroppy, a pawn in her family's power games, the original medieval poor little rich girl who decides to fight back and finds she's simply made her life worse is right up there for me.

So, obviously enough, is Tycho.

He's the most fun to write but also the hardest because he's not quite human, and I have to keep that otherness in mind. There's a strangeness to how he sees the world. And I have to remind myself—and the readers—that how he sees the world is not how the rest of us see it, for all he's got human failing and emotions in the mix.

The other one I really like is Duchess Alexa. I think there's a lot more going on with her than anyone around her realizes. How old is she? Why goes she always wear a veil? How come she looks so young? This is a woman who likes to watch the world through the eyes of a bat and poison her enemies. Yet is so devoted to her niece, Lady Giulietta, that she'll do anything for her. That's Alexa's weakness, of course. And she has enemies who'd be willing to use that.

introducing

If you enjoyed
THE FALLEN BLADE,
look out for

BEST SERVED COLD

by Joe Abercrombie

Springtime in Styria. And that means war.

*There have been nineteen years of blood. The ruthless Grand
Duke Orso is locked in a vicious struggle with the squabbling
League of Eight, and between them they have bled the land white.
Armies march, heads roll and cities burn, while behind the scenes
bankers, priests and older, darker powers play a deadly game to
choose who will be king.*

*War may be hell but for Monza Murcatto, the Snake of Talins,
the most feared and famous mercenary in Duke Orso's employ, it's
a damn good way of making money too. Her victories have made
her popular—a shade too popular for her employer's taste.
Betrayed and left for dead, Murcatto's reward is a broken body
and a burning hunger for vengeance. Whatever the cost, seven
men must die.*

extras

Her allies include Styria's least reliable drunkard, Styria's most treacherous poisoner, a mass-murderer obsessed with numbers and a Northman who just wants to do the right thing. Her enemies number the better half of the nation. And that's all before the most dangerous man in the world is dispatched to hunt her down and finish the job Duke Orso started...

Springtime in Styria. And that means revenge.

Duke Orso's private study was a marble hall the size of a market square. Lofty windows marched in bold procession along one side, standing open, a keen breeze washing through and making the vivid hangings twitch and rustle. Beyond them a long terrace seemed to hang in empty air, overlooking the steepest drop from the mountain's summit.

The opposite wall was covered with towering panels, painted by the foremost artists of Styria, displaying the great battles of history. The victories of Stolicus, of Harod the Great, of Farans and Verturio, all preserved in sweeping oils. The message that Orso was the latest in a line of royal winners was hard to miss, even though his great-grandfather had been a usurper, and a common criminal besides.

The largest painting of them all faced the door, ten strides high at the least. Who else but Grand Duke Orso? He was seated upon a rearing charger, his shining sword raised high, his piercing eye fixed on the far horizon, urging his men to victory at the Battle of Etrea. The painter seemed to have been unaware that Orso hadn't come within fifty miles of the fighting.

But then fine lies beat tedious truths every time, as he had often told her.

The Duke of Talins himself sat crabbed over a desk, wielding a pen rather than a sword. A tall, gaunt, hook-nosed man stood at his elbow, staring down as keenly as a vulture waiting for thirsty travellers to die. A great shape lurked near them, in the shadows against the wall. Gobba, Orso's bodyguard, fat-necked as a great hog. Prince Ario, the duke's eldest son and heir, lounged in a gilded chair nearer at hand. He had one leg crossed over the other, a wine glass dangling carelessly, a bland smile balanced on his blandly handsome face.

"I found these beggars wandering the grounds," called Foscar, "and thought I'd commend them to your charity, Father!"

"Charity?" Orso's sharp voice echoed around the cavernous room. "I am not a great admirer of the stuff. Make yourselves comfortable, my friends, I will be with you shortly."

"If it isn't the Butcher of Caprile," murmured Ario, "and her little Benna too."

"Your Highness. You look well." Monza thought he looked an indolent cock, but kept it to herself.

"You too, as ever. If all soldiers looked as you did, I might even be tempted to go on campaign myself. A new bauble?" Ario waved his own jewel-encrusted hand limply towards the ruby on Monza's finger.

"Just what was to hand when I was dressing."

"I wish I'd been there. Wine?"

"Just after dawn?"

He glanced heavy-lidded towards the windows. "Still last night as far as I'm concerned." As if staying up late was a heroic achievement.

"I will." Benna was already pouring himself a glass, never to be outdone as far as showing off went. Most likely he'd be drunk within the hour and embarrass himself, but Monza was tired of playing his mother. She strolled past the monumental fireplace held up by carven figures of Juvens and Kanedias, and towards Orso's desk.

"Sign here, and here, and here," the gaunt man was saying, one bony finger hovering over the documents.

"You know Mauthis, do you?" Orso gave a sour glance in his direction. "My leash-holder."

"Always your humble servant, your Excellency. The Banking House of Valint and Balk agrees to this further loan for the period of one year, after which they regret they must charge interest."

Orso snorted. "As the plague regrets the dead, I'll be bound." He scratched out a parting swirl on the last signature and tossed down his pen. "Everyone must kneel to someone, eh? Make sure you extend to your superiors my infinite gratitude for their indulgence."

"I shall do so." Mauthis collected up the documents. "That concludes our business, your Excellency. I must leave at once if I mean to catch the evening tide for Westport—"

"No. Stay a while longer. We have one other matter to discuss."

Mauthis' dead eyes moved towards Monza, then back to Orso. "As your Excellency desires."

The duke rose smoothly from his desk. "To happier business, then. You do bring happy news, eh, Monzcarro?"

"I do, your Excellency."

"Ah, whatever would I do without you?" There was a trace of iron grey in his black hair since she'd seen him last, perhaps some deeper lines at the corners of his eyes, but his air of complete command was impressive as ever. He leaned forwards and kissed her on both cheeks, then whispered in her ear, "Ganmark can lead soldiers well enough, but for a man who sucks cocks he hasn't the slightest sense of humour. Come, tell me of your victories in the open air." He left one arm draped around her shoulders and guided her, past the sneering Prince Ario, through the open windows onto the high terrace.

The sun was climbing now, and the bright world was full of colour. The blood had drained from the sky and left it a vivid blue, white clouds crawling high above. Below, at the very bottom of a dizzy drop, the river wound through the wooded valley, autumn leaves pale green, burned orange, faded yellow, angry red, light glinting silver on fast-flowing water. To the east, the forest crumbled away into a patchwork of fields — squares of fallow green, rich black earth, golden crop. Further still and the river met the grey sea, branching out in a wide delta choked with islands. Monza could just make out the suggestion of tiny towers there, buildings, bridges, walls. Great Talins, no bigger than her thumbnail.

She narrowed her eyes against the stiff breeze, pushed some stray hair out of her face. "I never tire of this view."

"How could you? It's why I built this damn place. Here I can keep one eye always on my subjects, as a watchful parent should upon his children. Just to make sure they don't hurt themselves while they play, you understand."

"Your people are lucky to have such a just and caring father," she lied smoothly.

"Just and caring." Orso frowned thoughtfully towards the distant sea. "Do you think that is how history will remember me?"

Monza thought it incredibly unlikely. "What did Bialoveld say? 'History is written by the victors.'"

The duke squeezed her shoulder. "All this, and well read into the bargain. Ario is ambitious enough, but he has no insight. I'd be surprised if he could read to the end of a signpost in one sitting. All he cares about is whoring. And shoes. My daughter Terez, meanwhile, weeps most bitterly because I married her to a king. I swear, if I had offered great Euz as the groom she would have whined for a husband better fitting her station." He gave a heavy sigh. "None of my children understand me. My great-grandfather was a mercenary, you know. A fact I do not like to advertise." Though he told her every other time they met. "A man who never shed a tear in his life, and wore on his feet whatever was to hand. A low-born fighting man, who seized power in Talins by the sharpness of his mind and sword together." More by blunt ruthlessness and brutality, the way Monza had heard the tale. "We are from the same stock, you and I. We have made ourselves, out of nothing."

Orso had been born to the wealthiest dukedom in Styria and never done a hard day's work in his life, but Monza bit her tongue. "You do me too much honour, your Excellency."

"Less than you deserve. Now tell me of Borletta."

"You heard about the battle on the High Bank?"

"I heard you scattered the League of Eight's army, just as you did at Sweet Pines! Ganmark says Duke Salier had three times your number."

"Numbers are a hindrance if they're lazy, ill-prepared and led by idiots. An army of farmers from Borletta, cobblers from Affoia, glass-blowers from Visserine. Amateurs. They camped by the river, thinking we were far away, scarcely posted guards. We came up through the woods at night and caught them at sunrise, not even in their armour."

"I can see Salier now, the fat pig, waddling from his bed to run!"

"Faithful led the charge. We broke them quickly, captured their supplies."

"Turned the golden cornfields crimson, I was told."

"They hardly even fought. Ten times as many drowned trying to swim the river as died fighting. More than four thousand prisoners. Some ransoms were paid, some not, some men were hanged."

"And few tears shed, eh, Monza?"

"Not by me. If they were so keen to live, they could've surrendered."

"As they did at Caprile?"

She stared straight back into Orso's black eyes. "Just as they did at Caprile."

"Borletta is besieged, then?"

"Fallen already."

The duke's face lit up like a boy's on his birthday. "Fallen? Cantain surrendered?"

"When his people heard of Salier's defeat, they lost hope."

"And people without hope are a dangerous crowd, even in a republic."

"Especially in a republic. A mob dragged Cantain from the palace, hanged him from the highest tower, opened the gates and threw themselves on the mercy of the Thousand Swords."

"Hah! Slaughtered by the very people he laboured to keep free. There's the gratitude of the common man, eh, Monza? Cantain should have taken my money when I offered. It would have been cheaper for both of us."

"The people are falling over themselves to become your subjects. I've given orders they should be spared, where possible."

"Mercy, eh?"

"Mercy and cowardice are the same," she snapped out. "But you want their land, not their lives, no? Dead men can't obey."

Orso smiled. "Why can my sons not mark my lessons as you have? I entirely approve. Hang only the leaders. And Cantain's head above the gates. Nothing encourages obedience like a good example."

"Already rotting, with those of his sons."

"Fine work!" The Lord of Talins clapped his hands, as though he never heard such pleasing music as the news of rotting heads. "What of the takings?"

The accounts were Benna's business, and he came forwards now, sliding a folded paper from his chest pocket. "The city was scoured, your Excellency. Every building stripped, every floor dug up, every person searched. The usual rules apply, according to our terms of engagement. Quarter for the man that finds it, quarter for his captain, quarter for the generals," and he bowed low, unfolding the paper and offering it out, "and quarter for our noble employer."

Orso's smile broadened as his eyes scanned down the figures. "My blessing on the Rule of Quarters! Enough to keep you both in my service a little longer." He stepped between Monza and Benna, placed a gentle hand on each of their shoulders and led them back through the open windows. Towards the round table of black marble in the centre of the room, and the great map spread out upon it. Ganmark, Ario and Faithful had already gathered there. Gobba still lurked in the shadows, thick arms folded across his chest. "What of our one-time friends and now our bitter enemies, the treacherous citizens of Visserine?"

"The fields round the city are burned up to the gates, almost." Monza scattered carnage across the countryside with a few waves of her finger. "Farmers driven off, livestock slaughtered. It'll be a lean winter for fat Duke Salier, and a leaner spring."

"He will have to rely on the noble Duke Rogont and his Osprians," said Ganmark, with the faintest of smiles.

Prince Ario snickered. "Much talk blows down from Ospria, always, but little help."

"Visserine is poised to drop into your lap next year, your Excellency."

"And with it the heart is torn from the League of Eight."

"The crown of Styria will be yours."

The mention of crowns teased Orso's smile still wider. "And we have you to thank, Monzcarro. I do not forget that."

"Not only me."

"Curse your modesty. Benna has played his part, and our good friend General Ganmark, and Faithful too, but no one could deny this is your work. Your commitment, your single-mindedness, your swiftness to act! You shall have a great triumph, just as the heroes of ancient Aulcus did. You shall ride through the streets of Talins and my people will shower you with flower petals in honour of your many victories." Benna was grinning, but Monza couldn't join him. She'd never had much taste for congratulations. "They will cheer far louder for you, I think, than they ever will for my own sons. They will cheer far louder even than they do for me, their rightful lord, to whom they owe so much." It seemed that Orso's smile slipped, and his face looked tired, and sad, and worn without it. "They will cheer, in fact, a little too loudly for my taste."

There was the barest flash of movement at the corner of her eye, enough to make her bring up her hand on an instinct.

The wire hissed taut around it, snatching it up under her chin, crushing it chokingly tight against her throat.

Benna started forwards. "Mon—" Metal glinted as Prince Ario stabbed him in the neck. He missed his throat, caught him just under the ear.

Orso carefully stepped back as blood speckled the tiles with red. Foscar's mouth fell open, wine glass dropping from his hand, shattering on the floor.

Monza tried to scream, but only spluttered through her half-shut windpipe, made a sound like a honking pig. She fished at the hilt of her dagger with her free hand but someone caught her wrist, held it fast. Faithful Carpi, pressed up tight against her left side.

"Sorry," he muttered in her ear, pulling her sword from its scabbard and flinging it clattering across the room.

Benna stumbled, gurgling red drool, one hand clutched to the side of his face, black blood leaking out between white fingers. His other hand fumbled for his sword while Ario watched him, frozen. He drew a clumsy foot of steel before General Ganmark stepped up and stabbed him, smoothly and precisely—once, twice, three times. The thin blade slid in and out of Benna's body, the only sound the soft breath from his gaping mouth. Blood shot across the floor in long streaks, began to leak out into his white shirt in dark circles. He tottered forwards, tripped over his own feet and crashed down, half-drawn sword scraping against the marble underneath him.

Monza strained, every muscle trembling, but she was held helpless as a fly in honey. She heard Gobba grunting with effort in her ear, his stubbly face rubbing against her cheek, his great body warm against her back. She felt the wire cut slowly into the sides of her neck, deep into the side of her hand, caught fast against her throat. She felt the blood running down her fore-arm, into the collar of her shirt.

One of Benna's hands crawled across the floor, reaching out for her. He lifted himself an inch or two, veins bulging from his neck. Ganmark leaned forwards and calmly ran him through the heart from behind. Benna quivered for a moment, then sagged down and was still, pale cheek smeared with red. Dark blood crept out from under him, worked its way along the cracks between the tiles.

"Well." Ganmark leaned down and wiped his sword on the back of Benna's shirt. "That's that."

Mauthis watched, frowning. Slightly puzzled, slightly irritated, slightly bored. As though examining a set of figures that wouldn't quite add.

Orso gestured at the body. "Get rid of that, Ario."

"Me?" The prince's lip curled.

"Yes, you. And you can help him, Foscar. The two of you must learn what needs to be done to keep our family in power."

"No!" Foscar stumbled away. "I'll have no part of this!" He turned and ran from the room, his boots slapping against the marble floor.

"That boy is soft as syrup," muttered Orso at his back. "Ganmark, help him."

Monza's bulging eyes followed them as they dragged Benna's corpse out through the doors to the terrace, Ganmark grim and careful at the head end, Ario cursing as he daintily took one boot, the other smearing a red trail after them. They heaved Benna up onto the balustrade and rolled him off. Like that he was gone.

"Ah!" squawked Ario, waving one hand. "Damn it! You scratched me!"

Ganmark stared back at him. "I apologise, your Highness. Murder can be a painful business."

The prince looked around for something to wipe his bloody hands on. He reached for the rich hangings beside the window.

"Not there!" snapped Orso. "That's Kantic silk, at fifty scales a piece!"

"Where, then?"

"Find something else, or leave them red! Sometimes I wonder if your mother told the truth about your paternity, boy." Ario wiped his hands sulkily on the front of his shirt while Monza stared, face burning from lack of air. Orso frowned over at her, a blurred black figure through the wet in her eyes, the hair tangled across her face. "Is she still alive? Whatever are you about, Gobba?"

"Fucking wire's caught on her hand," hissed the bodyguard.

"Find another way to be done with her, then, lackwit."

"I'll do it." Faithful pulled the dagger from her belt, still pinning her wrist with his other hand. "I really am sorry."

"Just get to it!" growled Gobba.

The blade went back, steel glinting in a shaft of light. Monza stomped down on Gobba's foot with all the strength she had left. The bodyguard grunted, grip slipping on the wire, and she dragged it away from her neck, growling, twisting hard as Carpi stabbed at her.

The blade went well wide of the mark, slid in under her bottom rib. Cold metal, but it felt burning hot, a line of fire from her stomach to her back. It slid right through and the point pricked Gobba's gut.

"Gah!" He let go the wire and Monza whooped in air, started shrieking mindlessly, lashed at him with her elbow and sent him staggering. Faithful was caught off guard, fumbled the knife as he pulled it out of her and sent it spinning across the floor. She kicked at him, missed his groin and caught his hip, bent him over. She snatched at a dagger on his belt, pulled it from its sheath, but her cut hand was clumsy and he caught her wrist before she could ram the blade into him. They wrestled with it, teeth bared, gasping spit in each other's faces, lurching back and forth, their hands sticky with her blood.

"Kill her!"

There was a crunch and her head was full of light. The floor cracked against her skull, slapped her in the back. She spat blood, mad screams guttering to a long drawn croak, clawing at the smooth floor with her nails.

"Fucking bitch!" The heel of Gobba's big boot cracked down

on her right hand and sent pain lancing up her forearm, tore a sick gasp from her. His boot crunched again across her knuckles, then her fingers, then her wrist. At the same time Faithful's foot was thudding into her ribs, over and over, making her cough and shudder. Her shattered hand twisted, turned sideways on. Gobba's heel crashed down and crushed it flat into the cold marble with a splintering of bone. She flopped back, hardly able to breathe, the room turning over, history's painted winners grinning down.

"You stabbed me, you dumb old bastard! You stabbed me!"

"You're hardly even cut, fathead! You should've kept a hold on her!"

"I should stab the useless pair of you!" hissed Orso's voice. "Just get it done!"

Gobba's great fist came down, dragged Monza up by her throat. She tried to grab at him with her left hand but all her strength had leaked out through the hole in her side, the cuts in her neck. Her clumsy fingertips only smeared red traces across his stubbly face. Her arm was dragged away, twisted sharply behind her back.

"Where's Hermon's gold?" came Gobba's rough voice. "Eh, Murcatto? What did you do with the gold?"

Monza forced her head up. "Lick my arse, cocksucker." Not clever, perhaps, but from the heart.

"There never was any gold!" snapped Faithful. "I told you that, pig!"

"There's this much." One by one, Gobba twisted the battered rings from her dangling fingers, already bloating, turning angry purple, bent and shapeless as rotten sausages. "Good stone, that," he said, peering at the ruby. "Seems a waste of decent flesh, though. Why not give me a moment with her? A moment's all it would take."

Prince Ario tittered. "Speed isn't always something to be proud of."

"For pity's sake!" Orso's voice. "We're not animals. Off the terrace and let us be done. I am late for breakfast."

She felt herself dragged, head lolling. Sunlight stabbed at her. She was lifted, limp boots scraping on stone. Blue sky turning. Up onto the balustrade. The breath scraped at her nose, shuddered in her chest. She twisted, kicked. Her body, struggling vainly to stay alive.

"Let me make sure of her." Ganmark's voice.

"How sure do we need to be?" Blurry through the bloody hair across her eyes she saw Orso's lined face. "I hope you understand. My great-grandfather was a mercenary. A low-born fighting man, who seized power by the sharpness of his mind and sword together. I cannot allow another mercenary to seize power in Talins."

She meant to spit in his face, but all she did was blow bloody drool down her own chin. "Fuck yourse—"

Then she was flying.

Her torn shirt billowed and flapped against her tingling skin. She turned over, and over, and the world tumbled around her. Blue sky with shreds of cloud, black towers at the mountain top, grey rock face rushing past, yellow-green trees and sparkling river, blue sky with shreds of cloud, and again, and again, faster, and faster.

Cold wind ripped at her hair, roared in her ears, whistled between her teeth along with her terrified breath. She could see each tree, now, each branch, each leaf. They surged up towards her. She opened her mouth to scream—

Twigs snatched, grabbed, lashed at her. A broken branch knocked her spinning. Wood cracked and tore around her as she plunged down, down, and crashed into the mountainside.

Her legs splintered under her plummeting weight, her shoulder broke apart against firm earth. But rather than dashing her brains out on the rocks, she only shattered her jaw against her brother's bloody chest, his mangled body wedged against the base of a tree.

Which was how Benna Murcatto saved his sister's life.

She bounced from the corpse, three-quarters senseless, and down the steep mountainside, over and over, flailing like a broken doll. Rocks, and roots, and hard earth clubbed, punched, crushed her, as if she was battered apart with a hundred hammers.

She tore through a patch of bushes, thorns whipping and clutching. She rolled, and rolled, down the sloping earth in a cloud of dirt and leaves. She tumbled over a tree root, crumpled on a mossy rock. She slid slowly to a stop, on her back, and was still.

"Huuuurrrrhhh..."

Stones clattered down around her, sticks and gravel. Dust slowly settled. She heard wind, creaking in the branches, crackling in the leaves. Or her own breath, creaking and crackling in her broken throat. The sun flickered through black trees, jabbing at one eye. The other was dark. Flies buzzed, zipping and swimming in the warm morning air. She was down with the waste from Orso's kitchens. Sprawled out helpless in the midst of the rotten vegetables, and the cooking slime, and the stinking offal left over from the last month's magnificent meals. Tossed out with the rubbish.

"Huuurrhhh..."

A jagged, mindless sound. She was embarrassed by it, almost, but couldn't stop making it. Animal horror. Mad despair. The groan of the dead, in hell. Her eye darted desperately around. She saw the wreck of her right hand, a shapeless, purple glove with a bloody gash in the side. One finger trembled slightly. Its

449

tip brushed against torn skin on her elbow. The forearm was folded in half, a broken-off twig of grey bone sticking through bloody silk. It didn't look real. Like a cheap theatre prop.

"Huurrhhh..."

The fear had hold of her now, swelling with every breath. She couldn't move her head. She couldn't move her tongue in her mouth. She could feel the pain, gnawing at the edge of her mind. A terrible mass, pressing up against her, crushing every part of her, worse, and worse, and worse.

"Huurhh...uurh..."

Benna was dead. A streak of wet ran from her flickering eye and she felt it trickle slowly down her cheek. Why was she not dead? How could she not be dead?

Soon, please. Before the pain got any worse. Please, let it be soon.

"Uurh...uh...uh."

Please, death.

VISIT THE ORBIT BLOG AT

www.orbitbooks.net

FEATURING

BREAKING NEWS
FORTHCOMING RELEASES
LINKS TO AUTHOR SITES
EXCLUSIVE INTERVIEWS
EARLY EXTRACTS

AND COMMENTARY FROM OUR EDITORS

WITH REGULAR UPDATES FROM OUR TEAM,
ORBITBOOKS.NET IS YOUR SOURCE
FOR ALL THINGS ORBITAL.

WHILE YOU'RE THERE, JOIN OUR E-MAIL LIST
TO RECEIVE INFORMATION ON SPECIAL OFFERS,
GIVEAWAYS, AND MORE.

imagine. explore. engage.